"EXTREMELY FUNNY AND ODDLY AFFECTING . . .

It's as if Carey had set herself the task of taking utterly ordinary subjects and making them far more inventive and stylish than a reader dared hope. . . . [A] novel so pleasurable . . . [we] find ourselves having epiphanies right alongside [the characters]."

—*The New York Times Book Review*

"The witty writing is clear and unpretentious, and love and money are examined from a variety of viewpoints; things are seldom as simple as they seem. . . . Readers have complete access to the thoughts and feelings of both sisters, who are fully imagined."

—*Library Journal*

"[A] wry, quirky novel . . . [Carey is] an engaging and often funny writer. . . . Her sharp descriptions of the sisters' various milieus give the novel its piquancy."

—*Publishers Weekly*

"Accomplished and insightful . . . Carey makes each segment engaging."

—*Kirkus Reviews*

By Jacqueline Carey

The Crossley Baby
The Other Family
Good Gossip

The Crossley Baby

The Crossley Baby

Jacqueline Carey

BALLANTINE BOOKS
New York

A Ballantine Book
Published by The Random House Publishing Group

www.ballantinebooks.com/BRC

Library of Congress Control Number: 2004092792

ISBN 0-345-45991-1

Manufactured in the United States of America

9 8 7 6 5 4 3 2 1

First Edition: July 2003
First Trade Paperback Edition: July 2004

For Cora and Thomas

With thanks to Ben Brantley; Ed Hirsh and the Guggenheim Foundation; Allen Feltman, Sandra Allen, and Maria Cornelius of Saint Dominic's Home; Michael Crane; Lisa Maillet of New York County Surrogate's Court; and real estate visionary Harley Brooke-Hitching.

The
Cork
Line

THE FEUDS WERE SUCH A JOKE. THE CROSSLEY GIRLS HAD laughed about them for years. Once upon a time their father had mentioned certain "disputes" shamefacedly, but later even he joined in the merriment. It certainly didn't matter to these three free-thinking, dope-smoking, miniskirted girls that a quarrel between heirs had broken up the original "Crossley's," one of the biggest jewelry businesses in Boston. Early photos made it look like a ratty old cigar box, anyway. And the girls relished details of other fights: Two maiden aunts had had a brick wall built down the center of their Victorian house in Dorchester, the better to avoid each other; back in County Cork, one Crossley and his widowed sister hadn't spoken for the last twenty years of their lives, although they slept in the same cottage and sat across the kitchen table from each other three times a day. There was actually a line drawn down the center of the table. Can you imagine!

When the two younger sisters, Jean and Sunny, shared a bedroom back in high school, Jean laid a strip of masking tape across the middle of the floorboards and called it the "Cork Line," as in "I don't care if you do open the window as long as the air doesn't venture over the Cork Line," or, about a guy Sunny had met at the Paw Valley Post Office, "Just keep Mr. Dick on your side of the Cork Line."

"I could swear I heard something just then," Sunny would say, turning the pages of a magazine with ostentatious languor. "But such a screechy sound couldn't have been human."

Even oddball Bridget, the oldest, picked up on the term. As an adult, Jean would occasionally mention the fact that Bridget's bedroom had not only been hers alone, but had also been the biggest in the house. Bridget was generally too distracted to notice, but once she said, "I have a Cork Line running down the center of my soul!" Jean snickered, but Sunny grabbed Bridget and hugged her and cooed at her and tickled her ribs until Jean finally said, "Yuck. Let's keep this PG," and Sunny said, "Oh, you just can't stand it that I'm so much nicer than you are."

The call, when it came, was between Jean and Sunny. It took place on December 18, 1990, shortly after lunch. Sunny wasn't planning to answer the phone; she was trying to figure out which cardboard carton held the bulk of the Christmas ornaments. She could find only a few of the most fragile, which had their own four-inch-square boxes tucked in among the holiday books and tapes. This was going to be the first Christmas since Sunny and her family had left the city. Bridget, who was scheduled to have a fibroid removed, would be coming up with her ten-month-old daughter, Jade, in a couple of days to recuperate a little before the twenty-fifth, and Sunny wanted to have put up as many decorations as possible beforehand.

It helped that Sunny's new house looked like an old Christmas tin: lit-up mullioned windows, a wreath on the door, a dusting of snow, an embrace of spruce. Because the rooms were still nearly bare of furniture, nothing commonplace interfered with the holiday setting. The pungent, sappy odor of evergreen drifted upstairs and down, thanks to the Scotch pine branches tacked over the arch to the dining room, the Doug fir Sunny's husband had cut on their own property, the basket of pinecones by the fireplace. That afternoon the kids were going to help decorate a gingerbread house she'd made from a kit. Three different sets of friends were expected up from the city around the day itself. Lists in her little loopy handwriting were scattered everywhere: Presents still to buy. Tips to be handed out. And lots of food. Ingredients for the marinade, ingredients for the pie crust, ingredients for the cookie dough. Eggnog, Burgundy, and a cheap champagne for the mimosas on Christmas morning. Already in a corner of the kitchen next to some stripped paneling (the house was a real fixer-upper) stood a large pile of holiday cakes and breads, olives and nuts, truffles and candy canes.

The ornaments were key—so important that an obscure hierarchy had evolved over the years. If Linc, who was five, got to put on the shiny fabric fish Bridget had brought back from Beijing one year, then Ruth, who was almost four, got to hang the butterfly. If Linc got the gingerbread boy, Ruth got the girl. There were also more complicated equivalences. The nutcracker, for instance, equaled both the pipe-cleaner bear and either the red-and-green-striped metal sled or Leon's white menorah, a nod to his cultural past. Then there were those ornaments the kids left for Sunny, including the red and silver glass balls from an ancient Woolworth's and a small, lacy brass frame that Jean had given them. Inside was a picture of Jean herself, eating a sandwich. In the hierarchy of relatives, it was weirdo Bridget who was on the top.

When the call came that December 18, the person at the other end claimed to be Sunny's sister Jean, but the voice sounded put-on. That is, Sunny could tell it was Jean, but Jean had the sort of strained tone she used to affect when she'd leave messages pretending to be a Hollywood agent or the president of the United States. It was as if Jean were calling up pretending to be Jean. Which was annoying, but odd enough that Sunny put down the manger scene she was unwrapping from its tissue paper and picked up the phone.

"Jean?" she said, implying by the confusion in her voice that she hadn't just been deciding whether to answer.

Jean said that something had gone wrong with Bridget's operation.

"Someday, Jean, you are going to go too far," said Sunny.

"I'm just telling you what happened," said Jean.

Something on the back of Sunny's neck began to rise. "What was it?" she said.

"They're being kind of cagey. But I think she's, well, dead."

"There's obviously some mistake," Sunny said.

"Really?"

"Nothing could have gone wrong with the operation," said Sunny. "It was very routine. She was supposed to be home in a few hours."

"Oh," said Jean. "I thought you knew something."

"Just tell me how someone could have died of such a routine operation. Bridget's been all over the world. She stumbled into a *civil war*, and she was fine."

"If you don't know anything . . ."

"I suppose she could have been in a car accident on the way to the hospital," Sunny mused. "It's possible."

There was a silence.

"Did they get her confused with someone else?" said Sunny in a sudden panic. She heard the intercom squawk in Jean's office.

Jean said, "Tell him I'll call him back."

Sunny struggled to remain civil. "You're at *work*?" she said.

"It's Tuesday. Of course I'm at work."

Sunny could have cut Jean open on an operating table right then and there, but the image that accompanied this desire—an everyday, real-life figure superimposed on a Dr. Frankenstein's laboratory—made her double up, and she found herself crouching on her knees, her face six inches from a cracked black diamond in the kitchen floor. "I have to go," she said into the phone, and hit the hang-up button.

Still doubled over, intently examining the gray curve of the receiver, she punched the memory button for her husband's office. "And how are you, Mrs. Dane?" said Brianna brightly. The receptionist. Sunny thought she'd been laid off.

"Connect me, connect me," said Sunny. And to her husband she said, "Jean thinks something happened to Bridget."

"Thinks?"

"The operation," she said.

"I'll be right there."

The drive up from Harlem would take more than an hour. Sunny hit the second button, which was for Bridget. There was her voice on the announcement, the same as always. "Bridget!" cried Sunny. "Call me immediately! You won't believe what just happened!"

One of the last few buttons was for Jean's office, but Sunny couldn't place which. She couldn't remember the last time she'd called her. Sunny hit the "9" and got a man's voice: "Poison Control. May I have the name of the child involved?"

On the second try, she got a double hello, first from Jean's receptionist, then from Jean herself, who had a way of speaking sometimes—holding the words way back in her throat—that drove Sunny nuts.

"Where did you hear this nonsense?" she asked.

"The hospital called me," said Jean.

"Where is Jade?"

"She's with the upstairs neighbor. Stew."

"I'm coming," said Sunny. "I'll pick her up. I'll call you back." She rested her forehead against the cool tile. "In a few minutes."

If Jean was angry—and she was, actually; incredibly so—it was at Bridget for not letting her find her a real job. Because Jean could have done it; no one in her family appreciated what power she held. She had wooed an executive away from his firm by reading a bird book that cost her $11.95. She had filled a six-figure PR job one summer day without leaving the Adirondacks. She had herself led a team that ended up recommending the new CEO of OxCon—a position that, with stock options, commanded millions of dollars. She never pretended to be surprised at her success. She had a vision. She could find previously unimagined fits between positions and people because she never saw square pegs and round holes, or even round pegs and round holes. Every element was more complex, with odd juts and indentations, yet more elastic, more vibrant, more erotic.

Bridget was not exactly at the level Jean was used to dealing with, but Jean knew lots of human resources people, had actually recommended many of them for their positions. She could have gotten Bridget anything she wanted. This despite the fact that Bridget had been without steady employment for years, despite her obvious unsuitableness for any sort of normal life. And a real job would have meant a real apartment in a real neighborhood, real day care for Jade, and, most of all, a real hospital with real doctors to take care of them both. Bridget hadn't graduated from college? She'd been in a hurry to grasp life with two fists. She'd wandered aimlessly all over the world? People who travel are more effective communicators. Her previous jobs were hard to verify? That just shows she was a real self-starter. In truth, Jean had always thought of Bridget as a person you could work around, and certainly there was use in that.

Even in high school, Jean had been able to predict the general shape of their careers. She'd often told her sisters she would end up supporting them. Their father may be struggling; their mother may be dead. But Jean had decided to be rich. "Just try not to get caught when I am competing for some particularly sensitive post," she added at one point during the Watergate hearings.

"Caught?" said Bridget, perplexed. "Caught doing what?"

"I have no idea," said Jean, "and don't tell me. It's safer that way."

Jean swept into the pale blue reception room and announced to Mary, the beautiful Vietnamese receptionist, "My sister's doctor just killed her. Who do we have on board for today? Cancel them all. Tell them the economy will only improve."

"Did something happen to Sunny?" Every part of Mary looked polished. Her straight black hair shone, her crimson nails gleamed, her sharp-collared, crisp white synthetic shirt was almost too stylish. There was no reason for her to be impressed by anyone.

"No. Bridget," said Jean abruptly. Mary had never met Sunny but was always telling Jean to say hello. Of course, Sunny had asked Mary all sorts of how-are-you questions, but they were bound to be fake; no one was that interested in someone else's receptionist.

Mary never mentioned Bridget, who had actually *been* in this office, in this very room. Maybe not often. But once. And she was hard to miss. At forty-two she was still "finding herself." After quitting a job with the city, she'd turned to more marginal employment—part-time waitress at a vegan restaurant, costume jeweler, occasional seamstress for experimental theater directors, New Age masseuse.

"I'm so sorry," said Mary.

"*You* have nothing to worry about," said Jean grimly. "But somebody else does."

The last time Jean had gone to Bridget's apartment on 7th Street was years before, not a memory she liked to relive. The only person who hadn't asked her for money on the way was a young fellow in jeans and a priest's collar, who had tried to give her clean needles out of the back of a brown van. It was terrifically embarrassing. "I'm just visiting my sister" sounded like every stupid lie she had ever told. What would she, an obviously successful person getting out of a company cab, be doing with a sister down there? Even Bridget herself wasn't a junkie, although it was hard to think of any other excuse for her continuing embrace of poverty. The priest had tried to warn Jean about HIV as if she'd never watched any television. She had never gone back.

In fact, Jean hadn't seen Bridget for months, and the last time they'd met it was by accident, on the Lexington Avenue bus. Jade had been hanging off Bridget's chest in one of those rampant Dresden blue pouches, definitely a Sunny hand-me-down. Where had they been heading to? Had Bridget even said? Jean tried to reconstruct the conversation. Bridget had no small talk. Sports, politics, the weather—no normal subject would do for Bridget. When Jean had asked after the baby, Bridget had replied by looking down at the top of the little head with its funny swirl of hair and saying, "Russians still think that cold air makes you sick." She had always spoken in irrelevancies. Jean may have tried to bring up Sunny, although Bridget tended to willfully misunderstand Jean's devastating remarks about Sunny's dependence on men and her move to the suburbs—both topics she should have warmed to. Ah, another memory returned.

Bridget had been stylishly, if cheaply, dressed in short squarish metallic-looking bell-bottoms and a zigzagged knit jersey top— the same sorts of clothes that she'd left all over her floor twenty-five years ago. From the straw basket she was using as a diaper bag she took a silver plastic clutch purse (empty, no doubt). A single black vinyl daisy protruded over the snap. While the doors pumped and hissed, she waved this purse as if to toss it away but instead said, "Recognize this?"

"Isn't that mine?" asked Jean.

Bridget laughed. "I found it in the attic," she said, meaning at their father's house out in Paw Valley. It was as if she had circled all the way around to the beginning of her life just in time to end it.

Outside her gleaming, polished granite midtown office building, waiting for the car service, Jean began to cry, but you couldn't tell, because the tears mingled instantly with the rain she lifted her face to.

Sunny showed great tolerance while dealing with the woman at Patient Conditions who claimed to have no record of a Bridget Crossley. "She was operated on this morning," Sunny said slowly, overenunciating. "And apparently there was some sort of problem."

"She probably hasn't been assigned a room number yet," explained the voice at the other end, a voice Sunny had waited through a ten-minute telephone tree to get to.

"All I want to know is whether she's dead or alive," said Sunny sweetly.

"I'm afraid I have no information about that."

All the sweetness disappeared. *"Well do you have a morgue?"*

"Maybe you should try again later."

Sunny kicked one of the Christmas boxes, ostensibly to get it out of the way in a hurry, and received a satisfying crunch in return. Bridget had said *just yesterday* she was looking forward to Christmas here. Sunny's stomach was shaky, gripped by a deep, cold fear.

By the time Leon arrived, Sunny had packed for the whole family. A cooler on the counter held juice packs, rice cakes, tubes of yogurt, and many other things she had grabbed and already forgotten. The suitcases were by the driveway, toppled all over one another in the crispy gray grass. She'd packed all the impossible children's outfits that Bridget had brought back from her travels but had never seen on Linc or Ruth—peasant blouses, kimonos, shorts with suspenders. Leon took one look at the luggage and said, "We're going to stay overnight?"

"I don't know." A thin gruel of tears ran down her face.

"Okay," he said. "Let me pee first." He was big, fair, thick armed, as steady as a sandbag.

At the kids' school, Leon stayed in the driver's seat while Sunny hopped out. Her hands, she saw, were trembling. Kindle had only a couple of dozen students total and lots of teachers, assistant teachers, and parent volunteers. "What's wrong?" asked one, seeing her face. Sunny just shook her head, saying she didn't know.

Linc was playing with the wood chips on the playground, so he was easy to roust. Ruth was in the classroom, trying to scrape paint off newsprint with a clothespin. Sunny slipped Ruth's jacket on her as they were going out the door. She couldn't stand to think about retrieving lunch box or mittens—it was too much; everything was too much—so she concentrated on diverting the kids' attention from these items. "Daddy is waiting in the car," she kept saying. "Hurry, hurry." It occurred to her then that she shouldn't bring them, but she couldn't bear not to.

In the car she leaned her forehead against the dashboard. The floor mat was ridged, and twin lines of dirt had accumulated on the sides of each depression.

"Are you okay?" said Leon.

"Yes," she said.

The kids were talking, but she couldn't distinguish the words. She would retrieve Jade. She would hug her and keep her safe. Stew would help her find out what kind of danger Bridget was in. He was, presumably, the father of her turkey-baster daughter, Jade. More important, he would be able to tell what was going on. He had been to medical school, all but the last year, which he'd quit only because he'd realized he was gay. He had broken off his engagement, moved to Manhattan, taken temporary work as a lab technician, and started to party. If he'd been ten years older, he'd have married his suitable young woman and become a doctor. Ten years younger, and he'd have had a gay wedding after graduating from medical school. But Stew's homosexuality demanded total devotion from him. He would be the perfect guide.

Jean tried to avoid hospitals, but sometimes her job made on-site visits necessary. She'd always been surprised at how normal everyone looked. Where was the anguish? The fear? The people here might as well have been changing trains at Union Square. The halls seemed to be lighter and brighter versions of subway tunnels, and she got the same sense that there was really nothing on the other side of the thick walls but earth. She could have been rolling along toward the social worker's office on castors. When she reached an open waiting room defined by a square of molded plastic chairs, Stew burst out of a door, baby first, and whispered excitedly, "Bridget told me she was supposed to have someone bring her home after the operation. But when I got here, there was no one left to bring."

Stew had a long, narrow face like a trowel, large, squarish lips, and a nose that was almost as thick at the top as at the base. His hair, which had been falling over his forehead in narrow triangles last time she'd seen him, was now sticking up in all directions. The kid he was holding must have been Bridget's, although babies, especially sleeping ones, don't have too many identifying characteristics. Even Jean could tell that his grip was odd. He was carrying the kid slightly away from his chest, as if positioning the bundle to drop it into a well.

"Ms. Crossley?" This was the social worker: short, young, Hispanic, with the little trained ponytail and discreet gold hoops of a debutante. The sort of person Jean would have been happy to introduce to a client. Clearly she could do much better than social work.

Stew looked around nervously. "I'm so sorry," he said. A sweet smell rose off of him.

"Please accept my condolences as well," said the social worker. "Won't you please come into my office? And Mr. Stew, would you mind waiting outside for a moment?"

"Why can't I go in?" said Stew.

Through the doorway to the social worker's office, Jean could see the padded chair she was expected to sit in—wine colored, seamed like a down comforter. It couldn't have been leather, but at least there was some resemblance. The lighting was dim, pleasant, as soothing as harp music. On the far wall a hand-stitched sampler announced, "Love is all you need."

"I didn't mean to exclude you," said the social worker. "It's customary to confine certain meetings to members of the immediate family, but there's no hard-and-fast rule. You're more than welcome to come in. Would you like me to hold the baby?"

"No," said Stew shortly, looking at Jean as if expecting *her* to. When the social worker joined in on this look, Jean picked up the baby as if that's what she'd intended all along. And she held it much better than Stew did, right next to her, like a sack of groceries.

As they started to move into the office, the social worker said, "Not everyone realizes how risky a hysterectomy can be."

"What?" said Jean, so loudly that the baby woke up and started to scream. Jean noticed the disapproving stares of two old white women, twin pyramids of flesh sagging over the sides of their molded chairs. She abruptly handed the baby back to Stew. "My sister didn't have a hysterectomy."

"Why don't we talk about it inside?"

"Put it this way," said Jean over the baby's cries. "Bridget was not *supposed* to have a hysterectomy."

"People are not always completely honest with their families," said the social worker, then added: "For some of the best motives."

"She believes in all that womanist stuff. She never would have got a hysterectomy for a fibroid."

"You need a lawyer," said Stew.

"Do I?" Jean asked the social worker.

"That is not the sort of conversation we're going to have," said the social worker pleasantly. "But it's up to you."

"I see," said Jean. "And what sort of conversation are we going to have?"

"I know you're upset," said the social worker, still smiling.

"Certainly that is my business," said Jean.

The social worker gently touched the thick blue pressed wool of her jacket, saying, "I just want to help!"

"Don't fall for it," said Stew.

"Oh, dear," said Jean. A nervous smile rose to her lips. Its inappropriateness frightened her, but at least she was sure it was not a sign of pleasure, not even deep down, where she had no intention of ever rooting about.

As if there were no longer any need for discretion, the social worker asked openly of Stew: "Is *he* a lawyer?"

"Why?" said Jean.

The social worker was just as sweet, just as calm, just as serious, just as absolutely sure she was right about everything, when she said, "Suing is not the first thing most people think of when someone close to them dies."

"Well, maybe they should," said Jean coldly, suddenly negotiating a deal. "I think it's time for us to go."

"I'm just back from the hospital," said Stew to Sunny when she came to his door, and as soon as she saw him and heard him speak, she knew that it was true: Bridget was dead. Sunny walked through the front room, with its couch and table and kitchen nook. She walked through the middle room, with its king-size bed, Jade asleep in the center. She stopped in the last room, which had been converted into a giant closet. She stood there for a while. Shelves built into one wall held stacks of nearly identical Izod shirts and blue jeans. Boxes of thick black plastic grids held different-colored underwear and socks. Opposite the shelves, on a dowel reinforced by a disembodied mannequin arm, hung dozens of sports jackets. Underneath was a long, skyline-shaped row of hiking shoes and work boots.

Eventually Stew came in and unrolled his hand to reveal a Medeco key. "It's hers," he whispered. "It's Bridget's."

The phone rang. It was Jean's husband.

Sunny took the handset from Stew. "Oh, Geoffrey, I don't know where Jean is. Have you talked to her?"

"Sunny? What's going on? Her office gave me this number."

"Hasn't she called you?"

"No. I've been here all day."

A loneliness washed over her that did not dissipate when Leon and the kids appeared. He had found a parking space a few blocks away.

"Could you go get the car again?" asked Sunny.

Leon stood watching her for a moment, not quite believing his ears.

"I need a ride to the train station. I have to tell Mr. Crossley in person. Can you take the kids home?"

Jade woke up when she was moved, so Sunny carried her screaming out to the car, up to the ticket window, down to the platform, up the steps on the train, down to the taxi stand, up and down, up and down, following a wave out to her father's home in Paw Valley, where he fell back inside at the sight of her, watched silently as she closed the hollow door behind her, and finally said in a hushed voice, "Did you and Leon split up?"

When Sunny told him about Bridget, his gaze dropped to her open jacket, where Jade was whimpering and scrabbling her feet against her stomach, trying to nurse.

"Oh," said Ed: a single falling breath.

"I want you to come home with me," said Sunny.

Ed nodded.

"Pack, and we'll take off," she said.

Sunny sat on the edge of his bed, drinking Madeira from a mug, the only liquor she could find. Jade was in her lap, having finally accepted some formula. Thank God Bridget had started giving her a supplementary bottle every day. Ed placed a change of underwear in a large hard-sided suitcase, then closed it up, imprisoning a lot of air.

"It's getting late," he said.

"I know," said Sunny.

Strapping Jade into the back of Ed's Toyota was like trying to put a seat belt around a garden hose. Sunny made Ed sit in the back and hold her. He did not object, although it took Sunny a while to get used to the brakes on his car, which grabbed and seemed to suck her down. When she tried to hit the turn signal, the windshield wipers went on with a dry squeak. The Toyota felt so light and tinny after the solid, lumbering van, she might as well have been driving a geegaw off a charm bracelet. In the mirror, she could see a car behind her open up like a bird taking flight! No, the wings were doors, which shut again. The traffic was thick and clotted, pulsing with a quicker thread that she found herself part of. Could she really have just wound down the road as slick as a snake? And why was she passing on the right? She slowed down fast, and an evil car in back passed with its horn blaring. Jade joined in screaming.

"Remember the baby," said Ed, as if he didn't care whether he or Sunny were killed. He had lost weight; he didn't look much different from the suit hanging on the hook by the window.

Sunny stopped at a discount store off the Belt Parkway to pick up a car seat for Jade, who had fallen asleep as suddenly as she'd fall off a pier. The one Visa card Sunny thought worked didn't, so she had to use American Express.

Then they all went next door to a diner, where Sunny and Ed looked out a long band of black windows, Jade snuffling a little as she slept in Sunny's lap. Tall stalks of sodium-vapor streetlamps illuminated a head-on row of cars, a pitched sidewalk, and a secretive trio of sawhorses.

"Bridget was a lot like me," said Ed.

"Yes," said Sunny, not sure what he meant and not caring.

She searched for the smallest item on the menu, as if she could not trust her mouth to open more than a crack. Who knew what would fly out otherwise? Finally she chose a cup of pea soup. She wouldn't even have to fit the whole head of a spoon between her lips; she could just sip.

"Are you absolutely sure about this?" said Ed.

Sunny nodded. "Stew saw . . . her."

"Because they make a lot of mistakes, you know."

Jade made an odd huffing noise, which caused Sunny's heart to rise to her throat. Her own children had never produced such a sound in their sleep.

"Bridget never had much luck, did she?" Ed continued.

"Oh, I don't know," said Sunny.

"In the end it seems like luck is the only thing that matters."

On the wall above the booth was a six-inch wreath, which sprouted tiny red berries on wire. One of the berries was misshapen, with little bumps on it. The table smelled sour.

Sunny looked down at Jade, who had gotten heavier and warmer as she slept in Sunny's lap. Holding her was like holding a bunny rabbit; Sunny could feel twitches and quivers running all through the little body.

"She has no mother," said Ed.

"No," said Sunny, examining the tamped-down face, the perfect arc of eyelashes. "But I'll take care of her."

If Ed was interested in the baby, he did not show it.

"Pie, please," he said to the waitress. Her clip-on nametag read "Sarah," which was the name of Bridget's best friend in junior high.

"Apple?"

"Yes."

"Or blueberry?"

"That's fine."

"Which one? Apple or blueberry?"

Ed looked at her, then muttered, "Forget it."

Sunny asked for a muffin, thinking of Jade. "And the check," she said, so they could hurry away.

"There's a minimum at the tables after five," said the waitress.

Sunny blinked at her, not taking in what she was saying.

"Just so's you know," said the waitress.

Outside, on her way to the car, still carrying Jade, Sunny stepped into a hole in the pavement.

What a lovely church! And such an interesting name: St. Marks-in-the-Bowery. Yes indeed. Poetry readings. Dance concerts. The Greek Revival spire even made it look like a real church on the outside, although the Episcopalianism it housed was a lot like the big, empty, renovated space inside. No doubt that was why Bridget had chosen it for Jade's christening. Not that there was anything wrong with that! It was the last Saturday before Christmas, and "Rudolph the Red-Nosed Reindeer" spilled from a nearby leather shop. Jean cast a benign eye on the filth stuck amid the cobblestones in front—the orange-tinted waxed paper (nice color), the mounds of sodden newspaper (unexpectedly 3D). Well, it was the slums, after all. Even this last thought Jean managed to slap into a cheery shape by the time it was done. For three days now her brain had occasionally stuttered through these slow, self-conscious impressions. It was not exactly that she was afraid Bridget would find her thoughts wanting, even if Bridget was tuning in to them, which she very much doubted. Alive, Bridget hadn't been particularly judgmental; she hadn't paid enough attention to details for that, relying instead on a blanket distrust of whatever was held to be a success in this world. Tellingly, she had been just as baffled by

Leon's work as Jean's; at least she hadn't fallen for Sunny's rhetoric. But Jean didn't want any misunderstandings, either. Often when she made some perfectly truthful remark, everyone laughed. While this was generally fine with her, it was not something she wanted to risk if a dead person might be listening in.

She caught sight of Stew, who was sneaking around near 10th Street, clearly avoiding her. Objectively speaking, she supposed, he was terrifically ugly, almost monstrous; but he had a magnetism that made her want to try to squeeze the life out of him. She pounced. "You must not have got my messages," she said.

"I was out of town," he said, his eyes careening away as soon as they slid near hers.

Out of town! Ha! Where would he go? Still, it was amazing how many people mooched their way through life. He was wearing a zoot-suitish, overly padded black jacket and snakeskin shoes. Jean could see chest hair at his neck. "I wanted to get your okay on the funeral arrangements."

"*My* okay?" said Stew.

"I wasn't sure about the music," said Jean, although actually Sunny had managed to handle that, despite her sprained ankle. "I thought you might know."

"She likes . . . ," he began, and then wet his squarish lips. "She liked . . ." Grief had heightened the seductively breathy overtones to his deep voice; there were new layers, new shadows. It was a voice you could get lost in.

Then Sunny was there, and she went ahead and hugged him, sort of mewing a little. She looked awful. She'd gained weight, not good for such a short, plump type, and she was still on crutches, her ankle huge in an Ace bandage and her face all swollen and blotchy and kind of yellow. Of course, she was cracking up. She'd admitted that she'd taken to reading the Bible while finishing off a case of dessert wine. Jean had never known a sane person to read the Bible. That was what priests were for.

Jean surveyed the triangle of cobblestones in front of the church. Geoffrey was still outside, talking to her father, who was gray-faced and sunken. Bridget had been his favorite, really; Mr. Crossley had distrusted people outside of his narrow circle in Paw

Valley, and it had been clear to him early on that Bridget would always need his protection. He teased her but spoke admiringly of
her superior virtues. He would often slip her a five-dollar bill,
folded lengthwise. Five dollars! Only an old man with his mortgage paid off could have thought that meant anything anymore,
even to Bridget. But he would come out of the kitchen with his
face lit up, his eyes sparkling, his hands still upraised as if to sus-
tain their secret bounty. A trick of memory superimposed this ra-
diant face on his present gray one, giving Jean such a stab in the
heart she thought for a moment someone had hit her. Thank God
for Geoffrey, who was leaning over her father in the cold now, his
brow furrowed, all his considerable intelligence brought to bear on
exactly what few words to utter.

At least there were a lot of people here. Many she didn't even
recognize. She must have assumed Bridget's friends were too cool
to go to funerals. A number of Sunny's friends had come as well,
both male and female. Jean had never had the time to make as
many friends as Sunny did, but if she, Jean, died now, the church
would be packed with business associates. Leon's real estate partner, Sergey Gustov, came up to her and said, with surprising bit-
terness, "Americans think they do not die, but see, they die."

The floor of the church was of the same shining blond wood as
a basketball court; it was surrounded by gray-carpeted risers and
banks of spotlights. The altar was on an imaginary foul line. Pots
of chrysanthemums and poinsettias had collected here and there
as if the service were a combination memorial and high school
"snowball."

Geoffrey held Jean's hand during the service. He was normally
stiff in public, and he clearly wasn't doing it spontaneously; he
had thought this through. It made her wish briefly that she could
be just a regular person now and then; it would be so much easier.
But he had to leave for Los Angeles right from the church. Had she
told him she had never been to a funeral before?

In high school, when many people mistook confession for
conversation, Jean always said that having a dead mother was too
embarrassing to talk about. If pressed, she claimed that the only
thing she remembered about her mother's funeral was how

jealous she had been of Bridget's new strap shoes. It had been decided—Jean never knew by whom—that Bridget was the only girl old enough to attend. Eight-year-old Jean and four-year-old Sunny had stayed at home with their next-door neighbor, now dead herself, who even then was so hard of hearing that the two younger girls could kick and pinch each other with impunity as she mutely said her ivory-colored rosary. Usually Sunny was a terrible tattletale, but that day she had been armed with a ferocious silence. The room might as well have been without air, the way no sound waves carried.

Later Jean had overheard Sunny asking Bridget what the funeral had been like. Bridget had taken so long to reply that Jean gave up and went back to her book, but then she heard Bridget say slowly, "There was no one there." When in fact lots of people had attended. Still, the phrase had spooked Jean; Bridget always sounded as if she were looking at the underside of a rock.

Jean wondered if anyone present was really envisioning Bridget in heaven. It was hard to imagine her belonging anywhere; even sitting in a chair in her apartment, Bridget had seemed to be slightly puzzled over how she'd got there. This sort of estrangement, however placid, was so exhausting it was no wonder the sixties hadn't lasted. (And why had no one managed to inform Bridget of that fact?)

Today Jean wore a dressy double-breasted black wool suit hooked at the shoulder. There was even a peplum—discreet, but a peplum nonetheless. It was a choice she regretted as soon as she rose to give her eulogy. She would have felt more like herself in a business suit. As it was, she looked as if she had stepped into a soap opera that Bridget was grimly eyeing at one remove. Bridget could never understand the appeal of a simple soap opera.

Jean paused up at the lectern before she started. Although she was used to public speaking, she had never before experienced these feelings of inauthenticity and insincerity that were repeatedly washing over her. Her awareness that she appeared to be struggling for control over her emotions only made these feelings worse. When she told a story about how a ten-year-old Bridget had jumped out of a tree, Jean secretly doubted that the act was evidence of the bravery she was claiming for her. It was probably self-destructiveness or a simple inability to connect cause and effect. Jean wished Sunny had agreed to speak, too. No one ever cared if she looked terrible.

As it turned out, though, there was another speaker. Once Jean had sat down, a man came forward with a sheaf of legal-size yellow papers curled at the top. "I'm going to read a poem for Bridget!" he declared loudly, nervously. He was fortyish, gaunt, crew-cutted, possibly insane. He would have been thrown out of any place Jean normally frequented. At first the strangeness of the situation demanded her attention, but the poem was impenetrable. As it droned on and on, she gradually lost the sense that Bridget was listening in to her thoughts. Instead Jean's lulled spirit seemed to rise slowly and join Bridget's watching one.

Sunny had been to Jean's new apartment only once or twice before. It was in a thirty-five-story Upper East Side building with a carefully pruned smudge of ivy on a small fountain out front. It also cost over half a million dollars—and was bought in part with the large profit she had made on the sale of her first place, a shabby two-bedroom near Columbia University, where she'd gone to college. This lavish reward for behavior of no benefit to the world rankled Sunny, Jean having acted just like those dreadful girls in school who wouldn't give up one boyfriend until they had another lined up. But for the first time Sunny realized that the apartment looked like one big overpriced funeral parlor.

Sunny hobbled into Jean's building with Stew and Leon, vaguely aware that Leon was describing the renovations he'd done on certain of his properties in Harlem. She noticed Stew's patronizing and forbearing demeanor toward Leon as if she were watching a TV show out of the corner of her eye. There was no question that Stew thought himself very broad-minded to be speaking to a landlord. Leon noticed nothing. Stew's expression of tolerant disdain did not alter as he registered the plump, white-gloved, lugubriously deferential doorman, the huge red imitation-velvet holiday bows over the fake lobby fireplace, the mirrored elevator with its waist-high handlebars, and the same starburst bronze-colored wall sconces visible whenever the elevator door opened.

As soon as the three of them reached the apartment, Jean was on them: "So what sort of name is 'Stew'?" She was in the doorway, effectively blocking their entrance.

"Sort?" said Stew, falling back. "Oh." He tried to focus, then drew himself up. "It's a very old American name."

Jean was long, rangy, and loose limbed, with a button mouth and short, curly dark hair like a spaniel's. Indeed, she kept at Stew a little like a dog with a bone.

"Isn't it a nickname?"

Stew grimaced, shook his head. But Jean was going to have this conversation if it killed her. "Is it your first name or your last name?" she continued.

Stew remained mute, with the rigid, falsely oblivious look of someone passing a crazy person on the street. Sunny, too, could not fathom what was going on. Was Jean simply irked that Stew had never acknowledged his turkey-baster baby?

To experience a rush of love upon seeing Leon took a preceding separation of at least a week. With the kids, just a few hours could do it. Sunny wanted to hug them both until her heart slowed down. But Linc was thirsty, Ruth had hit him, Linc had broken a wheel off her Barbie bicycle. Linc hadn't touched her dumb bicycle, yes he had, he had broken it, something had to be done about Ruth, why couldn't Linc have a little brother instead. "The more sisters the better, that's what I always say!" cried Sunny, but her voice cracked, and she had to stop.

Jade was sitting by the garbage can in the galley kitchen, evidently forgotten, mouthing a three-pronged metal rod. An antenna. Just one more piece of junk that Jean had sitting around this incredibly expensive apartment. Sunny began to choke on her own saliva. As she coughed and wheezed, she easily took the antenna from Jade, who put up no fight. Already Jade seemed to have given up some basic expectation or hope in these past few days without a mother. By leaning on one crutch and hopping a little, Sunny was able to put the lethal-looking metal on top of the refrigerator. Wasn't anyone else, maybe a person who wasn't on crutches, capable of doing a little monitoring around here? Where was Brianna, whom Leon had stopped to pick up on their way downtown so that she could baby-sit during the funeral? A rush of tears fell out, as if a cup had been upended. But she threw water on her face and said to Jade, with one hand on her oh-so-soft head of hair, "What a big girl." For a brief disorienting moment, she felt as if she were dead and she were comforting one of her own motherless children.

A woman with a thin forty-year-old face, spiked hair, and licorice red lipstick approached shyly from one end of the kitchen and said, "Hi, Jade." A friend of Bridget's, presumably. Sunny didn't recognize her. If she kept her head down, maybe she would go away.

"What a terrible time," said the friend.

"Yes," said Sunny, keeping her face averted. She was going to have to leave the room now. She couldn't stand talking. She'd let the kids watch TV in the playroom for three days straight. On Wednesday she'd turned the set off for lunch, and the silence had allowed such a clutch of thoughts to grow inside her head that she hadn't made that mistake again. From then on the four of them had crouched under a tangle of unzipped sleeping bags in front of the Cartoon Network, watching endless replays of death overcome, Sunny with her Madeira and the kids with a box of multicolored, sugar-coated cereal, the kind Linc and Ruth were normally not allowed to eat. Ed sat by himself in a chair that needed reupholstering.

The bottles of Madeira that Sunny had insisted Leon bring to Jean's were on the counter, along with the beer and the jug Chardonnay Sunny had known would be there and had known she would not be able to bear. A week ago, a Madeira would probably have made her gag, but now she was thirsty for it all the time, the kind of thirst that bestows the flavor of the drink on your tongue in anticipation. As the friend said something about the holidays, Sunny downed most of her first glass. She was leaning against the light blue Formica counter, and the weave of her skirt stuck to its lip. At Jean's, better not to think. Sunny poured out another glass of Madeira, listening to Jean's voice vying with a couple of male ones in the entryway.

The sound propelled Sunny out the other side of the kitchen, pinching the side of a wineglass between thumb and forefinger while curling the rest of her digits around the crosspiece of her crutch. She had almost reached the couch this way when Leon gently pried the glass away and put it on the coffee table beside the two-foot plastic Christmas tree that was the only visible concession to the holiday in Jean's apartment. "Jade," said Sunny. "Where's Jade?"

Place foot, drag ankle, prop crutch, drop bottom onto couch, lay crutches on cushion. Once she was finished, Jean was upon her, saying, "We have to petition the court to appoint a temporary guardian for Jade, so we can start a wrongful death suit. I had my lawyer draw up the papers, appointing me. It's just legal stuff. We've also subpoenaed the medical records. We are going to make them pay—enough so that it hurts. Jade will probably end up a very rich baby."

"This lawyer," said Leon. "He didn't say anything about having to establish paternity, did he?"

"My lawyer is a woman," said Jean with a small smile, raising her beer bottle as if it were the logical extension of her arm, her small round mouth fitting perfectly over the O of the top.

Despite her remarks, Jean wasn't breaking down sexual boundaries; she was simply stepping across them. She didn't disapprove of the patriarchs as long as she got to be one herself. Sunny closed her eyes. How was it that Jean could raise a bottle, talk, make plans, and Bridget could not? How was it that *Sunny* could still do those things?

Jean found it more painful than usual to watch Sunny with her children. There she was on crutches, and every time a kid asked for a glass of water, up she'd creak. Then she'd hobble around, spilling half of it as if no one else could adequately slake the thirst of a person under twelve. Ruth screamed for Sunny when her father tried to "make her a plate," i.e., put two rugalah on it. (For some reason, Bridget's friends, treating this event like a pot-luck supper, had brought various aluminum foil nests and black plastic takeout containers, which were now stuck randomly on the dining room table with the cold cuts Jean had got such a good deal on.)

Finally Sunny disappeared after a tottering Jade, ostentatiously carrying a disposable diaper between her index and middle fingers so she could still work the crutch, and a little group (of two) formed around Jean. "How come you don't have any juice?" said Linc. He was a solemn kid, wearing a miniature version of his father's khakis, identical down to the little pleats in front.

"Because I have soda, which is better."

"My mom doesn't let us drink soda," said Ruth. She at least had on an incredibly hokey A-line print dress with a pink fabric unicorn appliqué sewn on the front—an outfit impossible to find in an adult size.

"Take it up with your mother, then," said Jean. Neither of them moved.

"Do you have any stuff for kids to do here?" asked Linc. Why hadn't they turned to one of the men? Like maybe their father? They had probably been trained unconsciously to seek out wombs. Or was it already programmed into their DNA?

"Let me think," said Jean. She must be as brainwashed as the next woman, because although the situation made her a little nervous, she did see it as a chance to show off dormant maternal skills. It was too bad Geoffrey wasn't here to witness. But that creepy feeling of Bridget eavesdropping on her thoughts was returning. Didn't these kids realize their aunt had died?

"I know!" said Jean. "Felt-tip pens!" Fortunately she could find both black and red. She got paper from the printer and put it on the coffee table—two sheets. But before she'd crossed the room to get another beer, Linc was finished: On his paper was a big circle, not even closed, with two dot eyes. Jean narrowed her nice, regular-size gray ones, objects of much admiration. "It doesn't look like you spent much time on it," said Jean. The other sheet of paper—Ruth's—was blank.

"No," said Linc, either agreeing or disagreeing, she couldn't tell which. The low-level discontent he was displaying was consistent with either.

"How would you like to watch TV?" said Jean brightly. (And why hadn't she thought of it sooner? Hers was a splendid set, as big as a picture window.) Now she was the Pied Piper, kids trailing happily behind her. But the solution remained elusive, because she didn't have premium cable.

"Do you have any idea how much that costs every month?" she

said severely. "Not that I couldn't afford it, of course." She aimed the remote and began to click through the available programming.

Seeing a familiar face, she said, "I loved this when I was little," although she wasn't sure exactly which of the actor's hit sitcoms this was.

"Is it the kind of show where people you can't see are laughing?" asked Ruth.

"Yeah, a haunted show," said Jean, clicking on. "Wait. Was that Batman and Robin?"

"The real-people movie?" said Linc.

"Well, I don't know how real Batman and Robin are," said Jean.

Linc never seemed to crack a smile. "Is it a cartoon or does it have real people in it?" he persisted. "The real-people Batman movie is way too scary for kids to watch."

What a wimp! As if she was going to force them to watch it. Maybe pin their eyelids open, like in *A Clockwork Orange*.

This latest betrayal may have reminded Ruth of the earlier one, because she said, "I don't know why you don't have any juice."

"Don't fall for that stuff," said Jean, annoyed. "Juice is terrible for you. It will kill you if you drink too much of it."

There was something sinister in both Linc's seriousness and Ruth's petulance. They were ravenous, these kids—they were bloodsuckers, was the hard truth. Not that it was their fault. Sunny had made them that way. Jean managed to escape after promising that a show on how to paint foliage would soon turn into a cartoon. You had to be careful around them, clearly, or you were doomed.

She called the office and went through her messages with Mary. Competence was such a relief.

"How did I let you get away?"

God. More drama. This hissed statement had come from the hall, where Jean could see Sunny swinging herself slowly between the shelves of books by Catholics. Jean hung up the phone as Paul, one of Sunny's old boyfriends, probably the richest of the lot, caught her by the crutch. "Oh, Paul, honey," said Sunny. Who knows how she would have responded if Jean had not been there watching? Paul's tone had been explosive; you could feel the tension in the air. Jean had always been surprised that Sunny had married Leon instead of him.

Sunny thought she could make it from one minute to the next if no one else tried to talk to her or tell her how sorry he was. She stuck to family members whenever possible. Two or three would huddle together as if they were having a conversation—which they were not, whatever few words might be spoken. Then, after a while, the groups would reconfigure, just as at a regular party, and the silence would continue.

One thing Ed said was "I've asked Father Jim to say a mass for her."

Jean nodded. She was the only other Catholic, having attended mass every Sunday since the day of her wedding. Sunny wondered if a God you only pretended to believe in was much comfort. Or did Jean's usual ironic tone mean she was pretending *not* to believe.

Ed also said, "I don't want to be cooked. I don't understand why Bridget did. What do you think, Leon?" He meant, Do Jews believe in cremation?

A wail rose from the back of the apartment: Linc. Sunny hobbled toward him. Leon outpaced her. Ruth came running toward her down the hallway, crying, "Linc threw up! Linc threw up!"

Linc was outraged at his body's betrayal, but he said he was finished. Sunny slid down to the white ceramic bathroom floor and sat him on her lap, shooing everyone else away. A tile floor is chilly and peaceful. You are not expected to think or feel there. It is a good place to hibernate. Sunny's bandaged ankle stuck out nearly to the sink she kept her half-closed eyes trained on. A six-inch single spout and compression faucets with ridged caps. Much more expensive than anything Leon would use, but the same design. A white tile backsplash mottled with gray, a white wood cabinet housing the plumbing. Six fine cracks ran up the inner panel of the bottom of one of the doors, like lines emanating from an old lady's lips.

One crack was much farther to the left than the others and maybe a hair longer. The remaining five were evenly spaced. Her eyes divided and redivided them into groups. A sharp knock on the door. You cannot rest on the floor. You cannot look at the sink. It was Jean, who said, "Mr. Crossley is in a state. Stew denied being Jade's father."

In the living room, Stew, visibly upset and standing near the door as if ready to bolt, said, "You believe me, don't you, Sunny? I'm *gay*."

Ed was sunk in the club chair, deep lines between closed eyes, neck twisted, upper lip pulled skyward in a sneer, long yellow teeth exposed. The friends had all cleared out.

"I think they mean only in a biological sense," said Sunny.

"I'm not the father in any way," said Stew flatly.

The distaste in his voice grated on her but was ultimately convincing. Yes, she believed him. Then who was the father? She looked around as if for a clue but found none. She had got so used to Bridget's uncommunicative manner that she had rarely tried to reach behind it. Sunny hadn't been a bad sister. But had she been a good one? Bridget was a mystery to her. Sunny put out her hand, as if to catch something falling from the ceiling. "Do you know who is?" she asked.

"No," said Stew.

She would think about it later. "We have to go," she said, leaning heavily on her crutch. "Linc is sick."

"Jade is asleep." Leon.

"Leave her here." Jean.

"Don't be ridiculous." Sunny.

"I don't see why not." Jean.

"Don't look at me." Stew.

"The last thing the kid needs at this point is the stomach flu." Jean.

"Oh, oh." Linc, who ran for the bathroom, followed by Leon.

"We have to hit the road." Sunny. From the space beside the refrigerator she plucked a handful of plastic bags. "We'll take these."

"How about Mr. Crossley?" said Jean.

Ed's eyes were parted in slits. Why did they glitter so? Could it be the way the light from Jean's goosenecked lamp was falling? Sunny took him, left Jade.

Sunday morning she called and got Jean's machine. She

couldn't understand why Jean was taking so long to call her back, but she got sort of a kick, thinking about her trying to take care of a toddler. In the evening Sunny tried again, this time with more success. Jean said that they were all going to Geoffrey's parents for Christmas, that Jade was fine, and that she'd decided to keep her.

The
House
Without
a Back

chapter 1

THEIRS HAD BEEN A TYPICAL SEVENTIES FAMILY: ONE BARELY functioning parent, slouchy teenagers picking at one another, bongs, an Irish setter missing a leg, bell-bottoms in odd rusty shades like a color TV gone bad. Bridget was the person who made all the dinners, some close to inedible, many from a seventy-five-page *Introduction to Greek Cooking* that she'd found on the sale counter at a local department store. It was Bridget, too, who did the laundry—zealously, but sporadically enough that their father took to rinsing out his white drip-dry shirts in the sink and draping them on hangers all over the basement. Bridget also decided it was her duty to tell her sisters the facts of life, and although Jean was not very responsive ("What do you think I am, anyway?" were her exact words), Sunny was clued in well enough to remain without child throughout her high school years despite what Jean suspected was early and exhaustive sexual activity. (For a while, whenever Sunny came into their room, Jean would say, "Yes, slut?")

Paw Valley was a ramshackle town on the underside of Long Island. Their house was a yellow-brick ranch with a carport and a mangy lawn and a bristle of antennae up top. The single story had the proportions of a brick as well—it was about twice as wide as it was high—and its lines were all horizontal. The windows were set in a band; the roof was low and had the skimpy look of bangs cut too short. Aluminum seemed to dominate, although it was found only in the screen door and the slots for the various windowpanes. In front of the house, a couple of low, wide bushes as squat as golf caps lay on either side of a flagstone path. Behind it was the Long Island Expressway.

The yard was separated from the narrow, four-lane highway by a twenty-five-foot hurricane fence and a wide strip of tough weedy grass. The sound of traffic and the agitation emanating from it were constant. Every once in a while you'd hear a honk, a skid, and a crash. The yard was lit up all night by the oddly humming overarching streetlamps. Ed's bedroom was always dark because instead of curtains he hung thick white fluffy acrylic blankets. But the girls played happily in many of the yards along the fence for years. Then one day eleven-year-old Jean was in the backseat of a friend's car coming back from the new mall—the first in the area. Her friend's mother extended an arm straight out to the right, waggled her index finger, and said, "Look, there's your house."

Jean stared. She must have passed it hundreds of times without realizing it. And who would have noticed? The back of the house had none of the decorative elements of the front. The windows were high little slits. The concrete foundation was plain and shabby and bare all the way around. The place had the look of a mattress or a piece of furniture abandoned at the side of the road. She never forgot the sight. Even inside, despite the four walls around her, she got the disconcerting feeling of sitting in a chair without a back. But to Bridget's hippie friends, Jean declared, "I like to live near a highway. The better to escape."

Bridget was in high school. Her friends would often drop by because most mothers still lurked at home then, while Bridget's had been in the grave for several years. Sometimes the kids would offer Jean a hit off a joint just to see what she'd say in that voice that was already too big for her body: "I'm certainly not going to invite you to the White House when I'm president. Too risky." Or, "Try not to call the cops down on us. I have a future to think of."

They'd laugh and laugh, not meanly at all, until Bridget brought them up short with some remark like "It's a long way to

Washington, D.C. Fourteen hours, maybe." Bridget couldn't joke, and no one knew what to make of her. She never would have had so many friends if it weren't for her empty house. Once they were old enough to drive, they stopped coming, and Bridget didn't seem to notice.

In a neighborhood of largely blue-collar workers, Ed appeared each morning for years in a charcoal gray suit, a white shirt, and a dark red-and-blue-striped tie. He'd started working at a one-man insurance agency called Cosgrove, Inc., by chance; but when both his wife and Cosgrove died within a year of each other, it began to look more like fate. He seemed to belong among the bereaved and maimed, ministering to their secular needs. He kept the "Cosgrove" name, and although his new clients were few, he had a lock on the old ones. Not to go to him would have been to upset the small-town Catholic order that prevailed in Paw Valley.

The girls often heard him say "I insure people, not things" to describe the nature of his work. At first, this seemed a moral stance: an assignment of relative importance. His business philosophy was encapsulated in another of his sayings: "I'll always get along all right because Catholics are short-term optimists and long-term pessimists." (Translation: They figure they can come up with the money for life insurance now, especially since it will pay off soon enough.) And every one of his most gravely pitched conversations included "For you I'll put a rush on that check." He couldn't have put a rush on all his disbursements, although he apparently believed it each time, and probably the statement was more of a balm than an actual hurry would have been.

What the girls did not hear, ever, was any kind of sales pitch. He was incapable of a spiel. Or maybe he thought it out of place in his holy calling. In any event, all three girls knew that the business was slowly fading away but assumed that their father was right— that it would take forever to totally expire.

When Jean learned later of the typical insurance salesman's reputation, she got a great kick out of it. "Mr. Crossley can talk the last nickel out of a widow's pocket," she said.

Ed, who had long ago given up trying to make any sense of Jean's mirror-reversed-in-mirror remarks (it's so true because it's so false because it's so true), simply smiled.

There was some controversy about when exactly Jean had started to call their father "Mr. Crossley." Jean claimed that she had always referred to him that way—which was true in the larger sense—but Sunny said, "No, no, I remember you calling him 'Daddy' just like a regular person," and Bridget said in her slow hesitant way, "I think it was when you decided you were no longer a member of the family." Preposterous. Especially since Sunny and Bridget had started using the term, too, behind his back.

Actually, it was when he got a new gray briefcase. Jean was probably in junior high. "Very nice, *Mr.* Crossley," she said, spotting it. He always kept several freshly sharpened pencils in it and a pack of Wint-o-Green LifeSavers.

Bridget was at Hunter in 1970, but when the school was thrown into chaos after the shootings at Kent State, she didn't bother to return. Ed had been furious when he heard that certain classes had been canceled. "Rich kids crack up their parents' cars," he said. "That's first. Then they spit on their education." He was referring to a friend of Bridget's who had totaled a Saab on the LIE the summer before he was arrested demonstrating on the steps of Lowe Library. This was illogical in about a dozen ways, but Bridget just looked at her father with those big, fixed eyes as if she had no idea what he was talking about. She rarely argued with anyone. Still, Jean doubted that Ed had forbidden Bridget to go back to school in the fall. It had probably been Bridget's decision—her reading of his desires dovetailing with the slipperiness of her commitment. This despite Jean's reminder that it would be very easy to get good grades if everyone else was on the battlements.

Because Paw Valley was not too far from the city, Bridget had wandered in and out of the house even when she was enrolled in college. Once she was officially back at home, she was there only slightly more frequently. She often stayed at the houses of friends who took a class or two while they all planned trips. That year she spent six months in Asia, having left with $400 sewn into various places on her jeans.

"Oh, yes, India," said Jean. "Poverty can be so enriching there." It was irksome, the way Bridget did not understand that the family had no money. She never felt the lack of it. She left the room if Jean was forced by the peculiarity of the dinner to go pick up some pizza or a hamburger; Bridget had some incomprehensible rating system for food that precluded takeout. She didn't smoke. Her clothes were really all rags, floppy, baggy, with designs so faded they could have been washed up by the sea. Her long black curly hair simply flowed unchecked. She rarely listened to music. She bought only secondhand paperbacks with titles like *The Lotus and the Snake*. In the top right-hand corner of the title page would be a penciled figure: 10¢, 15¢. She did occasionally go to the movies, but they were free, shown in an international studies classroom at a community college one town over. It's not that Bridget was happy without money. She was always in a sunken state that implied an indifference to happiness. She was quiet; sometimes she didn't appear to have any emotions at all.

Sunny never seemed to feel poor, either, because people—especially boys—were always giving her things. It spoiled her. The transistor radio, for instance, was a present from the school bus driver. Who ever heard of a school bus driver giving a kid a gift? It was old, true; and the guy himself had tinkered with it, so there was no battery cover. Plus he was very weird, bald, but with a low-lying cirrus cloud of hair settled about each ear. Still, it boggled the mind.

When Jean asked Sunny in no uncertain terms why he had given her the radio, she said simply, "He already has another one," refusing to see how odd the gesture was.

When Sunny was younger, she would wander over to a neighbor's house and come back with a dozen chocolate-chip cookies or a loaf of banana bread wrapped in aluminum foil. She was everybody's daughter. If she was missing at dinnertime, she could be in any kitchen on the street. Jean kept waiting for her to turn sullen and covetous, like a real teenager, but she never did.

Jean knew exactly what she needed: Frye boots, maybe a belt with a real silver buckle, a new pair of swim goggles, and a dark green anorak with a drawstring hood from L. L. Bean. She was clearly bigger than Paw Valley, with its pinched lawns and constant bake sales, but it was annoying to have to postpone proof.

By junior year she was always looking around for a way to make a few dollars that did not interfere with what she referred to as her "long-range goals." Although she managed a town rec program during the summer, she didn't work during the school year, because studying was more important. (Jean often turned off the top forty station on the bus driver's radio, saying to Sunny, "If you want me to support you in your dissolute old age, I'm going to have to get into a good college." Sunny would just laugh.)

Then Jean noticed a neighbor kid, pampered Lydia Hayden, run crying down the street after the Italian boys on the corner ganged up on her and teased her and frightened her. Jean decided she would walk her back from school for a small fee. That afternoon, when Mrs. Hayden went into the backyard to hang up her wash, Jean, who had been reading her social studies textbook in a twisted old aluminum lawn chair, called out, "You ought to hire a bodyguard for that girl."

The Hayden lawn was as thick as a mattress. The LIE was obscured with a curtain of knotty vines that clung to their portion of the fence. Everything was new: tricycles, barbecue set, above-the-ground swimming pool. Kids tumbled about. Besides, Mrs. Hayden had clothespins between her lips. She was no match for Jean.

Picking up eleven-year-old Lydia and twelve-year-old Sunny in the afternoon meant a slight detour from the high school over to the new brick middle school. Also, Jean couldn't accompany the girls in the morning, because she left early for swim practice. But, as she had pointed out to Mrs. Hayden, the girls really didn't need her then; all the troublemakers were rushing off to make the second bell or hiding in anticipation of their truancy. Sunny got into the habit of walking Lydia to school, anyway.

Everyone knew that Lydia was happy with the arrangement because she got to walk with the always popular Sunny, but neither Jean nor Sunny thought this irregular. Mrs. Hayden could hardly pay Sunny to be Lydia's friend. As Jean saw it, she was paid for her organizational skills as much as anything. Who would have even *thought* of such a source of income?

One Friday afternoon a couple of weeks into this arrangement, Mrs. Hayden, instead of just pressing a few crumpled bills into her hand at the door, asked Jean to come to the kitchen by herself. Jean was wary, but she was not one to back down from a challenge. She had never been in the house at all. The dining room was dark and looked as if it had never been used. In the kitchen two playpens, one with three little kids in it and one with none, were pushed against the far wall under the phone. Jean wondered how you could reach over them to answer it.

"I'm so grateful to you girls for looking after Lydia," said Mrs. Hayden. "And I know it must be hard for you girls, raising yourselves. . . ."

"So many things in life are so dreadfully hard," said Jean mournfully.

"Oh, yes," said Mrs. Hayden, not sure at first how to take Jean's exaggerated tone of voice. "Would you like to sit down?"

Jean declined, settling her books over one hip.

Then Mrs. Hayden plunged on: "I know Sunny, and I know what a kind and generous nature she has."

"How true," said Jean.

"And I know there could never be anything improper going on between her and the Walker boy. But I worry when I see him going over to your house all the time when your father isn't home. Young people don't always know how things look."

"Oh, dear," said Jean. "This is very serious." If Sunny screwed up this arrangement, Jean would never forgive her. She supposed Mrs. Hayden had seen the graffiti on the bridge that spanned the highway: "Don & Sunny 4ever."

"Maybe I should talk to her?" asked Mrs. Hayden with feigned concern.

"Let me think," said Jean. What exactly was going on here? Mrs. Hayden couldn't think Sunny was corrupting her precious daughter. After peering out the window at the Haydens' new wood-sided station wagon, Jean said, as if struck by an idle notion during her meditations, "I didn't see you at church last Sunday."

Sunny didn't understand the power of religion. She was too young to have been affected by nuns before their mother died, and afterward their father stopped attending mass. He took Jean only because she insisted she would go straight to hell otherwise—which she would.

But Mrs. Hayden felt the power. Jean could feel her trying to figure out how the remark was meant, but Jean's face, casually averted, was all smarmy innocence.

"I was feeling poorly," said the woman.

As soon as Jean heard the response, she knew that Mrs. Hayden was defeated—and that Mrs. Hayden was aware of it. She was lost as soon as she had to justify herself. Jean assumed the excuse was valid, but that was irrelevant. She hadn't even had to mention "the way things look."

She gave Mrs. Hayden a bland smile. Now she had to figure out what the woman really wanted. "Maybe Lydia would like to come over sometime," said Jean. "As a sort of chaperone."

"Oh, I'm sure she'd love to." Bingo.

Jean's triumph over Mrs. Hayden was invigorating in a way. Still, there were a whole lot of people who would never have been put in Jean's position. People with mothers, for one. Or people with money. If the Crossleys had not been a known poor family, Mrs. Hayden wouldn't have dared utter a peep. She was too timid and conventional, like most of the world.

Sunny had already left for home, so Jean had to wait until she got there to tell her to cut it out.

"Cut what out?" said Sunny, who was making herself a sandwich by putting a slice of American cheese between two slices of white bread. Even in an oversize hand-me-down zip-up yellow jersey, she was as cute as an Easter bonnet.

"You know what I mean," snapped Jean. She dropped her books on the pink Formica top of the kitchen table.

"I know that you're a psycho," said Sunny, without sounding particularly riled.

"What are you doing with the Walker boy?"

"Physics," said Sunny.

"Go tell Mrs. Hayden, why don't you," said Jean, watching Sunny bite into her sandwich. The two pieces of bread sprang apart. "She's about to call Planned Parenthood."

Sunny giggled. "For Froggy Walker?"

Jean nodded grimly. "I set her straight."

"I might have kissed him once or twice. He's awfully sweet. I hope you didn't make your usual mean remarks about him."

Jean rolled her eyes. She opened a small paper bag left on the table. Inside was a container of black olives. So Bridget was around somewhere.

"But don't expect me to get mad at Mrs. Hayden," said Sunny. "I don't see how I can. Don't you remember when she bought a dozen boxes of Girl Scout cookies from me? And then handed them back when I tried to deliver them. She pretended to have just started a diet. I think they were all Thin Mints, my favorite."

"Watch it," said Jean. "Someday you're going to get yourself into trouble that I can't get you out of."

"Jean!" hooted Sunny. "You didn't get me out of any trouble!"

Jean looked gratified, as if Sunny's laughter had been what she was seeking all along.

chapter 2

THE FALL THAT SUNNY WAS A JUNIOR IN HIGH SCHOOL, SHE stopped off to visit Jean at Columbia on her way to New Haven, where a world government conference was being held. Sunny was always touring Washington or voting on issues in some hilly suburb. Whenever a student at Paw Valley High School had to be picked for "leadership qualities," it would be Sunny. The phone rang all the time.

Ed called her "my popular daughter," which was not quite the accolade it might have been on another parent's lips. And Sunny didn't value it much. From time to time she thought she would rather be exotic, like Bridget, or maybe caustic, like Jean.

She did a lot of listening. She was amazed at the problems people thought to have, each as intricate as a snowflake. A boy broke up with a girl—sad, but at least simple, right? Never. A good-bye could be looked at a hundred different ways. Or if a girl kept having fights with her mother, a description of one skirmish would involve a reworking of all the others. Discussions would branch off, intertwine, head backward.

The house in Paw Valley was a lot quieter without her older sisters, Bridget having finally gotten her own place in the city. Sunny would cook a ground-beef casserole or a quick-fix lasagna, which she and Ed would eat a few nights running. If they sat down at 5:25 to eat dinner, they would finish in time for the local news at 5:30. Every couple of weeks Sunny's boyfriend—whichever one it might be—would take her out to El Topo, her favorite restaurant. It was a relief not to have to share a bedroom. Jean was tall, her elbows stuck out more than other people's, and she was so loud; she was always making a fuss. She'd taken up far more space than her half. (For some reason Bridget was never asked to relinquish her room, the biggest in the house, after she left.)

"Where's the Cork Line?" said Sunny, looking around Jean's dorm room when she first arrived.

But this room was obviously Jean's through and through. It took Sunny a while to realize why: A boy could have lived there. There was nothing on the walls. No jewelry or makeup or perfume adorned the chest of drawers. The clothes flung about were jeans, sweatshirts, dark-colored jerseys. Jean had always scorned purses; instead an L. L. Bean backpack slouched on the desk. Through an opened sliding closet door you could see a basketball among the running shoes. Well, Sunny felt right at home. She'd been in a lot of boys' rooms, even one dorm room, thanks to a summer fling with a boy from NYU.

She dropped her black shoulder bag on the floor and reached out toward Jean.

"I hope you don't expect me to hug you or anything," said Jean, shying away in mock terror.

Sunny ignored this as she flipped the right point of Jean's collar out of her sweatshirt so it would match the left. "You've got to have both in or both out," said Sunny. She stepped back to examine her work, then tucked both points back behind the selvage of the sweatshirt. "In, I think," she said.

"I wanted it that way," Jean protested, but she didn't bother making any adjustments.

She looked different, out on her own like this. She used to be skinny and quick, all nerves and wires. She'd had a way of voguing as she made her pronouncements—throwing a couple of words over one shoulder or tossing her hair. She was still slender, but somehow more solid; her gestures were more than just light and sound. The navy blue athletic jacket she had on at least looked as if it might have been worn playing softball or field hockey now. Not that Jean would ever have done anything of the sort. She was far too contrary or brittle or self-involved or something to join an actual team, unless you counted the high school swim team.

What the appeal of the look was, Sunny didn't know. She herself had no interest in any kind of sport, except an occasional dip to cool off while sunbathing. Of course, some people considered athletic success the only real success, but Jean wasn't one of them. Even when she watched football or basketball on TV, she had a tendency to use the English term *good at games* with its more patronizing air. "He's so terribly good at games" she would say of a quarterback or a center, and it was hard to take him seriously ever again. There were people who found this annoying, but Sunny had no use for them. They were a dreary bunch.

"Don't get comfortable," said Jean. "We have to go ambush someone."

Jean's dorm was on Riverside Drive. While the two girls snaked their way through the sparse crowd on the sidewalks, Jean described a friend of hers named Bessie. "She is the funniest person in the world," said Jean, which made Sunny a little nervous. No girl in Paw Valley had been funnier than Jean, and Jean was usually so critical.

"Is that who we're going to meet?" asked Sunny as they passed through Columbia's tall iron gates.

"*Waylay*," said Jean. "Not meet. But no, Bessie is very unlikely to be up at two o'clock in the afternoon."

Up to the right was the administration building, which Sunny recognized from TV: Student protesters had made the sweeping gray steps famous. No one could have been more different from them than Jean, who greeted three separate boys dressed the way she was. She had a punchy syllable or two for each.

"Come on!" She practically bounded around the corner of a long, narrow building nearby. "Ah," she said, sighting a stocky, red-faced bluff man with a blond beard in a perfect **U** around his chin and cheeks. "Mr. Boudreau!" she called. "What a coincidence!" She introduced Sunny, who was still surprised by the sprint and was trying to conceal her quickened breath. "You must take all of Mr. Boudreau's classes," said Jean with her usual arch manner. "There is no one better."

"What nonsense you talk," said the fellow, beaming. In his brown corduroy pants and sports jacket, he looked like an Afrikaaner Santa Claus. He huffed, he twinkled, he waved a fat-ringed, pudgy hand. Sunny wouldn't have been surprised if he'd reached out with it and patted her on the head. "Of course I look forward to working with any sister of yours."

"There you are," said Jean as he hurried off. "Perfect opportunity for a compliment."

Sunny was doubtful. "To me, it sounded like you were making fun of him," she said.

"Me?" said Jean. "Never."

"So is he a good teacher or what?"

"Didn't you hear what I said? Do you think I'd lie to get a good grade?"

Sunny laughed. "Are they all the best?"

"To their faces?" said Jean. "Absolutely. Each and every one of them."

From where she stood, Sunny could see dozens of students strolling here and there amid delicately caged windows and chained-off swaths of dead grass. "I don't know how you get away with the things you do," she said.

Jean nodded happily. "Heaven help the world if I decide to use my talents for evil instead of good."

Jean was in an airily good mood all afternoon. She even told Sunny that if she studied *very hard* from now on, she might get into a decent college. At night they went to a frat party across 110th Street in a brownstone with American flags hanging out of two of the second-story windows. The cheap hollow dark-colored door, which had a hole where its lock should have been, looked odd beside the elegant old curves of stone. Jean pushed her way in as if she'd been doing it all her life.

The first thing Sunny saw when she walked in was an

elaborately turned banister with some supports missing. Jammed up against the gap was a huge stereo speaker, which stood on a step at about ear level. The front room was similarly handsome and battered. There were no curtains. On a cigarette-scarred coffee table in front of a plaid couch was an inflatable snake with red lipstick painted on its two-dimensional black plastic line of a smile.

By the archway to the kitchen stood a group of boys, one with his back to the door. Behind his back was his arm, which was waist high, stiffly perpendicular to the bare floor. In his hand was a bottle of beer, which he was hitting rhythmically against his bottom. It was as if he were hiding it from the people he was talking to or maybe slyly offering it to Jean and Sunny as they entered.

Jean ignored him; she ignored everyone, sort of the way she would at home, although she walked as if she were on stage. In the kitchen she took two bottles of beer from a six-pack on the counter, bypassing the keg on the broken blue linoleum by the back door. There were even more guys in this room, with three young women shoved up against the refrigerator.

Jean, who settled herself in a corner, had yet to speak to anyone, although she was clearly scanning the crowd. Sunny couldn't tell any of these boys apart. She had a similar problem with war movies. At least here the tiered young men were all wearing athletic jackets and running shoes rather than military uniforms. Their hair was short on the sides with a sort of ruffle on top. They were clean-shaven. They were of average height and build, as if there were too many of them to waste time on distinguishing characteristics. They had neutral, small-town, midwestern accents. Many were slack jawed, but not much actually came out of their mouths aside from generic shouts of greeting. What was amazing was how well Jean blended in. She not only wore the same clothes, she was as tall as they were, and she had adopted a similar slouching stance.

Sunny said, "So what are we waiting for?" but Jean didn't bother answering.

Finally, when one meaty young woman appeared in the doorway, she came to life. "Hey! You took out the old lawn mower, I see." No hair on the other woman's head was longer than three-quarters of an inch.

"Yeah," she said, running her hand through her scalp as if feeling for something she'd dropped.

"This is my sister," said Jean.

"The heartbreaker?"

"Jean," said Sunny warningly.

"So how many orgasms have you had today?" said the short-haired woman.

Jean let out a whoop of laughter.

"Who, me?" said Sunny.

"This is *Bessie*," cried Jean, still overwhelmed.

This was the funniest girl in the world? Well, there was lots of humor these days too hip to be funny; maybe Bessie's was an example.

Now she was shouting vaguely at the other side of the kitchen, "Hey! Stop that man! He stole my beer!" No one seemed to pay any attention. "Ah, you can have it!" she called, making a dismissive wave with her hand and then pretending to have caught a fly with a last snap.

Sunny kept taking small sips of her beer, which was now warm and tasteless.

"Are you looking at my penguin pin?" Bessie asked her. And before getting any reply, she continued, "I always wear my penguin pin."

Without unhooking the piece of jewelry, Bessie pulled it from her chest, straining the fabric of the turtleneck and contorting herself in order to thrust it only inches from Sunny's face. It looked weird with the athletic gear she sported.

"I *love* my penguin pin," said Bessie.

One of the animal's eyes was caught midwink. "Very nice," said Sunny.

"So how old are you?" asked Bessie loudly. And when she heard that Sunny was sixteen, she said, "Ah, a woman's sexual peak."

It was hard to believe that Jean the prude would talk to this person by choice, let alone admire her. Jean made fun of Bridget's rock magazines and radical newspapers for their—what did she call it?—their "outspokenness." She wouldn't have been able to *read* the advice columns, with their solutions to fascinating new difficulties: Insert a tampon after intercourse to keep semen from running itchily down your leg. It is possible to remove pubic hair permanently.

"Well, I've slept with a lot of guys myself," said Bessie. She began to point apparently at random through the crowd. "Him. Him. Him. And him."

"Really," said Jean with mock interest. "Chip Phillips, too. How was he?"

"He had the hands of a karate master," said Bessie, and Jean burst into peals of laughter again.

Then, for the first time, they were addressed by one of these guys, a fellow who may have had a slightly squarer jaw than the others. He said to Jean, "I saw you sucking up to Boudreau today."

Jean said, "My, my. 'Sucking up.' Where did you learn such colorful language?"

Sunny was mortified. If Jean hadn't been making fun of the teacher, then she certainly had been sucking up to him. Right? Did it matter that she made fun of herself at the same time?

Everything was upside down here. Jean had always gotten along with the teachers in Paw Valley the way anyone did who wasn't setting fires in the bathroom. But they *laughed* when she told them they were brilliant. So did everyone. "Look at the way Mr. Teeples forms an 'A,' " Jean would say to Sunny, waving a successful lab report. "Look at the vigor of the second, downward stroke and the careless grace of the crosspiece. And the plus sign! My God! It's a poem!" How could anyone have taken this seriously? Jean's little face would be screwed up in a parody of critical attention. It was hilarious.

Of course, Jean's whole stance was overly (absurdly) Goody Two-shoes (proauthority, antisex, and so on). Bessie, on the other hand, was nasty, although she did sometimes sound as if she were trying to copy Jean, as in: "I love the gents. I really do. Look at how they *stand*, for God's sake, sort of off-kilter, with all that baggage in front."

Half an hour later you still couldn't say that Jean and Bessie had been integrated into the crowd of boys, but enough words had been exchanged for a challenge to be laid down. Jean, in offering a helpful hint on chugging, had told one guy that you didn't actually "drink" the beer. Offense was taken, and a contest was enjoined.

The next thing Sunny knew, both Jean and her competitor had upended their beers over their open mouths. The boy was drinking very fast; you could see his Adam's apple pumping away. But Sunny could see what Jean meant by "not drinking." It was as if she were pouring beer into a glass. There was a final, frightening moment when she seemed to be unable to get her breath, but by the time the boy finished and looked around to see what had happened, her face was composed again.

"Beat by a girl."

"I don't believe it."

"Hey, Deep Throat."

"Wow," said Sunny. She had heard of Jean beating everyone down at Carmichael's, a bar just across the town line from Paw Valley, but she had never seen it.

Jean was still talking about it on the way home. "That was the captain of the swim team, you know."

"Really?"

"Not that he's the best swimmer," she added with overtly false modesty.

"Do you always go to parties with so many boys?" asked Sunny.

"The way I look at it is this," said Jean. "If I'm going to have a stupid conversation, I'd rather it be about sports than about hairdos."

"Right," said Sunny, glancing pointedly at the shapeless wavy mass of hair on Jean's head and summoning up an imitation of Bessie's tone: "Of course, you could probably use a few tips."

Jean's face collapsed in an exaggerated frown. "You don't like my hair?"

"It's just a little . . . formless."

"I can't believe you don't like my hair." Under a streetlight, Jean pulled a few curls straight so that she could examine the last few inches. "There's nothing wrong with my hair. I can't believe you're so cruel."

Because she couldn't help rushing in to reassure at such a time, even when the hurt was at least masquerading as a put-on, Sunny said, "I still can't get over that chugging contest. You were amazing."

"Yes," said Jean. Then, in a rare moment of sincerity, she began to tell Sunny how Bessie, too, was beating those guys at their own game. "She really puts all of that sex stuff in its place," she explained.

Is that what Bessie was doing? Jean almost made it seem worthwhile. But it was the novelty of hearing Jean talk this way that was disarming.

"I guess she hasn't really slept with any of those guys," said Sunny.

"God, no. I don't think she's ever slept with anyone."

"Well, she wasn't very nice to me," said Sunny.

"It's just that Bessie will say the thing you think even before you think it."

Sunny shook her head.

Back at the dorm, Jean took a splayed-out toothbrush and a huge jagged bar of white soap from a cubbyhole in the communal bathroom. Sunny had brought her toiletries in a clear vinyl packet that had originally held two little rows of bath salts. The different-size bottles and jars in it now fit together as snugly. She put the gaily colored item on the bright white enamel of the sink next to Jean. "That soap is going to dry out your face," she said.

But Jean was looking at her reflection in the punishing light, lifting her chin first one way, then the other, as if to make sure nothing had gone awry since she'd last checked. "My hair just looks like hair," she said. She squeezed a tiny drop of toothpaste on her toothbrush, way too little to do any good. But before Sunny could point this out, a coed wearing a long blue quilted bathrobe padded in, and Jean asked, "What do you think of my hair?"

"Well, I don't have my contacts in," said the other girl, blinking as if to confirm the truth of her statement. She moved in closer, apparently oblivious to the way Jean stiffened in response. "Why, what did you do to it?"

"Nothing," said Jean.

"Oh," she said. Then she summoned up the proper feminine reply: "Your hair always looks very nice."

"See," said Jean to Sunny.

chapter 3

The summer before Sunny's last year at Harvard, she bought a dozen cocktail dresses from a thrift store whose proceeds went to cancer research. It was in a wealthy suburb near the more industrial and commercial town of Paw Valley, and evidently she was the same size as a lot of little old ladies who had once lived there. The dresses were smoky blue, black, pale yellow. They had fans of blue silk over the bodice or dropped shoulders or matching hats. People reacted in different ways to these clothes. Jean asked her if she was trying to look like Elizabeth Taylor in *Butterfield 8.* "You do understand, don't you, that she was one of the bad girls?" said Jean with mock gravity. This was flattering, but Jean saw everything in such simple terms. Ed shook his head when he first saw her, saying she reminded him of his mother-in-law, the old battle-ax, long dead. And Sunny herself was afraid the effect might be a touch matronly. With her short, round, curvy body, she looked like a pocket-size mother, the sort you could take out, tell your problems to, and then put away and forget about.

People continued to confide in her, maybe because she was such an actively sympathetic listener. If a fellow told her he was depressed, she would put her hand on his leg, look into his eyes, and say, "How can I help?" Then the guy would apologize or cry or clam up or (once or twice) wind up in bed with her.

Sunny loved it. She left the door to her room unlocked so that anyone could come in and wait. She let it be known where she studied in the library. Over the first few years, the campus had become a collection of niches: the spot in the Yard where Dennis Fitts told her how awful his older sister was, the dormitory stair on which Sunny had been standing when a law school student had become roughly ardent, stumbled, and broken his toe; the cafeteria table where she often ate breakfast with a girl who felt out of place because her father was in prison for bribery.

One time a fellow in her American intellectual history seminar, a member of the Christian Fellowship whose sweetness gave Sunny hope for the future of religion, came to her for advice on his love life. He had a desperate crush on a girl in their seminar. "I can't eat, I can't sleep," he said in anguish.

Since the seminar had only one other female in it, a nondescript music major named Phoebe, it wasn't hard to figure out whom he was referring to. Sunny was gracious. Young men often declared their love for her in oddly indirect ways. "It may be easier on you if you get it out in the open and talk about it with her," she said.

"Oh, no, she'd be shocked," he said. "She'd be repulsed."

"I can assure you she won't be," said Sunny kindly.

The next time she ran into him, he said that her advice had worked splendidly and that he and Phoebe were going to a prayer breakfast later that week.

Sunny told this story with great glee in the dining hall. *"What a comeuppance!"* she said merrily.

To which a snub-nosed, rubber-skinned fellow on the far side of the table said, "I think I may die of a crush on somebody in this room, and her name isn't Phoebe." This was Paul Walsh, the roommate of a guy who'd taken Sunny to Truro for spring break the previous year. Paul was looking straight at her—into her, really—and his meaning was unmistakable. That night he took her to a French restaurant. The next day he bought her a pair of high-heeled boots.

For Christmas vacation that year, Sunny went back to Paw Valley as usual but ended up spending most of her time in the city with Paul. His parents' town house was one in a series of similarly clean, toothsome buildings facing Carl Schurz Park. You had to be careful on the first floor because each of the paintings on display was protected by two electronic beams, one vertical and one horizontal. Paul said that this was why he spent most of his time in the basement, where he drank cans of soda from the stacks of six-packs kept in the refrigerator under the stairs and where he did lines of cocaine off the side of the pool table.

If it got late—and it often did, since Paul liked after-hours clubs—Sunny would spend the night on the couch at Bridget's on East 7th Street. Bridget's apartment was in a four-story, city-owned sandstone building, and she had already lived there for years, so she didn't pay much rent. Because it was in the back, it was dark and quiet and airless. The furnishings were hippie Gothic. The couch was a well-worn tasseled rose-colored brocade. Cushions of spoiled velvet were scattered on top of it, a black-spotted mirror draped with peacock feathers hung above it, blousy silk flowers sprouted in a tarnished silver teapot beside it. The bedroom was separated from the living room by strings of shiny black rosarylike plastic beads. Ghosts haunted the reception of the old black-and-white TV. Various ferns and scheffleras lined the windowsills and filled pitted stone funeral urns on the floor. The place was pretty in its way, but it made all Sunny's fabulous vintage clothes—even the nubby pink wool suit—look a little shabby and decayed.

Bridget had a boyfriend, a small, curly-toed, jut-chinned college adjunct who claimed to be half Cheyenne. He was rarely around because, Bridget explained, he was uncomfortable in strange apartments. That was all right with Sunny; she was happy not to stumble on him in the middle of the night.

Instead it was Bridget's upstairs neighbor, Stew, who would often drop by for a few minutes and sip some herbal tea or all-natural fruit juice. The first time Sunny had met him she'd been going off to the revival house nearby, so now every time they ran into each other, he listed the movies he planned to see when he got the time.

"Another film I'd like to see is *La Ligne Dangereuse*," Stew was saying late one morning when the buzzer rang, indicating that Paul had arrived to pick up Sunny.

Paul bounded up the two flights of stairs and then lavished obviously sincere compliments on the neighborhood. He had been sneaking down here since the age of twelve. Sunny could tell that Bridget was charmed—as anyone would be.

Stew, who had been eating Bridget's zucchini bread in silence, said, "The earrings you chose for Sunny are exquisite." He was referring to Paul's Christmas gift to her. "I used to buy my fiancée jewelry back when I thought I was straight," Stew continued. "Did you get it at an estate sale?"

"Grant Peacock," said Paul.

Stew nodded. "I almost got a gorgeous cameo ring there once," he said. "The setting was white gold."

Sunny was reminded of Stew's previous existence—what seemed to be a fantasy consisting of the "debs," "top med schools," "Jack Russ terriers," and "Snug Harb Beach Club" that snuck into his conversation between the titles of French films. Stew did not measure himself by the standards represented by these abbreviations—he, after all, had been forced by his homosexuality into a more exciting fallen world—but he often seemed to be looking with skepticism at the kinds of heterosexuals he now found himself among. Paul clearly was a welcome change.

"I hope you can both come to our New Year's Eve party," said Paul, exuding energy into the moribund room. "The parents always have such a good time that it's fun to roll in and out."

"I'm sorry," said Stew severely. "I have a date with a dance floor. I plan to be standing in a crowd with my arms outstretched listening to everyone scream out, 'It's raining men! Hallelujah! It's raining men! Amen!'"

"More power to you," said Paul, unmoved. "But you'll come, won't you?" he said to Bridget, and curiously enough, she did.

Sunny was proud of herself for not minding that Bridget, who really was an odd duck, would be meeting Paul's parents when Sunny herself had seen them only a couple of times. The first time she had run into his mother, it was in the wide hall at the top of the stairs on the second floor of the house. Sunny and Paul were coming out of his bedroom, and even though they had been doing nothing more than looking for his high school yearbook photo— they made love only in the safety of the basement—Sunny was a little flustered. Her greetings were a little too loud. She felt as if she'd bubbled up and was now effervescing over the side.

"My dear," said Mrs. Walsh, grabbing Sunny by the elbow-length sleeve of her secondhand black-and-white silk sheath dress. The older woman seemed slightly tipsy, although it was only the middle of the afternoon. "You're so pretty. I hope you're coming to our New Year's Eve party?"

"I would be glad to."

"I have a handsome son, don't you think?" Now she grabbed him.

"Of course," said Sunny, although she didn't think so. His looks were blander, more affable, than that. "That's because he has a beautiful mother," she added.

Paul's mother sighed and patted her ash blond hair, which had the lovely waves and rolls of a pediment on top of a curio cabinet. "Yes, my husband married me for my looks," she said simply.

Sunny nodded; she was used to people telling her the truth. But Paul said, "Oh, Mother, please."

Sunny was a little nervous about how Bridget would fare with such rich, relatively conventional types. In a way, Bridget was a social asset. She seemed equally out of place everywhere, and her taciturnity often looked like self-possession. Sunny just hoped Bridget wouldn't be miserable. Once or twice she was on the verge of discouraging Bridget from coming.

On the night of the party Sunny passed up her *Butterfield 8* cocktail dresses for something a little more ladylike—a longish, full-skirted Italian tea dress with a matching slate blue wrap.

"I remember when all the beautiful young girls would wear gowns like that to garden parties," Paul's father said gallantly at the door.

Later, a younger business associate of his said with admiration, "What sort of dress is that, exactly?"

His wife was more patronizing. "*I* don't think there's anything wrong with wearing out-of-season clothes."

"Oh, I never worry about that," said Sunny happily. Drinking with adults was a pleasant novelty, and good manners forced them to listen to her opinions, which were always lively.

Bridget, on the other hand, was ostentatiously silent. When an elderly wag said of her flimsy pale yellow drawstring silk pants, "I see you wore your pajamas," she simply looked down at them as if wondering how they got there.

Sunny said, "Bridget bought those last time she was in Nepal."

"She gets all her nightclothes there," said Paul, mercifully making Bridget laugh.

But even Sunny got a little bored eventually. There were only a dozen or so people there, and the twinkly perfection of the Christmas tree, perhaps because she'd seen it all week, was beginning to look a little forced. Both Sunny and Paul were happy to see Henry and his new girlfriend, Clare, at the door, and no one was sorry when Paul announced in his slightly bullying way that it was time for all the young people to go downstairs to listen to the top forty countdown on the radio. Two brothers—friends of the family who were still in prep school—accompanied them, as did Bridget, of course, although she was considerably older than the others. The wag threatened to come, too, but in the end did not.

Henry Clark, a tall, thin, cranelike young man, was the roommate who had taken Sunny to Truro the year before. They'd had a great time, so Sunny was curious about Clare, a delicate, aspiring singer with matchstick bones under her thin pale skin. She was pretty and blond and had a way of enunciating her words more carefully than did other, more ordinary people. For whatever reason—a similar curiosity or just plain listlessness—everyone listened in on the conversation she started up with Bridget. Clare had studied the Alexander technique and wanted to know all about Bridget's recent switch from Swedish to craniosacral massage.

"So give me one of your astonishing massages," said Paul.

Sunny had kicked off her slingbacks; her petticoat-swollen skirt rose about her. She did not think anything would come of his suggestion.

"I'm not sure that I can do it here," said Bridget, looking around at the ashtrays (both Paul and Sunny were smoking), the half-finished drinks, the sprawl of brothers on the black leather couch. That, anyway, was where her gaze fell, but she also, somehow, indicted the bar with its little stainless-steel sink, the entertainment center with its shelves of board games and record albums, the black butterfly chairs, the butterscotch-colored octagonal leather ottoman, the gold wall-to-wall carpet. Not that Paul noticed or would have cared if he had. His behavior could be erratic, but he was safe as houses in one respect: He was almost impossible to insult. He simply didn't see it.

He popped open two cans of beer and shook them slightly for the young brothers' benefit. "Come and get it," he said from the other side of the room. Once they'd scrambled off the couch, protesting, he sat down alone on the center of it, unbuttoned his cuffs, and started to pull his shirttails out of his pants.

"What are you doing?" said Sunny.

"I don't give *backrubs*," said Bridget. "You don't have to take off your clothes."

"I would love to see how you do it," said Clare quietly.

Bridget threw a low, veiled glance at Sunny.

"Don't do it if you don't want to," said Sunny.

"No, no," said Bridget, lines crossing her forehead like railroad tracks. "It's okay."

"What do I do now?" said Paul.

"Loosen your clothes so I can get to your sacrum," said Bridget, putting a palm on her brow as if to smooth it out.

"What's a sacrum?" said Paul with alarm, looking up over his right shoulder at Bridget, who was now moving in on him. Clare was right behind her.

"Hey, I bet I have a sacrum, too," said Henry to Clare, who ignored him. Paul was on his back now, obscured by the women.

"Why don't you put a pillow over his eyes," Bridget suggested to Clare.

With Clare now at his head, Sunny could see Bridget slip his ankles between her thumbs and forefingers. "This will be more of a sketch than a full portrait," said Bridget. Up on the couch, crouched at his feet, she glanced over, saw the unyielding sofa cushion balanced precariously on his nose, and said, again with her hand to her brow, "That isn't going to work. Sunny, give me your shawl."

So the Italian wrap was tucked over his eyes.

"What if I start to laugh?" asked Paul.

"I'll hit you," said Clare.

"No one is going to hit anyone," said Bridget. And to Paul she said, "Ordinarily we would be able to work through any ticklishness, but I'm not sure that we can here."

"Maybe you can give me a massage later?" Henry said to Sunny, trying to be light and jocular and instead sounding awkward and uncomfortable.

"Bridget is a professional," said Sunny. She, too, had failed at the light tone she was aiming for.

"Your cerebrospinal fluid has its own rhythm, which can become unbalanced," said Bridget in a slight singsong.

Sunny was afraid Paul would react with a joke and Bridget would take offense. But his voice was neutral when he said, "Well, I'm certainly unbalanced."

"What I'm doing is lightly holding certain key areas," Bridget explained to Clare. "To redistribute the fluid."

Sunny wondered how long this would take. She hoped that Bridget would have the sense to cut it short. She watched Bridget crab-walk down the couch to lay her hands on his right thigh. Wherever Bridget placed them, the fit seemed snug, as if they had become so soft and moist they took the form of whatever they touched. "Everyone has a tough tangle of muscle fibers running all over the body," she was saying. "They're like a bowl of cold spaghetti. What I try to do is add a little sauce to loosen them up. So I go where the body calls me. It's very intuitive. You see how different this is from Swedish massage. I can't tell anything if I'm just sliding over the top of the skin." Bridget was now at the pelvic muscles, and Sunny was sure Paul had an erection, which Clare was looking right at. Sunny closed her eyes.

"Ah, I feel a hot spot over your spleen," said Bridget. "Basically your body should be the same temperature all over. But I'm being called here. You are in some kind of pain. Like most of us. It's not unusual. It is very easy to tighten up in reaction to life, to let your muscles go rigid, to stop up your spinal fluid. I'm helping you unwind this tension. I go very deep. Follow along with me. I can lead, but you have to accompany me."

Even the brothers were quiet now, though whether it was out of interest or drunkenness, Sunny didn't know. The next time she peeked, Bridget was astride Paul, with her hands cupped tenderly on his chest.

"Now your heart is calling me. I can feel the heat. It's as if you have an iron buried in your chest. This definitely has to be worked through. You should be feeling the release deep inside you, under your skin. I'll only be able to go so far now. I hope you're feeling like a wet noodle. It's a good feeling, a happy feeling. It doesn't matter how old you are, your body can always learn to react in a more natural, open way."

Out on the street nearby and in scattered spots far away, a cacophony burst forth—horns blatting, firecrackers sputtering, party crowds dimly roaring. "Happy New Year!" cried Henry, grabbing an unopened bottle of champagne from the bar.

Bridget's hands were off Paul now, but she was leaning over him, her seriousness and the urgency in her posture suggesting a sudden, odd intimacy.

"Happy New Year, Henry," said Sunny, giving him a big wet kiss on the forehead.

Bridget, evidently just realizing who Henry was, laughed. "You all jump in and out of bed like puppy dogs, don't you?" she said, amused at last.

chapter 4

JEAN'S FIRST JOB OUT OF COLUMBIA BUSINESS SCHOOL WAS VP of marketing at a small pharmaceuticals company. "Drugs, at my age," she said. "Who would have thought?" But she found the winning of the position more fun than the position itself. To plan the attack had been heaven. At Lord & Taylor, where every item of clothing might as well come with a certificate of authenticity, she bought a boxy Jones New York navy blue suit and a cream-colored blouse with an attached scarf. She developed a precision in tying this into a large bow that belied its apparent floppiness and rivaled the composition of any necktie; each side of the silky stuff peeked exactly one inch over the second button of the hip-length, square-shouldered jacket. Day after day, as she practiced her knot, she stored up an appropriate mix of amusing and earnest-sounding things to say. She beguiled those middle managers; then she slew them. It was only a matter of months, however, before she suspected that they had gotten her cheap. The precious suit, the jacket of which was now tucked out of sight at the far end of the closet, had been all wrong. And the self-scarf! Don't get her started.

So two years later, when an executive recruiter called her about a low-level vice presidency at a larger, more diverse company, she agreed to talk to him. Again she enjoyed the interviews, but this time she was more cautious about the job. In the end, the recruiting firm itself hired her. It was in fact her idea, but they thought it was theirs. She felt as if she had finally shot out into the world, like a caged greyhound.

When Jean was hired at Crough & Co., there were already half a dozen people at the firm doing basically the same thing: research, some consulting, support work of all kinds. She took it as a matter of course, however, when she was the one chosen to head a new search after only a couple of months. The name partner, a loose-limbed WASP named Matt Crough, called her down to his office to meet with a representative from St. Lucia's Children's Hospital in the Bronx, Ms. Amy Roth.

Roth, a thin, trim, cricketlike woman, began by explaining how important the hospital was to the area, managing to sound sincere despite her appropriately chirpy voice. She acknowledged that certain problems with staffing had resulted in a rise in patient complaints. This was probably an understatement. The hospital's difficulties had figured in the news lately, and Jean had even heard jokes about the CEO's conversion to Christian Science; it was the only thing that could explain the extensive cuts in medical services. But Roth was saying that the board was committed to quality care and had set aside several million dollars for improvements at this hospital alone. Certain departments were being eliminated; others were being beefed up. In surgery they were going to hire five additional physicians and a new chief. To oversee the changes, to galvanize the staff, and to restore the reputation of the hospital, the CEO had decided that they needed no less a personage than Edgar Davis, M.D., head of surgery for Brigham and Young Hospital in Boston.

How to bring up Julius Krill, Crough & Co.'s biggest competitor and the recruiting firm that St. Lucia's corporate parent usually employed? Companies rarely moved from Krill to Crough. Because Krill was older and bigger, the change would be considered a step down. Crough himself was being suspiciously silent.

"Well, you've certainly made the right choice, coming here," said Jean.

"As I explained to Matt," said Roth, "we have used Julius in the past, but my CEO is very, very keen on Dr. Davis, and we happen to know that the Krill firm has a no-raid agreement with Brigham and Young, so they can't get him for us."

So why weren't they just asking Davis himself? That's what Jean was wondering, but she said, "How lucky for all of us."

"Yes," said Roth. "It's not that we don't want a full search."

That at least showed some sense. Dr. Davis was a man of great prestige and power, in his sixties, at least. Outside of the diet book trade, there weren't many famous physicians, but he was one of them. Why would he leave a teaching hospital in Boston, where he had lived all his life, for a similar job at a smaller and much shakier place in the Bronx? Privileged New Englanders were often idealists, mused Jean. There might be something in that. Oh, well, she would figure it out. "What kind of salary are we talking about?" she said.

"We are prepared to pay him twenty-five percent more than he's making now. At the very least."

This was cheering, but only moderately so. She simply had to say something. "Dr. Davis may not realize what a splendid opportunity this is."

"My CEO wants Davis," said Roth flatly.

Sitting there, Jean had a thought that almost made her laugh out loud. Her boss must have heard the jokes about his conversion to Christian Science! Nothing could stop them like an alliance with grand old man Davis.

"One Edgar Davis," said Jean, "coming right up."

But the guy was not to be found. Fortunately Jean did not have the experience to realize how truly difficult he was being. She tried to go slow at first, calling the hospital and his home at various times of the day. Occasionally she talked briefly to a nurse or his wife. A couple of times she left her name, but he never called back, not even when she left a more detailed message. Once, after being put through by the hospital operator, she heard a deep male voice say "Dr. Davis," and it took her a while before she realized she had been connected to a *Valentine* Davis rather than an *Edgar* Davis.

When Crough offered to select and interview the other candidates for the search, she began to suspect that she had been given the "leadership" role because the firm did not want to waste the time of an actually valued employee. Well, she would show them. She read up on Davis, and an old interview in a magazine designed for physicians' waiting rooms made her decide that she should appeal to his ego as well as to his principles: He and he alone could save this hospital. It was worth a shot, anyway. She stopped calling. There was no point in getting a reputation as a pest. Then he'd never talk to her.

Instead she got clearance to fly to Boston, where she showed up at the doctor's office. He was out, said his receptionist; surgeons were often busy saving people's lives. Was there any message? That afternoon when Jean dropped by, she caught a glimpse of him hurrying down the hall arm in arm with another white-coated figure. She decided to give it another day, leaving a message for Crough when she knew he'd be out to lunch. She switched hotels, closing out her stay at the Hilton with her company card and using her own, rarely employed Visa card for the Marriott-Copley, where a medical conference was starting up. The head of Brigham and Young was going to be honored with a dinner and a plaque on Thursday night; Dr. Davis was bound to attend. She called up Brigham PR and got herself invited.

As a group, doctors were remarkably lean and fit; in the elevator they always seemed to be carrying gym bags rather than the medical bags Jean remembered from TV. Doctors were not very social, however. Listening to their conversations could be quite painful. She recognized a couple of other executive recruiters, men who specialized in the medical profession. One—the younger—was from Krill's office. "Who are you after?" he asked. She told him she had come to the conference for her health. On Tuesday, outside a lecture on plastic heart valves, she noticed the nametag on a tall black man with a square jaw and an equally squarish forehead: Valentine Davis, M.D. On impulse she handed him her business card and asked him to fax her his résumé. It was one of only three cards she distributed; they were not, after all, takeout menus, to be tossed out in bundles.

That evening, the first person she saw at the ballroom was Krill's man, who said, smirking, "How's your health?" She refused to be lured inside, however, because the little folded place cards were lined up in alphabetical order on a thickly draped table by the door: Dr. & Mrs. Edgar Davis, Dr. Valentine Davis . . . According to the numbers on the cards, she and Edgar were seated on opposite sides of the room. She spent the time winding back and forth purposefully through the crowd. He and his wife did not show up until the main course had been served, after the speeches had begun. He looked much older than his photos; a lot more of his hair was gone, and he was beginning to waddle rather than walk. Still, he looked the part, hawk nose, forthright stare, big bushy eyebrows. Jean was trying to decide how to approach him when the honoree sat down amid much applause, and Dr. Edgar was on his way out the door.

Jean sprinted after him. "Dr. Davis," she cried as the double doors swung shut behind her. She seemed to be panting. "I've been trying to get in touch with you, and I've come all the way from New York for the honor of meeting you."

The great man turned. "Don't come too close," he said.

"Let's go, Edgar," said his wife, her piled-up blond hair trembling slightly.

"I told you not to come too close, young lady," he said. "I can see through your clothes."

Jean plunged on. "I'm afraid you've confused me with someone else. I'm here as a representative of St. Lucia's, in the Bronx. They need you desperately—"

"I warned you," he said, his voice now high and shaking. "I cannot be held responsible for what happens now."

Jean just stared.

"He's retiring next month," said his wife fiercely, pulling on his arm. "Why can't you leave him alone."

But Jean had no intention of following this sad old couple anywhere. She wanted to lower the wattage on those silly wall sconces out of respect for her dear departed career. She wanted to sink down to that bloodred carpet with the vomit-pink cabbage roses and keen and wail and gnash her teeth in the forgiving darkness. Instead she found herself opening her door with the key card, ordering a beer through room service, and watching a basketball game between two teams she could not have identified the next day.

It was evidently some kind of senile dementia, she decided; his wife and staff were covering up for him. Of course, it wasn't a disaster; candidates didn't pan out all the time. But it didn't matter that what Jean had been asked for was a miracle. All anyone would remember was that she hadn't pulled it off. It was infuriating. Crough couldn't have known the details, but he must have known that this task the insectlike Roth woman had set on her was impossible to turn down, yet impossible to fulfill. "The scales have fallen from my eyes!" Jean shouted in her hotel room, but it did no good. After just a few hours of sleep, she took a 6:00 A.M. flight back to New York, and there waiting on her desk in the offices of Crough & Co. was Valentine Davis's absolutely splendid résumé.

She immediately got on the phone and made a reservation for the first flight back to Boston. She was feeling very, very persuasive. By Tuesday morning, the time of the next meeting at Crough's office, everything was in place. Roth had brought an assistant, a burly, silent type who came off, oddly, as a bodyguard. Crough, with a satisfyingly benign look, let Jean lead.

"Before we get to the rest of the list," she said. "I want to tell you about the new Dr. Davis." She could feel the eyebrows rise at this point, but it didn't faze her. "As I made my inquiries about Dr. Davis at Brigham and Young Hospital, a lot of people thought I meant Dr. *Valentine* Davis, who is an up-and-coming surgical star there." Well, there had been the switchboard operator. And the last part of the statement was certainly true. "The talk about Edgar is of a totally different sort. Unfortunately, he is retiring because of severe health problems. It doesn't look as though he has long to live, although of course that's confidential." Throw in a little pathos; that will keep them far away from him. "Here is a fax he sent me, thanking St. Lucia's for their interest and suggesting Dr. Valentine Davis instead." That was all Mrs. Davis would agree to; an actual recommendation would have risked a follow-up.

Jean handed out copies of the letter she had composed for the old man's signature. She also passed out copies of Valentine's résumé. "I spoke to Dr. Valentine Davis at length. He is young and so has not garnered the medical awards the more venerable Edgar Davis has, but his achievements are extraordinary, considering his age. And his relative youth means that he still has the energy to transform a big department. He would also be a far more appropriate symbol for a hospital in the Bronx, being tall and black and very handsome."

"Yale," said Amy Roth, reading the name of his alma mater. Jean could *see* her thinking, Affirmative action.

"I myself went to college on a football scholarship," said Jean. "And look at me now."

Roth pursed her lips as she glanced back and forth between the pages of the résumé.

"If you can't get Edgar, the next best thing is his protégé." Okay, a slight exaggeration. "And obviously Krill could never get you Valentine, since he is also at Brigham and Young, which Krill has to keep their hands off."

"I'll take it to the board," said Roth, snapping the catches on her briefcase to lay the documents inside. But as soon as she had started to examine them in that intent way, Jean had known she had her.

Jean went back to her office, stood on the foot-high heating register, and gazed at the geometrical smorgasbord of flat roofs, bulging water towers, and right-angled parapets. For years she'd had the sense that she was waiting for a certain sort of life to begin. It was as if she'd had to grow into her own style. And now it had happened. She was sure that if she jumped out the window, she would bounce right back up.

By Thanksgiving Jean was heading another search for a leading teaching hospital. Still, the Davis switch-over continued to delight her, and that was the story she told over the turkey dinner out at Paw Valley. She could tell that Sunny and Mr. Crossley were pretty impressed. Bridget probably was, too, although she was still busy finishing the gravy. When she brought it to the table, she looked at Jean with those big whirlpool eyes and said—not even joking, she had no sense of humor—"I have a friend named Davis. Maybe you can get him a job."

It was frustrating, the way no one truly understood. She called Bessie's family's south shore home and asked for Bessie, even though it was Bessie who answered. Well, she sounded pretty different. And she said, "Yeah, the cow's in the shed," evidently referring to herself. She had started law school and dropped out, taken a job selling time shares and quit, gone to Japan to learn the language but returned early.

Jean did not like to drive but figured she could make it in her father's car as far as Hicksville—or even out to Bessie's house, if necessary. When she suggested a rendezvous, though, Bessie was unexpectedly negative about the idea. So Jean launched into the Davis story right there on the phone.

"Yikes, a headhunting firm just for sex maniacs," cried Bessie, managing to be both illogical and extremely irksome. Jean loathed the term *headhunter*.

She returned to the city the next day.

chapter 5

SUNNY MOVED A LOT. SHE COULDN'T BUY MUCH, BUT AS her ex-boyfriend Henry pointed out when she transformed her dorm room with a swath of Thai silk, she always found the most comfortable seat in the house. This was after she and Paul had broken up a couple of times. Finally one of the splits stuck. Just before graduation, Henry was offered a spot in a large, student-filled apartment on upper Broadway, but he was heading east to the London School of Economics for two years, so he suggested she take the place. Instead, at the last minute, she moved in with a boy named Jed White. Why, she could not fathom five months later.

But what an effect on his loft! When she moved in, plates, silverware, cans of food, and boxes of pasta and cereal littered the kitchen table. By the time she left, they were up in cabinets where they belonged, the mattress was off the floor, the walls were painted toothpaste blue, and all the lightbulbs were covered with white globes. When he objected to her departure, she offered to leave him two pots and a frying pan. She had already bought him a copy of *The Joy of Cooking* as a going-away present. He threw it on the floor. It was a miracle the binding did not break.

Sunny went to stay with Bridget on East 7th Street, which was convenient, because Sunny had started to pick up some money tutoring high school students in the Village. But she didn't really like living with Bridget. It was not surprising, perhaps, that the black-spotted mirror, brocade couch, ghost-ridden TV, and rosary-bead curtains hadn't changed over the years. But neither had the plants. They were always in the same place, in the same urns, and they never seemed to grow. Sunny kept a spare toothbrush in the exact same spot in the medicine cabinet for five years.

One problem was that Bridget had still not got over her awful boyfriend's return to St. Louis. The breakup should have freed her to find someone more suitable but instead seemed to immobilize her for an entire two years. She still went on trips to various parts of Asia—Thailand, Beijing—but she looked as if she'd been put away in the early seventies and hadn't been exposed to sunlight since. Her clothes often smelled a little musty. She rarely referred to her feelings, as if she weren't quite sure she had them, but she did occasionally complain, "Now that Randall's gone, everyone here is exactly the same." For a while she was involved in a politically oriented women's drumming group, and Sunny thought Bridget might even find a lesbian relationship, but apparently she did not. When Sunny stayed with her, she scoured the appliances, put up shelves in the closet, and brought order to Bridget's dressing table. Bridget, on the other hand, was felled by menstrual cramps for days and seemed to move in and out of the apartment through osmosis.

After six weeks Sunny's friend Dennis, an architecture student who knew almost as many people as she did, told her about a place in Murray Hill that would be free for a month. With its framed posters of soothing cultural events (a Haydn concert series, an art show in Santa Fe), it reminded Sunny of a dentist's office. But it made her realize how much her own place meant to her. She still didn't have much money, because she was tutoring part-time, but she found what she at first considered a really dreadful hole beyond Avenue A—a railroad flat she soon became quite fond of. The toilet in the hall was hers alone; all she had to do was break through the brick wall in her bedroom to get to it from her apartment. She also dissolved the lime encrusted on the high, wheelbarrow-size bathtub in the kitchen, put in screens, and found a narrow night table at a flea market just big enough for one Tensor lamp.

Paul, who was now a mortgage bundler at 110 Wall, stopped by while she was stripping the floors one evening. He knew the area well because he used to buy coke two blocks away. "You don't belong here," he said. "Why don't you come live with me?" At this point the invitation was a surprise. Paul had a large white studio that looked a little as if it had been molded out of plastic. The staircase that turned a corner up to a loft bed was fenced off at banister height by an extension of the two far walls. Speakers hung in cunning spots above dark blue wall-to-wall carpeting. It was a real bachelor's pad.

"Marry me," said Paul. Not the sort of proposal you could take seriously for an instant.

"Oh, Paul," she said. "I'm never going to get married. What a horrible bore that would be."

A few nights later, as she drank Gibsons with Dennis at the French Club on Avenue A, he, too, told her she should marry Paul.

"Curious that you should mention it," she said, although she didn't take Dennis's advice too seriously.

Dennis had looked impossibly young in college—like a twelve-year-old, really—and had displayed little sexual or romantic interest in anyone. It had always seemed impolite to Sunny to broach such a messy subject with him. But now that he had come to New York, his fresh boy-next-door looks were paying off. He was already crowing about the interest he generated in gay bars. It was hard to keep him off the subject, to which he returned now, wide-eyed: "But do you think he could really have been a film producer?"

At this point Sunny was being pursued by Cap Turcotte, who flew to Washington every other week; Gerald Sherry, who owned a collection of Groucho glasses; Martin Fay, who had to quit his job when his colleagues all turned into monkeys in suits; Jack Shaw, whose father owned a department store; Ari Mufta, who'd had half his stomach removed; and Brendan Dobbs Duff, whose talents were wasted as a photo librarian (everyone thought so). Bridget was calling more than usual as well, to find out where Sunny had put this or that item when she was tidying up the apartment on 7th Street. Bridget never complained, but the calls themselves seemed faint reprimands, so Sunny would always add firmly, "Shoes belong in your closet," or the like. Sometimes it was easier to just sit and drink with Dennis, musing over career plans that never quite seemed to gel. She wanted to help people, but she couldn't see exactly how.

A few nights later she said in a gap in the conversation, this time at the Blue-and-White, "I'm just not interested in a job or a career per se. Why should I waste my life being a lawyer? I have a little more self-respect than that. And I have trouble imagining myself in any of the helping professions. I could never become a social worker or any of those poor overworked cogs in a bureaucracy. But there must be something for me to do. There are so many unhappy people in the world."

"You can help *me*," said Dennis, laying his forehead on the lip of the bar.

"Why, what's got into you?" asked Sunny, running her hand over his rust-colored brush cut.

The height of the bar stool, the way his legs were twisted around the supports—both made him look even more boyish. He had been carded that evening, and the drinking age in New York State was eighteen. "My sister's getting married," he said miserably.

"So?"

With his eyes half-closed, he told her he couldn't bear to tell his parents of his homosexuality. "And my grandmother is seventy-eight!" he cried. "It would kill her!"

"So don't tell her."

"Oh, but they'll suspect."

"You never worried about this before, did you?"

"But I didn't know before. Not really." He threw an anguished glance in her direction. "It's not that I won't tell them eventually. Maybe ease them into it. I know them, though. First I have to at least look like I'm trying heterosexuality."

Sunny raised her eyebrows.

"They think homosexuality is something you can talk yourself out of."

"Maybe a little education is in order," said Sunny.

"Actually, I want you to come to the wedding as my date."

"Ha!" Her single laugh was more of a shout. Several men turned and gave her the eye.

"You don't have to lie. Just don't say anything to contradict any delusion they might have. They won't ask you any questions, because they'll be afraid of the answers."

"So then when you do turn out to be a homosexual, you can blame it on me?" asked Sunny.

"No, no," he protested. He swore it would be fun. It would be a real change for her; she didn't get out of the city enough.

"I do nothing but leave the city for the weekend," she pointed out. "Jack just took me to Vermont."

"Oh, that doesn't count," said Dennis.

He probably meant nothing by this, but Sunny saw with a jolt that in a way he was right. She had never gone away for the weekend by driving past Paw Valley. She had a brief vision of speeding in Dennis's BMW through the tangle of Nassau County, leaving dust on the exposed shambles of her old house, and being deposited triumphantly among the shore birds in Amagansett. "Okay, dear heart," she said. "But I think you're stalling. And I hope you realize you're going to have to put out."

As it happened, Dennis's route did not take them anywhere near Paw Valley, but the morning of the wedding was cool and pleasantly damp, and the pared greenery lining the highway gave Sunny an expectant thrill. This was the way she was used to seeing a vacation begin.

Dennis drove straight to the church, where he had to seat his mother at the beginning of the ceremony. Sunny found herself in the front row—at the very core of the wedding—among people she had never met before. Both parents hugged her and introduced her to everyone in the vicinity as "Dennis's college sweetheart." Under a large tent on the country club lawn, Dennis's mother would pat her as she passed and say they were going to have a long talk soon. Once she asked if Dennis was eating and sleeping enough. Sunny said yes. Dennis's sister, who was tall and loud, said in passing, "Oh, I know we'll be great friends," and then on the way to the limo that was to take her on the first leg of her honeymoon, *she threw Sunny the bouquet.*

It was great fun, but exhausting. Sunny was glad when it was time to leave for Dennis's summer house, an overgrown clapboard cottage on a few acres of land. His parents retired early, and she and Dennis lay outside on a hammock strung between two black oaks. At first Sunny tried to find a more comfortable position, but she soon gave up because the weave of the hammock was so loose that her heel or elbow kept working its way through the holes. The crickets sang. The night was soft and warm, the temperature of bathwater. With her eyes closed it was hard for her to tell where skin left off and air began. She fantasized idly about having a big house that all the Crossleys and their friends could visit for holidays, one with a long dining room table and a dozen extra chairs. And a sleeping porch, maybe, crowded with cots. Jean would organize card games because she was so good at them. Also, they would have Scrabble, Stratego, Clue. She felt Dennis kiss her on the side of the mouth.

"Don't be a tease," she chided, waving him away.

"I'm not," he whispered. He looked ghastly in the moonlight, as if he were in pain.

"Oh," she said.

She was keenly aware of the slippery, ladderlike embrace of the hammock. She walked one of her hands up the next to establish some purchase, then froze in surprise as Dennis kissed her again. Gay or not, he was not her type. With his surprisingly brawny body, his fountain of freckles, and his skin as pale as frozen fish, he could have been any one of her many cousins.

"Shall we go indoors?" he said, whispering still.

"I thought you'd never slept with a woman." Now she was whispering, too.

"I never have."

A wave of tenderness engulfed her. Her bottom sank even lower into the hammock as she tried to lift her head.

In his bedroom, looking at the spread with its appliquéd clipper ship, she said, "Are you sure you want to do this? How about your parents?"

Dennis nodded grimly in answer to the first question and shrugged at the second. Their lovemaking proceeded in quick, logical, bloodless fashion. When he came, he rolled over on his back and looked at the ceiling, one arm laid across his forehead. He did not seem to have heard of a woman's pleasure, which was just as well. It would have been too embarrassing. But if satisfaction was not part of her experience, a feeling of accomplishment was. She felt the way she did when she'd just scrubbed out the tub.

"Thank you," said Dennis.

Sunny giggled.

He added, "You really are very nice."

"Well, so are you."

"No, I mean it," said Dennis. He cocked his head and gazed at her with an uncharacteristically moony expression, although he was no longer touching her at any point. "You have beautiful eyes, you know. Maybe we could go away again."

"Mmm," said Sunny. "Don't you think I'm worth at least a trip to the Caribbean?"

"I didn't mean—" he said. "You didn't *have* to— I mean, I hope you didn't just because—"

"Oh, Dennis," she said, laying her fingers lightly on his lips, which felt like her first—and only—gesture of physical intimacy with him. "I had a very nice time."

chapter 6

When evaluating candidates, Jean often spoke of "fit," using the word in an unusually physical sense. She had a certain firm image of herself, standing with her weight on one leg (making it wholly fantasy, since in real life she would be sitting down), legal pad in hand, dark shoulder-length hair curled under slightly, one eye on the interviewee and the other on the space around him.

She was wary of a person who seemed at pains to fill that space. Also of someone who was at odds with it. At one point Crough criticized her for passing over a certain Tod Hampa, who had turned a car rental division around in three years, and Jean said, "The guy was tearing holes in the air every time he moved."

"What?" said Crough.

"Believe me. It was painful to watch."

"I don't like metaphysics in the office," he groused, but she didn't cross him often, so he let it pass. A couple of weeks later, at the end of one of his in-house morning meetings, he said to her, "I just heard that Hampa went AWOL with one of the company cars and ended up in Alaska." He shook his head. "Sad."

"I won't let it go to my head, sir," she said.

She knew she had really scored when the tone of Crough's

response was an imitation of hers: "I fear it is already too late for that, Miss Crossley."

Matthew Crough was president and part owner of Crough & Co., which boasted a dozen or so recruiters, all of whom worked fairly independently. Jean knew that some thought of her as an apple-polisher, but those who did were all people who had tried it themselves and failed. They couldn't see that Jean operated on a whole different level. She flattered Crough not by agreeing with him constantly, but by acknowledging that they both knew what was going on behind her words, even if it was generally nothing more than "Isn't it ridiculous that I'm being nice to you because you are more powerful than I."

Jean went to the Bahamas once for the weekend with a fellow recruiter named Tess Dixon, but the trip was not a success. Jean couldn't forget how much it cost, and Tess kept trying to ferret out Jean's assessments of their colleagues' abilities, earnings, and futures. Although Jean mentally adjusted even more detailed analyses of her rivals daily, she was not about to share her insights with Tess. Too late, she realized that Tess had some idea of getting closer to Crough through her. But even if Jean had pointed this out—with the necessary chaffing, of course, to cover up the fact that she was deadly serious—it would have been impossible to explain to Tess how off base she was. Jean's tone worked with Crough because she had convinced him he was in on the joke. What the joke was, exactly, was not clear, but who cared? Every time she opened her mouth, she was trying to create a sense of conspiracy. Usually she succeeded.

Crough often referred to her handling of the disastrous employment of a certain financial expert, Francis Rio. She had lured Rio from a small Catholic hospital in Providence to a much larger, public, New York–based institution that was so riven by factions, he was fired from the job before he began. He was rather bitter when he called from his new home, surrounded by unopened boxes, not sure which room he was in. "Do you remember when I asked you if this was for real? You assured me that it was." Jean pointed out that her promise had not stopped him from negotiating a substantial golden parachute, which was being forked over without a fight.

"And they paid for the move," she added.

"Can they get us our old house back?" he asked quite unreasonably. "And our old life? Now that our new one has disappeared?"

Clients generally drop recruiters who witness them behaving foolishly or meanly. To forestall this, Jean called each of the different factions at the client company and said, "What terrible things have happened to Rio! He's been forced to move out of the sticks into a fabulous new house! To accept a fantastic sum of money for doing nothing! I don't know how he's going to stand it!"

"I don't know how he's going to stand it!" Crough repeated now, sticking his beaky nose around the open door of her office. He was passing on a new client to her, so the remark was not really apropos of anything, but his jokes—the old-fashioned sort, designed to put people at ease—trumped all others. The bad news was that this client, a fledgling pharmaceutical company head-quartered in Stamford, Connecticut, actually expected her to go up there to see firsthand what a different type of corporation it was. There were two partners, both young, both named Joe. They'd gotten into generics in the early eighties when the field was opening up, and they'd had some spectacular success with a "me-too" drug, but their profits started to decline as they expanded. Their executives were not used to handling the larger staff and bigger budget. They needed a strong, experienced manager, a real leader. The wanted "the best," and they were "willing to pay for it." But they also wanted to impress upon Jean how fun-loving and progressive they were.

This much Jean ascertained within ten minutes of meeting them. It helped that they were both named Joe, which was the source of much humor. ("Jean, Joe; Joe, Jean; Joe, Jean; Jean, Joe.") Also, the idea of the start-up had come to them while they were watching some vintage rock-and-roll concert, the exact nature of which was the subject of more bantering. Amid all this friendly ribbing, the Joes explained how their revolutionary concept of boss-employee relations was directly responsible for their success. On the tour, Jean did not point out that the main difference between their operation and others she'd seen was its untidiness and disorganization. The manufacturing of their biggest seller had largely moved to a new plant down south, but mysterious remnants remained; R&D sulked in a converted garage; and office staff had been added willy-nilly through a sprawl of prefab buildings. Outside, a large chained dog slept on a slab of concrete. "I'm not sure your methods are working on him," said Jean.

It was never a disaster if Jean's target—colleague, client, or candidate—did not know what to make of her for a moment, as happened with the Joes now. The fitted navy blue suit, which changed her gray eyes to a cool blue, was formidable. But as soon as she smiled, they were all the more charmed. She knew her way around the world, but she was one of them, a real kidder. The two Joes sat at a conference table with their shirtsleeves rolled up and their feet propped up on the polished wood, echoing each other like clocks chiming. They described job sharing, a company bowling team, and an agreement with the local day care center as if no one had ever heard of these features before. But their obvious happiness and pride were infectious. "Jean will make everything better," she promised.

After a couple of months she sent her first choice—an older, highly seasoned man—up to Stamford. "His attitude is all wrong," said one Joe on the phone after the meeting.

"Really stiff," said the other, who was also on the line.

Then she sent up another candidate. "I don't think you understand this place," a Joe fretted.

"And the free spirit that prevails," said the other. Clearly they were afraid she was sending them old fogeys with no idea of how special their company really was.

This gave Jean pause. It was true that she had always been a witness to, rather than a participant in, the psychodrama of "her" generation. *She had no parents.* Or virtually none. No matter what showed up on the parade of sitcoms, being raised by a single father was a lot like being raised by no one at all. For Jean, rebelling against authority just didn't have the same old zing. (There was no excuse for Bridget and Sunny's having turned out the way they did.) Jean had turned her singularity into a strength. But sometimes it made her feel left outside like that hideous dog sprawled on the concrete.

All day she turned the problem over in her mind. That night, as she tried to sleep, she pictured a hundred Joes all in a frenzy, trying to stab their fathers while leapfrogging over their backs. The idea made her tired, but she could find no rest. At one o'clock in the morning she was still so wakeful she found herself staring at the light bleeding in around the edges of the window shade. (And how did she think she was going to go to sleep *with her eyes open*?) Her mind had strayed from the Joes to what she would do someday when she was an unqualified success. She would sleep, for one thing. And maybe have a nice, leisurely dinner first.

In the meantime she could not flag, even for a moment. Although she was of course absolutely normal, she was aware she had a sense of mission that most other people did not have. She had always projected herself into her splendid future by sheer will, and that took a lot of sacrifices. Which were paying off. She might not be Crough's equal yet, but she was in a world that even as an eleven-year-old girl she had known she belonged to: perfectly regulated temperatures, an expense account, a discreet and beautiful staff (here she was thinking particularly of Mary, the Vietnamese receptionist, who dressed better than many of the clients), phone calls that could move people hundreds of miles.

The next morning she went into battle. First she convinced the next candidate, who was fifty-five years old, of how much he should want this job. "These children have very big allowances," she said. That was so he would not be offended when she told him to reduce his three-piece suit to two, exchange his white shirt for one with contrasting cuffs and collar, and add a hint of unruly curl to his hair. "You don't want to look as if you might take those allowances away," she explained. Then she called the Joes and told them that she had someone special, but he was so hot, they were going to have to come into the city to meet him.

The Crough firm leased part of a floor in a typical midtown glass-and-steel skyscraper. The interior decoration was ornate but drab—like the design of a dollar bill. The walls of windows on the outer rim of offices made the entire place feel at first open and aboveboard and accessible. But the real work was done in the conference rooms, which were on the inside and had no windows. In fact, it was a rule that no one ever opened a door to one of these rooms without knocking first. No outsider was allowed to walk the halls without an escort, and entrances and exits were carefully calibrated to prevent accidental meetings of any sort. This secrecy did not seem excessive to Jean after she had been at the firm for a while. No one with a job wanted his superiors to know he was seeking another, and in the long run it was better for Crough, as well, to be careful about whom it gave away information to. More important for her purposes was how automatic this was. Let the Joes see how an office could operate in the same smooth efficient predictable fashion as an adventure ride in Disneyland. And let them associate it with a man who may have more experience but whose clothes showed how relaxed and youthful he really was.

Jean told the candidate to come in early, because she figured she was going to have to bring him down one more notch, in the spirit of the professional woman's rule: Take off one piece of jewelry as you leave the house. Finally, as a last-minute inspiration, Jean called Bridget, asked her to lunch, and told her to wear her leather pants because the restaurant they were going to was rather fancy. As if any place outside of an S&M bar would require leather. But Bridget believed anything.

It all went beautifully—even the Bridget part, which was a bit of a risk. Jean was gambling that the Joes felt so successful that they would not be afraid they were like Bridget but would see her as an opportunity to show how cool they still were. Jean saw the phenomenon every evening at Grand Central, when the most expensively dressed young men clapped the scruffiest on the back: "Hey, remember that Grateful Dead concert? Wow. Was I fucked up or what." Et cetera.

After the interview, Jean escorted the happy group to the reception room, where Bridget, as neither client nor candidate, had settled with impunity. The cascading black hair, the snug white thermal underwear she wore as a shirt, and the navy blue polish she wore on her nails all labeled her as a free spirit. The leather pants also let you know (misleadingly, as it happened) that she could do her traveling in comfort. "Bridget! Bridget!" Jean cried, throwing an arm around her. Fortunately Bridget did not seem surprised by this effusive greeting, and she put her hair behind one ear in a gesture that looked like the beginning of a responding hug. Jean hastened to introduce her to the Joes, and Bridget remained relatively poised despite her surroundings. Jean had been counting on this. Bridget didn't seem to be able to distinguish between many people and so maintained that same air of slightly bewildered self-containment with a cabbie or a millionaire. There wasn't much time to chat, which was just as well, but Jean sensed that the Joes liked Bridget right off. And the candidate, who'd been warned, was attentive and relaxed with her, forming a sort of *tableau vivant* of how well he'd behave with the Joes' very special employees.

Jean was in an excellent mood when she came back from her lunch with Bridget. Bridget never got the details of her triumphs right, so telling her about them was a little like speaking down a well, but Bridget didn't feel used, either. She'd just said, almost to herself, "But how can you be sure people are going to do what you expect them to?"

Ah, the phone. Because Jean was expecting the Joes with good news, her "Hello" was especially bright and confiding.

"Hey, old buddy."

It took Jean a moment to place the voice.

"Bessie," she said with a warmth she certainly did not feel. Although Mary would use the intercom to inform her if the Joes were trying to get through, she suddenly felt the press of unfinished business.

"Long time no hear," said Bessie.

Yes, yes. "What have you been up to?" said Jean.

"Funny you should ask," said Bessie. "A little of this, and a little of that. Looking around a bit."

"Uh-huh. Like what you see?"

"Sometimes, sometimes."

"So. Are you still living on Third?"

"Oh, no. The city started getting me down. I'm back at the 'rents' for a while."

"Well, it's very green out there."

"I've been thinking over my employment options."

Jean thought fast, tapping her fingers on the desktop theatrically. She couldn't remember Bessie's latest venture, but certainly one had been in sales. "I know you've gone far beyond sales," she said.

"You got it. I went to work for a credit card company, but I had a difference of opinion with my boss."

"Happens all the time."

"Tell me about it. Anyway, here I need a job, and I'm thinking, who do I know who has lots to spare? Well, you can guess where my thoughts turned. My old friend Jean."

Jean laughed as carelessly as she could. "When was the last time you ran a hospital, Bessie? Or put together a P and L for an entire pharmaceuticals division?"

"Just thought I'd ask," said Bessie quickly, and hung up.

Jean went back to work, but she found it hard to concentrate. She'd tried to keep her tone as light as usual, but she now had the uneasy feeling that her words had not been worthy of her. They had not really been clever enough. When the Joes finally did call to congratulate her on finding such a confident, experienced, yet open-minded candidate, Jean's victorious mood was largely gone. Still she managed to say, "Money is the fountain of youth," which the Joes took rightly as a compliment on their ability to pay. She knocked off at an apparently civilized 5:30 and ran into Crough by the elevator. "Miss Crossley," he said with a formal bow.

"Mr. Crough," she said. Her tone was equally grave. Then she asked, "Have you ever had a friend from college call up and ask you for a job as if you were doing personnel for some backwater manufacturing concern?"

"God yes," he said in his impressively hollow voice. But then he told a story about an old classmate's trying to feel him out about who was doing the search for the CEO of Univor. "Can you believe it?" he roared.

Of course, Crough's idea of sly ego stroking was letting the client beat him at squash. Jean looked at his light round tortoise-shell glasses, his ship's-prow forehead, his slack rich-boy's mouth, and felt a pang of jealousy. Crough wasn't stupid, really. On the other hand, he sometimes didn't seem to have any mind at all.

"She ought to know what I do by now. I told her often enough."

"Nothing confidential, I assume," he said with a chuckle.

Something Jean could at last laugh off wholeheartedly. "I have heard that the younger generation thinks of money as just a way of keeping score," said Crough. "What do you make of that, Miss Crossley?"

"It's nonsense," she said. "I wear money, I eat it, and I sleep in it. I find hundreds particularly comfortable."

Crough had, unknowingly, come up with the perfect consolation: She could finally afford to talk the way she always had. Thank God she was no longer expected to have opinions about rock music!

She often thought of her eleven-year-old self getting that glimpse of the back of her childhood home, so painfully naked and no-account. Now she could buy good shoes, new sheets, a covered mirror for her purse. She didn't have to think twice about throwing away a jar of salad dressing she didn't like—not that she ever would.

So she went to the designer floor of Bergdorf's. When a young woman about her age asked if she'd like some help, it took Jean a moment to isolate the way in which this saleslady sounded different from others she'd dealt with in the past. This woman was—*respectful*. Not just polite or friendly, but *respectful*. Jean realized she'd never heard it before. Jean was wearing a calf-length camel-hair coat she'd bought the week before, and she was still in her brisk, down-to-brass-tacks work mode. The saleslady obviously thought of her as a successful, wealthy, and decisive potential customer. And when Jean said, smiling, "Oh, I'm just here for the air," she took this sally as a tribute to herself rather than an indication that she'd wasted her time.

You knew you had money when you didn't even have to spend it to feel its satisfaction.

chapter 7

SUNNY WAS HAPPY NEAR AVENUE A FOR A WHILE, BUT THEN she told an old college roommate about an empty apartment upstairs. What a mistake! Time to move on—again. Sunny didn't think much either way about the decision until she started to pack. Then she felt as if she'd absentmindedly taken off a finger and given it away.

Her next apartment was way uptown in a building south of Morningside Park. It was seven stories high, dark brick, almost cubic, with light-colored stone quoins and a huge arched rectangle of pointed black iron bars covering the recessed entryway. Inside and out, the strongest impressions were of size and age: tall, discolored hallways, a ponderously creaking elevator, ample apartments with bowed plaster walls. Sunny had a room on the back of the fourth floor. A month or two before, when the place had gone co-op, the leaseholder had bought it at the insider's price in hopes of turning it over in a year. Sunny had never met this person, who actually lived in Long Beach, California. Instead she dealt with an education student from Paw Valley who had decided at the last moment to move in with her boyfriend instead of living there herself.

Sunny deposited what few household goods she retained from the furnishing of past apartments in three cardboard boxes at

Bridget's. All she needed to bring to this new place was one duffel bag and one garment bag. Her cocktail dresses had largely been replaced by black spandex, so both pieces of luggage were light. Still, she may not have detoured quite enough around a bear-shaped, frowning man just outside the building. When she realized he was cursing, she said cheerfully, "Hey, fuck you, too."

The man looked up in alarm. "I wasn't talking to you," he said. "I was talking to myself."

Inside the new sublet she sat for a long time, resting her head at an uncomfortable upward angle against the shabby old wing chair. With her eyes on the ceiling, she could not remember what the fabric looked like. The room—one of two—was full of unfamiliar objects and strange furniture, as particular as shoes worn down by another's walk. She wondered briefly what it would be like to watch the same TV for a whole year in a row.

As she sat there, she gradually became aware of a teardrop-shaped stain over in one corner of the ceiling. It had probably been there a long time, she told herself. But it kept bothering her, so finally she pulled over a small, highly polished pedestal table, clambered up on it, and checked the stain with her fingers. It was wet and spongy. She went upstairs, to the apartment above, but no one was home. Downstairs in the lobby, she mentioned the leak to a gray-haired woman wearing a baby blue jogging outfit and asked if she knew anything about the people who lived above her.

"Leon's down in the laundry room," said the woman in blue.

"I should talk to him?" asked Sunny. The super, she assumed.

The woman nodded, as if this were obvious. "Leon will know what to do."

It was the guy from the street, examining a drain in the floor. He looked exactly the same: torn jeans, smudged pink T-shirt, worried expression. When Sunny explained the problem, he said, "Oh, yes. You're Diana's sister-in-law, right?"

Sunny sighed. Was she really supposed to be someone's sister-in-law? Or was this a trick? Why wasn't he mentioning their meeting out in front? "I'm Sunny," she said. She was not worried in the least about her own hold on the apartment—there was always a better sublet somewhere—but she did feel some responsibility toward the others involved, and she had no idea how irregular the arrangement was. So she was wary.

"I'm Leon," he said. "The sponsor."

Sunny was not familiar with the term; she thought it might have something to do with getting an alien a green card. He didn't sound foreign, but you could never tell. "Well, we don't need to get in touch with anyone before we fix a leak, do we?" she said.

"Oh, no," he said, stepping back. "Come on."

In the elevator, as his eyes followed the light through the transparent numbers over the door, he said, "I'm redoing a place up on a Hundred and Thirty-seventh Street now, and it has to be completely rewired. You wouldn't believe what these people have been living with. Broken windows, caved-in ceilings, rat holes the size of fists. Leaks there have been going on for years." He glanced at her.

"Really," said Sunny. He seemed cheerful enough about the work itself. Maybe he'd been cursing because his boss had been giving him a hard time.

Her suspicions seemed to be confirmed when he said, "You can't expect tenants to take care of something that a landlord won't."

"How true," she said politely.

After a pause he said, "So how is Diana?"

"I don't really know," she said.

Leon nodded, apparently satisfied with this reply. He was about a foot taller than she, with short fairish flat hair and a blandly rectangular face. Now that he wasn't cursing, he had the mild air of someone who had looked so strong all his life he'd never had to prove anything. In her apartment, examining the stain, he said, "As long as we can pinpoint the source, I can fix this up tonight." He asked if she'd be around. He was standing up on the table as he spoke, circling slowly as he felt the plaster with the gentle tips of his fingers.

That evening he arrived wearing a new black T-shirt. He said the plumber had found the leak on a building pipe rather than an apartment pipe, so his fee would be billed to the co-op. "Did you get in touch with Diana?"

"No."

Why did he keep harping on Diana? Maybe he really was a spy

for the management company, or whoever ran this place. Sunny watched him as he mixed the plaster, holding a plastic bucket between his knees and piercing and patting the white goop with a trowel.

"I always liked to make things," said Leon when he caught her watching him. "I never thought of it as work. More like art."

"Really," said Sunny. A very unusual attitude for a super, she thought. "Where are you from?"

"Jersey," he said, purposely revealing a trace of a local accent. "You know it?"

"No." After a pause she said, "You want some help?"

Leon said he was fine. As he tamped the plaster into the hole, Sunny crossed to her window and looked out as if she were interested in other people's roofs. She did not turn around when Leon said, "Diana and I may have had our differences, but as far as I am concerned, the past is forgotten."

He dropped heavily from the table with his hands up, backs out, like a surgeon. "Your sink?" he said.

When she handed him a towel decorated with a cat and a mouse napping together, he said, "How does Diana like the West Coast?"

"Oh, Diana, Diana, Diana," cried Sunny. "Why do you keep pestering me about Diana?"

Leon was taken aback. "It's just something to talk about," he said.

"Oh, I know," she said, quick to placate.

"I know you must be busy," he said stiffly.

"How should I know what I'm doing when I can't figure out what you're doing?"

He stood stock still. "What do you mean?" he asked. "What do you think I'm doing?"

She hadn't realized she'd jettisoned her suspicions of his spying until she said, without hesitation, "You're coming on to me."

"I guess," he said. He looked at her hopefully. "Well?"

"Why don't you have a beer," she said. Because now she felt she did know what sort of person he was—someone to whom she could tell the truth. For the moment, anyway. "Or do you have to work?"

"Oh, I allow myself a break every now and then," he said.

Sunny uncapped two bottles of beer with a cat-shaped bottle opener. She poured the beer into two tall glasses ringed with profiles of cats' heads.

"You like cats?" he asked.

"I don't even know any," said Sunny, resting her glass on her thigh. "I don't know whose stuff this is. And I don't know who Diana is, either."

"Diana?" repeated Leon, puzzled. "You mean your sister-in-law?"

Not the savviest person in the world, clearly. "I'm just subletting from someone who's subletting," said Sunny. "At least I think that's what's going on."

"Ah," said Leon, coming to life. "Well, you're lucky, then. Diana is not a nice person. Not at all. I couldn't understand your being her sister-in-law, you seemed so different. I mean, you're a *tutor*." He suddenly looked doubtful. "That part's true, isn't it?" Sunny nodded. "I would not even want to repeat some of the things she said to me. And about perfectly respectable people in the building, too."

Sunny looked at his smiling mouth, his thick, sloping shoulders, his furrowed brow, and asked, "How respectable are you?"

Leon was an exhausting lover. He wanted to get everything right. Did she like these gentle strokes of the thumb? Or something harder? Where? There? Did she know how beautiful she was? Did that feel good? Did she like to be admired? Could she turn all the way around? Did she prefer this pinched? Or flicked softly with the tongue? How did that feel? Should he cut his fingernails? Did she do this a lot? Could she stand up? Did that feel as right to her as it did to him? How about this spot? Higher?

It was a bit irritating. She felt as if she were stuck in stop-and-go traffic. At the same time, it was a devastatingly effective tease. By the end she thought she would die.

Afterward she gazed at the intersection of wall and ceiling that Leon had repaired and realized that from now on this particular angle would represent joy. Her confusion over who rightfully belonged in this fold-out couch only intensified this feeling.

"Why were you talking to yourself when we first met?" she asked.

He asked her what she meant.

"On the street, in front. I was walking by with suitcases, and you were cursing."

"That must have been some other lunatic," he said. He paused, then admitted, "Although it does sound like me." His grin was sheepish. "I get distracted. And I worry a lot about stuff."

"Like what?"

"Like I had a new front door put in up on a Hundred Thirty-seventh Street last week, and it's already busted. Today when I got there, I saw it was being held open by a pipe I'd had to strip."

"Oh, dear," she said, not paying a whole lot of attention. "But why don't you just let the landlord worry about it?"

"I am the landlord," he said.

"You're the landlord?" she repeated.

"Yes," he said.

"Oh," she said.

"You sound surprised."

"You mean you own that building, and you're the super here?"

"I'm not the super. I'm the sponsor. I used to own this place, or the bank and I owned it, and then I converted it. Now I just own one of the apartments on the top floor."

"Then why did you fix my ceiling?"

"To get in your pants, I guess. It sure worked, didn't it?"

She had not realized what her image of him had been until she felt it shift. She had thought of him, she now realized, as a guy from across a divide, a sort of Lady Chatterley's lover. Or maybe some pampered son brought low by drugs or a gnawing guilt. There was a great deal of romance in either image. But a landlord? A small-property owner?

"I'm a Jewish slumlord," he said.

"Oh," she said, inspired. "You're an idealist."

He perked right up. "No, no," he said. "Not an idealist. A realist. I know it can work. If you figure . . ." He spoke of rent rolls and maintenance costs. Whenever he mentioned a number, he ticked it off on his finger, as if that would hold it there.

The numbers inspired her to ask, "How old are you, anyway?"

"Thirty," he said stiffly. Jean's age. He was insulted again, she supposed. So why was she so relaxed about it? The exchange was oddly natural and open. It was as if he already trusted her enough to reveal his every little hurt. "So how old are you?"

"Twenty-six."

The lobby was a cheerful place the next morning. The black man unlocking his mailbox was smiling. So was the white woman propping open the door with her booted toe as she lifted her bags of groceries inside. Sunny grabbed the door for her. Outside she noticed that people on the street, too, looked more pleasant. "Hi! How are you?" That man and that woman were overjoyed to see each other! With happy authority, Sunny pointed the way uptown for a youngster who reminded her of one of her students, the one who tried the hardest. This was New York? The visible squares of sky were a brilliant blue; sun glinted off bike spokes and window shields; and there was a new sexiness in the air, like a recently discovered muscle. A gaunt man with a beard walked a beloved dog. A tender roar engulfed a sports bar. Lovers were entwined everywhere, faces lit up at the mere fact of flesh, the beating of one heart confirming the existence of the other. Sunny was floating through it all.

At the fruit-and-vegetable market she didn't have enough money for her purchases, but she barely noticed. "Oh, my." She flashed a great smile. "How embarrassing." Although the only reason she could say this was that it wasn't true.

SUNNY WAS SURPRISED WHEN PAUL CALLED. HEARING HIS voice was at once intensely familiar and jarringly out of context—like seeing a soap opera star on the streets. Could it really have been only last Tuesday that he'd made her listen to the new Spoonie Gee? Could it really have been just a few months since she'd been stripping the floor on Avenue A? Paul asked her if she wanted to get away for the weekend; Monday was Memorial Day, apparently. It was hard to believe he didn't know that the world had passed from shade to light, that the buildings were standing straighter, that the stars—missing as always from the city skies—had found their way into her brain, where they dazzled her. Sunny felt a brief pang of regret—for what, she wasn't sure. Not for Paul or Dennis or weekends out of town, certainly, although she thought more fondly of them than ever. Maybe she already missed some childhood notion of vacations or intrigue or leisure.

"Paul," she said, trying to adjust, "I think I've fallen in love."

"Oh?" he said, his voice already receding; this was no longer the one she knew so well. "Who is it this time?"

She had, perhaps, used these same words on previous occasions. But this disjunction only bewildered her more. Paul sounded hurt—at least hurt enough to be sarcastic. He may have assumed that she was making a choice between him and some unknown other, but was this even true? Paul generally became churned up over her only when her interest waned. And even if you assumed that she did have two clear options, she did not think Leon was the superior in looks, intelligence, or charm, except in the abstract way that even she knew was produced by love, not vice versa. She could think of no way to pass this on to Paul, however, without appearing to damn him with faint praise. Nor was she choosing the poor and virtuous over the rich and spoiled. Sunny didn't care that Paul did some coke; that would pass. And she was hardly picking the calm over the agitated, if Leon's "Fuck you" on the street was any indication of his underlying stability.

What she told Bridget was that she fell in love with Leon because he would have helped her strip the floors instead of asking her to marry him, as Paul did that day. Sunny grew so fond of this insight, she repeated it to Dennis, who said much later, after Leon had asked her to marry him, "You're lucky he wasn't in a floor-stripping mood instead."

For a man who spent his time transforming other people's apartments, Leon's own place was absurd: a broken-down sofa from his parents' family room, a nail-studded oak table he'd found on the street, a lovingly restored proscenium arch separating the two. He would pace back and forth through it as he talked into his cell phone. When he cooked, he took hours, apparently unaware of any labor-saving devices, and produced sliced vegetables so equal in size he could have used the tape measure he kept in his pants pocket. Fortunately Sunny was accustomed to making do with a limited range of sublet utensils. She could measure a cup of rice with her eye, shake rather than spin the salad, use a fork to grate cheese.

During their third or fourth evening together—their acquaintance was still laughably short—she had a thought as she looked over the *Science Times,* which was spread out on the oversize table. She was standing up, as if she had not completely committed herself to her reading, and, indeed, her mind kept wandering, first to Leon's side of his phone conversation and then to the future. As he said, "I am more interested in finding out whether it's working," she did not exactly picture a "happily ever after" scenario, but she did suddenly recognize what being a grown-up was going to mean for her. Although it wasn't exactly what she expected—it was both more splendid and more tawdry, not a BMW in sight—she understood that it was hers, as fateful as fingerprints. Not that she felt old; she felt buoyant. She also felt scared, yet sure; wistful and elated; intensely present, but dreamy and dizzy, plunged into what at times could be called nothing less than an out-of-body experience. Maybe that's what love was, the only emotion large enough to hold all these contradictions.

Although she had already told others of these feelings, she still hadn't mentioned them to Leon. When she was with him, she was too busy sorting out who he was. He was so different from the boys she knew. He made decisions quickly; he took care of people; he spoke and acted with unusual authority. She had to pester him for information about his mother, whom he managed to call once a week and visit once a month without thinking about in between. Paul, Henry, and even Dennis occupied their families' worlds; the contours of their lives were determined by what space they were given to fill. Leon seemed to have made up his life out of whole cloth. Accustomed to a professional class of those who worked for others, she was confounded by the idea of just going out and starting a business. And a business that housed the poor! Extraordinary.

Sunny might have gone uptown sooner to see his buildings—he was in the process of buying a second, next door—but she discovered that she was weirdly tired from staying up with him night after night. They talked for hours, about entrepreneurship in the eighties and how moral it could be, about Sunny's tutoring, about the future of the city. It was more than a month before they finally walked uptown. The day was going to be unusually warm for June—even in the early morning, you could tell—and she would rather have taken the bus. But she didn't want to look as if she were afraid, even to herself. As they set out, Leon's bright red T-shirt bobbed nonchalantly beside her.

She had never simply walked into central Harlem. She was used to the neighborhoods around Columbia. But it was as if she had always been on an invisible tether. Yes, she had been farther east than Amsterdam, where they were walking now. There was that restaurant at Malcolm X Boulevard and 110th. And she had been up the West Side to the green market, which was past 120th. But each of these had been brief forays, more like quick grabs. She went straight in, did some business, and went straight out, always within easy shouting distance of more familiar territory.

This walk was disorienting. She had never seen the hills of Harlem, which were as steep as several stories of stairs. They made her feel as if she'd passed into some other type of city, maybe San Francisco, which she had also never seen. School would be out for the year soon, and the kids, who were marching off in twos and threes, percolated with that seasonal agitation. They were cocky, eager, feckless. On one corner a group of girls in dark blue parochial school uniforms talked loudly about teachers. "No, he hates me," said the smallest, cracking her gum. "But Ms. Bernard, she loves me."

Sunny tried to see the area the way Leon would, as a collection of buildings and tenants. The materials around here were similar to those in the rest of the city: sandstone, concrete, brick. Lots of brick, because that's what the projects were composed of. No granite. The tracks for the metal gates on the storefronts were familiar. Many of the brownstones were shabbier than what she was used to, and the detail, more elegant: fanlights, sidelights, arches, buttresses, even gargoyles.

The people comprised a narrow band of the crowds you would see anywhere in Manhattan. She didn't see a white face besides theirs. A couple of guys studied her with interest, but that was certainly not unusual, and mostly she and Leon were ignored the way they would be in any neighborhood.

As waves of heat began to radiate off the pavement, Sunny felt her head twirl a little.

On the block of Amsterdam before Leon's street was a liquor store, an abandoned auto school, a glass-brick church, a locksmith, and a party shop. At the corner was a salon featuring Unisex Hair Styling and African American Hair Braiding. The door was propped open, and out on the sidewalk in front was a row of hair dryers, necks lolled back. The sight gave Sunny a sour, choked sensation in her throat, but within the dim store two women in light blue smocks moved about purposefully—cleaning, maybe. And beside her Leon was as solid and self-possessed as ever, obliviously

silent. She closed her eyes for a moment. Despite a thin meander
of breeze, her hands and forehead were clammy.

"Look, a hat store," said Leon, pointing to the other corner. "I
think that's why I chose this street. Lucile's Fashion Hats. Only
black women still wear hats. For church, of course."

"Hey, Leon." This quiet greeting was from a hatless, youngish
woman flanked by two girls. All three were in jeans; all three wore
gold hoops in their ears, the woman with the most had five up one
rim. Sunny wondered if she'd heard, if she'd taken offense.

"Good morning, Mrs. Austin," said Leon.

"Good morning." She looked at Sunny with an appraising cock
of her head. Her hair was flattened into a helmet; her lips were
painted a cinnamon red.

"This your lady?" said the older of the girls, a slim teenager with
a neat topknot of knife-thin braids.

"Yes," said Leon, warily, glancing at Sunny. "Yes, I guess she is."

"Nice to meet you," said Sunny. For some reason just standing
there made her feel sort of weak. She wished she could start walking again without appearing rude. Even the little girl was staring.

"You don't look too good, honey," said Mrs. Austin.

"I'm just hot," said Sunny.

"Oh, okay," said Mrs. Austin. "You have a good man here. When
Leon came in, I didn't know *what* to expeck. I never seen no landlord before. I figured they be as white as ghosts. Or maybe transparent. Though I did expeck one might dress better. Oh, see, he
blushing. Leon, *we* don't care how ratty you dress."

When they'd moved on, Sunny asked if they were tenants.

"All three generations are," said Leon. "It usually depresses me
to see such a young girl with a kid." So Mrs. Austin was the grandmother of the littlest one? Sunny had assumed she was the
mother of both. She felt Leon's eyes on her as he said, "I don't
think anything could bring me down today, though. The world
looks different when you're in love."

"Oh, yes," said Sunny. She was acutely aware that this was
the first time he had said these words. A white Styrofoam takeout container skittered in front of them. She felt as if she were
floating.

"You've noticed that, too?"

She took his hand. "Yes," she said. "Right away." Her head was swirling off her neck, as if her happiness were making her sick.

Leon's building was the last in a row of four brownstones. It had an odd old grate in the sidewalk by the door, which he was pleased to see was closed and locked for a change.

Standing on the stoop, Sunny felt a stab of hunger so deep, it could not possibly be contained inside her small round body. She knew this hunger. She recognized it from college, when she'd ended up having an abortion, an awful procedure she hadn't been the least prepared for, despite Paul's holding her hand. She had sworn she would *never* do it again.

Everything—red shirt, black doorknob, bright yellow fast-food wrapper—drained to gray, and Sunny started to go down. She was aware of every minute, though, so how could that be called fainting? Still, there she was, on the cracked concrete, and Leon was sliding his hands here and there underneath her, as if he couldn't make up his mind about where they belonged.

Sunny said, "Oh, no." She closed her eyes. "Oh, no."

chapter 9

FOR SEVERAL YEARS NOW, JEAN WOULD BUY THE *TIMES* AND
The Wall Street Journal every morning at the newsstand near the
103rd Street subway stop. During the quick trip to 96th Street,
she had a chance to glance at the headlines. Then, once she
switched to the express, a low-level ticking of her brain would
begin, an offhand and automatic mixture of judgment and predic-
tion devoted to finding a seat amid the crowded car. Stand where
two sets of seats lie perpendicular to each other, thus increasing
access. Stay away from that man in wingtips; he's sure to go all
the way to Wall Street. A kid in a uniform is good; he's liable to
get off soon, and that must be his mother with him. Two seats becoming free meant that Jean would get one even if there was
someone nearby who was more deserving (unlikely) or more
shameless. Once settled, she would find momentary peace in the
relaxation of limbs, back, stomach, feet.

Soon, however, she would start to check out the other people in
the car. Occasionally she would notice a particularly pleasing color
of lipstick or a book on existentialism among the less prosperous
riders, but most of her attention was focused on the other profes-
sionals in the car, specifically the females. She would pick out
these rivals instantly with her eyes, then assess them. Generally
they could be dismissed. But this one might have a lovely old

locket; that one might have an unusual Fendi handbag. Then Jean's equilibrium would be off. These distinctive elements would chafe her brain until she found some way to minimize them. She would think, Probably inherited, doesn't count, or, Looks like a gift to a mistress. Once the car had been neutralized, she would seek out her own handsome, competent, successful reflection in the black window across the way, then begin reading her newspapers.

But the morning after Jean learned of Sunny's impending marriage, she could not find peace so quickly. Her eyes kept catching on wedding rings. It was surprising how many of them there were in a city where you were supposed to be single. Not all of these ring wearers got on at Times Square, either, with the rest of the commuters from New Jersey. The rings had gotten thicker through the years, maybe because of the new eighties affluence. Or maybe because everyone was boasting a little louder. There was a guy hanging on to a strap next to her with a wedding ring that could have been used as a length of pipe.

The first glance around her office that morning did not bring her the satisfaction it should have, despite that wonderful pile of trade publications on her desk, bristling with Post-it notes, every one representing a person just waiting to be plucked from a space that was too small for him.

The woman in the medical technician's uniform who wheeled the breakfast cart down the hall every morning brought her, as usual, a bagel with cream cheese and a light coffee. "Nourishment!" she called in happy, accented imitation of Jean's famished cries of delight on her first day of work. The word still seemed to crack the woman up. She smiled broadly, chuckling a little; she evidently thought Jean was just great, a real joker, so funny, a real American. And the woman herself looked like one of those crosses between Arab and Asian—Pakistani, perhaps—so who said that humor had to be culture-bound? But look at that—a wedding ring.

Of course she needed a husband, considering the job she had. Half of the women in the subway car who wore wedding rings were probably underpaid and overworked. Secretaries, or whatever they were called nowadays. Jean was different. She traveled light. She always knew how much she had in her money market account and her IRAs. She always carried at least $100 in cash with her. She kept a toilet kit, underwear, panty hose, a rolled-up wrinkle-free skirt, and a cashmere sweater in the bottom drawer of her desk. And Sunny *had* to get married. It wasn't the same thing as just plain old getting married.

Fortunately, Jean's first call of the day was from Gilbert Blakely, executive VP of HealthQuest Services, Inc. There was nothing surprising about this, but it was still gratifying; Blakely was the most powerful person yet who had contracted for her services. "I hear good things about you," said Blakely, and Jean said, "All true, of course." Blakely had an explosively expiring laugh, like a truck braking.

They agreed to meet at the Hotel Morengo for a drink the following Tuesday. By then, Jean had a map of HealthQuest imprinted on her brain. She could feel it pulse up there as she walked through a revolving brass door into the uptown side of the hotel lobby, which occupied the whole center slice of a block in the East 50s. The huge room was cut up by banks of palms, rounds of upholstered chairs, a screen or two, a mysterious few steps lavishly carpeted in blue, a four-man registration desk, and a concierge in a cage. If you listened closely, you could hear the music of the spheres—a low, crackling hum of information exchanged, deals made, crises averted. It was exactly the sort of place Jean was happy that she felt comfortable in, and she was there as herself, not as a wife.

The bar was about halfway down on the right, divided from the room by clay-colored planters. Although she was fifteen minutes early, she could see that Blakely, whom she recognized from trade photos, was already there, sitting at one of the larger walnut tables with a younger, thinner, paler man. Blakely was fifty, short, thick necked, broad shouldered, and barrel chested. He looked like a safe that had just fallen on somebody.

Jean picked up a bottle of beer at the bar, then loomed over them. Neither of them wore a wedding ring. "So," she said, "are you fellows friends of the bride or the groom?" It had just popped out. Idiotic, of course, but that was not always a mistake.

A look of alarm crossed the younger fellow's face, but Blakely let out that same booming "Ha-a-a!" and said "You must be Jean

Crossley." He added an aside to his companion: "Women can never get their minds off marriage."

"The marriage between employer and employee is always in the forefront of my mind," said Jean smoothly.

She didn't catch the other guy's name, and she was too rattled to ask him to repeat it. He was wearing a midnight blue suit and a pink tie—the band uniform look. "He's writing me up," said Blakely. "Follows me everywhere, right?"

"Everywhere I can, Mr. Blakely."

"Is that all right with you?" Blakely asked Jean.

"I can watch my tongue if you can watch yours," she said, now more than a little nervous about her opening remark. If only she had waited a bit to check out the lay of the land.

"We don't have much choice about it," said Blakely. "His father is one of our biggest suppliers."

"I certainly don't want to interfere," said the young man. Jean noticed now that his smile was pasted on. He looked more un-comfortable than she was, which reassured her somewhat.

"Sit down, sit down," grumbled Blakely. "Don't you know when you're being kidded? Miss Crossley certainly would." His whole big red face contributed to his grin.

"Please, call me Jean."

"Jean," he repeated. His aggression had a showiness that Jean assumed was due to the journalistic scrutiny. She wondered if her own remark would make it into the article. How it looked would depend on the context. It was wonderfully madcap, she told herself.

"We've used Julius for years," said Blakely. "And they've never come up with a serious female candidate for an executive position. I think it's time we did something about it." He beamed at Jean in a self-congratulatory fashion, as if his were a bold and daring statement.

"Sounds good," said Jean. All PR. Didn't reporters get tired of it?

"That's why I specifically asked Matt for you."

Like there was some kind of "old girl network." Oh, well. Jean had picked up new clients for crazier reasons. How about the fi-nancial officer who'd gotten her name a few months before from a fellow *inmate*?

"We're looking for a new VP of planning and development," said Blakely. Mostly fund-raising, in other words. Not going out on a limb to put a woman in that spot. "We are committed to getting the best. Male, female, or in between."

"Ah, yes," said Jean. "In between. Well, I'll see what I can do."

"You know," said Blakely meaningfully. "One of those men who think they're women. *Or one of those women who think they're men.*"

"I'm not sure I understand your point, sir," the reporter said stiffly, and the other two looked at him in surprise.

An awful thought crossed Jean's mind. Was he trying to *protect* her? So what if Blakely had implied she wanted to be a man? Couldn't he tell how tough she was? How accustomed she was to executives who mistook moronic insult for humor? Why, these men were everywhere; she could have dealt with Blakely in her sleep. Did she seem that uneasy? Did she look as if she'd get hurt playing with the big boys? She couldn't let this reporter even hint at such a thing.

"It will be especially easy to find people interested in working at HealthQuest," said Jean. "As Mr. Blakely well knows."

"Gil!" cried Blakely. "You must call me Gil."

It had been sheer instinct, to prompt him to give up his Christian name, but it seemed to have worked. The reporter retreated.

"Of course, the most interesting people don't know they're looking for new jobs yet," said Jean.

"But you know," said Blakely. "You know better than anyone."

So what if his tone was close to a sneer? Maybe even was a downright sneer? He probably hadn't talked any other way for years.

"Yes," said Jean simply. She eyed the small black tape recorder sitting in the center of the table. She wouldn't have noticed what a jerk Blakely was if it weren't for this reporter. And now, in addition to keeping Blakely happy, she had to convince the reporter that *she* was happy. That she was *right* to be happy.

"Are you familiar with the executive recruiting industry?" she asked him.

"Maybe you can answer a few questions for me at some point," he said, which was a good sign. He struck her as rather timid, not the sort who was going to write some slash-and-burn exposé, but she couldn't be sure; this was not an area she had any experience in.

The meeting was over soon enough, and Jean said she had to walk over to Third Avenue—i.e., against traffic. She generally did this to avoid being put into a taxi by a male client. She disliked the whole feeling of being looked after, handled, squared away. It seemed especially inappropriate to be treated that way by someone for whom you were supposed to be working magic. Jean was the one who should be in charge, at least of that aspect of his life. So she invented a trip to Third, the doorman got Blakely a cab, and she found the reporter walking beside her.

He blended in well, much better than Blakely would have. His face was almost generic-looking. "So where are you from?" he asked.

"Paw Valley," she said. Meaning, tough-girl territory.

"Ah," he said.

"Do you know it?"

"I'm afraid I don't," he said. Then, before she could decide how to proceed with her damage control, he said, "So I guess you're used to people like Blakely."

"Sure," she said. "But he's not from Paw Valley." Her response was disingenuous. Hospital administrators tended to come from areas like Paw Valley, within sight of the city but not participating in its riches.

Jean couldn't tell if this was what the reporter had meant, however. His mind was elsewhere. "I'm not used to men like that," he said. "Still, I'm always interested in people who behave in ways that seem bizarre to me."

"What are you trying to get me to say?" she asked. "That Blakely is bizarre? Because he's not."

"Oh, no, no," he said. "I was just thinking out loud."

Although he had what would register as regular features in a photograph, there was something annoyingly tentative about them. His darkish hair, too, just lay there. Maybe he needed a haircut. He wore one of the most innocuous suits imaginable. But the pink tie was revealing. A pastel color, even in a tie, should have

seemed mild. But it did not. A pink tie was only pretending innocence. Actually, it was a little like a white suit: a thumb in the eye.
Take that. Despite his Milquetoast manner, this man had vast
rocks of stubbornness submerged under the surface.

"I live for the search," said Jean, regretting her words as soon as
she spoke them. Not that they were false, exactly. In fact, maybe
they weren't false enough. They were . . . pointless.

But he was just nodding, rubbing his chin, vaguely distracted,
perhaps self-absorbed.

"You don't seem very much like a reporter to me," said Jean.

"No?" he said, looking at her for what seemed like the first time.
"Well, maybe I went into the wrong line of work. What would
you suggest?"

"Mushroom farmer," she said.

"No, I mean really," he said.

They had stopped at the corner, much to the annoyance of the
people parting behind them. "Really," she insisted. "Mushroom
farmer."

"Oh, well," he said, opening his arms to display his palms, then
folding them in on himself, grabbing an elbow in each hand, as if
to say, "If you can't even talk straight to me about that . . ." He
was definitely younger than she was, also at least an inch shorter.

"Look at the time," she said, although she made no show of consulting her watch.

The fellow turned his wrist slightly to actually check the face.
"It's only six," he said. "A whole hour or two before my bedtime.
How about it?"

How about what? Was he suggesting they spend that hour together? And had he placed some small emphasis on the word *bed*-
time? Jean had been hit on before during the course of her job, but
the efforts had always been pretty crude. This was more confusing than anything else. His body language was not in the least se-
ductive; his arms were folded against her like a shield. Besides,
most people would say that he was pretty good-looking, more at-
tractive than the men she usually went out with. Why would a
young fellow like that be pursuing her?

"You want to interview me about Blakely?" she asked.

"If you like," he said. "My apartment is right around the corner. I think it's presentable."

This seemed awfully forward for such a mild-mannered fellow. But his arms remained folded. And she knew she could handle him. Besides, Sunny wasn't the only one in the family used to men. So she agreed.

His apartment was farther away than he'd said but still within easy walking distance. Their conversation was attenuated, even dreamlike. She was succinct about her job. *Then she talked about the weather.* She loved the weather.

The building was a brownstone, pretty dilapidated considering the area. The contrast between it and the completely renovated half-of-a-floor apartment it housed made Jean feel as if she were stepping into a world as self-enclosed as a snow dome. There was track lighting, an exposed brick wall, a polyurethaned floor, a couch cinched with big gray slipcovers.

"Would you like some coffee?" he asked. Once inside he seemed to have lost his confidence, which restored her own good spirits.

"Decaf?" she asked.

"Oh. I don't think I have any. Well, let me make sure."

She started to follow him into the kitchen and saw too late that it was no bigger than an airplane bathroom. He was backed up against the refrigerator, buckling slightly. *He was afraid of her.* Jean grabbed his hand. Then, as if he'd made a minor but key miscalculation in the physics of movement, he kissed her so hard she almost toppled over. Her arms were around him; his unsuspected beard scraped her lips and chin.

"I don't—" he said, but they weren't letting go of each other. Then, in a low voice, he said, "That's my bedroom."

Turning, Jean could see through a half-opened door a shimmer of light lying across a faraway floor. "What's your name again?" she said.

"Geoffrey Ferris," he said, as if resigning himself to his fate.

"Geoffrey Ferris," she repeated, backing toward the entryway. "I'll give you a call, Geoffrey Ferris."

chapter 10

JEAN WAS WAITING FOR GEOFFREY FERRIS IN THE BAR OF THE Hunting Lodge Hotel. Jean liked to sit in bars alone. A woman can be more truly alone in a bar than anywhere else in the world. In a bar, her aloneness can fill the whole room. Jean was smoking a cigarette at one of two knotty-pine banquettes and looking at the blue line drawing of "The Hunting Lodge Hotel" on the front of a book of matches. Hunting Lodge Hotel. Who had put together two words for the same thing rather than think of an actual name? It was as if you lived at the Residency Apartments. Or set out to dine at the Café Restaurant.

Sunny and Leon were having a rehearsal dinner in a room at the back of this inn, which, although not far from her father's house, only Sunny had ever heard of. Jean had arrived early; now she was late. She *had* called Geoffrey, as she'd said she would, and she had asked him to accompany her this evening. He'd said he would be flying in the night before from Seattle, but he would try to make it. So really she was only sort of waiting for him. The conversation had been a tad awkward—even she had to admit that—and she wasn't sure whether he had said he would call her today to finalize the plans. It was a not unpleasant limbo, waiting for someone you weren't sure would arrive. She certainly had no time for a needy, demanding date, and today at least she was happy to have an excuse to sit.

She'd had some vague intention of joining Sunny, Bridget, and their father when they arrived—they were all coming in the same car—but as soon as she'd heard their odd, muffled, fitful voices continue on down the corridor past the door to the bar, she'd somehow ordered another draft instead. Despite Sunny's swelling stomach, she was surprisingly traditional. A rehearsal dinner? After rehearsing what? A little tune from *Oklahoma!*, perhaps? "I'm just a girl who cain't say no. . . ."

The bartender, who was leaning idly against a back cabinet, was a college boy in khaki pants and a white Lacoste shirt. A costume, of course. He was pretending to be a boy who did not have to spend his weekends working in a bar. He was pretending he *wanted* to work in this bar—for authenticity, for manly experience, or to pick up girls. Jean used to have to wear such costumes. One of the nicest things about starting a real job was that she got to graduate to a uniform: suit, pumps, smart handbag.

A waitress outfitted in black pants and white shirt—a uniform in the more traditional sense—came in and handed the boy a drink order. With a round cork tray under one arm, she managed to seem both good-humored and very impatient. She said, pointing, "It's supposed to be Dutch gin."

Oh? That must be Bridget's.

With new interest Jean watched the boy start to line up the drinks. He was even more of a neophyte than she'd assumed; he had trouble with the spigot for the draft beer, and he pointlessly moved the first glass he filled a few inches away from him. His original placement had not been confident, true, but adjusting it only made it worse.

There were two beers, Bridget's gin and tonic, and—could those be two sodas? Jean went ahead and asked. The waitress glanced over, as indifferent as a traffic light.

"Seven and Sevens," said the boy, still hobbled by a civilian's manners, or maybe just pleased at his mastery of at least that recipe.

Seven and Sevens? What kind of family was Sunny marrying into? Jean closed her eyes, ostentatiously shuddering to think. Of course Jews didn't drink. (Except for the ones Jean knew.) Maybe that was the only cocktail they'd heard of? A third Seven and

Seven now joined the others at the bar. That was a lot; it did make you suspicious.

"Seven and Sevens," she repeated, her eyes open but her neck still slumped against the tall back of the banquette. The elusive Geoffrey had drunk Scotch at the Hotel Morengo.

Even if you didn't count the forty minutes before the rehearsal dinner that Jean had been waiting for him, he was now late for the dinner itself. It was possible that the plane was delayed. Very delayed. Still, he should have called. Of course she was hurt and all that. She had feelings. On the other hand, if he had showed up when he said he would—or if she hadn't halfway expected him—then she would now be an ordinary person sitting with a dreadful pack of Seven-and-Seven-drinking in-laws in the other room. Instead there were rhomboids of sunlight on the floor, faintly Viennese *Third Man*–ish Muzak filtering in from hidden speakers, and a tormented, slack-jawed bartender played by a future teen heartthrob.

A pay phone on the wall near the bar had been so placed to be used by her, Jean, at this very moment. She had a sober smile for the bartender—enough to let him know she was still on the planet, not enough to encourage him to move down to within hearing distance as she sauntered over to the phone. She dialed the number on her surreptitiously held matchbook, listened to the single ring out at the front desk—it was, as she'd always suspected, a beat earlier than the ringing sound in her ear—and left a message for Sunny saying that she was tied up but she'd be there as soon as she could.

As she moved away from the phone, that same waitress, minus her tray, scurried down the hall, presumably with her message. An unexpected bonus.

"Another?" said the boy.

When Jean turned to indicate the beer still sitting at the banquette, she saw that it was indeed empty, so she said yes. "Aren't you awfully young to be working here?" she asked. This was cast over her shoulder on her way to her seat. She had no intention whatsoever of getting into a conversation with him.

"No," he said, hurt.

Now she was supposed to be careful of the feelings of a kid who could still be offended by remarks about his youth. It was hard not to be *jealous*. But let's see how long it took to buck him up again. "You look so much like that guy on TV," she said. This was always safe. Everyone thought he looked like someone on television.

"Which one?"

"You know," she said. She took in the kid's most obvious physical characteristics. "Kind of sandy brown hair?" She crept the tiniest bit out on a limb: "Tough guy? But sweet underneath?"

The boy mentioned an unfamiliar name.

"That's it!" she said.

"Other people have told me that," the boy allowed. "Of course, I don't see it myself."

"It's hard to see yourself as others see you," said Jean, barely sustaining her interest. Besides, the two of them were speaking across a space of some ten feet, not exactly the way to be inconspicuous to any stray relative driven by injudicious Seven and Seven drinking to wander up and down the corridor.

Jean could have tried to track Geoffrey down after his plane was due. Sometime before noon, to give herself a little leeway. But that would have been undignified. He had a voice, he had a phone.

The waitress returned with a fistful of drink orders. Evidently other customers were starting to drift into the main dining room. The restaurant-frequenting crowd must have grown out here: more money, wives working. Naturally the Crossleys had not eaten at restaurants when Jean was a kid, but she couldn't remember anyone else doing so, either.

This time the order with the Dutch gin and the Seven and Sevens included a Scotch Jean recognized with a pang. Geoffrey had arrived. Jean pictured him stiffly greeting all those people to whom he had nothing to say. He would not be comfortable. He knew no one.

Still, she did not move. Rise up like a cornstalk, signal for a check, calculate a tip, and so forth? Forget it. So she said to the bartender, "I grew up around here."

"Oh, really? Where?"

He did seem eager to talk, so she went through the whole process of extracting and lighting a cigarette, to build up the suspense, and then told him where the house was, stressing the ugliness of its situation, the proximity to the highway. "But now I live on the island of Manhattan," she said with exaggerated satisfaction. Her tone became even more ironic, as if nothing could be more ridiculous, when she added, "That means I am *very* rich and successful. I never buy just one egg, I always buy a dozen."

As she spoke, Jean caught out of the corner of her eye the appearance of a woman in a spectral forest green crushed-velvet dress. It was a curious length, not to the floor, but a few inches up from the ankles—a length you might have found on a nightgown. Pressed above one ear was a large white crepe-paper flower twisted with green floral wire. It was only moments before Jean realized with a start that this was Bridget. She had used the same velvet for the cushions in her apartment.

Jean said nothing, maybe because of her surprise, and Bridget, oddly, said nothing to her, either, although she could not have avoided seeing her. Bridget also probably registered the significance of the nearly finished beer glass. But she said only, "I was looking for the bathroom." Always that thin little voice.

"Down the hall, to the right."

Bridget nodded gravely and left.

Jean had got a call from Mr. Crossley just a few days before, asking her how she thought Bridget was taking Sunny's wedding.

"What do you mean?" asked Jean.

"Bridget is a very sensitive girl, and it must be hard for her to see her younger sister marry before she does."

"How about me?" said Jean with an unreal wail. "What about my feelings?"

"Oh, you're different," said Mr. Crossley.

"That's so true," said Jean, pleased. "I really don't care at all."

Now that Jean had been spotted in the "Hunting Lodge" "Hotel," she obviously should join the others. It would look too peculiar otherwise. But she found herself still under a spell, sluggish and heavy-headed.

Then she had an idea: Call Bessie. Jean seemed to be at the phone as soon as the thought struck.

"So guess where I am? My sister's rehearsal dinner."

Bessie had been surprisingly easy to roust, considering how long it had been since they'd spoken. She was still at her parents' house out here on Long Island.

"The one who doesn't like me?" said Bessie. Ah, as sharp as ever.

"Just another example of her terrible taste," said Jean. She swallowed the rest of her beer and placed the bottle, leaning slightly, on top of the phone.

"I guess it's no surprise I wasn't invited to the wedding," said Bessie.

"Just thank your lucky stars. There's a whole gaggle of relatives, clucking and pecking and squealing and wiggling."

"Sounds as lively as a barnyard," said Bessie coolly. "Too bad I'm not there. I'm such an animal lover."

"I actually haven't made it in yet. I'm having a couple of drinks in the bar first."

"Oh, so this is one of *those* calls."

Against Jean's better judgment, she said, "One of what calls?"

"One of those 'I'm drinking, so I'll call up everyone I've ever met' calls."

"You must have met a lot more people than I have. I never get calls like that."

"Maybe your friends are saner than mine. They always were, weren't they?"

Jean was feeling a decided chill. She had forgotten how impossible Bessie had become. She briefly considered asking her old friend what was wrong, but she was not willing to be quite that insulting. "Well, I guess I better go, then," she said.

"Right," said Bessie sarcastically. Why say "right" sarcastically? It was idiotic.

Of course, Jean should have left then, but the baby bartender was right there, a bouquet of wineglasses in one hand. With the other he was sliding the glasses, upside down, in the slots above him. "Whatever else you do, get to the city, it will save your life," she said to him.

"It's kind of crowded there for me," said the boy, his eyes dropping momentarily from the tracks above him.

Jean put her hand to her face in mock horror. "Don't you realize you're surrounded by water? No one's going anywhere from here except through the city."

"I thought I might fly to Phoenix."

"Oh, Phoenix," said Jean, dismissing him. "Let's take a peek at the check." She tapped her credit card smartly on the bar. "See?" she said. "A *gold* card."

By the time she got to the private dining room in back, everyone was finished eating. Her entrance wasn't so bad. A lot of names. And kisses. And handshakes. And squeals. No one asked her why she had been holed up in the bar. But then Geoffrey waved. *Waved.* Waving was what you did when you cruised past a stranger's boat in the harbor. Waving was what you did to a TV camera from the stands at a long-decided sporting event. Oh, and waving was what you did when you saw the woman you had just tried to kiss in a galley kitchen. Who had abandoned you to a pack of her relatives.

"We ordered you the chicken," said Sunny, who indicated a plate of food that looked like a plastic replica of itself.

One of Leon's sisters said to her clearly beloved brother, "But get back to your story. What did the exterminator do?"

A maintenance story. Oh, good. Soon they would be talking about lawns. *And no matter what I say he keeps mowing down the peonies.* Ha, ha, ha.

Jean had never met Leon's family before. All three sisters were little round-faced, round-bodied rubber balls like Sunny, just not as pretty. Sunny could have been a fourth, the one the parents could get rid of without a dowry, thank God, while the others were forced to work at various real jobs. College librarian. Psychiatric social worker. Director of paralegals. Not glamorous. But real work, unlike anything Sunny had ever done.

Although Jean was pointedly listening to the Dane contingent, she was most aware of the discussion going on between Geoffrey and Bridget, who, as maid of honor, was sitting on the other side of Sunny. Geoffrey was wearing a dreadful beige sacked-out tweed jacket, but no one in this crowd was going to notice. At one point she heard him say, "The reason I've gone as far as I have in this business is certainly not my style or my contacts, God knows, but my skepticism."

What business? The magazine business? How far exactly had he gone? But Bridget was talking to him, which was a surprise. Bridget could be extremely withholding. She often did not converse with you so much as force you into a monologue, which was especially difficult over the phone. She had once told Jean that she would like to talk to her hairdresser the way other women did, but she could never think of anything to say.

As female cries rose again from the Dane end of the table, Jean wondered idly what it would be like to marry a cream puff like Leon, object of so much female adoration: mother (even to hear her cry of "Oh, Leon!" was embarrassing), sisters (the conversation had turned to day care, not lawns, big difference), and probably many worthy ex-girlfriends, all much plainer than the beautiful Sunny. Leon clearly thought he had lucked out. That would be flattering. But to push and not to feel any push back? What was the point of that? All you'd find was the endless assurance and comfort and give of a pillow, and maybe that wasn't even him you were touching but one of his many female fans crowded around him.

"Not for two months," said Sunny when another Dane sister questioned her about her due date. "But already I can barely reach around my stomach to shave my legs."

"They can get positively European," Leon put in.

"Oh, Leon!" The mother again. And twitters.

"Hairy," he said in a stage whisper.

"I don't think you should have an opinion about that," said Jean.

Leon was surprised. "Really? And here I thought I was being so attentive and caring. As a new man, I thought I was supposed to talk about cooking and grooming and all that stuff."

"Not until you start shaving your own legs."

"And how do you know I haven't?" he asked.

Geoffrey liked this. Although Jean was still trying to avoid looking in his direction, she could feel him laughing with the others. She would have liked to say that expressing an opinion about someone else shaving her legs was very controlling, but she sensed that her audience had moved on. Sunny, however, who was not quite so attuned to the lightness of the moment, tromped right in: "Jean will argue any position at all," she said. "Just press a different button next time."

Typical younger sister remark. Best to ignore it.

"I always like to be able to see different points of view," said Bridget in her slow way. "I figure if I can't understand the other

side, I don't know my own very well." Bridget tasted her words
before she spoke, so it sometimes seemed as if only embarrassed
pauses gave her enough time to frame and then express her
thoughts.

"So where have you been?" Sunny asked Jean. "Hiring the president of Peru?"

When Geoffrey joined in with his own questioning glance, Jean
realized that Bridget had not mentioned seeing her in the bar. She
tried to catch Bridget's eye, but her face was as blank as a mirror.

"I was missing you all terribly," said Jean in her most ingratiat-
ing voice. She gave Geoffrey an especially evil smile. "Naturally."

chapter 11

SOMETIMES SUNNY FELT AS IF SHE WERE LOOKING AT LEON from a great distance. She had been through labor with this man, but in some ordinary sense she still did not know him. His favorite color, for instance? She hadn't a clue. She didn't know whether he liked the taste of, say, eggplant. She had never seen him eat it, but then, he hadn't eaten lots of different foodstuffs in front of her; their acquaintance had been relatively short.

In the seventies he'd been led down from SUNY Buffalo to the city by the same obscure ache that had deposited so many young people in little enclaves on the Upper West Side, in the East Village, and down on the Bowery. By chance he ended up near Columbia University, not far from where Jean lived. Restlessly casting about, he took a couple of evening classes and ended up volunteering at Homes for Hope, a nonprofit organization that was spasmodically renovating a building in central Harlem.

Even with his limited experience, Leon could tell how badly the project was run. No one had any clear idea of how many volunteers there were or how many were needed. Sometimes more than a dozen, mostly students, would stand around for hours and joke and flirt while waiting for someone to tell them what to do. They didn't seem to think they were wasting their afternoons. Clearly these were social occasions. At other times, no one but Leon would show up, and an administrator, harried by nothing more than his own incompetence, would wave his hand here and there in the building, hinting at vast areas of undefined work to be done. The shipment of supplies was ill-timed; the quantities, ill-judged. Although Leon had no access to the books, he soon wondered if any but the most cursory records were being kept. Sometimes he was able to assist a plumber or an electrician, who would grumble about the disorder. Anyone would have thought he could do a better job running a renovation. Leon, with his natural curiosity and gifted hands, decided to try.

He scouted around and found a city-owned brownstone close enough to City College to be a fairly safe bet. Only half of the apartments had tenants. Assuming full occupancy, the rent roll stood at $1,200, but it was not clear how much of it was in arrears. At this point Leon had been selling software for several years, and he had almost $10,000 saved up. His mother gave him $15,000 from what was left of his father's life insurance. With this, he paid off the back taxes on the building and put in completely new systems. The rewiring he had to hire out, plus the major plumbing, but the rest of the plumbing he did himself, and everything else he did with only occasional assistance from a fellow in the neighborhood.

Leon was lucky. In the early eighties business became interested in the city again. If he'd waited a couple of years, he would have had to come up with much more money. The building might have been out of reach. Also, the tenants were, by the standards of the neighborhood, fairly solid. The lack of records had obscured a strength rather than a weakness. Because he was still selling software part-time, Leon often had to work straight through until midnight, and he rarely took a weekend off, but why should he mind? The place was gorgeous. A new refrigerator was put in every apartment. Most got new stoves and toilets. When he put an ad in the *Daily News*, he actually showed a one-bedroom to a man in a bow tie who worked in an art gallery. Not that he was interested in a new clientele. All of the old tenants stayed. Once the renovated apartments were filled, he turned the building over and more than doubled his money, if you didn't count his time (and he tried not to).

With the proceeds, he bought a brownstone in Manhattan Valley. And then another. He stopped selling software completely. He turned over those two buildings and did a few conversions farther downtown, starting with the building he and Sunny lived in now. That wasn't as much fun. Because of the larger purchase price, he had to hire out nearly all the work, the banks demanded more oversight, and he felt he didn't have enough control over the property.

His dream, as it evolved over these few years, was to buy as much of a block as he could. The paperwork required from a landlord was so complicated that it was impossible for a small entrepreneur to comply with. This was the major reason he hadn't held on to his rental buildings for long after the renovations. But on a larger scale, with office help, it would change from impossible to merely onerous. A larger scale would also mean better deals on goods and services. And his buildings would have to be near one another, because a single brownstone was too vulnerable to the crack house on the one side, the rats on the other.

His first step he made almost without realizing it. After turning over the Hamilton Heights building Sunny had seen when she was pregnant, he bought two smaller sandstones on East 111th Street from an old-style Jewish partnership. At the closing, which was a few days after Linc was born, he mentioned his interest to the sellers' lawyer, also Jewish. ("So what else is new?" Leon said to Sunny that night.) The lawyer asked to see some baby pictures. Then, walking Leon and his attorney out to the ancient elevator, he said, "I represent another owner who's in the process of selling two similarly sized buildings on the same block. For ten thousand I can steer the sales your way." Leon asked for a site check immediately.

"Ten thousand dollars?" said Sunny when she heard. "You mean like a *bribe?*"

Leon shrugged.

"Wow," said Sunny. "I don't know." Her head might as well have been stuffed with cotton.

The apartment, too, was all padding. She contemplated Leon's rough world from a nest of baby comforters, fresh cloth diapers, quilts, lambskins, and little hooded towels. That morning, as Leon had looked over the new prospects, she'd nodded off with a phone in her hand, too exhausted to dial. Even now her eyes were half-closed as the baby, tucked tight into a receiving blanket, nursed under her big soft pink jersey. For a moment she had a keen sense memory of her own sucking. Could it be that she was really remembering what it was like?

"I know it's going to work," said Leon, and he launched as usual into a lot of figures. "This is the beginning of everything."

"How nice," said Sunny.

The next day, as she looked groggily at the ceiling, an expensive, British-made, navy blue baby carriage was delivered—a present from Paul. The handlebars reared up at disconcertingly vertical angles, as if to remind her of properly trained nannies wearing sensible shoes. A person—unlike anyone in real life—who could relieve Sunny of some of this awful responsibility.

In two months Leon owned four buildings on 111th Street. That was when he purchased an apparently useless one-story former machine shop in the middle of the block with the intention of converting it into an office. No more trying to concentrate at home while Sunny walked a sleepless baby. Her friend Dennis, casting about for architecture jobs, drew up the plans. Work began, and as Leon was supervising the removal of several years' worth of rubbish, a young Nigerian woman, Gloria Smith, showed up with the rent for all the Nigerians in his buildings. The cash was in a sealed business envelope. She did the same on the first day of the following month. The third time he asked her if she wanted a job. She started before the renovation was complete, sitting carefully at a desk amid the chaos, recording rents, registering complaints. This freed Leon to work on the endless forms required by the banks and the city.

There were problems, certainly. Vandalism in these tenements was much higher than he'd expected. When he went in at night, extension cords would be running from his hall light fixtures into apartments that dealers were involved in somehow—not as tenant, usually, but as son, grandson, boyfriend, or even nephew. When Leon hired a tenant as super for each building, however, the abuses did drop some. No problem looked insurmountable. Leon knew there were many decent people trapped amid the horrors of the neighborhood. They had been waiting for him at his first purchase, up near City College. Now he wanted to create a stronghold for more of them in East Harlem—a whole block of safe, clean housing.

He left every morning at 6:00 when the baby woke up—before the paper was delivered. He returned before 5:00. (He didn't like being uptown later than 4:00; it was asking for trouble.) In between, Sunny washed and dressed and fed the baby over and over and over again. Often she took him out in Paul's carriage. She became friendly with a few other mothers over in Riverside Park. She listened to them talk and tried to join in. No one had heard of Spoonie Gee. She went out to lunch a couple of times, but it never really worked. The insistent and fragile presence of the baby made it hard to focus on anyone else.

There could be no break in her vigilance. Her skin was always alert to change—in air pressure, sound waves, anything. If sharks could have a couple of extra senses to detect prey, then new mothers, who are equally ferocious, can develop some as well. Danger lay everywhere. Subways had deadly chomping wheels and struts, cruelly noisy brakes. Kidnappers lurked in shaded doorways. One bent old woman in a supermarket told Sunny to put the hat back on her baby if she absolutely had to open the door to the frozen food compartment.

Sunny started to see Bridget more often during this time. She was feeling particularly kindly toward her oldest sister because when Bridget and Jean had come to the hospital, right after Linc was born, Jean got on the phone to check her messages, and Bridget said, "That's a *real baby*," the only comment that pinpointed exactly how curious the situation was. Bridget did not visit as much as Sunny thought she should, though. She never baby-sat. The Upper West Side was a long way from the East Village. And Bridget seemed to wander rather than walk, giving the forty-five-minute subway trip the languorous pace of one of her journeys to the Far East. (How she ever managed to do as much traveling as she did, Sunny could not fathom.) But Bridget did make it uptown more often than Sunny brought the baby downtown to visit her, so Sunny was grateful.

When Linc was a few months old, Bridget, who did not get

cable, came up to see Leon interviewed on a cable show called *Real Estate Now*. It was an early spring day, freakishly warm, before the buds on the trees had popped out, but when a vague promise of growth was everywhere—even in the asphalt and crumbling concrete. They didn't look so different, after all, from the park's hard-packed, well-trodden paths or the squares of soil below the trees lining the streets. The distinction between organic and inorganic was not so clear in this season. Could it be warmer inside or out? It was hard to tell. Bridget kept her Sherpa vest on while sipping chamomile tea in the living room, waiting for the show. Yet to bring Linc to the fruit-and-vegetable market that morning, Sunny had retrieved cork-soled sandals she'd last worn before she was married.

Bridget had brought a much used but still brilliant gift bag with an apricot-colored dahlia on a hot pink background. It contained a little Native American drum. She was always giving Linc little gifts—sometimes very little gifts, like a tube of aloe vera no bigger than a baby's finger—but gifts all the same, often useful ones.

This was a change. Back when Sunny was single, most of the guys she knew had picked up checks, bought her clothes and jewelry, even loaned her money for the rent. There were exceptions: She paid for Martin Fay after he lost his job; also Brendan Dobbs Duff, who never seemed to have a dime. And sometimes it was fun to pull out a wad of recently acquired cash from her perfectly round purse and shell out for Paul or Henry or Dennis. But basically the flow of money was in the one direction, male to Sunny. In turn, Sunny would purchase for Bridget or Ed little items like a Dustbuster, a salt-and-pepper set, a wedge of cheese. Neither could see what was needed—even if Sunny pointed it out—and both were in the habit of not buying things.

Reversing this flow of presents did not make sense. Sunny wanted to tell Bridget that she, Sunny, who had never had access to more than a few hundred dollars at a time, now had a joint checking account—which didn't include Leon's business accounts—of tens of thousands of dollars. Not that she felt the money was hers, or even Leon's. It seemed to have materialized with the baby, so it must belong to the baby. And it wasn't for spending; it was more padding. But it still meant she could not appreciate gifts as she once had.

Leon pretended to be a hardheaded businessman, but the truth was, he had a messianic streak, no matter how much he tried to deny it. He had told the producer of *Real Estate Now* that he wasn't prepared to give specific numbers. "No one expects you to," he was told. Nor would he talk about how dangerous the neighborhood was. "We're not that kind of show," came the reedy reply.

It was Sunny's theory that Leon was the only slumlord who'd ever been willing to go on TV, so she had advised caution. Suppose someone had heard about the bribe? Okay, it wasn't a talk show that thrived on controversy. But Leon's eyes had lit up at Sunny's (gentle) use of the word *slumlord*. It was a word he used himself in a more sarcastic spirit, but from anyone else, even Sunny, he saw it as a challenge—and more of an insult than he cared to admit. He hated it when people didn't like him. Sunny wasn't afraid that he would lose his temper on the air, exactly. But she was afraid that he would be made unhappy and that others would see this.

She sat Linc in the corner of the couch, where he sank back in the typical Buddha fashion of babies. Then she turned on the television she and Leon had bought when they married. It sat on a tower of two other nonworking TVs, which were being used for support only. On top of the latest TV was the cable box.

"This is exciting," said Bridget, settling herself farther into the nubby weave of the couch. "I feel like I'm about to watch the inaugural address."

Linc began to fuss, so Sunny absently let him nurse as they waited for the show to begin. An ad for an adjustable mattress came on. Crank it up, crank it down: It was as thick as sleep. Then: Leon. He looked bigger than normal, sort of stunned, like a football player off the field.

"I'm here with today's guest, Leon Dane, a landlord with extensive property in East Harlem." The interviewer was skinny, blond, mild mannered, with a prominent Adam's apple and earnest eyeglasses. This would be fine. Sunny put Linc back in the corner of the couch.

The first question: "Why East Harlem?"

The property was cheaper. He could buy more. The challenge. The satisfaction. As Leon spoke, the phone number of the studio appeared in a black band at the bottom of the screen. So it was a call-in show. Who knew what nut would respond? She should have told Leon to get his hair cut. It looked like a thatched roof, the way the middle section stuck up.

"I didn't know it was a call-in show," said Sunny to Bridget.

"Well, um . . ." Bridget glanced down at the floor, then up at the ceiling in a characteristic gesture. "It looks like it is."

The baby started to cry. He'd slumped over to his side, so Sunny straightened him up, balancing his weight over his bottom again.

No one was calling in, which seemed to embarrass the interviewer. His questions were innocuous: "How many units?" "What about the vacancy rate?" "What are the most challenging features?" Linc was crying again, drowning out the answers. She stood and rocked him as she watched. Sunny had suggested that Leon simply announce that he was a do-gooder and be done with it. Leon had refused—"I am not," he'd said, frowning—and this vow, at least, he was sticking to. Why should he have to announce his good work?

When a call finally came, it was technical, about a form required by the city. The voice was female, Brooklyn.

Leon gave her a form number but said he had to double-check. "The paperwork is so complicated I don't know how someone who owns a single brownstone, for instance, can manage it. In fact, I do the books for a landlady who runs the luncheonette around the corner. She gives me free coffee."

Sunny rocked faster. Please, please, she prayed, do not offer to take on this woman's paperwork. But fortunately the phone was already disconnected.

The interviewer again: "I know you've converted residential buildings in more established areas." White areas, he meant. "How does that compare with owning rentals in this more marginal neighborhood?" Where Hispanics and blacks lived.

"This is more fun," said Leon.

The interviewer was pleased, called for a commercial. A Cadillac in a showroom, with leasing figures. "I'll get us some cheese sticks," said Sunny. She propped up Linc, who'd sort of listed again behind her. "Would you watch him?"

"That was good," said Bridget about Leon's remark, or maybe the whole show.

It started up again with the same shot of Leon, to the left, and the interviewer, to the right, in chairs catty-corner to a low, square table. Sitting at a similar angle on the gray, deep-cushioned, roll-armed Castro convertible, a wedding present from Leon's mother, Sunny felt she had the best of two worlds: access to a realm of consequence and physical proximity to her child.

Another call, polite but challenging, male, firm: *How can you possibly make a profit?*

"I don't think I should use specific numbers," said Leon. Then he did anyway, counting them off as he always did on his fingers: purchase price, mortgage, interest, maintenance, rent rolls.

A third call: *How do you deal with the vandalism?*

Only Sunny would be able to tell from Leon's answer how annoyed he was. He did assume higher damage rates. But he still felt that others exaggerated the problem, even though he was furious that the windows he'd just replaced at 205 had already been broken—a fact he did not mention.

A belligerent, hectoring tone, probably white: *Isn't it true that you have blocked the latest Tenants Action initiative for self-funding?*

Leon seemed to glow like a radioactive spill. "I do not think that I should have to collect 'dues' "—he spat out the word— "from my tenants, many of whom are on welfare."

As proposed, the dues would come out of any rent increases passed over the next five years. Aren't you more worried about your pocketbook?

"How can I deal with this?" cried Sunny, springing up to pace. Then, not even aware she'd turned around, she dove for the floor as Linc fell into her outstretched arms. He had tumbled off the couch, and Sunny had caught him so fast that she had no memory of the fall.

"Wow," said Bridget. "How did you *do* that?"

Now that Linc was safe, he began to scream.

chapter 12

SUNNY HAD BEEN TRAPPED IN THE APARTMENT FOR A week. Linc had started off cranky, with a bit of a cold, then developed the croup. For two nights, he slept beside her in bed with the humidifier on so high that the next morning the comforter was as slick as an oilskin and the wallpaper had started to peel. Sunny slept only in snatches, fearful that one of those awful breath-robbing coughs would be his last. When she finally emerged from that thick damp gloom, the bright blue day made her blink. Even the traffic gleamed. She hailed a cab, intending to go to Macy's. Instead she found herself giving Leon's office address.

At the light the taxi driver, a heavily jowled Arab, turned around to say, "Go around the block?"

"Why?" asked Sunny. "Can't you just go across on a Hundred and Tenth Street?"

"No, no, too far east," he said, indicating the unwanted direction with a wave of his hand.

Had he misheard the address? "I *am* going east," said Sunny. "To East a Hundred and Eleventh Street. Not west."

The driver pointedly studied her and Linc in the rearview mirror, then fell silent. Sunny tried to maintain a certain outraged dignity but felt guilty nonetheless. Although she was not about to commit the cruder crime (buying drugs) that the driver suspected her of, she did feel that what she was doing was wrong somehow. It couldn't be too dangerous for Linc, she told herself. Not if Leon went over there every day.

Squat, plain, and historically shabby, East Harlem was very different from the splendid ruin of Hamilton Heights. It had the strong horizontal lines of a place like Jackson Heights but was more deserted. Fast-food wrappers spread-eagled by the wind fluttered against the chain links of a fence. The many gaps between parked cars revealed refuse that had collected up against the side of the curb—takeout containers, cups, pint bottles, crack vials. Although it was after noon, most storefronts were sealed off with rolled metal sheeting; garage doors set in brick were locked tight; windows were covered with security grates. When would they be open if not now? At the end of Leon's block, Sunny saw a dozen people in front of a six-story sandstone—the tallest building in the area. Although a couple of figures were settled on the stoop, most were standing in indifferent groups. There were more females than males, but the difference in number was slight, and most looked neither young nor old, belonging instead to some midrange that defied more specific expectations.

Next to the old machine shop was a brownstone with an open window. From it a young man with a battered ear muttered, "Why bih, why bih," at her.

Through the door she could see Leon looking into the opened drawer of a filing cabinet: intent, oblivious, competent, dear.

"'Why bih'?" Sunny said to Gloria as she buzzed her in. "What does that mean?"

Gloria looked embarrassed. Oh. White bitch. "*Non, non,*" she said with the gently nasal overtones of West Africa. "Don't pay attention to him. He's nothing. A dealer. Small time."

Leon's face was clouded with alarm. "What's wrong?" he cried.

"I just thought I'd visit," said Sunny, embarrassed despite her resolve.

"It's time I see the little one, *non*?" said Gloria. As she took Linc in her arms, she corrected herself. "Oh, *non,* the *big* one, the *big* one." She laughed, shifting his weight to her hip. "You look like your daddy, *non?*"

Leon was pleased. "He has my forehead," he boasted, posing with fingers as calipers, and for the first time Sunny saw the resemblance; the isolated forehead pulsed with pride.

"How come there are so many people hanging around outside the big building at the end?" asked Sunny.

Gloria made a face, then flapped her thumb against stiff fingers to indicate idle chatter.

The floorboards of the office were the original ones: wide, rough, unevenly spaced. The wall was a bumpy white-painted brick. Gloria's desk was the first one you saw as you walked in; Leon's was directly in line with hers, only farther back. Each had a student's desk chair, battered and scarred, beside it. At first Sunny was going to sit beside Leon, but the grittiness of her fatigue demanded more space. She dropped into one of the chairs lined up under the long, low front windows.

Leon picked up Linc and threw him over one hip, then the other, snorted on his belly, and finally turned him upside down so that he could look at him sideways. The baby soon started to cry.

"Oops! Your turn!" said Leon, handing the boy off to Sunny. For Leon, the baby could have been a piece of equipment for a sport with rules so arcane that no one could expect him to master them. "You've picked a busy time," he said. "It's the first of the month. Not that it's as busy as I would *like* it to be," he added.

Through the haze of her fatigue Sunny did not understand right away, then realized he was talking about the rent being due.

"Have you had lunch?" he said.

"Yes," said Sunny, trying to quiet the baby by patting him on the back. "Can't I just sit and watch for a while?"

The wooden chair was not comfortable, but it was tolerable once Sunny laid her jacket and Leon's over it. She stuck Linc up under her pullover and let him nurse.

"I don't know how interesting we plan to be," said Leon, resting his bottom against Gloria's metal desk. "How about you, Gloria, do you plan on being very interesting?"

"Luisa is here," said Gloria, as if in response.

The woman Gloria buzzed in was not unusually heavy, but

she walked slightly tilted back, as if her breasts and belly required it. Her shoulders were sloped; her feet and hands were delicate. She carried a huge black satchel of a pocketbook, lumpily weighted down with who knew what. She was in her forties, but looked almost grandmotherly, dressed in black slacks and a white shirt with a frill at the neck. Beside her was a young girl with legs as thin as pipe cleaners sticking out from under a long gray sweatshirt.

This must be the part-time bookkeeper, the one with the heart condition who occasionally took in temporary foster children. She seemed to be continuing a monologue she'd started on the street. "I told them and I told them"—tole them and tole them—"you cannot place a child"—chile—"without more notification." Her accent was a softening, really, as if a ripe piece of fruit were interfering with some of the harsher sounds of the English tongue. "I have to prepare the sheets or whatever. I like things clean. I like to buy a present. I like to welcome a child." She threw a questioning glance at Sunny but ignored her when she got no explanation for her presence.

"And who is this?" asked Gloria, leaning over her desk for a better view of the girl, who was about as high as the desk and as tough as a nut, but blurry, with unkempt hair and watery features that looked as if they'd leaked under the skin.

"This is Alba."

"Nice to meet you, Alba," said Leon.

"It looks like you got a good one this time," said Gloria.

Alba did not smile. She did not frown. Nor was her face frozen in any abnormal way. It was as close to blank as Sunny could imagine.

"Alba's birth mother is in Florida," said Luisa, "and her regular foster mother went on vacation with, you know, the rest of the family. A foster mother, I believe, may *want* to take her foster daughter to Puerto Rico with her, but sometimes she has no money. So I get to raise Alba for a week." She raised her brows at the girl.

"Money, money, money," said Gloria to Sunny. "She talk like a bookkeeper, *non?*"

"Someone's got to keep us in line," said Leon. As he introduced

Sunny, she switched breasts, managing to distribute Linc's weight better over her arm and stomach.

Luisa was magisterial in her response, possibly offended because she had been kept in ignorance unnecessarily. She walked in her stately fashion to a far desk, dropped into the chair—still with shoulders and head angled back—and said in loud but measured tones, "Leon is a good landlord. I know. I work here, and I live here. Before, the tenants live in filth. I keep my apartment nice. I have my own bedroom, and then there is the living and another little room. I clean it, I fix it up all the time. But the halls, they was dirty and broken. This is not a Third World country, I said. Come on. This is America. You cannot see it here. Then Leon purchased the building. He put in new refrigerators. He put in a new front door, new mailboxes. He put in new windows, but then one night they were broken. Whatever. So the building was like sixty percent better after Leon purchased it. Now it is one hundred percent better. I see it on the books, it is not what he was supposed to do. But he did it. Now he must be careful."

"Everyone likes Leon," said Gloria. "Pretty much."

"Pretty much?" said Leon happily.

Linc had mercifully fallen asleep on the second breast.

"Do you go to school?" Sunny asked Alba.

The child's face did not register the question.

"Can't you answer the lady?" called Luisa.

"I hate questions about what I do," said Sunny, meaning it as a pleasantry, but realizing it was true. Here she was an adult, and she had yet to hold down a full-time job.

"Alba!" Luisa's voice soared. "Sit next to me."

"Do you have any children?" Sunny asked Gloria.

"No," said Gloria, barely suppressing a shudder.

"It can be really fun," said Sunny. She sounded wistful.

"Some kinds of fun I can wait for."

"You wait until you have a man that does what he has to do," said Luisa. "A man that can give you what you need."

"She believe in true love," said Gloria. "The more money, the more true love, *non*?"

Although Leon was leaning back as if all this whirl of talk had nothing to do with him, he was clearly glad to be in the midst of it. He was a man who liked female companionship.

Gloria buzzed in an anxious, tentative woman and her teenage son. The boy was handsome and magnetic, a natural leader. But while Sunny admired his lithe, scornful posture, Leon told him to stop horsing around in the bathroom so that the toilet wouldn't have to be replaced again, and Gloria scolded him for not being in school.

"He feel bad," said the mother in a soft, high voice.

"He looks all right to me, *non*," said Gloria.

Her plump cheeks, fire-red nails, and elegant knot of tight braids all expressed disapproval as she ostentatiously wrote out a receipt. Sunny tried to count the fan of bills with her eyes.

When mother and son had left, Luisa said, "You have to think with your head, and so many people they do not think with their head, they think with their heart."

"She has no head, *non*," said Gloria, shaking her own.

"*Everyone* have a head," Luisa corrected sternly. "Though some work better than others, I believe."

"One bad man after another," said Gloria. "Where does she find so many, that's what I want to know."

Luisa nodded. At last, something they could agree on. "The son going to be just like the father," she said.

As if to prove he did not belong in such a category of masculinity, Leon said, "Are you all right there, honey?"

"Did she really pay only twelve dollars?" Sunny asked him. Twelve ninety-five was the price of her current lunchtime favorite, an open-faced melted cheese sandwich topped with arugula and slivers of black olives.

Gloria and Luisa eyed Leon, evidently wondering what his response would be.

"Welfare pays us directly twice a month. Mrs. Mafeo just has to make up the difference." He lifted his hands, which had been hooked under the top of Gloria's desk, and began to rub them together. "What made you come by?" he asked.

"I don't know," said Sunny.

She leaned her head against a slat between the windows and closed her eyes again. She had plenty of money—enough, anyway, so that she could go out and buy Linc three new pairs of pants without thinking about it. She had a husband who was usually at home at night. Yet sometimes she was so stressed out, she wanted to disappear into the witness protection program. She didn't know how a single mother survived.

chapter 13

YES, YES, YES. JEAN *HAD* INVITED GEOFFREY TO THE rehearsal dinner to show she could catch a man as well, if she happened to want to. The trouble was, she couldn't forget him.

Jean considered her taste in men reassuringly boring. She liked to go out to an expensive dinner now and then with a guy in a well-tailored suit who could talk a little business. All very sane: matchmaking according to salary. She was not interested in commitment, because she didn't know how far she was going to go. Someone like this reporter just didn't figure in. He didn't behave the way a man was supposed to. He was actually more aggressive than he appeared, but sneakily so.

It didn't help that Blakely's search took a curious and ultimately infuriating turn. Oh, it was easy enough to track down a few possibles and throw in a man for contrast. But then she heard of a woman named Christina Tonnelli, chief operating officer at a two-hundred-bed hospital in Akron, who was keen on moving to the city. Preliminary inquiries were not inspiring. Although Tonnelli immediately agreed to fly east for an interview, Jean did not see how she could interest someone at Tonnelli's salary level. Blakely was offering a slight step up in pay, but higher prices in the New York area would mean an actual loss of purchasing power. Normally people would suffer such a cut only for blue skies or purple mountains or green grass or some other colorful nonsense. Also, Blakely's hospital was larger, so while the position might involve more responsibility, the title at least was a definite diminishment. The move would look bad on a résumé. Jean was more frank than usual as the phone conversation came to a close, but Tonnelli was not to be discouraged. She arrived for an interview the next day *an hour early.* What was wrong with this woman? She looked healthy. And sane. No makeup. She wore black square-toed shoes that she must have chosen for their practicality, although actually they were very modish; all the Hollywood starlets were wearing them. Was she about to be fired? But she accepted the possibility of being mentioned in a magazine article matter-of-factly and didn't care a bit if anyone contacted her current employer. "Oh, they know all about it," she said cheerily. Finally, Jean, pretending that the interview was over, asked her about her family.

"My daughter has been accepted at Juilliard," said Tonnelli.

Jesus. How extraordinary, that a woman would throw her career away for her daughter's. But it wasn't Jean's job to save idiots from practicing suttee, so she forwarded Tonnelli's name to Blakely along with the others.

In the midst of this process, Geoffrey called up and said he had to check on some of her physical characteristics for his article. No kidding, he really said that. Then he trailed off, giving up on whatever banter he'd been attempting. "I suppose that's sexist." His voice had grown faint.

"Why?" she barked.

"Oh, maybe it's not," he said. She had the peculiar sense that he was having this conversation with himself rather than her.

"Have you had dinner yet?" she said.

"I don't usually eat what normal people would call 'dinner,'" he said.

"Who does?" she said, not to be bested. "But we have to eat something, and every once in a while it might as well be dinner." She suggested a seafood restaurant that another fellow (a property manager) had taken her to, and Geoffrey agreed.

When Jean arrived, he stood up to greet her, revealing a bulky tweed sports coat over a pink-and-white chalk-stripe shirt. Ridiculous. And his face was drawn and closed. Beyond ridiculous. Insulting.

"What's wrong?" said Jean, as the waiter held her chair for her.

"Nothing," said Geoffrey.

"Don't you like the restaurant?"

Geoffrey slid his eyes to the waiter, presumably in a vain attempt to quiet her. "It's okay."

A disaster. Thank God this sullenness had revealed itself early. "I'm sorry," Jean said to the waiter. "Our plans have changed."

Outside, Geoffrey said tentatively, "Is everything all right?" Odd, Jean had forgotten what he looked like. She didn't usually go out with such regular-featured boys.

"Passable," she said.

"Why did we have to leave?"

"Did you want to stay?"

"Not really."

Jean abruptly entered a drugstore and bought a handful of financial magazines. Geoffrey tactfully waited outside. When she rejoined him, he looked at her with nervous concern. "Is it some kind of woman thing?"

"Some kind of woman thing? Yuck! Yes, it's some kind of woman thing, I guess, to want to eat in a place my companion likes."

"Oh," said Geoffrey, startled.

A young girl darted in front of them, clutching her cardigan to her chest with crossed arms. Geoffrey said, "We could go back. I didn't mind it."

"It's too late now," said Jean.

"Did you really leave because of me?" asked Geoffrey.

"What do you think?"

"I don't know what to make of you!" he cried. "You seem to say one thing and mean another!"

Jean sighed.

"Are you mad at me?" he asked. A curiously direct question, coming from him. They had started walking east, fast, as if trying to escape their own footsteps, a woman in a $500 business suit and a man dressed as if all his luggage had been lost.

"Honestly," said Jean with disgust. "Why would I be mad at you?" Although of course she was, at this point.

"I thought maybe . . . On the phone you sounded as if maybe you were . . . " They were practically running.

"The problem is, we don't really know each other."

"You didn't take me very seriously when we met, did you?" asked Geoffrey.

"I don't know what you mean." Jean had stopped suddenly beside a menu taped to a window: a lot of different burgers. Through the glass you could see the bar, with its spill of standing patrons.

"Do you think this would be all right?" asked Geoffrey.

"I don't know," said Jean.

The one time she'd slept with a guy, she'd felt like throwing up afterward, although that had probably been because of all the wine she'd drunk. (He had been a French exchange student, and she had finally gone to bed with him after his farewell party.)

"Well, it's all right with *me*," said Geoffrey.

Once they were seated in the restaurant, the conversation developed the more natural rhythm—natural to Jean, anyway—of question and answer. What she wanted to do was tell him about that stupid Christina Tonnelli, who had recently sent her an announcement for her daughter's cello recital back in Akron. Scrawled in pen across the back was "Next year, Juilliard!" But no matter who had waived confidentiality, Jean did not feel she could go into the subject. So instead she fell back on questions designed to efficiently elicit character, expectations, and expertise. She was not used to asking personal questions, which were out of bounds at work, but details did creep in: He came from Georgia. (A surprise, because he had no southern accent, not even a slight slowing of speech.) His father ruled both family and surgical supply company with ruthless politeness. His mother was a housewife; his sister, a nurse. He was only a couple of years younger than she. He liked to play the piano.

Geoffrey's questions, on the other hand, were as dutiful as those of Jean's job seekers. For instance, he asked her how her cheeseburger was.

She said, "I don't think this place is known for its food."

"Why not?" he said.

"It's a singles bar," she said.

"You're kidding," he said, looking around. "But it doesn't look any different."

"Different from what?" asked Jean dryly. See, she was having fun.

But he threw her off base again by saying, "I'm never going to be a success in the way you think of it."

"How do you mean?"

"I'm never going to make a lot of money."

"I think you're taking a rather narrow view of me." Jean *always* took into consideration elements like prestige and satisfaction; Crough even thought of her as woolly-headed at times, though she was usually proved right. The conversation had jumped way off track.

"Listen," she continued. "You seem like a very nice person."

"Uh-oh," he said.

"Why do you say that?"

"Nothing good ever starts like that."

"But you are nice."

"I know you think I'm nice," he said. And, indeed, his regular features, long furrowed brow, and unassuming hair did seem to radiate decency. "You think I'm nice and harmless. Inoffensive. Passive. Not at all the sort of take-charge manly businessman you're used to. Blakely is the person you liked to cross swords with. I'm not complaining. I'm just trying to figure this out. If I'm right—and, really, there is no point in denying it, certainly we are beyond that—if I'm right, then why did you ask me to dinner tonight?"

His eyes were indeed mild, but they were completely focused on her. For some reason she couldn't be sure he liked what he saw. "Well . . . ," she said.

"This is just a suggestion," said Geoffrey. "And you don't have to take it too seriously if you don't want to. You could try coming over again."

He was sitting stiffly, not using his space comfortably at all, which gave Jean the strength to turn the tables on him. "But why would you want me to?" she asked.

"Because you look like all those teenage girls I used to dream about, back when I was in junior high," said Geoffrey fervently. "Hair tucked behind their ears, chins up, laser smiles, long coats, longer legs. Coming out of their Key Club meetings. Oh, *the Key Club*." He slumped forward under the burden of the memory. "My adolescent heart still aches."

God, he was handsome. Even his clothes couldn't hide it. His eyelashes must sweep halfway down his cheeks. Jean suddenly reached across the red-glassed votive candle for his hand. To clasp his hand palm to palm, she found herself turning her own wrist as if preparing to arm wrestle. Not something she wanted to risk. This was not *at all* what she had planned.

chapter 14

BESSIE WAS GOING TO HOUSE-SIT JEAN'S APARTMENT WHILE she was away. It had been a couple of years since they had last got together. When Bessie had called up from her parents' house on Long Island, she referred to "adventures abroad," and it is often easier to get back in touch with someone when you have been away yourself. She said that after all that freedom and excitement, the 'rents were getting on her nerves. "It's not like I have plants to water or cats to feed," said Jean. (Here Bessie cooed in mock sympathy.) "But you can always stay here for a couple of days." Jean was surprised, nonetheless, when Bessie agreed. You couldn't even set up a meeting in that short a time. Jean herself was rarely in her apartment. Sometimes she felt she did not so much live in it as find herself encased in the idea of it. It was in this sense just a blueprint and a series of numbers.

But Bessie was enthusiastic. She said she'd bring a six-pack the night before Jean's flight. Jean hesitated, saying, "I need a lot of beauty sleep these days."

"Hey," said Bessie. "Not as much as I do."

When Jean answered the door that evening, Bessie's fingers were indeed hooked through the top of a six-pack. Cradled in her other arm was a small philodendron in a pot.

A honking, wailing ambulance out on Broadway suspended

them in its overwhelming noise for a couple of minutes. When it had dwindled away, Jean said, "Nice-looking plant."

"Just get me a knife and fork," said Bessie.

Then her eyes swept the living room, and she cried, "Hold everything! I'm having a Proustian experience here!"

"You're awash in memories?" said Jean. She and Bessie had shared the apartment while Jean was in graduate school, and she couldn't remember if Bessie had been back since.

"Drowning," said Bessie. She sighed sentimentally. "We had a lot of unhappy years here."

"How true," said Jean. Bessie was as funny as ever, but Jean had forgotten how exhausting she could be. Well, she could always excuse herself and retire. When they'd settled themselves in the living room, she asked, "Is the plant a, uh . . . gift?"

"Can't have you resigning yourself to the lonely life, can we?"

Jean's eyes fell to the coffee table. This was when it would have been convenient to have a framed photo of Geoffrey next to the magazines. She would have to look into it.

"So where are you off to tomorrow?" said Bessie.

"Conference," said Jean. "I'm going to give a paper called 'How to Find a Job You're Not Remotely Qualified For.'"

There was a long pause in which Jean wondered if Bessie thought she was being serious. At last Bessie said, "I can't think of a better person to do it."

"Actually, there won't be anything half so interesting."

"'New Perspectives on Human Resources,'" said Bessie. "'The Happy Manager: Fact or Fiction?' 'How to Hunt Heads and Live to Eat the Brain.'"

Jean hadn't noticed before how pale and unkempt Bessie appeared. These couldn't have been the same sorts of clothes she used to wear: Unflattering light blue cotton pants with a thick elastic waist. A smudged off-white golf shirt. Flat sandals in which her feet were strapped like a body on a gurney. Worse, Jean could tell she'd spent a lot of money on this stuff. Maybe Bessie had shut her eyes during the selection process. She'd always had a curious idea of her looks.

As Jean searched for something to say, her eyes lit upon the

Hermès scarf tied, bafflingly, to one handle of her bag. "Nice accessory," she said.

"Just something I picked up to impress my old friends," said Bessie, pointedly examining the well-worn jeans and snug black turtleneck that Jean had changed into as soon as she got home from work.

"Ah, yes," said Jean. "I dressed up myself. Nothing is too good for my college chums."

"So I see," said Bessie. Had she always had that habit of ducking her head and gazing at your lips when you talked? "I guess your job turned out pretty well."

"Yes," said Jean. "I am a great success. That's why I'm in these fabulous new digs."

"I never should have left this place," said Bessie. "But bartending school beckoned. I didn't know then that further education is always a mistake."

Bartending school was perhaps the only type that Bessie had not tried.

"I'm surprised you knew where you were when you walked in," said Jean. "Look. Poster *in a frame*. Split in the seat of the couch *covered with an afghan*. Rug *without one stain in it*."

"It's funny to think of you finding jobs for doctors," said Bessie, taking a long final pull on her beer. "I always had to help you with your biology homework."

"I never took biology."

"Yes you did."

Jean got up to pluck two more beers from the refrigerator. Clearly Bessie was on some kind of warpath.

"I thought you might be moving on," said Bessie, who had followed her into the kitchen. "A person with a job like yours."

"I don't believe there *are* nicer places," said Jean.

"What do you make at a job like that?" asked Bessie.

"Hard to tell," said Jean. "What with bonuses and all."

"Ballpark."

"I really don't know." This she said over her shoulder as she returned to the living room.

Bessie, defeated, gave up and started rolling her beer bottle between her opened palms. "I remembered this place as bigger," she said.

"It was bigger," said Jean. They were still standing, squaring off.

Now Bessie was closing one eye and sighting her over the top of the bottle. "Hey, remember when I first told you about this place?"

"Not really."

"Sure you do. I'd just heard about it from Joe Valley, whose sister was moving out."

Yes, Jean recalled something like that. "Whatever happened to him?" Finally, they were sitting again.

Bessie shrugged.

"How's life been treating you?" asked Jean.

"What can I say? Rush, rush, rush!"

"I hear you. Who's got time to be happy?"

"Yeah," said Bessie. "I've been thinking about it and I decided to quit the rat race, settle down, and raise a couple of kids."

Bessie had never held a job for more than six months in her life.

"Ha! Gotcha!" cried Bessie, recovering her initial enthusiasm. "You should've seen your face!"

"All right, all right, no double callbacks," said Jean.

"What does *that* mean?" exclaimed Bessie happily. "Sunny still married?"

"For now."

"The last time you called, you were hiding from her wedding."

"The rehearsal dinner, you mean."

Bessie nodded absently. "I'm what you would call 'in between engagements.'"

"Ah," said Jean.

"In the literal sense."

"Well . . ."

"Yup," said Bessie, nodding.

"Juggling fiancés?" She couldn't be serious.

"What can you do?" said Bessie.

Jean leaned back, crossed her legs. "I have a boyfriend."

"Really," said Bessie. "Did you score yet?"

For the first time, Jean giggled.

"I see you have," said Bessie.

"You didn't hear it from me," said Jean.

"He probably has a big job, too."

"Sort of."

"So you'll definitely be moving on pretty soon," said Bessie.

Jean grew wary. "What do you mean?"

"Big job. Big boyfriend. You'll be hard-charging your way into a new apartment," said Bessie, "and if so, it would very nice if . . . I thought it would be very *symmetrical* if . . . you gave the lease to me. Considering everything."

"Bessie, I own this place," said Jean. "I bought it about a year ago."

There was a silence.

"At the insider's price, I suppose," said Bessie bitterly.

"Yes."

Bessie rallied and said with bright, false cheer, "Well, don't tell me what you paid for it. That would be too much, even for an old trooper like me."

"It was ridiculously high, actually."

"Let's just drop it," said Bessie. "Forget I said anything. It was just a thought. I have a lot of thoughts. They careen all around my brain. I can't stop them. They keep getting loose and banging into things. Here, there, everywhere." She started to wave her hands wildly. "Flit, flit, flit. See, there goes another one." But it was the beer bottle that went flying off. It hit the wall headfirst and re-gurgitated a bit of beer onto the plaster before crashing down and rolling in a crazy circle on the floor.

chapter 15

Sunny LIKED TO HAVE EXCUSES TO GO TO THE OLD machine shop that had become Leon's office. When she got pregnant for a second time and could never shake her hunger, she decided that what the place needed was food. One of her few memories of her mother was a visit the two of them had paid to a real estate office near their home; Sunny must have been four. In the waiting area was a low, modular couch made of plastic aqua pillows, a kidney-shaped coffee table with a speckled top, and a heavy white china pedestal bowl filled with little chalky mints. Sunny ate them as her mother talked to a lady from the church.

Sunny wanted to re-create this sense of haven at Leon's office but couldn't bring herself to put out candy. The diets around there were already so poor. Nor did she know where to find a bowl with a pedestal. But once when she was in the supermarket she spotted a thick wooden salad bowl, very handsome, which had the added advantage of being difficult to break. Without thinking she put it into her cart next to Linc, who preferred the roomy back to the little retracting seat up front. The next day she bought a bag of organically grown Macouns on Broadway near her apartment. Two bags would have been better, but she couldn't manage them and the diaper bag. Instead she crammed a package of unshelled peanuts into the net that hooked over the back of Linc's stroller. Through the mesh you could see enough of the red, white, and blue lettering to think of ball games, state fairs, and zoos.

Brianna, the new receptionist, laughed when she caught sight of the lumpy bag of apples under Sunny's arm. "You're always trying to feed us, aren't you?" said the girl. She was really young—just out of high school.

"What else did I try to get you to eat?" asked Sunny.

"Some mix."

"Oh. Trail mix."

"For the fat or like that." Brianna was Puerto Rican but had almost a Valley girl accent.

"It's a fatty acid called omega-3," said Sunny. "Raw peanuts are an excellent source." She was in too good a mood to point out that the coffee and sweet roll that Brianna had got on the corner would do her no good at all. Besides, the luncheonette was the one Leon filled out the city's forms for, so Sunny knew it could use the business.

She unbuckled Linc, who immediately threw off the characteristic stroller hunch and took a few tottering steps. "Is this my big boy?" cried Gloria, the only other person there. When Leon had managed to buy up most of the block, Gloria had been promoted to office manager. Her new desk was back near Luisa's empty one. (Luisa worked part-time at a number of different places.) On top of all the desks were matching phones with a palette of transparent buttons that lit up to indicate which lines were in use. It was very modern. But the Nigerians still gave Gloria their rent after hours before the first day of the month. They never communicated in any other way, never complained. One refrigerator didn't work for weeks before Leon got wind of it.

When Sunny offered Gloria an apple, she said, "I don't eat things"—tings—"that are red and green like that."

"You eat tomatoes," said Sunny.

"Tomatoes are good when they're just red, no green," said Gloria with finality.

"So where's Leon?" asked Sunny, sitting at his desk, glancing at the extremely boring paperwork, and swiveling back and forth in the secondhand ergonomic desk chair.

"With Sergey."

"Oh, right." In fact, that was why Sunny had chosen today to come in. When Leon had needed extra cash for a sandstone across the street, he'd brought in a man named Sergey Gustov on this one investment. Sunny was aware that the new partner was going to be around looking at other properties, and she'd wanted to see what he was like.

Linc gummed several apples, but the super who'd come in for cleaning supplies turned one down, as did the grandmother of the drug dealer on the first floor, as did the beautiful Dominican cleaning lady whose neighbor in 2B was bothering her.

"Maybe you should eat one yourself, in front of everyone, and pretend to like it," said Gloria at the end of a phone call.

"I forgot the peanuts!" cried Sunny. She shook some, rattling, into a brittle plastic hat textured to imitate straw, a souvenir of Gloria's from the last city council election. As she turned, she caught sight of a stranger through the grated window of the door: hair unruly and flecked with gray, a well-shaped beard, shoulders pushed forward, hands thrust into the pockets of a black leather jacket so that the bottom corners were pointing at her. Maybe five or ten years older than Leon.

"Ah, beautiful," he said as he was buzzed in. "Another beautiful woman. Leon, you always have beautiful women in the office. That's why"—vy—"I love to visit."

Leon, who was right behind Sergey, also walked with his hands thrust into the pockets of his pants. Sergey made him look different somehow, a little foreign. Learning of Sunny's identity, Sergey cried, "Leon, you never tell me you have such a beautiful wife, by the way." By the vay. "And baby! Such a handsome, handsome baby. A baby which is the *best* baby."

Linc had found a small plastic bottlecap, which Sunny didn't think was small enough to swallow, but she was keeping an eye on him anyway.

"Yes," she said. "He is the best baby in the world."

"My darlink is at home," said Sergey. "She—how do you say it? Puts on creams all day."

"Well, I put the creams on my kid rather than on myself," said Sunny.

"Oh!" cried Sergey with delight. "Smart *and* beautiful! What a wife! Why did you not tell me about your wife? Beautiful women in office, beautiful woman at home. Go here, go there, all the time, beautiful."

"Hi, Sergey," said Gloria.

"Gloria," said Sergey. "I must kiss you." Which he proceeded to do. "It is custom. But not Brianna. That I get in trouble for. She is young girl. Too young."

"Sergey and I have just been looking at 236 and 238," said Leon, "to plan out a course of action."

"Very pretty buildings, by the way," said Sergey. "Very pretty. And Leon is good partner. He is Jew. So, he is good with money." Oh, dear, thought Sunny, even as she laughed.

"I know," continued Sergey, "because I am Jew also, by the way. Maybe not so much in beginning, but then to leave Russia, I have to go to Israel first thing. So, now I am real Jew. Much, much better at money."

The black leather jacket, the gray slacks, the gold ring—Sunny realized now that these were all probably expensive items, more expensive, in fact, than the sorts of clothes the rich people she knew would wear. The gleaming gray slubbed pants she could imagine on the more stylish of Dennis's gay friends.

Because the plastic hat was still in her hand, Sunny offered it to Sergey.

"Ah, *nuts*," he said. "A very interesting hat. With nuts."

"Have some," she said.

"Yes, I will"—vill—"but later," said Sergey. "In Russia, by the way, there is no landlord by law. So everyone is landlord, but illegal landlord. Everyone has apartment, rents to other people, gets invisible money. You have that? Invisible money?"

"We prefer the visible kind, actually," said Leon.

Gloria said to Sunny, "A lot of kids allergic to peanuts, *non*. A girl in my niece's class got into shock last year. She was in the hospital for the night. But she feel okay now."

"Oh," said Sunny.

"In your country, what costs one hundred dollars?" Sergey asked

Gloria. "In Russia, nothing costs one hundred dollars, because there is *nothing to buy*. Nothing! Look everywhere"—vare—"doesn't matter, nothing."

"Let's just put these peanuts away," said Sunny, shaking them back into their red, white, and blue plastic bag.

Just in time, because suddenly Luisa was at the door with her nephew Felipe and Alba, who was still her foster child. Alba had stayed with Luisa for over a year now. Her original foster parents had simply refused to take her back, and although Luisa thought they should be punished in some way, there wasn't much anyone could do. One of the social workers had mentioned trying to deal with the birth mother in Florida, but nothing came of it. Luisa didn't mind keeping the girl for now, but the agency kept telling her that if she wasn't willing to adopt, Alba was going to have to be placed in a home where such was a possibility. It wasn't fair otherwise. And Luisa certainly couldn't adopt; she couldn't afford to give up the fees associated with foster care. "I add up every penny," she told Sunny at one point. "I make each pile for something, you know, a little for electricity, a little for food, a little for my heart medicine, and then I put the piles into the envelopes, and it works, but I got to do a lot of shuffling from envelope to envelope at the end of the month."

"Sunny!" cried Felipe in a little piping voice, bouncing from foot to foot. The boy could have been built on a spring.

"How landlord baby Linc?" said Alba, bending over him.

"What?" said Sunny.

"Landlord baby Linc" was a perfect concept: It sounded like a government program. He was, after all, already replicating. (Sunny would never have gotten pregnant a second time if it hadn't been for the first. It had to do with mass production and maybe marginal rate of return if Sunny remembered her intro to economics class—or rather the notes she'd copied from Henry.)

The aptness of the term, however, was not what surprised Sunny. She had never heard Alba speak before. Alba had a low, creaky, unused-sounding voice, all the more magical because of those qualities. "Why, Linc is just fine, honey," said Sunny. "Linc is just fine." And to Luisa she cried, "She talked to me!"

"Can you speak in any other voices?" Felipe said to Sunny.

Sunny *knew* she should have taken Spanish in college. *Why* had she wasted all those years there?

"No," she said earnestly. "But I'd like to."

"You can't talk like this?" said Felipe in a high, cartoon-inspired squeak. "It's easy. You just scrunch up your mouth."

Alba giggled. Another first.

The doorbell. This was getting to be quite a party. But a pall fell over the room when Brianna buzzed in a truly skaggy-looking woman: wrists like broom handles, a tremulous mouth, old jeans with legs as floppy as garbage bags and a big fold at the waist secured by a rubber band. Her hair was a puzzle, sort of like a bath mat—short, but it didn't look as though it had been cut, even badly. It looked as if it had stopped growing. To Brianna she kept saying, "I have it"—or was it "I've had it"? She was moving with her shoulder foremost, eyes down, as if plowing through the air itself were difficult. The crowd must have intimidated her, but she also had a paralyzing effect on them.

"Let me see what you have right now in your pocket, Mrs. Arboleda," said Leon loudly as if her main problem were that she was hard of hearing.

As Mrs. Arboleda began to aimlessly pat the loose thighs of her jeans, Sunny looked down at the firm crisp parabolic curves of the apples.

"Just put your hands in and see what you can find," said Leon.

Muttering in Spanish, Mrs. Arboleda pecked at the fabric of her jeans, eventually coming up with a few crumpled bills.

Gloria moved forward and plucked the bills with the very tips of her fingers, pinkie extended. "Eight," she said briefly to Leon.

"Bring us the rest tomorrow," he said.

The silence continued as Mrs. Arboleda made her unsteady way back to the door, but once she was outside, Sergey said in a stage whisper, "Tell me. Was that Miss America?"

Only Luisa refused to laugh. "I love my babies," she said, still caught in the previous mood, "but my sister, you know, she should not have had Felipe. I mean, she should have had him later. I love him, but she could not go back to school, and you have to go back to school. To get a good job. And she is seventeen years old when she had him, and this fact is not sinking into her head. That it is not good for her and the child.

"I can help my sister sometimes, but who could help me? That is why I have to think about doing for Alba. I have to put the child first. No matter how much I may love a girl like her. A smart girl who knows herself. You have to think with your head." Luisa pointed to her temple, watch crystal facing out, index finger poised to bore into her brain.

chapter 16

SUNNY ORDERED TWO CASES OF PERRIER-JOUËT FOR Bridget's baby shower. Martinis would be a bit much, she decided, but she wanted to insure the festivity of the occasion. Most of the guests were not familiar with babies and just wanted to have a good time while adjacent to a new and exciting experience. Sunny knew this because she'd ended up inviting a number of her own friends. Bridget had displayed a curious reluctance about the shower and had kept giving excuses for why she hadn't come up with a list of people to invite. Finally, she gave Sunny three names: one neighbor (Stew) and two clients. So Sunny turned around and simply invited everyone she could think of, male and female.

Of course, any single woman was completely free to have a child. Bridget seemed to think it natural for an unconventional type like herself to do so. And no father was that big a help around the house. Women like Sunny who didn't have a job did all the domestic chores. A man who was completely supported by his wife maybe did half. But no one who was pregnant knew what she was getting into. Did Bridget realize how much everything cost? How desperately she *needed* these presents?

The apartment was an appropriate place for a baby shower, since Leon's makeshift bachelor collection of hand-me-down furniture and up-to-the-minute audio equipment had been transformed over the years into a tight pack of primary-colored plastic. Taking up almost as much space as the dining room table was the red vinyl tent nearby, door flap tied open to reveal two saucer eyes, all that was distinguishable on a twisted, unzipped sleeping bag. Through the large archway and down two steps to the right was a three-foot-high blue basketball hoop and matching easel. Under the window was a kid-size red-and-yellow sedan you had to propel with scrambling feet, like a car on *The Flintstones*. Next to the couch was a single kitchen appliance with stick-on burner decals, a swinging refrigerator door, a sink the size of a Pop-Tart, and a microwave with a revolving tray. This had been a Christmas present for Linc, but Sunny had to trick him into playing with it, since he never did much more than dish up the plastic pepperoni pizza, and she had to discourage Ruth, now three, who cooed happily over little culinary delights for her various dolls and stuffed animals.

"Baby" decorations wouldn't have been noticed here, so instead Sunny decorated with a tropical theme. The dining room table had a thick green raffia skirt. Scooped out pineapples were used as serving bowls. Paper parrots brilliantly patterned with vermilion, lime green, and cerulean blue hung from the ceiling. She ordered six pounds of shrimp and an immense poached salmon from Citarella. On Saturday evening she made three salads, one pasta, one green, and one (tropical) fruit. On Sunday morning she made Leon pick up an armful of breads. It was a lot of work, but worth it, to give Bridget's baby a head start in life.

Bridget had finally succumbed with regard to the shower. Sunny had really given her no choice. With hesitantly expressed but equal persistence, Bridget had insisted she help. Sunny then told Jean she should come early to set up, too—just to let her know what a real sister would do, even though Jean did not qualify. Jean said she would try to come, obviously not meaning it at all (her sigh told Sunny that she was waiting for a far more important call), and then she showed up just the same.

So what to do with them? Bridget was slow even when she wasn't pregnant, and Jean had no domestic skills. What Sunny really needed was someone to tip the florist, who had just buzzed, but she couldn't trust them to do it, because God only knew what either would consider sufficient. So she sent Leon.

Bridget was sitting on the couch with Ruth on her lap and Linc beside her, peering in her ear for some reason. Bridget looked good pregnant. Her skin was dewy, and her cheeks were pink. She was wearing a pair of loose drawstring pants with silver threads running through them and a big black baggy sweater that sloped over her seal-like bulge. It was just like Bridget to look somehow off and stylish at the same time.

"You have hair in your ear," said Linc.

"I know," said Bridget. "I need an awfully little comb for it."

Jean was hovering uselessly. "I got you a very nice present," she said. "Cost a fortune. Would you like me to tell you what it is?"

Only Jean, living in a world of capable, well-paid, able-bodied single people, would be so proud of something that fit in a box. Sunny just hoped it was useful. Still, she was pleased. An expensive gift, no matter how irrelevant to actual life it might be, was a fitting tribute to the importance of the event.

"That's nice," said Bridget. "But I don't need a lot of stuff. I never have."

"Well, the baby has to wear something," said Sunny, taking the ginger flowers and bird-of-paradise from Leon, who had just walked in.

"It's so embarrassing to hear the mothers in Tompkins Square Park talking about where they bought their baby clothes," said Bridget.

"Maybe," said Sunny. "But they were probably up all night with screaming babies. You should cut them a little slack."

"I don't know that we really want to give mothers *more* slack," said Jean in her usual joking tone. "I hate dealing with those women at work. Always canceling at the last minute because their kids are sick or something."

"Really," said Sunny, who would have been profoundly irritated if she'd had the time. "Why don't you go get me a knife?" She smiled. "To trim the stems."

Jean was incapable of finding such an item, so Sunny was still hugging a glass vase to her breasts when she answered the door. Good: Stew was the first guest to arrive. "The whole thing is pretty amazing, isn't it?" she said.

"It sure is," said Stew, trailing behind her down the hall. Standing around with all the Crossley sisters, including Bridget, he said, "I thought Bridget was very closed off and depressed when I first met her. It's hard to believe now. She's such an uninhibited, caring person. We've gotten awfully close over the years."

"I guess so," said Jean, with an overtly significant glance at Sunny.

The buzzer sounded again, but Sunny did not feel she could leave this conversation, and Leon seemed to be handling the door okay for now.

"I couldn't believe it when she told me she was pregnant," said Stew.

"Really?" said Sunny. That was interesting.

"It was the last thing I expected," he said.

"Will wonders never cease," said Jean.

"Well, she isn't exactly *young*," said Stew. "Speaking of which, who is that with the woman in the red dress?"

"You mean Paul Walsh?" asked Sunny.

"Your old boyfriend Paul?" said Stew. "Really? Wow, he certainly has changed."

Had he? Sunny hadn't noticed. "I'm sorry Geoffrey isn't here," she said absently to Jean.

"He's in Boston," said Jean. Then she announced to Stew, "My husband, Geoffrey, wrote about me in an article a couple of years ago. He said that as a recruiter I played the 'wisecracking best friend' to 'the often rudderless client.' Not bad, is it? That's why I married him."

Sunny wondered why Jean had brought this up. "Do you think I should have had a shower for you when you were married?" she asked.

"Certainly not," said Jean. "I didn't need one."

The living room had begun to fill up comfortably. Linc asked several times if he could have some soda "because it was a special occasion." Since Sunny had said yes the first time, she didn't know why he kept asking. Henry came with Clare. In the dining room Sunny overheard Brendan Dobbs Duff telling the two of them in patronizing tones about some success that he had been within a hairbreadth of. Both he and Henry thought they were being kind, talking to the other. Dennis brought the star of an Off-Broadway show. A lot of the conversation in the rest of the room was about who exactly had heard of this guy. By now Sunny was planted at the door to greet guests and accept presents, so she was the first woman to be kissed when Sergey arrived. His wife, short, chic, and firepluglike, rolled her eyes—not about Sergey's effusive embraces, it turned out, but about the candy box he held in his hand. "I told him, you cannot give chocolates for a baby," she said with scorn.

"This is for mother," Sergey protested, kissing Bridget, who blushed. "See, she likes. But your other sister, she is afraid." Indeed, Jean had slipped away.

"Jean doesn't need you," said Bridget.

Implying that Sunny had needed him—or at least his investment? The reference seemed an oddly pointed one.

But here was Gloria, carrying a package as big as a suitcase. Sergey moved forward to kiss her, Bridget retreated down the hall, and Sunny ended up with Gloria's gift, whose particular yielding firmness Sunny recognized right away.

"Pampers," said Gloria with a trace of nervous defiance. "I always bring them to baby showers."

No one else would have brought such a homely gift, but Sunny felt a curious pang of gratitude she hadn't for any of the other offerings. Bridget was going to need plenty of diapers.

If Sunny had had any hint that Bridget was going to get pregnant, she wouldn't have left all her old baby stuff at Leon's office for his tenants through the years. Thanks to this party, though, Bridget's baby might end up with even more cunning little possessions than Linc and Ruth had had. Most guests appeared to have followed Sunny's directions on what to bring. Paul had walked in with a stroller, although Sunny had given him other, less expensive options. Clare's soft, limp package, wrapped in yellow tissue paper and sporting a many-fingered silver bow, had to hold receiving blankets. And Dennis must have brought many outfits, if the size of the box was any indication. Sunny briefly regretted not giving the relatively well-heeled Sergey any suggestions. She hadn't really expected either him or Gloria to show up, although it was true that Bridget had been to Leon's office several times. Once she'd dropped off the keys to the van with Gloria and learned details about family members in Lagos that Sunny had never heard of.

Sunny could tell that Bridget was embarrassed by all the largesse. Fortunately, this was hard to discern through her usual quiet, neutral affect, but Sunny did notice her take Gloria's hand and squeeze it before retreating with Sunny into the bedroom. It was getting hard to fit all the gifts on top of the blanket chest. Sunny dropped the diapers near the larger packages on the floor.

She was still contemplating the pile when Jean joined them. "You know, I should have invited Bessie," said Sunny.

"I thought you didn't like her," said Jean.

"That's not true."

"Well, she couldn't have come anyway," said Jean. "As she's dead."

Sunny laughed.

"Stew didn't get you anything, did he?" Sunny asked Bridget.

"No," said Bridget. "I told him not to."

"Why?"

"I told all my friends not to bring presents."

"But this is a *shower*."

"I know," said Bridget uncomfortably. "But they don't have any money. I can't expect them to buy me stuff that they wouldn't buy themselves."

"I certainly hope that my demise will not be the occasion of such merriment," said Jean.

"What?" said Sunny.

"Although of course it has its funny side," said Jean.

"Bessie is really dead?"

"Yup."

"Dead to you, you mean."

"She's finished. Not alive. Kaput."

Sunny could not make sense of Jean's tone. "How did it happen?" she asked.

"She drove her car in front of a commuter train just outside Huntington Station."

"Did you hear about this?" Sunny asked Bridget.

"I barely knew her anymore," said Jean loudly. "We hadn't seen each other for years, and then a while back out of the blue she came over and asked for the lease to the apartment."

Bridget shook her head.

"It was a lot of nonsense," said Jean. "What was I going to do? Give her an apartment I'd bought for two hundred grand?"

It was a shame that Jean wasn't a normal person. If she would moan about her feelings of guilt, Sunny could tell her it wasn't her fault.

"You don't think her suicide is connected, do you?" asked Sunny.

"Of course," said Jean sarcastically. "People are always driving themselves in front of trains for the love of apartments."

"Jesus," said Sunny, glancing at Bridget.

"Acute apartment anxiety has only recently been recognized as a mental illness by the American Psychiatric Institute."

Jean was really on a roll. She was hard to watch.

"It's considered a leading cause of suicide in women between the ages of thirty and thirty-nine, you know," said Jean. "Nothing will push up those statistics like a drop in the vacancy rate!"

"Don't you care?" said Sunny, eyeing her with disgust.

"If only I had known then what I know now!" cried Jean with mad irony. "I could have got her the help that she needed!"

Almost
Home

chapter 1

It was a good thing Jean had a certain detachment from her emotions. She never used to sit in a taxi on her way home from work with her heart in her mouth, her right arm draped desperately over her briefcase. Of course, the juddering lurches of the taxi would give any sane person pause, but on one or two nights in late December, her heart had threatened to leap right out of her chest.

After Bridget's funeral, when Jean had told Sunny she intended to keep Bridget's baby, she'd also said they were going to see Geoffrey's parents for the holidays. This happy family trip was a fiction. Geoffrey still referred to it during his call from Los Angeles the morning after the funeral, but he then added that he had to stay on the West Coast until Christmas Day, so Jean knew the visit was not going to happen. In the past, she would have been changing plane reservations daily, fuming about advance booking deadlines. But she had learned that Geoffrey often spoke of things that *ought* to happen rather than *would* happen. She figured she could always get a full-price ticket at the last minute if necessary; an expensive ticket that exists only in the planning stages costs no more than a cheap one that will also never exist in any other realm.

Whether or not Geoffrey realized that the trip was a fiction,

Jean didn't know and had stopped trying to figure out. While listening to him, she offered no alternatives or suggestions. She did not pretend to believe in the trip, exactly; she simply accepted the theoretical construct, however temporary, that Geoffrey seemed to need. As a result, Jean wasn't lying to Sunny, strictly speaking, and the possibility of the trip bought her some time. Despite her clearly stated intentions, she knew that Sunny expected her to return Jade.

There was no real reason that Jean and Jade shouldn't stop by the Danes' on Christmas Day. Neither Leon nor Sunny was likely to retain Jade by force. But Jean hadn't spent a holiday with Sunny in several years. And she hadn't gone this far in the business world by courting trouble. She planned to spend the day alone with Jade in her apartment. It would be great fun. They would attend a mass at which everyone sang carols, eat at a smart restaurant, and watch heartwarming holiday movies on TV whenever they felt like it.

So far, she had not seen a whole lot of the child. She had spent the Sunday after the funeral winnowing through possible candidates and then interviewing exactly one baby-sitter, who was far too expensive because Jean had had to go through an agency owing to time constraints. There would be time later to look for another. Oneika was her name; she'd been born in Guyana; and she had a classy-sounding English accent. Luckily Jean was more qualified than most to make such a fast hire.

"So when do I start?" Oneika asked.

"Right now," said Jean.

"And where is the girl's"—gull's—"room?"

"She doesn't exactly have a room yet," said Jean. When she felt Oneika's distrust mount, she added, "My sister just passed away a few days ago."

"I am very sorry to hear of that," said Oneika, all of her suspicions melting away.

Judgmental, clearly. Well, Jean was ready for her: "I have a lot to learn from you." *Exactly* what you say to a subordinate in a new situation.

On her way to work later that day, Jean opened a charge account at Baby Nation, where she picked out a German-made crib for nearly $1,000. She was going to add a tiny barn-red sweater, but it turned out to cost $295. Fortunately, Oneika spotted a couple of one-piece outfits at the drugstore while picking up the baby nail clippers, baby formula, baby bathtub, baby thermometer, baby Tylenol, baby diapers, baby wipes, and other baby items that she'd insisted upon. Jean gave her enough cash to go back and buy the outfits as well, although she expected they would be rather cheap looking, and they were.

Only a couple of days remained to buy presents before Christmas. Jean saw no reason to go to FAO Schwarz, and it was not cost-effective for a person like her to wait in line at Toys "R" Us. But once you started looking, there were toys for sale everywhere: on the street, at the grocery store, even at the corner newsstand. Remembering how Linc and Ruth drew after the funeral, Jean bought a box of crayons at the drugstore Oneika went to. She also chose a large yellow metal truck, to avoid gender stereotyping, and a red mesh bag of wooden alphabet blocks. There was one baffling item, a kind of double-barreled cootie-catcher made of various different types of colorful fabric. It caught Jean's eye because "9–18 Months" stood out in bold black letters, and Jade happened to be ten months old. Well, it was bound to have instructions.

Jean had got used to the mornings. Jade woke her a little earlier than she was used to, but once she was accustomed to the crying, which Oneika told her was normal, the hour became rather pleasant. Jean had been surprised at how light and pliable Jade felt when she picked her up out of the fabulous white wood crib. Jean did not know how to lift her at first, but whatever she did, Jade seemed to expect it, hooking her little arm around her neck. And Jade was so keen on drinking the bottle that Oneika had prepared the night before, and she was so happy after she was finished. The disposable diaper was sometimes alarmingly hefty and puffy, but that Jean left for Oneika.

Generally, by the time Jean got home at night, Jade would be asleep, and Oneika would be reading a magazine. Once when she returned early, Jean caught Oneika "preparing" the bottle. It turned out all you had to do was use a church key on the can of formula and *pour it in*. Ha! That testing-it-on-the-wrist stuff didn't seem to hold in this day and age. People were often mysterious about what they did to cover up how easy it was.

Christmas Eve was the first time Jean spent many waking hours with Jade, because Oneika insisted on leaving at 3:30, even though it was a Tuesday. By 4:30 Jean had learned the central question in child care. People with less intelligence, less keenness of eye, and less strength of character often avoided the most difficult question in any field by branching into more frivolous controversies—in this case, bottle vs. breast, or "talking" vs. corporal punishment. When the real question was: What did you *do* with a baby? You couldn't have a conversation with one, you couldn't take one to a bar, you couldn't even watch TV with one.

For a while Jean tried to talk to Jade, promising her that *It's a Wonderful Life* would be on soon and briefly describing the dance floor opening over the swimming pool, one of her favorite scenes of all time. But what point was there? Jade didn't know what a swimming pool was. As far as she was concerned, gymnasium floors might part over pools every day of the week. It was no surprise there were books like *Heather Has Two Mommies*. At least a kid would know what a Mommy was.

You could see why adults got so excited over such blank slates. If you told a baby that "glip" meant water—and managed to remember the word yourself—the baby would accept it eventually. Oneika's ideas of what "glip" might mean could cause a little confusion, but Jean was sure she could get away with it. Not that she'd be interested in actually carrying out such nonsense. Still, it was something to occupy her otherwise rather empty mind.

By the time *It's a Wonderful Life* did start, Jade was tearing little pieces off the dust jackets from the books by Catholics shelf. When the swimming pool scene came on the screen, she was lying on her stomach, howling. Why, Jean had no idea. There was no reasoning with her. Fortunately, Jean knew most of the dialogue by heart, so she wasn't missing much. She tried giving Jade a bottle. No. Maybe there was a diaper problem? Babies were always crying about their diapers on old TV shows. So Jean undid the snaps on the drugstore outfit, which showed small dogs on sleds in a pattern reminiscent of wallpaper. Curiously, the dark blue shirred bands at the ankles of the outfit did not have snaps, and there was no way to undo them. Jean managed to untape the diaper and look inside. Nothing. Oh, well. She'd put on a new one anyway. Still screaming, red face knotted like a fist, Jade squirmed away as soon as Jean took her hands off her and lurched into the hall, leg fabric flapping. Now what?

Best not to dwell on the night. Jean usually went to midnight mass on Christmas Eve. This year, because Jade would be asleep by 9:00, Jean would have to forgo that intoxicating whiff of mystery. The trouble was, Jade did not fall asleep by 9:00.

The evening had not gone too badly. Jean had amused herself by feeding Jade a little baby food jar of plums, with a nod to the "visions of sugarplums" that would dance in her head. She changed her into what might be nightwear, because it was in a different pile, though she was aware of no other distinction. Then, for hours, Jade did not sleep. When Jean first brought her to her crib and tried to lay her down, she scrambled back up again. It was awkward, trying to keep Jade off her feet, so Jean soon gave up. Jade kicked and clung, a little explosion of fury. It's not that Jean wasn't stronger, but smaller phenomena can make themselves felt in unbearable ways. How about the sucking of mud at your feet? Or think of how fiercely a tick can attach itself to your skin.

Jade was so persistent. She cried and cried, whether Jean was in or out of the room, and Jean, who *never* got headaches, felt a bad one creeping in around the edges. As it turned out, she could have made it to midnight mass, but by that time she was too tired and cranky to do anything. Sometimes Jade's little eyes would start to close, and then, suddenly, they would pop open, little piercing blue devil eyes. Jean had no idea when she finally slept, although she woke at the regular hour, with a sandpaper brain. If Jade thought she was going to best her with a little sleep deprivation, however, she did not know her foe. Once when putting together a list of overseas candidates, Jean had survived solely on snatches of sleep in the afternoon, which everyone knows doesn't count.

When she took Jade to mass the next day, she learned that a couple of teenagers cared for young children down in the basement during the service so the parishioners would not be disturbed. She was tempted to offer one $100 to come home with her; on Christmas morning, maybe it would have to be $200 for *one hour*—but of course that was just a joke, she wasn't as pathetic as all that.

Jade was not interested in her presents, which Jean had to unwrap for her. The toy that looked like a cootie-catcher came with no instructions, and Jade had no more idea of what to do with it than she did. Jean poked it and pulled it, but it didn't seem to move the way a cootie-catcher did. Finally she took Jade out for a walk in the stroller. As soon as Jade fell asleep, Jean headed quickly for home, gestured frantically to the doorman when he wished her an overloud "Merry Christmas," and waited through several trips for an empty and thus quiet elevator. She did not dare move Jade from the stroller but lay down within sight on her wonderful bed with its firm new mattress.

Soon Jean heard the click of the bolt being withdrawn from the lock on the front door. Then familiar footsteps, the slight scrape of the swollen hall closet door, a rattle of hangers. Footsteps again—past the bedroom door, although it was open a crack, the light was on, and Jean hadn't seen Geoffrey since Bridget's funeral. Plus it was Christmas, after all.

Geoffrey went to his office: the drop of a briefcase, a muttering of his answering machine. Dialing. Was Geoffrey returning one of his phone calls? The springy dull note of a quick hang-up, then more dialing. Maybe he was trying to call his parents to explain why he wasn't at the airport.

Jean crooked her neck to check out Jade, sleeping on in her stroller, her little head slumped to one side, one perfect curl about the size of a quarter plastered to her temple. Jean was tempted to try to find another holiday film on TV, but to move—to make that decisive break between "off" and "on"—seemed somehow to betray herself and to give in to that elusive husband of hers. Instead she put her hands behind her head and wondered what the hell Geoffrey thought he was doing. The phone calls were finished, and still he hadn't emerged. Could he be working? Jean made twice as much money as he did, and she didn't need a home office. Oh, well. Useless to complain.

Footsteps again. Toward the bedroom. No, past the bedroom. To the bathroom. Characteristic gurgle of the toilet flushing; she'd heard it a million times. Footsteps. The slightly hollow sway of the bedroom door.

Jean watched him look at her, do a slight double take.

"Jean?" he said.

"Yes, Geoffrey?"

"I thought you were asleep."

"And why did you think that?"

"Well," he said. "You're in bed."

"I was resting."

"Oh," he said. He sat on the bed to unlace his shoes, facing away from her. Hard to believe she had often admired Geoffrey's self-containment. She could tell he'd been expected to go into the family business, for instance, but he'd been as deft at slipping out from under that mantle as he'd been at shrugging off her questions about it. He never even acknowledged his mother's persistent efforts to please him.

"What's that?" he said, finally noticing the stroller. "Is that Jade?"

"Yes, it is," said Jean. She didn't feel like giving any details.

"Jade," he said wonderingly. "What's she doing here?"

"I thought I'd take her to visit your parents," said Jean in an inspired move.

"Oh, dear, that's too bad. Everything got out of hand."

"These things happen," said Jean, because she truly did not need a lot of coddling—even though in this particular instance, if she could have killed him by simply pressing a button, she probably would have.

"They asked me to wish you a Merry Christmas," said Geoffrey, unfastening his top button and tugging his shirttails free of his waistband. So he hadn't forgotten what day it was. "Apparently you've got a big fan in Gilbert Blakely. He called them out of the blue and asked all sorts of questions about you."

"Really," said Jean with pleasure, sitting up. "I wonder what that's all about. . . . Probably ensnared in the tendrils of my beauty."

"No, that's me," said Geoffrey. Not a bad follow-up to the good news about Blakely.

"Did they say what sort of questions?" asked Jean.

"Just general, I think."

"Next time maybe I should talk to them myself."

"You can take over all the talking to them, my share, too. I think that's a great idea." He was actually fond of his parents—in the instinctive, easy, and remote way you'd be fond of a favorite sports team. Still, exaggerated agreement was always a deft maneuver.

Jade woke up with a cry as sudden and total as if something had dropped on her head.

"When are you going to give her back?" asked Geoffrey.

"Watch this," said Jean, hurrying off to the refrigerator to get a bottle. Jade thrust it high into the air with a practiced sweep of her elbow, her eyes flicking here and there as her little throat started to pump. "See," said Jean. "A born chugger."

chapter 2

THE DAY AFTER CHRISTMAS SUNNY PUT THE KIDS AND two toys apiece—presents they'd yet to tire of—in the backseat of the van to drive down to pick up Jade's stuff. She probably could have left them with Ed, but he had spoken only a couple of sentences in the last day or two, and besides, she didn't want to walk into the apartment alone. Linc and Ruth were both young enough to exude pure life in the unfiltered way they could also express pure anguish or pure joy. When the wipers started a peculiar loose-jointed crawl across the windshield, just checking their little faces in the rearview mirror made her feel safe.

Bridget's apartment was stuffy—as always. The tops of the peacock feathers and the blue shoulders of the glass vase were dusty. Where to start? Sunny had six unconstructed boxes with her, and six more in the back of the van, parked only a block away. First she opened the hall closet, but instead of depositing her coat in it, as usual, she pulled coats out. Then she wrapped Bridget's Christmas decorations in tissue paper: a string of musical notes cut out of red aluminum, candles scented with peppermint or pine, the real pinecones that Jade had helped spray with gold paint at Sunny's house two weeks ago. But this would not do; she was pretending the packing was seasonal.

She went to the kitchen and opened the refrigerator, thinking she should throw away the spoiled milk, but there wasn't any, because Jade didn't drink it yet. On the counter next to some dried flowers was a small dropper-topped bottle labeled "Ceanothus Tinctoria" in letters that flowed like ivy. This was the herbal medicine Bridget had used to try to shrink her fibroids. Sunny lost her breath for a moment.

Better to go straight to Jade's things. They had sprouted here and there, tender and bright amid the stylishly seedy apartment like new crocuses in a bed of dead leaves. A pile of little shirts—lemon yellow, periwinkle blue, and cotton candy pink—glowed on top of an ancient glassed-in bookcase. The top two had been shower presents from Dennis. A little balding brown bear, a favorite from Bridget's youth, sat with an expensive-looking Russian matryoshka doll on the gargantuan lap of the oversize bear that had been Jean's present. Sunny showed Linc how to transfer various rattling, jingling, and popping toys from a shelf on the changing table—a shower present from Sunny and Leon—to a fresh carton. Yes, it would have been faster and neater to do it herself, but there was no point in hurrying your life away.

"I thought baby Jade was going to live with us," said Ruth.

"She is," said Sunny. "She's visiting your uncle Geoffrey's parents for Christmas, but she'll be back any day."

"Cool," said Linc.

A truly wonderful child, thought Sunny as she admired his freckled nose. She had trailed thankfully after the children all Christmas Day. It was like the Christmas she'd quit smoking. Distracted by assembling a train set or checking the roast, she'd forget the death for a minute. Everything would be under control, she would think, if she could just take care of that one problem nagging in the back of her mind—what was it?—and then it would rush back out at her, its black sweep all the darker because of her momentary forgetfulness.

All she had to get through now was New Year's Eve. After that, a nice long blank winter, as peaceful as the grave. The kids were too young to stay up till midnight anyway. But the idea of the holiday evoked a fizzy spurt in her brain, and Sunny thought uneasily of the evening so long ago when she'd brought Bridget to the party at Paul Walsh's house. It was strange to think that Stew was not Jade's father after all. It could be anyone. Although of course it wasn't Paul. The idea was ridiculous.

She crossed to Bridget's desk, where a calendar sat next to the phone. Names and times were scattered through the boxes: appointments for massages. Bridget's handwriting was low-slung and scalloped, like a child's drawing of waves. On December 18, written with the same-size letters, the same thin, cobwebby lines of ink, the same wispy hopefulness, was the word *operation*. Sunny abandoned her task, gathered her children and the one filled box, and fled back to her house in Rockland County.

At first she just sat in the living room wrapped in a child's sleeping bag. High on the wall across from her was a hole from which three colored wires stuck out like desiccated fingers. Should they be shoved back behind the plaster? Sunny didn't know and never remembered to ask Leon when he had the time and attention to give her a straight answer. At least the kids couldn't reach that far up. Beneath the wires was a special chair (nail-polish red, back like an oyster shell) that Dennis had told her to buy several years before, although even at a discount it had been shockingly expensive.

The whole house had this same bewildering mix. The inner metal structure was wearing through the fabric of the fold-out couch. Next to it was a gorgeous inlaid trunk from Bali, a wedding gift from Bridget. The floor was dry, dull, scratched, pitted, and scarred. It was made of unusually long pine planks, however, which for some reason was a plus, and over them was a fine old Persian rug from Leon's grandmother. The fireplace had not been emptied in years, but who noticed, when an intricately detailed carving of leaves, flowers, vines, and fruits extended the entire length of the mantel. Everywhere you looked, your eye sought out possibilities.

By the time Leon returned from the office that evening, Sunny was rearranging Ruth's room to accommodate a port-a-crib and the pint-size foam rubber chair that Ruth had received for Christmas. "What are you doing?" he asked, holding a bottle of wheat beer.

"Making room for Jade," she said.

"I hope she comes with her own bank account," said Leon.

"Leon!" cried Sunny. But her natural sympathy soon overtook

her disapproval. "Are the banks still being skittish?" The loans on his buildings were all balloon mortgages, which had to be refinanced after five years. Some were due soon.

Leon nodded. He looked at the blue-and-green swirls and new age–inspired sentiments on the label of the microbeer. "You never buy things on sale, do you?"

"I don't know," said Sunny. "I never thought about it."

"Aren't you supposed to compare the prices?"

"Why?" said Sunny.

"To save money."

"I don't see what difference it would make."

"A businessman knows that a nickel here and a dime there really do add up."

"Life adds up," said Sunny.

"I don't mean this as a criticism," said Leon. "It's just interesting, that's all I'm saying. You're not at all profligate."

"I see," said Sunny.

She went back to the playroom to tell the kids to come to dinner. The playroom was the one place in the house that felt fully furnished, as most of their old co-op was in there now. Linc was using the art software on the computer. Ruth said, "Mommy, Linc won't give me a turn, and he promised."

"I did *not*," said Linc, outraged.

Ruth seemed to be using the magical word *promise* to stand for an abstract idea of fairness rather than anything Linc may have actually said. But there are some arguments better left unraveled.

"Come on," said Sunny. "I need someone strong to help me with your granddad."

Once Linc was willing to give up the computer, so was Ruth. They all creaked up the stairs to the guest room. Sunny had not gotten around to stripping the shag carpeting in there, and the futon sat directly on the floor. The futon cover was the same grassy green color as one of the greens in the rug, so it looked like an even softer, somewhat elevated part of the floor. For the kids, it was ideal. They could tumble, nap, and wrestle with impunity. But Ed was still trying to right himself, flapping like a fish on a line, when Sunny and the kids crowded through the door.

"You take the other hand," said Sunny to Linc.

"*I can do it*," hissed Ed, waving them off.

Dinner was yellow rice and black beans with avocado, watercress, and a few shrimp. Leon was pleased. Sunny realized that this was because he thought the meal was inexpensive, which it probably was, although she wasn't sure.

"Do I *have* to eat this shrimp?" asked Ruth.

"You have to try it," said Sunny.

"How much do I have to eat?"

"This much."

"This much?"

"More."

"How about this?"

"I can't even see that little speck of shrimp."

"Well, just look down. It's right there."

"Eat these two pieces, and that'll be enough."

"Did you know that cockroaches can live for ten days without a head?" said Linc.

"Last time it was ten hours," said Sunny.

"Ten days," Linc insisted.

"Isn't that interesting," said Sunny. She could feel Ed suffering, eyes closed, hands in his lap. For some reason this seemed to be a criticism of her children, though she couldn't see why.

"How has business been out on the Island?" Leon asked Ed. "The rich made a big fuss in eighty-seven, when the stock market crashed, but really it's the poor who suffer. Two more of my tenants were laid off right before Christmas. Some present, huh?"

"May I have some Perrier?" asked Ruth.

"What do you say?" Then Sunny corrected herself, because it didn't matter whether Ruth said "please." "You have to drink your milk first."

"I want to save it for dessert."

"There's plenty more."

Ed came to life with a creak, like an old windmill. "Only the very naive believe that hard work is rewarded now," he said.

"You may be right there," said Leon, although Sunny knew that he did not believe this—that despite his moodiness he was in his own odd way one of the most hopeful of men.

"Can't you make one of them a super?" said Sunny.

"I've already got a waiting list," said Leon.

"Where's the baby?" asked Ed suddenly. "What's her name . . . Jade?"

"She's with Jean," said Sunny.

"Jean?" echoed Ed, puzzled.

That was all he said, but Sunny was struck with shame. She hadn't even tried to call Atlanta to wish Jade a Merry Christmas. Of course, the baby wouldn't understand. But still . . . The problem was that Sunny had not even tried to think of Jade as her daughter. She would never have left Linc or Ruth at Jean's, no matter who was sick. She had never left either of them anywhere. To think of them alone in the dark was unbearable. And now Jade was left without anyone who couldn't stand to give her up.

That night, in their king-size bed—big enough for everyone—Leon said, "I don't suppose you could ask your father for a little money."

Sunny raised an index finger against her lips in alarm, then got up to close the door. "Be careful," she said. "He might hear you."

"He couldn't have heard me," said Leon, his face instantly expressing concern. "Isn't he in his room?"

"You never know. But I don't mind working around the house," she said, letting her eyes rest on the lopped-off boxes that held her clothes. "It keeps my mind off . . . everything."

"I'm not talking about the house," said Leon gloomily. "I'm afraid things may get a little tight around here."

Sunny shrugged. "So?"

"A little tighter than might be comfortable."

Christmas was always expensive. If she thought about it long enough, she could make herself uneasy about one or two of the purchases. But she had made them coolly, routinely. More troubling were her memories of the last few days: putting the flowers on American Express, giving the organist a check, tipping the minister in cash. She had been fevered, desperate. Maybe that was why she would not deign to think about these out-of-pocket expenses for more than two minutes in a row, let alone mention them to, say, Jean, who was paying for the cremation out of the estate.

"I am certainly not going to start worrying about money at this point," said Sunny. She decided not to mention using her card to buy the unconstructed boxes at the rent-a-truck place out on the highway.

"Yes, you're right," said Leon. "Money is just a fetish after all. At least your father isn't *costing* us anything."

"He doesn't have any money, anyway," said Sunny absently, once again thinking of Jade. "He's such an old man. It was so terrible watching him try to get up off that futon. I was hoping we could buy a frame for it."

Leon sighed. "Maybe next week," he said.

chapter 3

Valentine Davis called Jean on Thursday, sooner than she'd dared hope. Jean knew that she was awkward when asking for favors, which was regrettable. She believed in paying her own way, of course, but the social glue resulting from non-monetary exchanges could be invaluable. Small requests she could handle. If she asked a client for the correct time (even though her Rolex was 100 percent reliable), or for advice on where to have lunch (though she was rarely in an unfamiliar city), she received with the answer recognition as a different but still real person, using up minutes in her own way. Larger requests—borrowing an umbrella to dash across the street, say—might result in greater bonding, but Jean had found them beyond her. And a request when she actually wanted the favor itself—forget it.

So it was with special trepidation that she had called Davis to ask him if he knew of anyone qualified to go over Bridget's medical records. Of course, what she really wanted was for him to go over the records himself, and when she told him matter-of-factly about Bridget's death, he offered to immediately. She almost didn't believe it when she got off the line.

Now here was his voice, both rough and soothing, like the lick of a cat's tongue. Jean had answered the phone on her way into her office, at the reception desk, because the beautiful Mary was spending the week at a spa in Baja California. Mary's desk, like all of Crough & Co., was curiously neat, bedecked, and empty.

"What's the prognosis, doctor?" asked Jean.

"I think you may have reason to be upset," said Davis in such modulated tones that she worried she'd been too flippant.

"I knew it," she said, sitting down, pulling a green "While You Were Out" pad toward her still fine-looking camel hair coat.

"'Patient presented with a twelve-week intramural leiomyoma,'" said Davis, obviously reading from a document in front of him. "That's the fibroid being taken out. She was scheduled for laparoscopic surgery. You know what that is?"

"No."

"A laparoscope is an optical device that makes it possible to perform surgery without cutting a person open. Sort of a tiny camera. It's an amazing tool. The physician inserts a tube into the abdominal area and introduces the laparoscope through it, so he can see what he's doing. Then he puts his instruments through another tube. These are very sophisticated, nothing like the old scalpel. They make incisions with electrical current."

Jean clicked off a memory: Bridget saying they were going to "look through my belly button." Yes, that made sense.

"You can see what you're doing in a television monitor by the patient's feet," said Davis. "This is still catching on, but it's going to revolutionize a lot of surgical fields. Hospital stays are shortened considerably, and so is recovery time. Insurance companies love it. It's much cheaper and generally safer, because there's less bleeding and less trauma to the site. But in this case something obviously went wrong. The operating room record states, 'Electrical interference made continuing the procedure problematic.' They must have been freaking out in there."

Jean stared at the top of the reception desk. At the edge lay a garland of shredded red foil. Beside it was a stuffed bear with a red-and-green ribbon around his neck.

"I can't tell what happened," said Davis. "There might have been a problem with the insulation on the electrode. Or it could have been a more general problem with the current. Either way the surgeon may have accidentally burned areas outside the scope of the camera and been completely unaware of it. The field of vision is very limited, after all. In any case, the mention of electrical interference in the operating room record is very, very suggestive.

"A postoperative report indicates that the patient complained of 'right lower quadrant pain and light-headedness.' A different writing says, 'Patient difficult, complains of headache.' Maybe you don't want to hear this."

"I do," said Jean. Bridget difficult? But she was so passive. The situation must have been insufferable.

"At ten-fifteen—that would still be A.M.— 'Abdomen rigid, difficulty breathing.' I'm skipping some. At eleven oh-five, 'Patient confused.' Then another operating room record for a laparotomy a few minutes later. That means they opened her up to find out what was wrong. A Dr. Guild with a Dr. Yankel assisting. They found massive internal bleeding. She died before twelve."

"She bled to death," said Jean, unconsciously laying her left arm, in its heavy sleeve, over her own belly, armored with camel hair.

"Yes," said Davis.

"They're going to fry."

"Accidents happen," said Davis. "She wasn't on any blood thinners, was she?"

"Oh, no, she didn't really believe in modern medicine. She never took aspirin or anything like that. It was embarrassing."

"Laparoscopic surgery is very new," said Davis. "Very exciting. I had to do some calling around to even hear about unintended electrosurgical burns. I guess I don't know why the electrical interference didn't act as a red flag."

"You're wondering how much experience this doctor could have had with the procedure," said Jean.

"I am," said Davis. "I'm also wondering why she had the procedure at all."

"What?"

"I don't like to second-guess another physician's plan of care, but I find the records here confused at best. Do you know why there are so many different doctors listed? The facility seems to be the same."

"An HMO, I think."

"Ah," said Davis.

"You think she shouldn't have had the hysterectomy?" said Jean. She was incredibly hot. Her hair was stuck under her coat collar. Sweat was gathering on her neck.

"It's a controversial subject," said Davis. "I'm familiar with it because statistically African American women have higher rates of TAH, or total abdominal hysterectomy, than the general female population. Some researchers claim this is medically justified, some argue that it's not. Let's just say I have a suspicious nature."

This is what happens when women don't have the economic clout to protect themselves, thought Jean.

"Bridget's records go back for years. Normal Pap smears. Heavy bleeding. Excessive bleeding. Menstrual pain. Pretty ordinary stuff, I would say, but I'm not the one who spoke to her. On 4/24/84 an ultrasound indicated an intrauterine mass 'consistent with a leiomyoma or polyp.' Histological examination showed it was a myoma. That's just another word for fibroid. At one point it is described as fourteen-week sized. Here's another—ten-week sized. At another point, twelve or fourteen. That's compared to a fetus, by the way. That's how fibroids are characterized. On 5/18/87, 'Pelvic pain. Possible degeneration of myoma.' I don't see any follow-up. It increased in size during the first and second trimesters of her pregnancy. After delivery, it reverted back. Next thing you know, hysterectomy is recommended, just months after the birth.

"Why then? I don't get it. I don't see the complaint that led to the procedure. The mere presence of a fibroid that size isn't usually considered enough. Not in this day and age."

"The doctor said her pelvic organs were a 'mess,'" said Jean.

"That's not a scientific term I'm familiar with," Davis said dryly.

"We're talking about a double whammy, right?" said Jean. "An operation both botched and unnecessary."

"It is possible that she had the operation precisely because it is new and exciting," said Davis.

"Because the doctors wanted the practice?"

"Yes."

And who was more vulnerable than Bridget, a single mother living in a poor part of town? This was the sort of thing women like Sunny never took into consideration until the worst had happened. Being a "nice" person was no protection against anything. Well, Guild and Yankel didn't know who they'd tangled with. . . .

Within the hour she was at the offices of Danny Briccoli, who had won a $5 million judgment for the mother of a stillborn baby. He was over six feet tall, solid and pale, with thick lips in a white face and inch-long hair that was so blond it was almost white.

"I'm an executive recruiter," said Jean, the tendrils of her hair still wet, her coat in her lap. "I place a lot of doctors. I don't think I have unrealistic expectations of medicine."

Briccoli nodded, pulled up his chair, and offered her a small metal box of throat lozenges. "Who's to say what's realistic?"

Jean relaxed a little. This was what being a grown-up was all about. Here, she felt, she could regain some control over the monsters of the last couple of weeks. This man would cage them, price them, build up a moat made of money. He reacted not at all to the most damning of Jean's revelations: Bridget gave massages for a living; Bridget was a single mother; no one knew who Jade's father was.

All these facts fit neatly—innocuously—into the hundreds of questions Briccoli asked, many indistinguishable. Other facts became less important because they were not elicited by this lengthy interrogation. Jean did not tell him that her guardianship of her niece might be subject to review. She did not tell him that Sunny might balk at the lawsuit if Jean was the person to ask her for help. She did not tell him that the father could step forward at any time.

In the end Briccoli said, "I like it. Juries love to give money to orphaned babies. And there's no wiggle room in death."

Although Jean knew what he meant, and she was perfectly fine in every way, her face must have contorted somehow, because he said, "Excuse me. My wife says I'm very shallow. I don't know whether it's true, but I don't see what difference it makes. She loves me anyway, and it doesn't interfere with my legal skills."

"Probably helps them," said Jean lightly. This attorney was the perfect weapon. He would see that no one got away with killing members of her family.

When she got back to the office, she made an appointment with Amanda Pennington, adoption attorney to the stars.

chapter 4

SUNNY WAS HAVING A PLEASANT CONVERSATION—HOW was your holiday, it must have been fun to have a little one around, etc.—but she could sense that Geoffrey's mother, on the other end of the line, was not enjoying her part as much. Behind that slow, hospitable accent lay a quizzicalness, even a mistrust.

So Sunny said, "I wonder if I could talk to Jean."

"I'm afraid Jean's not here"—hee-ah—said Dorothea Ferris, already sounding relieved.

"I'm sorry I missed her," said Sunny.

"Yes?" said Mrs. Ferris, tensing up again.

"When did she leave?"

"Well, she never did come down. Those two are so busy all the time."

What?

"I thought this year would be different, but it wasn't. Geoffrey had to spend Christmas on an airplane, poor thing."

As Sunny's blood rushed to her head, Linc plucked at her sleeve. "Can I have a snack?"

"Yes," said Sunny.

Linc looked sideways at her. "Can I have a chocolate orange?"

"Yes," said Sunny.

She called Jean's apartment. To the machine she said, "Merry Christmas. When can I come pick up Jade?"

What should she do? She couldn't simply show up and take the child. Especially from a third party like a baby-sitter. Who knew what further damage that would cause. Next she called Crough & Co. Jean was at a meeting. Finally she looked up the number for *Entrepreneur* magazine and asked for Geoffrey.

"How nice to hear from you, Sunny," he said, friendly but surprised, a little remote.

"Geoffrey, I have to see you," she said.

A pause. "That sounds good," he said. Anyone else would have demanded to know what was so important. Geoffrey would never involve himself enough to pry. "Do you want to call and make arrangements with Jean?"

"I'd like to see you alone." This was true, she suddenly realized.

"Oh," he said. "All right. How about lunch next week? Is Tuesday good for you?"

"I was thinking about today."

"I have too much work to do, Sunny." A little scared, maybe.

"It's important."

"You can't talk about it over the phone?"

Could she? "No."

"You can come to my office, then. Of course."

If she saw him in person, she was sure she could figure out exactly what Jean was up to. The sincerity and magnitude of her emotions were bound to win him over.

She knocked on the guest-room door and when she got no answer opened it a crack. Ed was sitting on a lone desk chair, trimming his nails. "I have to talk to you," he said.

"Yes?"

"Maybe you should sit down."

"Okay." She half sat and half squatted on the edge of the futon.

"A smart fellow like your husband could go work for a corporation now," he said. "He's got plenty of experience."

"That's an interesting idea," she said. "But right now I have to go out for a while."

The kids were in the living room, side by side on the couch, curiously quiet. "What are you two eating?" she asked. Without waiting for an answer, she added, "We're going to see your uncle Geoffrey."

She decided to stop and buy a copy of a book on child care at Rain Forest Books near their old apartment. This took longer than she had hoped. Parking was easier than usual, but both children, it turned out, needed a book as well, and choosing was difficult.

The *Entrepreneur* offices were on lower Park Avenue in a massive stone building with a recessed entryway. The receptionist's desk faced the wall rather than the door, so her back was to anyone entering. Her reaction, when she turned, was of astonishment, as if she had never seen a child before—and two, why, will miracles never cease. Geoffrey's reaction was similar, though not as marked.

"Linc! And Ruth," he said. "I didn't expect such delightful company, or I would have had something for you." There wasn't much room in his partitioned office. He began to remove a pile of publications and loose papers from one olive green padded chair, glancing around as if he might have neglected to spot another. He was a nice-looking fellow, a little dull, maybe, with his uncertain brown hair and inoffensive features, but he'd always seemed kind.

"Wait," he said. When he disappeared, Sunny gazed out the window—past the advertisement for butter painted on the side of a brick building, above the jaggedly canted skyline, and into the brilliant blue of the morning sky.

Then he was back, carrying his hand at an oddly limp, curled angle. "One for you," he said. "And one for you." You couldn't tell what was in his conjuror's grasp until he had dropped a small rustling nugget into each of the children's hands. Linc, with more experience of adult treats, refused his, but Ruth unwrapped the shiny gold cellophane. Hard candy. Well, Sunny was right beside her, in case it became lodged in her throat. Sunny gave Geoffrey a smile as big as his wall clock. "How nice," she said, wondering if she was risking her own child's safety in an attempt to secure another's.

"How is Leon?" asked Geoffrey. He was clearly encouraging her to speak up, but he was being nice about it; he wasn't about to throw her out of the office.

"He's fine," Sunny began calmly, sitting on the one empty chair and depositing her children around her.

"You know I'll help you any way I can," said Geoffrey.

"Ble-ech." Ruth made an exaggerated, noisy grimace of distaste. Sunny plucked a Kleenex from among the crayons, scratch paper, and packs of raisins in her purse. "Spit it in here." She enfolded the broken-backed candy in tissue.

"Of course I love my sister," she continued in that "the other shoe is about to drop" tone that often precedes bad news.

Geoffrey put his hands behind his head. "So do I," he said, tipping back far enough in his office chair to test the coiled springs. He was not being flippant, really; nor was he issuing a warning. Despite such traces—he had picked up a lot of mannerisms from Jean since their marriage—his statement was curiously matter-of-fact.

"You know how hard Jean works."

"We have dinner together maybe once a month," said Geoffrey with a rueful chuckle.

Was he *proud* of that fact? "I see," said Sunny.

"Maybe twice," said Geoffrey.

"Well, that may not bother you. But Jean doesn't have time to look after Jade properly." She handed over the book on child care, still in its paper bag.

"Oh?" he said, unwrapping the paperback and looking dumbly at the cover.

"Jade belongs with me," said Sunny, and when Geoffrey didn't respond, she went on, "It's not that I have anything against women working, God knows. But people who don't have kids can't have any idea of what a commitment it is. The time it takes. You don't have a life of your own anymore—" She stopped in frustration. She couldn't pursue that line, or he'd think she couldn't handle a third child. All she'd uttered was the simple truth, but its enormity was impossible for the childless to comprehend, rendering it useless as a deterrent.

She tried veering off a little. "Time is *crucial*. You can't be a mother in nooks and crannies, because kids don't fit into nooks and crannies. Oh, you can cram them in. An adult may be a hardened package, but a kid is different. You can always twist and mold and shave and amputate a kid's spirit until it fits anywhere. That doesn't make it right, though."

"Of course not," he said, still bewildered.

"Jade, you understand, is in a fragile state. She needs someone who will be with her all the time. She needs people she knows well, not people who just happen to be related to her. She needs a sister and brother. And a big happy home."

"I thought baby Jade was going to live with us," said Ruth.

"She is, honey."

"Sunny," said Geoffrey with some decisiveness, but then he trailed off into "I . . . uh . . ."

He didn't know anything about it. "Jean told you how she's decided to keep Jade?" said Sunny.

"A little." A lie.

"She hasn't had time?" Here Sunny was being polite. She suspected it was more than a matter of hours in the day. "That doesn't bother you?"

"Jean doesn't trust me," said Geoffrey, "and I'm not sure she has any reason to."

What? He was smiling politely, as if they were still exchanging banalities. Yet he had never said anything like this to her before and did not seem to be confiding in her.

"Am I not supposed to mention that?" Geoffrey spoke with the same deliberateness he always did.

"I don't know," said Sunny.

"I don't like to complain," said Geoffrey. "One morning when we parted at the Columbus Circle subway stop and I saw her hurrying away, I realized I was going to marry her." He shrugged. "It was very mundane. But I didn't feel I had much choice."

Now Sunny was confused. "But will you help me?"

"Everyone knows you're the expert on motherhood," said Geoffrey ambiguously.

"Please."

"Sunny, you know I think you're great," he said, putting his hand lightly on her knee. "I'll see what I can do."

chapter 5

JEAN CAME HOME EARLY THAT NIGHT, NOT MUCH PAST 7:00. By the time Geoffrey got in, she was focused on the towers she was building out of Jade's books, each of which was a bound collection of half a dozen thick squares of cardboard about the size of cocktail napkins. A word or two and a picture adorned each page, the images revealing a definite slant toward the juveniles of all species. Because of the wall-to-wall carpeting, the books had to be splayed out considerably before they could stand, which meant the second story of the tower had to be equally opened up; and so forth. Construction could take a while; demolition, by Jade in her drugstore pajamas, was a matter of seconds. Still, Jean was happy to have found something that Jade liked to do. And you could not call it a waste of time because it left part of Jean's mind free to monitor Geoffrey's progress to the living room.

"Hello, Jean," he said.

"Hello, Geoffrey," she said, not bothering to get up from where she sat cross-legged on the floor. Her two knees, encased now in black leggings, stuck out from either side of her and formed the same rounded angles as wire hangers.

She began to read the closest of the books out loud. Amazing, the way Jade was riveted by these texts, although Jean did read them with a great deal of feeling. "Tall, short, up, down, in, out . . ." Well, so much for that one. The weight of Jade's little head on her arm was about that of a Rolodex. Jean was afraid to move, for fear of dislodging it. She used her left arm to retrieve another of these page-turners.

Geoffrey poured himself some blended Scotch—not the Lagavulin she'd just given him—unbuttoned his sports jacket, and sat on the couch. "So how was your day?" he asked.

Very peculiar. He had *never* not checked his messages before talking to her. Usually he didn't even say hello.

"Absolutely splendid," said Jean in a neutral tone.

"Anything new?"

"Tons," said Jean, sticking to her wait-and-see policy.

Geoffrey nodded twice. He looked at Jade as if he were going to make some further remark, then thought better of it and stood up, evidently to retire to his office.

"How was *your* day?" asked Jean.

"Excellent," he said.

To his back, as he was on his way out, she said, "You're not curious about Jade?"

"What about Jade?"

Clearly he knew something.

"I've been thinking that we need the pitter-patter of little feet around here," said Jean.

"Jean," he began, standing uncertainly in the doorway. "Are you angry about Christmas?"

"Why would I be angry about Christmas?"

"I don't know." He poured himself more Scotch.

"I had a fine Christmas," said Jean. "Of course my sister had just died, but other than that, it was fine."

"I saw Sunny today," he said.

"Sunny? Where?" A play for time.

"She came to the office." He passed Jean a white paper bag that he'd left by the liquor. "She asked me to give you this."

Jean carefully drew out the paperback, flinching when she saw the title: *Now That I Have a Baby, What Should I Do?*

It had been a mistake to let any situation develop in which it was possible for Sunny to tell Geoffrey about Jade first, that much was clear. But there was no point in wasting time on regret now.

"She seemed to think you were planning on keeping the baby."

"This is not the right company for that kind of conversation," said Jean, looking significantly at the little head beside her.

Jean did not know any babies to compare Jade to, and she thought the whole notion of "personality" was overdone. But she had become familiar with the "Jade-ness" of certain specific arcs— in at the temples, the fold of the eyelid, and the crease in the neck; out at the cheeks, the earlobes, and the sudden nose.

"I have been contemplating that course of action, yes," Jean added.

"And when were you going to consult with me, I wonder."

"As I said, I don't think this is the time. And there hasn't been any chance up to now, either."

Looked at properly, these statements were perfectly truthful. And they had the added benefit of putting off the inevitable conversation, which Jean had no idea how she was going to approach.

As Geoffrey sat back down on the couch, he made the sounds men always seem to employ to do such a simple thing: a whiff of pants legs being pulled up, a crack of knee, a jingle of keys. Jean noticed it particularly because it all seemed focused on Jade. He was perched on the edge of the couch, leaning over the both of them there on the floor.

"Jade, can you understand me?" asked Geoffrey.

"Of course she does," snapped Jean. "What people say has very little to do with what they think."

Geoffrey's smile was tight. "How true," he said.

Jean rose and advanced upon him, purposefully towering over his perching figure. "I'm going to go read Jade one of those stories in which everyone lives happily ever after."

Geoffrey was swirling the ice in his glass. "I don't know what to make of you sometimes, Jean," he said. "I really don't."

A dark chord struck in Jean's heart. "I know you still can't believe your good luck in catching me," she said.

"Yes," he surprisingly agreed. Light-colored corduroy pants rumpled at the knees, a tweedy sports jacket bagging at the elbows.

His sloppy clothes had led her to assume he was a more relaxed person than he had turned out to be. Even after several years of marriage, he was formal with her. Which was generally how she liked him.

Jean read to Jade in the bedroom. She'd checked the book out from the library on her lunch hour. It was about a snake that a sophisticated but pleasant-looking old lady received as a gift, and although this book did have more of a narrative line than the others, it, too, left plenty of Jean's mind unoccupied. What she had to remember was to avoid asking Geoffrey what he thought. To do so might commit him to opinions that could become inconvenient later on. She also had to appear to respect his point of view. Which in the larger sense she actually did. A difficult balancing act at best.

She looked at her watch as she came out of the bedroom, where Jade was crying in her crib.

"How much time do I have?" said Geoffrey.

Jean glanced at her watch again, as if to remind herself of why she had looked at it in the first place. "That's for Jade. I go in and pat her on the back every half hour."

"Maybe *I* should say good night to her."

"It will screw up the schedule," said Jean with mock censure. "But we can always start over." This with mock magnanimity.

Geoffrey went straight over to the crib the way he'd corner a subject at a cocktail party. "Good night, Jade," he said, patting her awkwardly on the shoulder. The little girl, who had been surprised into silence by their entrance, began to scream again. Jean felt some relief at the sight of an adult who knew even less about children than she did.

In order to direct the conversation, she started to speak as soon as they were both out of the bedroom. "I always said I didn't have time for kids. But I've found that time can be pretty elastic."

"Haven't physicists proved it doesn't exist?" asked Geoffrey lightly. Amazing, the control he had over himself. Jean had never been up against anyone in a domestic situation who had Geoffrey's strength. Sunny, Bridget, Mr. Crossley—they were all like water trickling through your fingers.

"Well, no one's throwing out the clocks yet," said Jean, looking at her watch again. They both listened to Jade wail.

"You want me to be a father," said Geoffrey.

To gain time, Jean picked her way around the coffee table and dropped to the couch. "Well, yes," she said.

"I kind of like the idea," said Geoffrey, moving in on her. "But I'll have to think about it. What makes you suppose we have the kind of relationship that can support a child?"

"I don't know what you mean," Jean said coldly.

"I'm not sure we see each other enough," said Geoffrey. He placed his glass on the coffee table as softly as if it had been lined with felt. He had huge hands. Jean's leggings were absurdly flimsy, just thick tights. He placed his hand across her hipbone. She felt every nuance as he gently strummed it. "I haven't seen you in so long," he said.

She tried to keep him to the point. "You're the one who has to travel constantly."

"Yes, we have to take more advantage of the time we have," he said, laying his ear across her belly button as if listening for something deep within. And there it was—a jagged piece of lightning shot right through her. Jade's wails grew louder.

"Am I supposed to sleep with you to get my way?" Jean spoke ironically, but her very words sent another flutter through her. Geoffrey unfurled the length of his body against hers. Their hands were clasped defensively in front, wedged between their chests, muscles tensed as if they'd wrestled each other to a standoff. Jade wailed on and on and on.

"Why not?" he said.

Marriage was the most intense power struggle Jean had ever known. She was no longer underneath him, but half on top. It was impossible to tell which way he was pushing, which way she was. He cupped her pelvic bone the way you would the hood of a car in order to open it. His uneven cheek scraped a nipple through her loosely woven sweater.

What would he negotiate away for the pleasures of her body? Almost anything, argued his single-minded hands, his insistent zipper, his goofily narrowed eyes. To be wanted so much was electrifying, nothing like Sunny's tawdry bargain with the devil. No one before could ever have felt such driving softness, such velvet relentlessness. Jean groped below his belt. That exquisite pressure; it was no different, whether she was pushing him away or stroking him harder. She twisted, and he fell upon her.

chapter 6

LEON AND SUNNY DROVE DOWN TO THE OFFICE TOGETHER on the following Monday. It had taken most of the weekend, but Sunny had at last found friends for the kids to visit so that she could help out. Brianna had been laid off after Christmas, when she agreed to try for her high school equivalency diploma, and in an attempt to ease back on Gloria's hours, Leon had encouraged her to take time off, too. It was just his luck that as soon she took advantage of this, he and Sergey were supposed to meet with the owner of the local travel agency. Judging by its elaborate signage, which left no space on the storefront unlettered, there was little this agency did not do. Leon dealt with it mainly because of its small fleet of gypsy cabs. The last time Leon had ordered one, the owner himself—a man who often boasted of surviving cancer—got on the line and suggested he come over to talk about a loan.

Harlem had not been softened by Christmas. The cold made the air look brittle; the buildings were hunkered down and gray. New arches of elaborate wires seemed to have sprouted periodically over 125th Street. No, those were arrangements of stars and snowflakes, presumably lights that did little to relieve the daytime gloom. But Catholic East Harlem was a bit more festive. The red and green garlands curlicuing across 116th Street were thick and furry, entwined with still furrier bells, bows, and trees. Occasionally a Santa or angel cutout could be glimpsed in a window.

"Don't buzz in anyone you don't recognize," Leon was saying. "You know most of the tenants—certainly all that might come by. You know everyone who works for me. Ask to see the credentials of anyone else. I suppose you have to let in any stray vulture from the city that shows you a badge, God knows why."

"I'll be fine," said Sunny.

"Luisa usually comes in on Monday," said Leon, "though she may not today, because of the holiday."

"How long is this meeting going to take?"

"I don't know," said Leon. "But Sergey wants to look at the property again, too. He's a little upset."

No one came in for the first hour; no one called. Sunny didn't even notice anyone walking by on the street. People must be spending the holiday indoors. The office was cold, but since Leon hadn't turned on the space heater before he left, Sunny decided not to, either. Instead she put her coat back on to sit at Gloria's desk and tried to read the newspaper.

It was hard to concentrate. Sunny hadn't thought twice after the funeral when Jean had said she was applying for guardianship of Jade in order to facilitate the lawsuit. It never occurred to Sunny that Jean might be interested in anything more. Maybe Jean wanted a ready-made family, one that she could effectively buy in a store. And the law was on her side—at least for now. Sunny didn't see where she could have stopped this whole bewildering chain of events.

At one point a stranger's face appeared ringed in the wreath over the grate barring the office door: darkish skin around the mouth, haunted eyes, tightly cropped hair that managed nonetheless to stick up here and there like a choppy sea. As a concession to Leon, Sunny walked over to the door rather than buzzing the fellow right in. What should she do? He held up a pen so that she could see it through the grate. A curious sort of ID. When she let him in, it turned out he was selling ballpoint pens by the gross. She managed to buy only a fraction of that, a mere dozen.

Later she filled out two work orders—one for a broken (apartment) lock, one for a burned-out (hall) lightbulb—and dialed the number of the super on call, who was curiously defensive, as if she were reminding him to do something again rather than asking him to do something for the first time.

When at last she spotted Luisa's moonlike head in the wreath, she felt a surge of warmth and relief. "Merry Christmas, Sunny!" declaimed Luisa as she rolled in like a float, trailing a solemn little boy in a white dress shirt.

"This is Roberto," she said, magisterially adjusting the gold cross on her chest.

Another foster child. Sunny had heard that Luisa had someone new, but the sight of him was a surprise.

"Roberto is a guest in my home until his father finds a bigger apartment," said Luisa. "His mother has had trouble, but he saw his father at Christmas, and he gave him a baseball and a glove. A very nice man. He was incarcerated upstate, whatever, but then he moved in with a girlfriend that he met through her brother in his drug treatment program. They had a child together, and they have a stable home. Now they have to find a bigger apartment because the apartment is still the one where the girlfriend lived by herself, and it's not big enough. Roberto will go to a nice new home with a little sister. Maybe by the end of January." With one stately hand Luisa pulled her ergonomic chair closer to her desk.

"But how is Alba?" asked Sunny. "Do you ever hear from her?"

Luisa slowly turned ninety degrees in her chair with the heavy certainty of a revolving door. "I asked the social worker about Alba, and she is fine. The goal for her is adoption, you know. She cannot live in limbo. She needs permanency. She has to find a home within a certain frame of time. She shouldn't be in placement too long. I cannot adopt. I cannot provide for the child. I do fine when I have the check, but when the check is gone, I cannot do for her. She is not just a companion for me. She is a person, a little person."

Sunny's heart, which had already sunk because of Alba, quailed further at the sight of Sergey with Leon. Suddenly she felt she wasn't up to his sort of aggressive flirting today.

"The child is my main priority," said Luisa stiffly as Sunny buzzed in the men.

"Ah," said Sergey as he entered. "I have solution to problem. Sell your wife. I am joking, by the way, but she is beautiful woman. She is Russian a little, I think." And to Sunny he said, "*You* can be poor. A beautiful woman can always be poor. But a man like me, I cannot afford it."

"No one's going to be poor," said Sunny. "What happened with the travel agency?"

"The terms are . . . unacceptable," said Leon.

"I could tell you that," said Luisa.

Sergey thumped his handsome forehead with the heel of his hand, then began to pace. "Banks, banks, banks. What do they want? Buildings are same. Same rooms, same halls, same people. What is difference? Nicer mailboxes. Did you show them mailboxes?"

"I don't think they care about the mailboxes," said Leon. "In today's market the buildings aren't worth what I paid for them. It's as simple as that. The banks don't have any sense of commitment. They can't see five years down the road. All they think about is the bottom line this month."

"Leon is not so Jewish," said Sergey to Sunny.

"Even Jews lose money when the market goes bad," Sunny pointed out lightly.

"No-o-o," said Sergey. "Not real Jews."

"If we can just refinance, we'll get over this hump," said Leon.

"Leon, Leon, you must think," said Sergey. "There must be a different way to skin a horse."

Leon just shook his head.

"Everything will work out," said Sunny. "It always has in the past."

"In the past?" said Sergey.

"That's what capitalism is like," Sunny persisted

Sergey snorted. "Who gets it, by the way?" he asked Leon. "If you do not get refinance, who gets the building? The city? The mayor? That black mayor who wears the white clothes?"

"The bank will take it over," said Leon.

"I am joking. I know that. So when the bank does not give you new mortgage, they get building. Why would they ever give you new mortgage? Why would they give anyone new mortgage? All they have to do is sit around, get building."

"I don't think it's quite as sinister as it sounds. They'll probably sell it at a loss."

"To me?" asked Sergey. "Will they sell it to me?"

"I don't know." Leon put his head in his hands.

"It's question. I have many questions. How about burn it down?"

"Sergey, don't even joke about it."

"If it's no good to anyone . . . It is no good to bank, no good to you, no good to me. Why should it stay up?"

"People live there."

Sergey snorted. "There are other places to live."

"I never would believe it when people kept trying to tell me how important money was," said Sunny.

"Americans!" Sergey called to Luisa, addressing her for the first time. "See. They are babies. All of them."

Sunny closed her eyes briefly. Maybe he would just go away.

"How do you pick dog?" Sergey asked her.

Was this a riddle? Sunny couldn't think of a response.

But Sergey didn't need one. "My wife, she thinks you pick dog because he's cute, he's smart, he can shake your hand," he said. "But I say no, doesn't matter, you pick rich dog. Get what I mean? Rich dog is much better."

"That's no solution," said Sunny. "My niece Jade is going to be rich, and it's causing endless problems."

"Bridget's baby?" said Sergey. "How is she rich?"

"The hospital will probably give her a whole bunch of money because Bridget's operation was screwed up. So Jean wants to keep her."

"Ah," said Sergey. "I met your sister Jean. She is not soft like you."

Why this should be as wounding as it was, Sunny did not know. "I am not soft," she said.

"Yes, you are. You are soft. And round. Very nice. That's good. You do not want to be hard like coffin lid."

"Well, I'm going to fight her," said Sunny.

"And how much money is rich? What money will the baby get?"

"I don't really know."

"See what I mean? Soft."

chapter 7

J EAN USED TO HAVE NO NERVES AT ALL. THEN, ONE DAY A
couple of years before, Geoffrey arranged for them to meet in
Chicago when she was flying out and he was flying in. On paper,
at least, they would overlap by nearly twenty-one hours. The airport hotel was less run-down than most. The three-story lobby
had a huge skylight, bromeliads in chromium planters, and chic industrial gray carpeting. Geoffrey was supposed to get there first,
but he had not checked in by the time Jean arrived from her meeting, so she left her bag in the room and went down to the pool to
swim a few laps. It was in the basement. The pool room was separated from the hall by a pair of glass doors that opened when you
slid the hotel key into a slot in the wall. The pool itself was small,
and you could walk around only three sides of it. On the fourth
side was a small ledge where the unused lane divider was strung.
There was a Jacuzzi, because hotels always had Jacuzzis, but Jean
had never liked them: all that heat and frenzy. Water should be
self-assured in its difference from air, as the water in a pool is—
heavier than air and, at the same time, more buoyant.

Jean slid slowly down the ladder. She'd never been much of a
diver, even in her swim team days. She started off with a slow
crawl, enough to crumple the still surface, did a nice flip turn at
the shallow end, and switched to a slightly faster, more shapely

stroke, arms cutting the water as cleanly as butter knives. She did another flip turn, not so nice, and did another couple of laps. A growing sense of a change in the light made her glance to the side as she turned again. A man in a dark three-piece suit stood on this side of the glass door, watching. She had heard nothing. Although the air in a pool room is full of odd echoes and curious amplifications, under the water you are deaf. She began to swim more slowly and warily, trying not to look in his direction. The next time she glanced over, he was at the very edge of the pool, still in his black suit. She told herself that he could not enter the water with all those bulky clothes on. But in the midst of her freestyle she kept sensing an invisible hand about to touch her on the back, so she had to switch to a sidestroke. By the time she reached the other end, the man was gone. She turned and swam the length of the pool underwater, and when she surfaced, there was Geoffrey sitting in one of the white plastic chairs at the shallow end.

"Did you see a guy in here?" she asked, pulling herself up, shedding water everywhere.

"What guy?" Geoffrey, who was wearing a sports jacket rather than a suit, handed her a beer. A glass of Scotch was balanced on his thigh. As soon as she sat in the chair beside him, wet and without a towel, he began to tell her the story of a coworker who was happily married but maintained a separate residence from his wife. "At first they lived in different cities, so they got used to it," he said. "When he was transferred to New York, he got a great deal on a studio apartment to write in. He moved his stuff in there and never got around to transporting it over to her place."

Jean looked blank.

"You'd like him," said Geoffrey. "He's very skeptical."

"Skeptical" was the term Geoffrey applied to anyone he liked and admired, including himself. This was very different from the usual generic term of praise: "nice." Sunny used "nice" whenever she liked someone, whether the meaning of the word was applicable or not. "Such a nice guy," she would say about a fellow who might be energetic, lively, lucky, kind, generous, or passionate—and not "nice" at all. Everyone Mr. Crossley liked was "smart," whatever his IQ. That was pretty common, too. Jean knew she used "funny." "Skeptical" was Geoffrey's alone.

"Am I missing something here?" asked Jean, looking down at her bright red Speedo suit and then around at the white-painted cinder-block walls before focusing back on Geoffrey and his sports coat. "I'm a little spooked."

"I thought something like that might work for us," said Geoffrey.

"You mean you want to get married?"

"Yes," he said.

So that moment had a happy ending. For a while it had been hard to shake the sense of doom she associated with the man in the black suit, but it eventually loosened its grip on her. She even started to wonder if Geoffrey had entered the pool room to watch her and then gone up to change. When she asked him, though, he reminded her that he didn't own a three-piece black suit. Maybe not. But she didn't trust his memory of the day; it did not seem to have stuck.

Jean liked to think of Geoffrey's past as remarkably similar to her own. Working-class Long Island and newly upper-middle-class suburban Atlanta may have been wildly different, but Jean imagined that Geoffrey had moved through his surroundings the way she had through hers—already half-disappeared into the future, thus with plenty of room to maneuver around petty disappointments and more narrow minds. In this sense neither Jean nor Geoffrey had much of a past, just a present.

The morning Jean was supposed to meet with Amanda Pennington she became aware of his gaze as she carefully hiked up her skirt and unrolled very sheer, unblemished panty hose up her thighs. He made it clear that he liked to look at her put her clothes on almost as much as he liked to look at her take them off, and she was always aware of his particular watchfulness. His eyes were not tunnels or X-rays; they could have been made of protective glass. You couldn't see into them, and they didn't try to look into your soul the way some bright blue ones did.

Normally this did not make Jean nervous. She didn't know what made today different.

"You mustn't be late for a lawyer who's been in *People* magazine," he said.

Well, she had mentioned reading about Pennington in the checkout line at the supermarket a while back. "I have never been late in my life," said Jean.

Out on the street she was seized with the conviction that she would never get a cab. But she did, and she found comfort in all the familiarly frantic traffic, that noisy, unthreatening construction work, and those dear buildings inhaling and exhaling crowds of art lovers and health care workers and actuarial experts and general corporate drones. She wasn't all that late—only twelve minutes, maybe even ten—but again she felt anxious as she was ushered into Pennington's office.

The greetings were easy. As Jean spoke the familiar words, she was vaguely aware of an equine aura in the room: a little ceramic show horse with a hatted and booted rider; a photo of Ruffian; a mustang carved out of grainy-looking stone. "My little hobby." Pennington waved a languid hand and laughed apologetically. Then Jean noticed all the soft, thick, expensive leather: desk set, wastebasket, briefcase, shoes, belt, saddlebag pocketbook.

"I have been awarded guardianship of my niece," said Jean, managing to take a seat without any overt display of nerves. "The process was pretty straightforward. But I'm thinking of adopting, and my attorney says if I want to go ahead with it, I should come to you."

"Good choice," said Pennington.

Jean was heartened by this cheery and self-congratulatory note, but then her eyes dropped to a discreet photo cube with a red-lipped smiling baby face on it. Pennington must be a working mother. This should have been reassuring, but somehow it wasn't. Jean was for a moment afraid that she would be asked something only a real mother would know. A nonsensical notion, of course.

"We have to fill out some documents," said Pennington. "I submit them to surrogate's court. At some point there has to be a home visit. I use a very nice, very professional woman. And that's pretty much it. If all goes well, the adoption will go through ninety days after guardianship was granted. It's a good idea to have legal counsel, but it's not a whole lot more complicated than that."

"How about if someone contests it?" asked Jean.

"What do you mean, 'contests' it?" Pennington cocked her head. Jean's heart leapt to her throat.

"Objects to you?" Pennington elaborated. "Or wants the child himself?"

"Wants the child herself."

"So we're not talking about the father."

"No. No one knows who he is." To try to calm herself, Jean plunged her nails into the palm of her right hand and forced herself to concentrate on the woman in front of her. Thin-faced, freckled Pennington might like horses, but even more important to her was to be thought of as a horsy type, a girl who could offhandedly choose a college because you were allowed to board a horse there. Who did she think would be taken in by all this folderol?

"Are we talking about a relative?" asked Pennington.

"Yes," said Jean.

"Wants to adopt?"

"Possibly." Jean was just light-headed. She hadn't had breakfast yet.

"The surrogate judge is keen on the parties working out an agreement between themselves," said Pennington. "I've seen her send people back out repeatedly."

"I don't mind a good fight." There, that was better, more like the old Jean. She concentrated on all the lessons that she was going to buy Jade, twice as many as pampered kids like the Haydens had taken for granted. Piano lessons. Ballet lessons. Yes, even horseback-riding lessons. "I think this other relative has had financial difficulties recently," said Jean, "and I'm afraid she may be interested in the considerable settlement my niece is due to inherit."

"I see," said Pennington, suitably impressed. "Start keeping track of expenses."

"Oh, I am," said Jean.

The attorney nodded, unsurprised. "You'll have to account for every penny you spend."

Penny? If the expenses kept up at the current rate, Jean would have to buy a bigger calculator. Number joke. Geoffrey claimed he could always make her laugh with a number joke. But the point was, Jean expected to have to throw a few bills into the pot. She was prepared to do so. She was not out to make a profit on Jade. The pursuit of lawsuits was not an efficient use of her time. But she felt she had to win Jade the money in much the way she would never leave a check uncashed.

"What if negotiation doesn't work?" asked Jean. "How would the judge decide then?"

"Theoretically speaking," said Pennington, "judges are not allowed to take into account sex, marital status, sexual orientation. Or unusual hobbies. Fortunately for me." A *joke* about the horse collection? God help us.

"I assume financial security would be considered," said Jean.

"Oh, yes." Pennington nodded. "And all proceedings are completely secret. Although a financial situation would have to be truly dire to make a difference."

Jean had run into that attitude before. As if any salary above $50,000 were the same. Well, it wasn't.

"Child care by a relative would probably be an advantage," Pennington added.

For a moment Jean felt Jade's little arm hook around her neck. "But she would never not give a baby to a woman just because she worked, right?" said Jean, trying to keep her tone light. "If she paid for a really great baby-sitter?"

"Of course not," said Pennington.

LEON SPENT THE FIRST EVENINGS OF THE NEW YEAR AT THE computer in the playroom, working on spreadsheets and visiting on-line banks. His two bottles of beer—one quart, one twelve-ouncer—would be up on the windowsill so that no kid could spill it into the keyboard. (This was the house's only hard-and-fast rule: No beverages by the computer.) He listened to "Drop me off in Harlem / Any place in Harlem . . ." and "Up in Harlem on a Saturday night / When the highbrows get together, it's just too tight . . ." over and over on the disk drive.

He had managed to cut Gloria back to four days a week, and she had started quarreling with a couple of the more difficult supers, men who had never liked being at the mercy of repair orders filled out by a woman. Just today a tenant had yelled at her about a bro-ken radiator that she had never heard of. Where was the work order? She told Leon he should be backing her up more. Then Luisa had called to see if anyone had seen Alba; the social worker had told her the girl had run away.

"My God," said Sunny, trying to have a conversation with him, although his eyes were already glued to the screen. "Did you help look for her?"

"Of course," said Leon. "She showed up at Luisa's right away, but I didn't know until I had already been out walking around for half an hour."

"At least Alba's all right."

"One guy I passed asked me what game I was playing. Just a stranger on the street."

"What does that mean?"

"I don't know," said Leon. "I suppose he meant it in an abstract sense. It was very hostile, though. It made me wonder myself." His eyes were still on the screen.

Sunny retreated to the living room, where the bills were spread out on the coffee table. Before she was married, she'd had one charge card, an American Express she'd gotten in college through her father. She rarely used it. It had to be paid off every month, and where would she get money a month later that she didn't have right then? Once, she'd bought a couple of airline tickets to Portland, Maine, for her and Paul, and Paul had reimbursed her. After she was married, and before she gave birth to Linc, she used this same American Express card to buy everything recommended in *Now That I Have a Baby, What Should I Do?*—both in the necessary and the optional lists. For a year or so, she put everything on this card, paying it off monthly.

Although Leon never questioned any purchase she made, she refrained from buying the clothes, books, and jewelry she had received as a single woman, when the expense of these luxuries had been spread among a number of different men. It seemed hard on Leon to suddenly saddle him with both her and a child.

By the time Sunny was pregnant a second time, she had switched to a MasterCard. Already Leon's real estate companies— one for each building—had gone through a number of cycles. Occasionally surprise repairs were necessary, some major. At 212, for instance, one bathroom floor fell through the ceiling below. No big deal, except that the reason it had broken through was that the previous owner had repaired the floor with concrete. Every time there was a problem, he poured a new layer. No one had noticed, including the engineer who'd filed the structural report. Leon had considered the evenness of the floors an advantage. Now he could see that every floor was a potential disaster. He had to remove concrete from every bathroom in the building and from some of the kitchens, too. For several months he used every spare dollar he had on this project and on the two new roofs that he'd at least known would be necessary. Finally he'd had to turn over a building to raise some capital.

Sunny got used to having lots of money and then no money and then lots of money again. It felt similar to the way she'd lived her whole life—no financial wherewithal herself, but occasional access to riches. MasterCard was good for this state of affairs, because you could defer payment until the coffers were full again. Who cared if the debt began to build back up as soon as you'd paid it off? Leon disliked consumer debt because it cost so much, but he couldn't see any way off the roller coaster, and he was generally too busy with his property to give it much thought.

After the stock market fell in 1987, the parched periods began to get longer, and Sunny accepted a Visa with a lower interest rate that started charging her the day after she made her purchase. That's what she used when she had no intention of paying down a debt any time in the near future. Either card was good for a quick influx of cash when necessary, although the interest rate on cash advances imposed by the MasterCard was, if not shocking to Sunny, because she didn't pay all that much attention, at least eyebrow lifting.

The bills laid out on the coffee table included American Express, MasterCard, and two Visas, one of which Sunny had accepted when Ruth was eighteen months old so that the family could go on their only vacation, to Chicago, where Leon checked out the buildings on the South Side. Over the years Sunny's credit limit had been raised several times, most recently—and providentially—right before they bought the house to try to save money. The debt the bills represented was considerable, but that was not what she was concerned with. One of the cards had been declined the day she'd picked up Ed, and she couldn't remember which it was. (She thought of them as keys. Carry a bunch, and if the first doesn't work, try another.) She thought she'd managed to pay the minimum on all of them last month. An outlay of a few hundred could insure access to several thousand.

Ed inched in just as she realized she hadn't bothered to pay anything on the MasterCard; that was maxed out, so there was no point.

"I don't want to disturb you," he said.

"You're not disturbing me," said Sunny. Indeed, she felt relatively relaxed now. She never looked at the bills without a beer in hand.

"Paying some bills?"

"In a manner of speaking." Throwing down a pen, one of those she'd bought at Leon's office. It didn't work very well.

"Jean called today," said Ed. "While you were at Ruth's dance class."

"You're kidding," said Sunny. This was news. "Did she leave a message?"

"She wanted to talk to me."

"Huh," said Sunny, startled now. She watched him take a seat. Ed had grown even thinner. With his strong tucked-in chin, shadowy temples, and big dark eyes, he looked like a praying mantis. His shoulders were hunched, his arms were folded back on themselves, and he quivered a little with suppressed emotion.

"It was unexpected," he said.

"I bet."

"She's very tense, isn't she?" he said.

"I guess so."

"You wouldn't understand because you're so calm."

Sunny couldn't help looking down at the bills. Well, she supposed that was true.

"Jean has always been an operator," said Ed. "I don't think you and Bridget ever realized to what extent."

"What do you mean?" Sunny imagined some underhanded childhood maneuver of Jean's that had been too subtle for anyone but a grown-up to detect.

But no. What Ed said was "She has always got what she wanted."

Sunny laughed. Had she really? Of course not. "She won't this time," she said.

Ed cocked his head. "She wants me to sign an affidavit swearing that the two of you would be equally good mothers."

"Oh," said Sunny. So Jean must have started the whole legal process involved in trying to keep Jade.

"I don't want to sign anything," said Ed.

Sunny was thinking furiously. On the surface, Jean's was a reasonable request. It looked as if she were simply insuring that Ed would not be forced into choosing between his two remaining daughters. Certainly Sunny didn't wish that, either. But she was suspicious. She tried to puzzle out her misgivings.

"I always tried my best to understand Jean, but I don't think I ever succeeded," Ed continued.

Jean certainly could not expect Ed to sign an affidavit in her favor, if only because she had no experience as a mother. She was probably just neutralizing him. That wasn't so tricky.

"Do you remember when we bought her that bottle of perfume?" said Ed.

Aha! Sunny looked down at the bills again. If Jean could show that she and Sunny had the same nurturing capabilities, then maybe she assumed the court would award Jade to the most financially stable of the two.

"We told her we tried to get her something feminine for a change," Ed continued. "I felt kind of bad afterward, as if we'd insulted her. Did you get that feeling?"

"Well, she never liked perfume," said Sunny, absentmindedly picking up pieces of rice cake off Leon's grandmother's rug.

"I was wondering when it would be convenient for you to give me a ride back to Paw Valley."

What did that mean? Was he going to leave? "You're welcome to stay here," said Sunny.

"It's time I got back," he said. "I have to check on the house."

She had not yet been able to provide the completely comforting family circle that she'd intended, but perhaps if he stayed . . .

"I'm sure the house is fine," she said.

He grimaced with exasperation. "Nothing is safe in this world," he said.

"You could ask one of the neighbor ladies to go over there."

His grimace developed into a groan.

"Why not?" asked Sunny.

"I can't be beholden to a neighbor lady."

So Sunny retreated. "Maybe we can play cards tonight," she

said, although she couldn't think of a game the kids would sit still for. When she was young, she had loved to play cards with her father. She had been honored to receive that kind of attention. Still, it was better that her kids were not desperate for it. Hearts? Not likely. Maybe Bridget would have some ideas. No, Bridget was gone.

chapter 9

THE WATERY WINTER DAWN HAD OPENED INTO A BRUISE-like purplish gray by the time Jean arrived at Bridget's old apartment on 7th Street. She had to wake up Stew to get Bridget's key. He handed it over willingly enough, then seemed to want to engage her in a conversation he couldn't quite acknowledge to himself. "So . . ." he said, wetting his squarish lips. And: "Well . . ." And: "Uh . . ." She decided it would be easier on everybody if she kept the key.

Jean peeked into each room, lingering in the doorway of the last because of the large padded-metal table. A massage table, not an operating table, but there was a kind of unsavory congruence. She tried to picture it as a scene of debauchery, but in truth she could not. Other people's sexual desires always seemed to her a little silly.

Sunny had evidently started to pack up but hadn't got far. Typical. She was capable of licking the sidewalk to keep her children's feet from getting dirty, but she had never done any real work. Finances were beyond her. Look, she had bought new boxes to hold Bridget's old stuff, a ridiculous waste of money. When Jean had moved, she'd used liquor boxes—mostly Scotch, in honor of Geoffrey.

In the bedroom, a drawer of Jade's clothes was open. Half were spilled carelessly into a box nearby. It was odd that Jean had not thought to come and get Jade's belongings before this. Some of the gifts she'd been given at the shower Sunny threw were quite nice. Jean herself had supplied a bear as big as a six-year-old. And it was always best to have a little continuity with the past, as long as sense was not sacrificed to sentimentality.

Jean didn't think she'd ever seen Jade in this apartment. No memory came to mind, and Jean did not feel like straining after one. She was relieved whenever she noticed variations between Jade's and Bridget's characters. After eating, Jade often ended up with food on the back of her head—evidence of a physical exuberance Bridget had lacked. And Jean couldn't imagine Bridget's gripping anyone with Jade's persistence. Even her crying, as annoying as it was, seemed to promise a forcefulness more like Jean than Bridget.

Mmm, that Chinese-looking padded outfit—was it a warm outer garment? Or just another set of pajamas? It was so hard to tell. Recently Jean had found herself in the middle of a meeting worrying whether Jade's fleece was equal to these brutal January days, because it was far flimsier than the heavy, noisy snowsuits of Jean's youth. Distractions of that sort would end once she had arranged her mind more efficiently. In the meantime, when Crough asked her opinion about the matter they were discussing, whatever that was, Jean was able to say promptly, "You know I always agree with you, sir," eliciting at least a few chuckles, although since she hadn't heard the preceding argument, she wasn't sure if the indifferent laughter was with her or against her.

The most efficient course of action would be to call Sunny when she had a question, but that Jean would never do. Even if Sunny weren't after Jade, she had studied every aspect of child care forward and backward only to be more smug about her lily-livered answers. She let her children run her family, her home, her life. They expected the world, and so far Sunny had been able to give it to them.

Jean wouldn't mind consulting Leon about child care, but he probably didn't know much more than she did. Sunny would have pushed him away—consciously or unconsciously—not wanting anyone to encroach on her territory.

By the telephone in the bedroom was a calendar full of appointments, all the males possible fathers. Except that there didn't seem to be any males, just females. There was an empty week after the handwritten word *operation,* then the names started up again. Those people were sure to have heard something by now, so there wasn't any point in trying to get in touch with them. She pocketed the loose change on the blotter.

Jean wondered whether Sunny regretted her marriage. Sunny could have had anyone, surprise pregnancy or not. It was bad enough to leave your fate in someone else's hands, but if it turned out that the person was as financially hapless as Leon . . . After speaking to Amanda Pennington, Jean had decided to find out just exactly how bad Leon's financial position was. She had been shocked by the credit report she'd ordered through Crough & Co. Even if some of the highest figures were misprints, she couldn't imagine how Leon and Sunny had managed to get hold of so much credit. Several of Leon's buildings were about to be foreclosed on. The balloon mortgages were due any day, and the monthly payments were way behind.

Sunny was unlikely to admit to doubts about Leon, though, even to herself. She wasn't the type. She was always so sure she was right. She really thought she was nicer than everyone else— which was hardly the advantage she assumed it was.

Of course, Geoffrey didn't make any more money than an auto salesman for twice the work, but Jean didn't need his support.

The phone on Bridget's ruined cherry desk rang. The old-fashioned sound—Jean was used to more of a hum—reminded her that she'd meant to turn it off days ago. Still, maybe it was Jade's father. That would be interesting.

Jean lifted the receiver, waited a beat, then said, "Hello."

"Hello, Jean." It was Sunny, who was proving to be a natural tactician. An unexpected visit to Geoffrey. A bull's-eye call to an apparently vacant apartment.

But Jean was equal to her. "Hi, Sunny," she said. Cordial, not startled.

"Stew told me you were there," said Sunny. Maybe not quite the tactician she could be. She shouldn't have explained; better to insinuate supernatural powers.

"You're up early," said Jean. It was strange to have this conversation, which of course she'd known was coming, in an unfamiliar apartment suffused with a not unpleasant but still oppressive and funereal floral scent. Jean sat on Bridget's old cane chair.

"So how have you been?" asked Sunny.

"Fine," said Jean. Her stomach was flipping around a little, but it was nothing.

"And how is Jade?"

"Jade is great," said Jean. "We're having a grand old time."

"Well, I'm glad," said Sunny. "Really. I am."

"The malpractice attorney wants to talk to you. Danny Briccoli."

"Sure. Whatever he wants."

Very smart, to nail Sunny when she was pretending to be flexible.

"It's only right that they pay for Jade's college education, considering they killed her mother," said Jean.

"Who, exactly, are you suing?"

"The doctors, the hospital. You haven't heard anything about Jade's father, have you?"

"No. It could be anyone at all." Sunny's chuckle was a little nervous. "For some reason Paul keeps flashing into my mind."

"*Paul*?" Jean's laugh was real. Rich, sexy Paul Walsh? "Maybe someone else wants to sleep with Paul. Or wishes she still did." Paul could be giving her the financial security that Leon was not.

The brief silence probably meant at least a partial hit. "Well, Paul certainly is as nice as pie," said Sunny. "Look. Why don't I come pick up Jade today?"

"No, thank you," said Jean. "We're fine."

"Mr. Crossley told me you called him."

Jean was pretty sure that he would sign the affidavit Amanda Pennington had prepared for him. It was possible that he liked Sunny more than he did Jean, but he didn't *love* her more. Just a few months before he retired, she'd opened a filing cabinet drawer in his office, wondering what it could contain. Inside was every report card the girls had ever gotten.

"This interest of yours isn't going to last," said Sunny. "It'll be confusing for the kid in the long run."

"Why shouldn't it last? I've spoken to a lawyer, and I'm going to go ahead and apply for adoption."

There was a silence. Then: "Really?"

Jean countered with a silence of her own.

"Try to put the child first," said Sunny sharply. "Think of what would be best for her."

"I am," said Jean. "I can give her all sorts of things you can't."

"Like what?"

"Honestly, Sunny," said Jean. "What makes you think you'd be such a better mother than I would?"

"Try not to be so ridiculous."

"No, really," said Jean.

"You're an incredible jerk, for one thing."

Jean hung up.

Very, very bad tactics on Sunny's part.

If Sunny wasn't nice, she wasn't anything. And Jean was going to do a *much* better job than she did. Sunny couldn't stand seeing a mother work because her self-esteem would not allow her to. Now that she was out of the marriage pool, where she'd got used to starring, she had to enshrine a series of fairly low-level caretaker skills in the sacred name of "motherhood." (Janitor, nurse's aid, teaching assistant—not a whole lot of challenges there.) Women with fulfilling employment didn't end up as full-time mothers, and why should they? They didn't have to fool themselves into thinking that their very presence was a matter of life and death. They didn't have to justify their nonproductivity with the mute declaration that otherwise their precious mites would turn into tattlers, whiners, biters, and bullies. It was insulting to the kids, if you thought about it.

Jean usually told the truth, albeit in a limited and amusing way. Sometimes she spoke the exact opposite of the truth with lifted eyebrows, but she considered this mere sarcasm, which was beneath her. Whichever route she took, however, she pointed what she said in one particular direction or other with the tone of her voice. In court, Jean figured, she would not be able to do that. She would not be able to "feel out" the judge; she would have to speak the full 360 degrees. The only way to deal with such a huge task was to be as exact as possible about every little point. It wasn't her fault that a lot of what she was going to say would not be flattering to Sunny. Family loyalty had always constrained her from elaborating on Sunny's fecklessness, her wantonness, her profligacy. Now Jean would be forced to tell the whole truth about Sunny's life—and her own. It was a striptease she looked forward to.

chapter 10

LATELY SUNNY HAD BEEN FORCED TO RETURN TO AN ODD version of her original, financially innocent state of pure American Express. All her other credit cards were maxed out, no more finagling was possible, and she had to assume that something would happen before her charges had to be paid for. She had reached this state once before, during the concrete floor fiasco, and she recognized that same relief in the sudden simplicity of it all. The only problem was that she couldn't get cash on American Express. But once she'd reached this point she was living in a pecuniary netherworld anyway, hiding currency in her sock drawer: She wasn't letting it anywhere near their black hole bank account. The good thing was that the card had never been declined, even when she'd been close to two months behind on the bill.

Leon had managed to stave off the repercussions of the 1987 crash only so long. Obviously Sunny should have accepted another card offer in the mail months before. But Leon had thought that they would pull through with more ease than they had. Only a year before the bulk of the mortgages were due, he had been confident of receiving refinancing. Even as late as last November, he'd come so close that one night they'd gone to celebrate, thinking it was a done deal.

Now she made no purchases anywhere that didn't accept

American Express. Groceries at the supermarket over on Route 6, yes, and anything at a department store was okay, including the all-white footed pajamas Ruth needed for the winter show, scheduled in February so as to avoid any religious connotation; also delivery of the *New York Times* continued, but magazines from the newsstand were out, as were movies and ice cream—all cash purchases—and no dentist, because he took only Visa. (Sunny put off her appointment, citing a conflict.) The quarterly payment to Kindle School had been made before the crisis hit, but they continued to nickel-and-dime her. When Henry called, Sunny was trying to explain to Linc why she could not buy any of the $25 T-shirts that his class was selling to promote worldwide friendship and peace, which was, she had to concede, a very good cause.

Henry had been working in trusts and estates at a small but well-established midtown law firm for several years now, and he had started sounding slightly perplexed, as if maybe he had gotten on the wrong train. Paul had married Clare last year, surprising everyone, and although Henry had never expressed any anger or regret over the event, Sunny couldn't help thinking that he feared life had passed him by. He had just told one of his wry, self-deprecating stories about looking for a co-op when Sunny heard rocket noises from the extension in the bedroom.

"*Buh*-h-h," said Linc, dwindling eventually to a guttural hiss.

"You just have to take a close look at everything," Sunny advised, ignoring the interruption. "Under the sink. In the closets."

"Guh, guh, guh, guh."

"Look at the grouting," she said. "If they didn't take care with the things you can see, they certainly didn't take care with the things you can't."

Henry sighed. "I haven't noticed my environment for thirty-two years. How can I start now?"

"Sssssssssssssssssss."

"Honey, it's hard to talk when the house has been turned into a launching pad," said Sunny.

"Why don't you come with me?" asked Henry. "Just this once? And show me what to look for?"

"I'd love to, but I'm not sure I can."

"Please?" said Henry. "I'll buy you lunch."

"Okay," said Sunny. "I'll bring the kids."

"Nnnnnnnyyyyyyyaaaahhhh."

"Oh," said Henry. "Sure."

That was how Henry, Sunny, and her two kids came to descend upon one tiny, two-leveled foyer near Lincoln Center the next morning. The real estate agent, a game, smiling blonde in her early fifties, and the doorman, who had a bristly black mustache as thick as a nail brush, were flummoxed until Ruth cried, "I take swimming lessons! I'm the best in my class!"

"I'll just bet you are, sweetheart," said the real estate agent, and when they'd all crowded into the elevator, she sang out gaily, "Breathe in!"

It was Henry who did not look at ease. He was standing with his back to the wall, his large shoes turned at an unnatural angle to save space.

"Wow," said Linc as he burst onto the hardwood floor of the co-op. Every time he took a step, a transparent wedge on the back of his sneakers lit up. "Where's all the furniture?"

"Henry can buy furniture for a dozen apartments," said Sunny.

"I like it the way it is," said Linc. "You can run in a circle." Which he proceeded to illustrate.

The renovation was standard, one wall of exposed brick for every three of Sheetrock. This was what you got after working sixty hours a week for ten years? Oh, well.

The real estate agent said, "I always like a place with southern exposure. It means more light."

"How true," said Sunny, who hadn't noticed that the apartment faced south. Of course, selling was the agent's job. Still, Sunny liked the dogged hopefulness that the remark displayed. Nita Altman was the woman's name. She was slightly plump, but not soft; her flesh had the smooth sheen of metal. And she wore a lot of gold: thick gold crescent earrings, a gold circle pinning a bit-and-tackle scarf around her shoulders, and gold buckles on her narrow navy blue, low-heeled shoes.

"Oh, look," said Sunny, trying and failing to raise the sash of a window. "Giorgio's is across the street."

"You know Giorgio's?" asked Nita.

"Sure," said Sunny. "Did I go there with you, Henry? Or was it just Paul?"

"It must have been Paul," said Henry.

"That restaurant has the best veal in the city," said Nita. It was expensive, Sunny surmised from her tone.

"Do you live around here?" Nita asked.

"No," said Sunny. "I used to live way uptown from here."

"Eighties?"

"One Hundred and Tenth."

"Fascinating," said Nita.

Sunny could tell she still didn't know what to make of her.

"The whole West Side is coming into its own," said Nita. "The Marlboro, which was really on the skids ten years ago, went over the two-million mark for a classic six this year." She was standing with her hip out, an odd bit of Mae West amid her implacable professionalism. "You can still get good deals on small places. It's the top end of the market that hasn't been shaken. A full twenty percent of the rental units in the area now qualify as luxury housing. Most of the renovations done nowadays restore apartments to their prewar sizes. You wouldn't believe some of the prices."

Yet she did not give the impression that she chafed at having to show around this relatively impecunious crowd. It was as if these high figures were more like daydreams to keep her going. She huffed and puffed as they walked the two blocks west to the next place. "You're a friend of Henry's?" she asked Sunny on the way.

"Oh, yes," said Sunny. "A very good friend."

The real estate agent nodded, although she was obviously not satisfied.

Since Henry seemed to think he did not have to take part in this conversation, Sunny said, "I bet yours is a very interesting job."

"You gotta like people, but if you do, you're golden," said Nita, apparently unaware of the echo of the precious metal on her person.

Sunny asked her how she got started.

"I was awarded the apartment in my divorce settlement," said Nita, "but I couldn't afford to keep it. The maintenance was too high. So I brought it to Skyline Realty, and I got to talking to one of the girls in the office, the result of which was, I ended up getting my real estate license with my first alimony check. It was a good thing I did, too, because that was the last check I ever saw."

"Wow," said Sunny.

Nita shrugged it off. "It's a long story," she said. "One day you're eating at Café des Artistes, and the next, you're lucky if you're doing dishes in the back. But you could do this work. I can always tell."

"That's nice to hear," said Sunny.

"I sent my daughter through Vassar College on this job," said Nita. "That's where Jackie Kennedy went, you know."

As you walked in the front door of the next apartment, a wall of friendly faces smiled back at you: father, mother, daughter, baby. There were maybe a dozen photographs of various sizes and in different types of frames. The little girl ran across an open field, sunlight on her legs. The couple held hands in a porch swing. Mother and baby tilted heads at mirrored angles.

In the living room was a soft, puffy, deep blue couch. On the coffee table stood another photo, this of a Christmas tree set up in front of the bay window that constituted one wall of the room they were in.

"It would be nice to have a family," said Henry wistfully.

"That would be a good place for a tree," said Sunny in a small voice. Their co-op up on 110th Street had never looked like this, she thought. Maybe if it had, they wouldn't have lost so much equity.

Even the children were hushed.

In the dining room, a small oval table polished to a shine and set with place mats suggested a nest of domestic bliss. The sleigh bed in the parents' bedroom had a quilt on top and a carved trunk at its foot. In the girl's room was a white wood crib pushed against one wall and a three-story dollhouse against the other: It was also wood, painted pink, with white gingerbread trim.

"I just *know* I can give Jade a happy life!" cried Sunny.

"Of course you can," said Henry.

"I want to play with that dollhouse," said Ruth.

"Oh, Henry, I'm not sure I'll get custody of Jade," said Sunny.

"Leon is having trouble refinancing his buildings. I'm not sure . . . I'm not sure we can afford a lawyer."

"Why didn't you tell me?" asked Henry, without taking his eyes off the miniature world of the dollhouse. "I can represent you."

"I promise I'll pay you eventually."

"Forget it," said Henry.

"It is a nice cozy place, isn't it?" said Nita.

Nita! Who had struggled as a single mother without background or education and ended up sending her daughter to the college "where Jackie Kennedy went." Sunny wanted to hug her.

Henry treated them to lunch at a retro diner where the boxes of the board games Sunny had played in her youth were displayed on glass shelves on the walls. She and Henry took turns exclaiming, "Chutes and Ladders! What a dreadfully repressive game!" and, "Lie Detector! I remember that!"

Sunny was supposed to meet Leon uptown. He had dropped her and the kids off earlier and then headed to his office to catch up on paperwork, an unfortunate necessity now that he spent his weekdays fighting with the banks. He smiled upon their arrival because he was always sensitive to others' feelings, but he made no attempt to cover up how harassed he felt.

When Sunny told him about Henry's offer, he said doubtfully, "Is that why you went with him to look at those apartments?"

Sunny couldn't believe it!

But fortunately there was a buzz from the door. "Hello, everyone," said Luisa, gliding in on her castorlike feet, trailing a very familiar child. "I thought I saw your car parked out front."

"Leon! Look!" cried Sunny, although of course Leon was right there with his eyes open.

Alba didn't smile; she was the same hard-bitten, blurry-featured little girl she had always been. But the sight of her made Sunny's heart leap.

"Hi," said Linc, eyeing her curiously. It was funny to think that Alba wasn't all that much older than he was.

"What do you know," said Leon, half rising up from his chair, his face lit up for the first time in months.

Alba stayed a couple of steps behind Luisa, but Sunny could tell from the way she peeked about now and then that she relished the attention.

"She walked all the way from her new foster home to mine, eighteen blocks, mind you," said Luisa. "She took a route I believe that went across on a Hundred and Thirty-fifth Street and down on Park. Not straight across. Not straight down. She kept looking and looking. It's different things she tried. You know, when Alba was born she was in the hospital two months before she was able to get out. That's how messed up she was because of the drugs in her system. She was born positive for cocaine and heroin. And syphilis. A child's mind can be affected. She can have learning disabilities. But this girl is smart."

"That's obvious," said Sunny. She would have hugged Alba if she could have reached her, but Luisa was unconsciously blocking her like a hedge.

"The child went in neighborhoods that are not safe," said Luisa. "A lady asked where she was going, and Alba told her, 'I'm going to Mama Luisa's.' That's what she called me, Mama Luisa." Luisa began to move herself, gliding frictionlessly over to her desk. "When I opened the door, Alba said, 'Hi.' I didn't see her for six weeks, a month, and this is what she says, 'Hi.' I thought she wouldn't remember me someday, but no: 'Hi.' "

"Did you miss Mama Luisa?" Sunny ventured to ask, afraid of what might have precipitated the flight and uncertain of what lay ahead.

"Roaches would fall down on her bed at night," said Luisa. "That apartment was like really roach infested."

"Yuck," said Sunny.

"I always believe a kid," said Luisa fiercely, although it had not occurred to Sunny that the description might be inaccurate. "Especially a kid like Alba. She's a little girl that doesn't speak a lot but that will tell you like it is."

Sighing, Luisa lowered herself into her chair with the surprising delicacy of a helicopter.

"You have to count," she continued. "One, her birth mother. Two, her foster mother that did not show up after her vacation. Three, that was me. And four, the new foster mother that has the roaches. I cannot give the child to number five. This is too many.

She will end up in therapeutic. She has to go back to number three, me."

"You mean you're going to keep her? How wonderful!"

Something like fear entered Luisa's eyes. "Alba is my main priority. I cannot do the good stuff for her I am supposed to. But I decided she is going to go with me because to go to number five would not provide stability. It's a relief, you know. I feel better that I have to do this. I want to make a home for her even though it will not be the best."

"Oh, Luisa," said Sunny. She had the impulse to hug her, too, although sitting at her desk, Luisa was as hard to get to as Alba. Sunny ended up patting her meaty shoulder with an open, hooked hand. Even at a moment like this, Luisa was formidable. "I know things will work out."

Sunny was happy. Life might have been easier if Leon's income had been steadier, she reflected, but it wasn't, so there wasn't any point in kicking about it. And she certainly didn't want Jean's tedious life. It would be like playing Candy Land without the delightfully unexpected surges and drops of candy cards.

chapter 11

Jean was in her office trying to decide whether to start vetting the résumés on her desk. Normally she would have sent them over to Alice, the head of research, but Blakely had asked her to do them personally, and Jean had agreed. Certainly the position was prestigious enough to merit her time. On the other hand, the work was routine, and Jean had fallen behind slightly in two of her current searches—nothing that anyone else would notice, but still worrisome. Lately she'd had to work harder for the same, or sometimes even less, compensation.

Business was not good. That was the unpleasant truth. Jean was getting résumés from people who would have (foolishly) high-hatted her two years before. One was topped by a smiling photo of the guy; another had gold borders. Next she'd probably get confetti. Once upon a time, this much churning would have meant more fees for the executive recruiters. Nowadays, too often, the departure of an employee meant not a job to fill, but a job gone. Positions were being cut by the thousands. CEOs were becoming famous for the numbers of the "disappeared."

Simply returning the calls of those laid off took endless time. No one will talk more than the unemployed. Not that Jean was making these calls for charity, God knows—never that. But she'd always been proud of taking the harder route, and she was too tough to stop now, even though she was older and could feel every cigarette she snuck and every hour Jade kept her up at night. She may have hated those calls, but she still kept dialing, kept chatting. She never commiserated. In the rare event she could produce an interview, she'd say, "So, are you ready to stop lolling about?" Or if she didn't, she might bark out, "I assume your lawn is nice and trim by now," or, "Discover any good hobbies lately?"

It was getting harder and harder to pursue her old strategy of reassuring the person who had behaved the worst. In this economy, you couldn't figure out who it was. Also, the guilty party often didn't recognize this status, so the effort was wasted. The days of "I don't know how he can stand it!" about Francis Rio, who was fired before he started, seemed long ago indeed.

Fortunately Jean worked largely in the top echelon, where people were firing rather than being fired. Oh, she still got stuck with the occasional "VP of Administration—Regional," a fancy sounding title for an administrative assistant. The money Jean made from that search paid for a week of Oneika, without overtime. Hardly worth it to open her door in the morning. But Blakely had put her over the top. Thank God for his patronage. Headhunting firms themselves had started cutting back. Julius Krill alone had dropped over thirty people. Krill! Who bought a little insurance at the same time by going public and blaming it on the stockholders.

Jean fully intended to get to Blakely's résumés, but she had to return a call first. "What did Dr. Kuskin say about Jade's temperature?" she asked Oneika, still secretly thrilled at the casual way she could pronounce the name of one of the best pediatricians in the city.

Geoffrey had suggested—risibly—that Jean ask Sunny who her kids' doctor was. He was forgetting that Jean talked to people associated with the health care industry all the time. By asking around, she learned to speak with awe of Dr. David Kuskin. The news that his practice was full did not give her pause for a minute. She assembled a dozen referrals—some parents of patients, a few fellow doctors, an administrator or two, all clients of Crough & Co. or their happy hires. She had even thought of including Blakely, but it would have been a waste of ammunition, and he was so high up in the hierarchy there was always the risk his name would not be recognized. When Jean finally called, she was able to secure a checkup for Jade in five months. In the meantime, she was officially a Kuskin patient.

"He told me to bring her in tomorrow if her fever doesn't go down," said Oneika.

It really was not hard to stay on top of everything if you knew how to choose subordinates and how to delegate. Oneika was very professional—still judgmental as well, but Jean didn't mind.

"They would like you to send Jade's old medical records before the checkup so they know what shots to give her," she added.

Okay. One more task before the résumés. Jean had taken Bridget's old check registers from her apartment the day that Sunny had revealed her true character. Where were they? Yes, here in the bottom drawer under some current files. Bridget was sure to have written checks to Jade's old pediatrician. All Jean had to do was copy out the names of doctors and figure out who did what. It would help with the lawsuit, too, she was sure.

There were deposits every month from a "LeSu" and a "LeSu Properties." Looked like child support to her. But wait a minute. *LeSu*. That was one of Leon's companies. "Le" stood for Leon, "Su" for Sunny. How could Jean have forgotten? If she moved, she would throw up.

Leon as Jade's father—ridiculous. Of course, it was always absurd to try to picture two people in bed together. Even Leon and Sunny, who seemed so physically attuned that they demanded consideration as Siamese twins, Jean had to picture lying doll-like on painted covers. To think of them going down . . . well, forget it.

It was true that there was something essentially malleable about both Leon and Bridget. Jean figured that both would be easy to push into bed, but she couldn't imagine either advancing on the other. It could have been one of those soap opera situations: forced by a sudden storm to share a single bed in a motel room, wet clothes strewn gratefully on the floor, a little shivering to ignite the flame. No, the idea was laughable.

Jade did resemble Leon somewhat, but Jean had read somewhere that all babies looked like Winston Churchill, and it could be that all babies looked like Leon as well, Leon being chunky and jowly. Still, the ears stuck out the same way. . . .

Leon must have pulled a Kevin Kline. What was that movie? The wife asked the husband, Kevin Kline, to sleep with the unmarried friend because the friend wanted a kid and didn't see how it was going to happen.

But then Sunny would know about it, and Jean couldn't believe she did. Sunny would never be able to keep a secret like that. She talked to everyone. Maybe Leon had done it on his own? Just donated his sperm? Either way, there'd be a paternity test . . .

No, this was more ridiculous than Paul Walsh being the father. It was fear speaking. If Leon was the father, that would strengthen Sunny's claim. Jean drew a deep breath. She stood up to unbutton her wraparound waist-length jacket, which she undid first on the far left and then on the far right. The gesture was one of Jean's favorites. It reminded her of discarding a gun belt.

Thank God she didn't know anyone who could be Jade's father. No one had even met Bridget. Except the Joes, of course, those pharmaceutical buffoons who'd come down from Stamford. The ones with the chained dog lying out on the concrete. Obviously there was no connection. Still, she did associate a feeling of disquiet with them. Where had that come from? Yes, she had "used" Bridget to show them how cool the candidate could be, but the idea of "using" someone belonged in high school, back with the distinction Sunny had made between "loving" someone and being "in love" with him. Besides, the ploy had worked terrifically well.

Jean picked up the phone and called the Joes. Both of them got on the line, which caused a few minutes of chortling confusion: "Is this Joe?" "Sure, this is Joe. Is that you, Joe?" "Yeah, this is Joe."

"Your manager still working out?" asked Jean.

"Sure," said one Joe. "He's cool."

"And how's business?" asked Jean.

"Can't complain," said the same Joe. "People still get sick in a recession."

"Sicker," said the other. "You're probably doing all right, too."

Of course she was! But it wasn't because executive recruiters in general were.

After they circled for a while longer in this fashion, Jean started to get off, adding, "My sister Bridget died."

Both Joes said something that, blended together, sounded like "Sorry to hear."

"I think you met her once," said Jean.

"Really," said one Joe.

"Huh," said the other.

Okay, they'd clearly never seen her again. That was all the information that Jean had been after. Yet their obvious indifference irked her. They thought they would never die.

"Yes, only thirty-nine years old," said Jean, shaving off some three years for the full shock value.

"That's awful," said one Joe, more heartfelt.

"What happened?" Also concerned.

"A botched operation," said Jean.

"Oh," said a Joe.

"Too bad." Already drifting away. The dead woman had had bad luck, nothing they had to worry about.

Jean noticed Matt Crough in her doorway. It was unlike him to wait patiently for the end of one of his subordinates' conversations, but Jean couldn't help wondering how long he'd been standing there in his slack-mouthed way.

"Uh-oh," she said into the phone. "Gotta go. The boss is here." She could have been a fifties comedian referring to his wife.

"Hi, boss," said Jean.

"Hi, Jean," said Crough. "Who was that?"

"The two Joes. You know. Up in Stamford."

"They have something for us?"

"Not yet," said Jean.

"I understand you're doing a new project for Blakely."

"There's no one I'd rather work with."

Crough nodded. "I wanted to make sure you had the time."

"Of course," said Jean, a little chilled but not showing it.

"Because I understand you left work early a couple of days this week."

Early? Oh, he meant before 8:00.

"You know me," said Jean. "It doesn't matter where I am, I'm working."

"Glad to hear it," said Crough airily. Crough, who left work at 5:30 every night.

chapter 12

LEON FINALLY ACCEPTED AN OFFER FOR HIS LARGEST BUILD-
ing, the only one not on his block. "It means taking a loss that
would have been unthinkable six months ago," he said. "But this
way we can regain our footing and focus on our core holdings."

Sunny was pleased by his use of the word *we,* although she
wasn't exactly sure to whom it referred. "Thank God," she said,
"that the worst is over."

She paid off American Express, paid down the other cards, sent
checks off for the other bills that were due, and accepted another
card offer through the mail, in case of further emergencies. Despite
heating subsidies, Leon's most pressing bills were for oil. December
had been an unusually cold month. After sending out those checks,
he performed financial triage on his buildings: those whose financial health would be sound for a little longer without any help (the
most recently purchased); those that were so close to the refinancing date that they could be saved only by a miracle (why send a
bank money when it was going to take the property anyway, once
the balloon was due?); and those that might actually be saved by a
quick infusion of cash for taxes and mortgage payments.

The Dane household, which had begun to feel parched and
creaky in recent months, was once again its true well-oiled self.
Even Leon was cheery. And what a relief, to be able to order class

pictures for the kids without worrying whether the checks were going to bounce.

The day after Sunny dropped her last payment into the mail, Henry FedExed her a copy of an affidavit he'd drawn up describing why Jade should live with the Danes. The child was intimately familiar with the household, which she had visited often with her mother. She would be blessed with an instant brother and sister who already knew and loved her. Jade's maternal grandfather was a frequent visitor. The family ate dinner together every night; they read out loud afterward; weekends were a happy cacophony of swimming lessons, music enrichment, and special programs at the Bronx Zoo. Jade would have the life that every parent would wish for his or her child, should disaster strike.

Mary Crossley Dane, also known as Sunny, was the person who made all of this possible. She was the most attentive, sensitive, and loving of mothers. She volunteered at the children's school (no mention of the fact that "parent hours" were required, but never mind). Although she'd moved to a new town only six months ago, a popular Cub Scout pack already met at her home, which was also a haven for neighborhood kids. The linchpin, as Henry pointed out, was that Sunny, despite an education anyone would envy, had sacrificed the immediate pursuit of a career to raise her children. She was always there—for comfort, for counsel, to share a passing joke.

At the moment, actually, Sunny was helping out at the office. Gloria had found part-time work at the Columbia University Library, and she was coming in only once a week now. As soon as Leon could afford to give her the severance he thought she deserved, he was going to have to let her go. But Sunny went in to East Harlem only during school hours, as long as neither kid was sick and she didn't have to help out in the classroom. She knew women with tennis dates that were less flexible than her commitment at Leon's office.

Sunny was in a remarkably good mood the next morning, although traffic, especially on the Tappan Zee, was worse than usual. At least according to Leon. Sunny had noticed that traffic was often "worse than usual," occasionally "better than usual," but never just plain "usual." Leon wasn't bothered—or even surprised. He did not have much time, however, to get to an appointment at yet another lending institution, part of his newly reenergized pursuit of refinancing.

Sunny gave Henry a call at his law office to thank him. He did not share Sunny's good mood. "Remember that co-op?" he said. "It turns out it was less than a thousand square feet. Why didn't we notice?"

That was true, come to think of it. The rooms had held only a few well-placed pieces of furniture. It was more like a series of department store displays than a place people lived.

"Where did the owners move their life to, I wonder," said Sunny.

"Garrison," said Henry gloomily.

The co-ops Henry had seen were nicer than the apartments on Leon's block, but they weren't *that* much nicer, thought Sunny. At least that's what she told Leon when he called in between meetings. "Of course, they're near stores where you can buy all sorts of expensive consumer items," said Sunny. "Fresh fruit and vegetables. And antique furniture. And designer clothes. Maybe that's what it means to be middle-class today. Proximity to consumption."

"Henry has plenty of money, and I don't think he needs your help," said Leon mildly.

Sunny was alone when Sergey dropped by. He looked different, grayer and more withdrawn—shyer, too, maybe, because it was just the two of them, although he started with the usual fulsome praise.

"It's nice to see you, too, Sergey," said Sunny. And it was. She felt equal to his onslaught for the first time in months.

"So your husband—he is away?"

"You know, at some bank," said Sunny lightly.

"Ah," he said.

"You want to sit down?"

He had been pacing without focus. Now he circled back to the chair beside her, eyeing it.

"Leon needs investor, rich investor," said Sergey.

"Like you?" said Sunny. It felt good to be able to tease him.

Sergey shook his head in disgust. "I am father," he said.

This could have meant anything, right? But Sunny knew instantly what he was referring to. She looked down blankly at the top of the desk.

"You can test me for my DNA. But I know I am father of Bridget's baby."

Sunny also knew that what he said was true. Bridget had always been excited by the exotic. And Sergey pounced as unthinkingly as he breathed.

"This is problem. For you. For me."

"Why is it a problem?" asked Sunny in a small voice. Clearly Sergey's claim of paternity was only the initial step of some monumental move on his part.

"My wife does not know about affairs. She knows maybe in back of her mind, but she does not know in front."

"I won't tell her."

"I know. You are nice, very nice. Too nice. Sometimes it is hard to talk about real things to nice people."

"Leon won't tell her, either. Even if you didn't ask him not to, he wouldn't. He never passes on stuff like that."

"My wife is fierce woman, with many brothers. I do not like to tell her any kind of bad things," said Sergey. "She gets upset."

"So don't say anything." Sunny couldn't stand the plaintive quality in her voice.

"I do not want to tell her about building at 222. How can I say, 'Bank is going to take'? She would not understand."

Sunny nodded fearfully.

"I have many buildings. I do not have many partners. But Americans like partners. Partners can listen. Partner can say, 'This tenant is very bad. This window must be fixed.'" Fix. "Very nice, to talk about things. I like to have tea, talk. So I try American way. I get partner. Good partner. But I do not get good building."

"Oh, but it is," cried Sunny.

Sergey's hand cradled his chin in what Sunny could only assume was a pantomime of thinking. He let Sunny take in this posture for a moment, then continued, "It may be good building, but then it is *secret* good building, and what does it matter? Other people must know it is good building. *Secret* good building not good."

"You can't give up hope," said Sunny.

"Hope? Hope? What is this—hope? You think hope is good thing?" He shook his head again.

"You have to talk to Leon," said Sunny. "He'll explain it to you." Where was he, anyway?

"Some other person, not so good judge of character, could think that Leon sold part of building because it was not good building. I know him; I know it's not true. But my wife does not know him. And I must agree, maybe Leon have little idea, little suspicion."

"Of course not!" said Sunny. Had he? And if so, was that wrong?

"I see why Leon does not have other women," said Sergey. "I could not do it, by the way, but when I see you, I understand."

"I don't care who you've slept with," said Sunny. "And Jade will be very well taken care of, I promise you."

"If you are chosen mother, that is true. My wife, I love her, but she would not be so good. Her feelings would be difficult. So I worry. What must I say to her?"

"Why say anything?"

"Yes, I do not want to tell her about building. Better if Leon can buy it back from me."

His accent was such that Sunny thought at first she hadn't heard him correctly. "What?" she said, and when she saw the way he looked at her, she knew she had been right. "You want Leon to buy you out?"

"Yes," said Sergey.

"Why would he do that?"

"Because he is good. And it is good thing to do."

A threat was surely there, but Sunny had yet to figure out the specifics.

"Better to forget everything," said Sergey, waving his hand. "DNA, Jade, hospital."

Sunny knew she was being dense, but she just could not understand.

"Better not to think about. Or talk about."

Oh. "You want Leon to buy you out, and in return, you won't sue for custody of Jade?"

Sergey threw up his arms. "Sunny," he said again. This time he sounded farther away.

The light in the office was very bright in contrast with the darkening of the windows. It was only 11:00, so a storm must have been seeping into the sky. One of the panes rattled; that was the wind.

She felt sick. This was not the sudden, doubling jolt produced by her first awful suspicions about Bridget's fate. Instead a bewildered numbness was coupled with a feverish visual clarity. The furniture was painfully, profoundly three-dimensional; the edges of the desk looked as if they'd slice your fingers open.

"I don't believe it," she said. "That's not what you're like."

"You think I make my money so person can lose it?" he said in a different, harder voice. "You Americans, you see nothing, everything great, very rich country. You nice American girl from Long Island, nice house, nice food, nice husband, everybody nice."

Could this be an accurate description of her? She supposed so.

"You think rich and nice are same thing. You eat your cake and have it, by the way. You think you must get money because you are nice girl? Why? Why should I have Leon to take my money and make disappear? Because he is nice? Because he helps immigrant people? How about me? I am immigrant person. Why is that good—to take away from me and give to colored people?"

"I think you should ask Leon these questions," said Sunny, surprised that her voice was steady and each word distinctly articulated.

"Yes," said Sergey. "For you to think just of the little baby."

"I will," said Sunny. "I always do. I think of her, and I think of Linc and Ruth."

"Bridget was very nice girl, too," said Sergey. He reached over and pinched Sunny's thigh. He grabbed too much flesh for it to be painful, but it would have been shocking at any other time. "She was real American girl, like you."

As soon as he left, Sunny picked up the phone and called Paul Walsh at work.

chapter 13

JADE WAS STILL AWAKE WHEN JEAN GOT HOME AROUND
9:00 P.M.; she could hear odd jagged cries through the door. It
turned out that Geoffrey had gotten home early. "Oneika and I
were standing in the hall, having a polite conversation," he explained. "I asked her how she was, and she said fine, and she asked
me how my day had gone, and the next thing I knew, the baby
was in my arms, and she was gone."

"Quite a magic trick," said Jean with her usual double meaning:
making fun of Geoffrey for his implied helplessness while also
wondering how Oneika had managed to pull it off. The last time
Geoffrey had got there first, he'd headed straight back for his
home office and waited for Jean. It was infuriating, the way he assumed he could slip through life. Still, Jade was not his child, and
Jean didn't want to upset his apparently fragile acceptance of her.

"How did it go?" she asked.

"Children are a good excuse to play!" said Geoffrey. He slid out
gamely onto the wall-to-wall carpeting but gave up when Jade did
not respond to a ball rolled across the rug or a wooden hammer
clattered on a xylophone (items Jean had thankfully taken from
Bridget's apartment during that one trip).

"She's pretty sick," said Jean magnanimously, figuring it was
worth reassuring him about his paternal capabilities.

After pouring himself some of the single malt Jean had given him for Christmas, he saved face by pretending to teach Jade how to shake hands, a charade that neither of them ever seemed to tire of, although Jean was often tempted to point out its similarities to training a dog.

"Ow-w-w-w," said Geoffrey, holding his right hand motionless in Jade's while writhing in simulated pain on the carpet. He was pretending to be incapacitated by her fierce grip.

Jade managed a wan smile.

"How about Chinese?" asked Jean.

"I've already eaten," said Geoffrey between gasps of pain.

Jean grabbed a beer from the refrigerator. It was not true that Jean did not like to relax. She liked to drink beer—ale, actually. In the English rather than the German family, although she never spoke of the English aloud as anything but "my ancestral enemies." She also liked to watch a little TV, preferably a snatch of trash with great actors in it, like *The Boys from Brazil.* And she still liked to swim, although she didn't particularly enjoy the pools in the city, even the one at the much admired Midtown Squash Club, where so many careers were made or broken. When she swam there, she was working. What Jean did not miss was having "friends." What was the point of a friend, after all, if she knew nothing about what you spent your time doing?

She picked Jade up out of the hold that Geoffrey was pretending was hers. "I spoke to *Dr. Kuskin* today," said Jean. Actually, she'd been in his waiting room for half an hour, then she'd had to leave for a meeting with Blakely, who canceled at the last moment. A month earlier she would have been perplexed by the relative equanimity with which the grown women around her idled away their time in a pediatrician's office, occasionally glancing through a handful of truisms in a parenting magazine. But now she recognized the stunned-love state that made your surroundings irrelevant. Besides which, it was interesting to compare Jade to the other babies in the room, all of whom were whiny, fat, lumpish, sullen, or slow. Jean was proud to be associated with Jade. And with Oneika, who sat as self-possessed as a nun.

"He called me from the consulting room," said Jean. "Jade has roseola. The only danger is that the fever might go up too high, so

I have to check on her every four hours through the night to make sure her little brain isn't cooking."

"That sounds scary," said Geoffrey with infuriating concern—infuriating because he was trying to slough it off on her.

"It's no big deal," said Jean, tightening her embrace around the baby. "I had it when I was a kid." She considered asking him to check on Jade once as well but decided against it, and of course it wouldn't occur to him.

The phone rang. Most likely someone pushing a credit card; you couldn't get away from those people in the age of easy-come debt. Jean did not bother to put Jade down and retreat to the bedroom, which she regretted when she realized it was Amanda Pennington, who said she'd learned earlier that day of an affidavit filed by a Mary Dane.

"That's my sister Sunny," said Jean. She should have known. A person like Sunny would not go to a notary public on a daily basis, and Briccoli had called earlier in the day to say that she'd sworn out a statement about Bridget's understanding of her surgery.

"I'm not familiar with the attorney's name," said Pennington. "But it seems serious."

"Who is it?"

"Henry Clark."

"That's an old boyfriend of hers," said Jean.

"Something I should know about?"

"No, no. She just has all these men wrapped around her little finger." Jean was on the cordless phone, so she could get over to the couch without dislodging Jade or the handset, while studiously ignoring Geoffrey's questioning glances.

"She's arguing the stay-at-home-mom position," said Pennington. "And I'm not going to lie to you. It can work."

"You're kidding," said Jean. Jade's body was as hot as an electric blanket.

"Of course very few things work against *me*," said Pennington. Her arrogance should have been annoying. But it was also reassuring.

"Good for you," said Jean.

"You mentioned at our meeting that she was having financial difficulties," said Pennington.

"Yes."

"You know your sister, and I don't, but I have been in this business long enough to know that people have a lot of different motives for pursuing adoptions. You also made reference at that meeting to the fact that your niece is expecting a sizable settlement. Is it possible that your sister wants to be paid off in some fashion?"

"She wants me to pay her off, you mean?" asked Jean.

"Is it possible?"

Of course it was possible. Yet Jean had not gotten where she was today by being a crude judge of character. "Put it this way," she said. "I don't think Sunny would consciously know that that is what she wanted."

As Geoffrey poured himself another drink, Jean pointed to her half-empty beer bottle with an imperious lift of the chin.

"I'll make sure her attorney knows she's going to have to account for every penny of the settlement," said Pennington.

The phone call ended before Jean got her beer.

As she fetched the new digital baby thermometer, Geoffrey asked, "What was that all about?"

"Sunny," said Jean.

"She still wants the baby?"

"I guess so," said Jean, thinking that maybe she could scramble herself some eggs. "You know what she's like."

"Not exactly," said Geoffrey.

"Spoiled," said Jean.

"Really? She seems to do a lot for her kids."

"Too much," said Jean. "That's my point." The thermometer beeped: 103 degrees. Bad, but not terrible. It was amazing, this technology.

"Ah," said Geoffrey. "Well, I'm sure you know what you're doing."

Jean narrowed her eyes. In her exhausted and hungry state, she found it impossible to figure out what he meant.

Jade was basically already asleep, so even though her eyes opened when Jean put her down for the night in her handsome German-made crib, she gave out only a few of those jagged cries, like a car staggering along in the wrong gear. (Not being a good driver, Jean had experienced this on more than one occasion.) Taking care of Jade wasn't work—Jean still wasn't willing to concede the point—but it was true that it had to be done in a way that, say, drinking English ale did not.

Jean was reminded of Blakely's canceling their meeting at the last minute. "Did your parents ever elaborate on what Blakely told them about me?" she asked Geoffrey.

"I haven't talked to them."

Jean sighed.

"Don't you talk to Blakely all the time?" he asked.

"I guess. We've missed each other a lot lately."

"I see," said Geoffrey, now fussing over her beer. "You certainly are very interested in him, aren't you?"

"He is my most fascinating client," said Jean. "Just as the second largest health services corporation is my second most fascinating client."

"But Blakely is so . . . creepy around you," said Geoffrey. "It's not right."

Jean was stung. She noticed that Geoffrey had been careful to keep his back to her. Did he not think she commanded respect at work? "He treats you like an errand boy," she pointed out.

"Oh, he still thinks of me as a kid," said Geoffrey, turning with the air of having weathered the worst. "That's different."

"He's used to huffing and puffing," said Jean.

"He 'gets off' on giving you a hard time," said Geoffrey. His mouth was overly careful while forming the unfamiliar slang.

So that's what he meant. Jean's reactions were unpredictable enough that Blakely no longer tried to shock her in any simpleminded way. But there was a sexual charge to their exchanges at times; it was Geoffrey who had opened her eyes on that score. Geoffrey was the one who had showed her how desire could lick under her every arch remark like the first tongues of flame under a log. Blakely may not have been an object of desire for any sane woman, but the process of thrust and parry still inched toward consummation—in rust rather than in fire.

"He can't get over being Papa Bear," Jean said to Geoffrey, who was alert, flushed, excited by the conversation.

Looking at him and listening to another crest of Jade's cries,

Jean remembered this wondrous truth: Geoffrey had agreed to let a baby into their lives in order to bed her, Jean—a champion chugger, swimmer, negotiator, etc., but hardly a femme fatale. Logically, he could have retracted his promise, but somehow Jean knew that he wouldn't, and he still hadn't. The thought of the power she wielded could still make her turn over in the dark sometimes and hook her leg over his thigh.

chapter 14

SUNNY HADN'T EATEN AT A RESTAURANT JUST FOR ADULTS in a long time. She didn't mind, usually, but it was pleasant to be entering this Wall Street lunch spot now. Big soft wet snowflakes had started falling in the eerie radiance outside. Inside were tracks of water and large fur-lined boots and a knot of men shoulder to shoulder at the coat check.

The walls were paneled in dark reddish wood with many prominent moldings—padauk, maybe. The work could not be duplicated today because wood was cut in standard sizes, all narrower. Funny, that she should start to appreciate the art of such places when she no longer frequented them. The whole restaurant was pleasantly dim. A small fire cracked and spat in a stone fireplace, too small to be an original. Sunny wondered what it had been. A podium holding the reservation book glowed under a minuscule halogen light.

Sunny's plan was to ask Paul Walsh to refinance Leon's buildings—or to see that it happened. She couldn't believe she hadn't thought of this solution before. Paul had a lot of power now. She was pretty sure she had heard him talk about foreclosing on Brazil and whether or not to save the peso. She hadn't paid enough attention. The work seemed to lack the human dimension that could have made it interesting. No wonder he was paid so much money, if that's what he had to do all day. In the future, however, she was going to have to care, because the consequences were so important.

She didn't know how exactly she was going to elicit this help from Paul. She might be able to simply ask for it. Over the years she'd found that people were very generous if you allowed them to be. The trouble was, she'd never traded on a friendship this way before. Henry had said he would represent her in the suit over Jade out of the kindness of his heart. It was possible that he was regretting it now, but that was another matter. Sunny had not deliberately prompted the offer, no matter what Leon suspected.

Paul was sitting against the wall under one of the nineteenth-century portraits of merchants. He stood up as she approached, and she was happy to see a few other heads swivel as well; it gave her courage. Paul had filled out, she realized. He had lost his twisty nervous energy. His movements were deliberate. There was a touch of gray at his temples. Well, it was all the better that he was a grown-up now, too.

Sunny had been surprised when Paul married Clare. She liked Clare, but through the years Clare had always seemed to be a girl who was doomed to hang out at the fringes. Sunny had expected Paul to marry a more vibrant woman from a different circle. This was New York, after all, which reeled with circles. How about the woman in the red dress he had brought to Bridget's baby shower? Marrying Clare looked too much like settling for second best. And it wasn't fair to Clare, either. Graceful and delicate, she would probably be somebody else's first choice.

"I was so pleased to get your call," said Paul.

The truth was, Sunny was willing to exchange much for the refinancing of those buildings. Just about any sort of favor. Preferably in a deep and sumptuous dark-paneled room like this.

"I've ordered oysters to start," he added.

As soon as he spoke she tasted them on her tongue: rubbery, juicy, with a tang of sauce.

"Do we need menus?" he asked, signaling for the waiter.

"What did I used to get here?" asked Sunny.

"Sole," said Paul.

Sunny smiled.

"How's Leon?" he asked.

"Fine," she said. "Although he's having some business difficulties."

"He can still make a killing with conversions, as long as he's careful."

"Well, it's a little late for that," said Sunny. "It's terrible, the way banks redline certain neighborhoods." Her whole body was heating up, particularly the core.

"Don't I know it," said Paul, opening his hands just above the table as if to catch a beach ball. "Can you believe the bank gave us a hard time about a mortgage on our co-op because of the area? The loan officer told me he wanted 'extra assurances,' so I told him where to get off. He was just a kid, too easy to bully, which meant I had to hold myself back. But he should have shown a little imagination. The district may be new, but I promise you, it will be the next SoHo. I can't wait to have you see it."

Paul had always talked easily. He was never ashamed—about the possibility of bullying, about holding himself back. To him there was no difference; he could be honest about everything. And Sunny was sure the neighborhood would be as hot as he claimed.

"I didn't know there was redlining in white neighborhoods," she said.

"The problem is, it isn't really a neighborhood yet."

The room was hot and smelled of wet wool. The window in the front had steamed over. Sunny felt as if an illness had descended upon her. She was paralyzed with desire for Paul Walsh. (Jean was right.) At the same time, she found it difficult to sit still. She kept squirming in her seat. This was called sacrificing her virtue? She wanted to throw it away. Her smile grew sickly.

"Though it's a perfectly legal residential loft," said Paul.

"Ah," said Sunny.

The oysters arrived. She leaned forward. Her lips parted for the fleshy shellfish. She licked them after it slipped down. Such an irresistibly flat taste.

"The value of property in East Harlem has plummeted in the last few years," she said.

"Marginal real estate everywhere has taken a beating," said Paul. "I ought to know. How else do you think we could afford our space?"

Marginal? "Paul, I'm sure your place is terrific."

"It's pretty nice," he said. "And you'll get a chance to see it soon."

"Oh, good."

"Since I couldn't get you to share my dream loft"—Sunny ducked her head a little and looked up at him from the corners of her eyes—"will you at least come to the housewarming?" asked Paul.

This was not going right.

"Clare is going to call you as soon as we settle the details," he said.

Not right at all. "How is Clare?" she asked feebly.

"You know," said Paul. "Overworked. Supervising a renovation of that magnitude is not easy."

Sunny realized she had no idea how to engineer the exchange she'd had in mind. Hers wasn't much of an offer, of course. She wasn't uncharted territory. But she knew Paul still wanted to sleep with her (although he might have been constrained by loyalty to Clare). And she was still willing to be pinned to a mattress herself. But she couldn't see a path to that point. She couldn't think of any words to use.

Finally she blurted out, "Can you help Leon refinance his buildings?"

The whole room slipped into suspended animation for a moment: no clink of silverware, no chatter, no scrape of chair legs.

"Has the market value dipped below the loan figure?" Paul asked.

"I'm not sure," said Sunny.

"It doesn't matter anyway," said Paul. "No one will touch it. A place like that is the first to be dropped in an economic downturn."

"East Harlem will never be chic like your neighborhood," said Sunny. "The buildings are little and ugly and shabby. But they're prewar. They're solid. They make good homes for people who need them desperately." She was giving up hope but made herself go through the motions. "I feel very strongly about this. I would do anything to see them saved. Anything."

But Paul wasn't paying any particular attention. "You can't lend more money on property than it's worth," he said.

"You know it will go back up," said Sunny. "Can't you open their eyes to what's right?"

"It doesn't work like that," said Paul. "And if I went around giv-ing unsecured loans, I'd be fired."

The crushed ice under the oyster shells was gray.

"I see," said Sunny.

Sunny had always had an easy fit with the world. This had not been narcissism. She was often intensely aware of the situations that others found themselves in. But it is not hard to deal with a predicament that can be summed up with a single word or phrase like embarrassment or need or injured dignity. Paul's reaction here was obscure. It had so many shades that her eyes blurred it into a bland hue. She could not puzzle each piece out, and she had lost the ability to intuit them. Worse, she could no longer figure out what to do because she didn't even know what she wanted.

chapter 15

JEAN FELT HOT AND SWEATY AS SHE WAITED IN THE FULL sun by her very own window. She was exhausted. Her stomach bounced somewhere outside her body—maybe outside the glass—and every once in a while she had to blink away a miasma that had surfaced in her field of vision. She knew it wasn't real because it remained stationary as the city rolled by beneath her. Plus the scale was all wrong. The miasma had the air of the microscopic; it looked like a trellis of flowering spores. She closed her eyes and felt as if she were rattling around in a tin box. Her teeth hurt. She tried not to think of how far behind she was in returning her phone calls. She tried not to think at all.

Fortunately, Jean had no reason to be nervous about the home visit itself. Her attorney had told her she'd never had a client flunk one. And Jean was an expert interviewer; she'd be able to stay two steps ahead of anyone. The idea that an evaluation told you more about the person asking questions than the person answering was a bit of faddishness Jean would never fall prey to. Yet there was some knife edge of truth to it. She knew that what she was dealing with was the character of the social worker and that any bias would most likely run in her favor.

When Nancy Phalen arrived, she was indeed everything Jean had wished for: brisk, trim, and efficient. In her sixties, maybe.

Dating back to a time when smart, ambitious women were channeled into unprofitable work in certain "caring" professions. Her suit was cheap but oddly similar to Jean's: shortish, blue, made of pressed wool. Not too fashionable, but not a simple copy of a man's, either. "Where's the child?" asked Phalen.

Jean blinked. It must look peculiar that Jade wasn't there. "She's with her baby-sitter. At the park. We can go find them."

"Later," said Phalen. "Shall we sit down?" At her age she needed to. She pointed to the black leather couch with a touchingly awkward-looking V of fingers, all swollen knuckles and engorged veins. Then she began reading from a description of her goals in the interview before her skirt actually hit the seat. Jean did not usually associate with the elderly. She tried to pay attention, but Phalen's voice was sort of wavery and scratchy, and it was hard to untangle the bureaucratic jargon. Too late, Jean realized she should have asked Oneika to tidy up a bit. She supposed she should hire a cleaning lady, but the expense had always seemed so unnecessary.

"There are no right answers," said Phalen. Okay, Jean got that. Also: "The evaluator's judgment is only as accurate as the facts on which it is based." A disclaimer! Jean had to sign on a line to show that the statement had been read to her, then initial mysterious places in the margins.

"Must be hard to deal with all that nonsense every time you talk to someone," Jean remarked.

"It's important that you understand the procedure," said Phalen. "We've had some problems in the past."

"I'm sure you have," said Jean gaily, then recognized the hostility of the words. Apparently she'd just told Phalen she was sure to have had problems. A lot of the sense of a statement lay in its pitch and tone, however, and both of those were full of the surface friendliness the situation demanded.

"Describe the child's relationship to you," said Phalen.

"Jade is my niece."

"Most people use this opportunity to think of a more emotionally descriptive term."

"Oh," said Jean.

"Well?"

"Well, that's what she is; she's my niece." Jean concentrated on keeping up her demeanor. She was more tired than she'd thought.

"You're married?"

"Yes."

"You live here with your husband?"

"Our hours often overlap."

Phalen tapped her clipboard with the deep purply pink of the pencil eraser. "Let's call that a 'yes,'" she said finally. The loose skin below her neck shook. "What hours do you work?"

"All the time," said Jean. "You have to keep your eyes open in my line. Day and night."

"Sounds exhausting," said Phalen dryly.

Jean shrugged, trying to focus.

"How is that going to square with your care of a child?"

"I'm sorry," said Jean, staring dumbly at her ankle. "I have a run in my stocking."

"Is something bothering you?" said Phalen. She did not sound friendly.

Jean flicked on the smile again, full power. "Not at all."

"And your child care arrangements?"

"I have an extremely expensive nanny named Oneika MacIntyre."

"Is that a problem?"

"Of course not. I make a lot of money."

"I see. Do you have meals together in your home?"

"Meals," said Jean, striving for charm. "Well, Jade does not exactly sit down to the Sunday roast yet, but she and I have a drink together after work every night. I have a beer, she has a formula. It's very companionable. I look forward to it, actually." That much was true. Silly enough to merit the frivolous tone, but still true.

"Do you ever use alcohol excessively?"

"I don't have time."

"How about drugs?"

"I'm thirty-nine years old."

Phalen glanced at her sharply.

"No," said Jean. "Although I am always flattered when someone tries to sell me some. It makes me feel young."

"What is your attitude toward discipline?"

"In favor."

"How about physical punishment?"

Clearly a trap, but it was hard to think through the implications when her head hurt so. "I would prefer something more useful," said Jean. "Sweeping, maybe. Like Cinderella."

"What do you think about parents' admitting they're wrong?"

"I am unlikely to have to deal with that," said Jean.

She was getting giddy; that's what it was. But she sensed no lightening of mood on Phalen's part; the questions kept coming.

"Have you read any books on child development?" she asked.

"Not if *Rosemary's Baby* doesn't count."

"Does Jade understand good table manners?"

"She already knows to drop her salad fork on the floor before her dinner fork."

"What do you think you should do for the child's education?"

"Vote Democratic."

"What do you think a parent should teach a kid before school?"

"How to get there?" Jean's words faltered, but her smile did not.

"At what age should parents start talking to their children about sex?"

"Whenever the parents have questions!" said Jean. Her face grew red and hot and tight. She thought she was laughing at first, but no, she was crying. The tears seemed to fly straight out, as if she were falling over backward away from them. "I'm sorry," she said, gasping. Astonished at her lack of control. "I'm sorry. It's such an old joke. Such a horribly stale old joke."

"Are you all right?" asked Phalen. Skeptical.

"I'm the one who's fine," said Jean, groping on the end table for the paper napkin she'd left there last night. On it was a slightly off-color, indented ring where her beer bottle had sat. "I am always fine. It's Jade who's had roseola."

The Phalen face changed instantly, got all soft and mushy. And she called herself a trained professional. "Would you like to put this off until some other time?"

"No, no," said Jean. "I'm just tired. I've had to check on her all through the night for a while now." Phalen was probably used to tears, she told herself fiercely.

"I can come back later."

"You can't," wailed Jean. "I've already put off a meeting." With Blakely. HealthQuest had made a play for another conglomerate.

"How hands-on would you say your parenting style is?" asked Phalen. "For example, if the child were making microwave popcorn, would you tell her what to do at every step? Or would you let her learn by trial and error?"

"I'm sure Jade would be much better at making popcorn than I am," said Jean. But now her tone was dull. Her words no longer had even a veneer of cleverness; they seemed to her simply true. There was so much she couldn't do. She had slept through the alarm the second night, slept through the entire half hour of beeping before the hand of the clock disengaged. Geoffrey had been in Houston, so she'd had no backup. What a failure she was. How could she have slumbered on while Jade's brain might have been cooking only a few yards away? As it turned out, she was fine the next day, but what if she hadn't been? Oh, how she missed Bessie. Jean put her head in her hands and wept.

chapter 16

WHEN LEON CALLED FOR THE FIRST TIME THAT MORNING, Sunny was unwrapping a bungee cord with which Linc had laced up several kitchen cabinet doors, using the creaky old handles as eyes.

"Any word?" said Leon.

"No," she said. The bungee cord was strung around her neck. The handset was cocked between neck and shoulder.

"I gave her my number, but still, she might call you."

"I know." Sunny grabbed Linc and unfurled his collar, the bungee cord taking on the look of a tailor's tape measure. Linc worked his loose tooth as he tried to shrug her off, grunting a protest.

"It's early yet," said Leon. "She said they'd call before four."

"I've got to get the kids to school," said Sunny. "Why don't I call you when I get back?"

"No, no. No need."

On the way back Sunny fortunately remembered to drop off the tapes before the video store opened; otherwise she'd have been expected to pay the fines immediately. At home she figured it was probably a good idea to have a quick bowl of cereal before Leon called again. As she pulled at the milk jug, a long liquid splash leapt out and laid itself across the damaged countertop in a

California-shaped puddle. The paper towels were still upstairs, from last night, so she tried to slide the milk into the sink with the palm of her hand. This didn't work very well.

The phone rang. "Sergey just called," said Leon.

"Oh, dear."

"I find it hard to even talk to the guy at this point."

"I know." Ruth's vitamin pill was still on her place mat where Sunny had put it that morning. And there was a mitten under the table.

"I told him I'd call him later," said Leon.

"You don't have to give in to him because of Jade." Sunny backed up—as soon as she'd done it, she couldn't remember why—and something crunched underfoot. Cereal? Or maybe some beloved toy, a tiny motorcycle or baby doll, seven cents' worth of plastic, but irreplaceable. No, worse: It was Linc's science project, due that day. It must have fallen out of his backpack. But how could she take it to school now?

"He's my partner," said Leon. "I have to deal with him, Jade or no Jade."

"I guess." Much of the bright green aquarium-style gravel had come loose; a distinct heel print obscured the fish's mouth. Up on her tiptoes, she slipped the tagboard on top of the refrigerator, into the salad bowl, and next to the bungee cord. As soon as she got the chance, she'd have to sweep, too.

"Uh-oh," said Leon. "Someone's here with his hand out. Got to go."

Sunny ate her cereal and emptied the dishwasher at the same time, which was easy, because her hands were free while she chewed and swallowed. She checked her watch. Just time for a full cycle of wash before she had to pick up Ruth and her friend Ariel at Kindle. The preschool was only four hours long. Sunny picked through the tangle of clothes on the bedroom floors, sorting as she went. Linc's comforter was discolored under his huge bear. Curious.

The phone rang. Leon again. "Recycling fines. Apparently the junkies didn't throw away their syringes with the plastics. 'Pass the word to your inspector friends,' I told the guy. 'You'll get no more money out of me. I'm judgment-proof.'"

"Is anyone there?" asked Sunny. "Luisa? Or Gloria?"

"I'm all alone," said Leon. "Not even the tenants are dropping by to complain anymore."

"I can be there in an hour. I just have to figure out what to do with Ruth." And her friend Ariel, come to think of it.

"No, we both have to stay by the phone."

Maybe she could still rescue the science project. She went searching for some quick-drying rubber cement and a pencil with an eraser that was unmarked but not so new that it could leave ugly pink streaks. Froggy Walker had actually sniffed rubber cement to try to get high. Sunny had been present. When was that? Twenty years ago? No, more like thirty. An engineer now, he detected underwater "land" mines. Which was at least possible. All of his colleagues who worked on land mines buried in the earth were chain smokers, he said. There. Not so bad. You could barely see the heel mark. She picked up the mitten, swept.

Sunny arrived at the Kindle School early so she could drop off the science project at Linc's class before picking up Ruth and Ariel. Linc's was the only one apparent in a sea of little faces. "Mommy," he said in surprise, then turned his back on her in mortification. He was not about to forgive her for prompting such a childish response.

A message was waiting for her when she got back home with Ruth and Ariel. Leon: "I've been thinking. Anything that's over what we paid would be all right by me. What do you say?"

"How about lunch?" said Sunny to the girls. "Some nice ravioli?"

"Yes, yes, yes," cried Ruth, such a dear child, always enthusiastic.

"You forgot your vitamin this morning."

The phone rang. "Did you get my message?" asked Leon.

"Yes," said Sunny.

"I know it means wasting all the money we put into it. And all the work you did. But the point now is a quick sale." Sale of their house, he meant. It was the last place they had any money at all.

"It makes sense," said Sunny.

As the ravioli simmered, she thought she'd try to deal with the laundry, which she'd never actually gotten into the machine. The basket was still in Linc's room. Oh yes, something about the comforter. Had he wet his bed after all this time? No, the patch was sticky. She turned back a flap, feeling around in the thin ooze. It wasn't blood, not dark enough. She pulled off several lumpy Lego vehicles, a pile of shabby, splayed-out cartoon books, and a bunny, toad, and dog, all compressed into cotton bricks. Revealed on the comforter were light-colored, maggotlike . . . no, that was only orange pulp. Linc had spilled some orange juice in bed. Which meant a whole other load of wash because the comforter was so bulky.

"Mommy!" cried Ruth from downstairs. "It dinged!" The timer.

Sunny doled out ravioli to both girls. By the time Ruth was halfway through hers, Ariel—a pigtailed blonde wearing an "I Love My Grandma" T-shirt—still hadn't picked up her fork.

"Don't you like it?" said Sunny.

Ariel shook her head.

"What do you want instead? How about a peanut butter sandwich?"

Ariel compressed her mouth into a thin line, then nodded.

"Okay," said Sunny cheerfully. "Let's go, then."

"Go where?" asked Ruth.

"I mean, go on. Go on with life."

"Oh."

Sunny had cut the sandwich into little roof shapes and placed it delicately in front of Ariel by the time the phone rang again. "One seventy-five," said Leon tersely.

"That was the offer?" said Sunny.

"Yes."

"Oh." It was lower than he'd ever feared. "That's not good, is it?"

"I'm going to tell them to shove it."

"Okay," said Sunny. She stood in the center of the kitchen, studying Ariel's untouched sandwich. Nothing was more deeply embedded in her brain than the shape of a piece of bread. "Be nice, though."

"You know me," said Leon.

The phone rang again as soon as she'd replaced the receiver. This time it was Jean, who sounded particularly tinny. She started talking about the importance of role models. It was hard to listen. "What kind of message do you think you're sending to young girls when you throw away your incredibly expensive education? You didn't even marry one of your rich boyfriends."

Sunny hung up.

"I think Ariel wants a *tuna fish* sandwich," said Ruth.

"How about it?" said Sunny. "You want a tuna fish sandwich?"

"Okay," said Ariel.

Sunny was tempted to add onions, celery, and parsley, which was the way she preferred it, but if she was going to make the kid a sandwich, she was going to do it seriously, as if the kid were really going to eat it.

Not that she did. Sunny also tried out a saucer of apple slices on the child before taking a few bites of the tuna fish sandwich herself.

The phone didn't ring again until she was hunting in a drawer for a plastic container to hold the leftover ravioli. All of the tops had holes punched in them, indicating that creatures had lived— and probably died—inside.

"They're calling back before the end of the day with another offer," said Leon.

"What happened to four o'clock?"

"There is nothing deader than a dead deadline," said Leon.

"I guess this is all part of negotiating," said Sunny doubtfully.

"I thought I'd seen everything," said Leon. "But I've never heard of such a low jumping-off point."

"Maybe the rules are different outside the city," said Sunny.

When the phone rang next, it was Ariel's mother, who said she'd had to reschedule a massage and could Sunny keep Ariel until dinner?

Sunny's heart sank, but what she said was "Sure." This meant that for the rest of the afternoon Linc would have to sit in the dangerous front seat, because there were only two seat belts in the back. Also, she'd have to choose between taking Ariel to the grocery store, which didn't seem fair on a play date, and scrambling around to find some dinner here on a day Leon would probably need something a little more bracing, like a big steak.

"You're a lifesaver," trilled the other woman.

"Ariel didn't really eat any lunch," said Sunny, then realized she was speaking to a dial tone.

Because it took half an hour to get to the Kindle School, it was already time to pack up Linc's swimming stuff and head out. En route, Ruth kicked the back of her seat nonstop, but it seemed silly to mention it when she and Ariel were having such a good time together. At the school, Linc proudly handed Sunny a bloody paper towel, the stiff accordioned kind dispensed from metal holders. Inside was a tooth. "How *wonderful*," cried Sunny, but she had forgotten his swimming goggles, so they had to go home to get them before going to the Y.

A message: "One seventy-nine." Far less than they'd paid. Well, there was no point in making Linc late for his swimming lesson, so off they went. But instead of stopping at the grocery store nearby, Sunny drove back home to make her call.

Waiting for her was another message, from a woman representing the magician Sunny had called a month or so ago to inquire about birthday party rates. There had been a cancellation, and was she still interested?

"We want chocolate milk," said Ruth.

Sunny tried to call Leon's office as she poured out two inches of milk for each girl.

"That's not enough," said Ruth.

Sunny remembered the spill that morning. "That's all there is," she said. And into the handset, as she wondered why Leon wasn't answering the phone: "Hi, honey, it's me. I know it looks bad, but everything will be fine, I'm sure of it."

"I can't drink that," said Ruth.

"That's not logical," said Sunny. "You can always drink less than you can. You just can't drink more than you can."

Ruth was unmoved. "It's too little."

"It's too little," echoed Ariel.

"All right, then, let's go to the store."

"No," said Ruth.

"How are we going to get more milk if we don't go to the store?"

"Get a cow!" cried Ruth, delighted with herself. "Get a cow!" An incredibly smart girl.

When Sunny tried to return the spurned milk to the bottle, most of it ended up on the counter where she'd spilled the rest that morning. She'd always planned on replacing these cabinets. Now she wouldn't have to. She checked her watch. Linc had to be picked up in twenty minutes. Could she do half of her grocery shopping before and half after?

Because of various tragedies (a misplaced tooth, an injured spirit) Sunny was still bringing in groceries (just milk and dinner, purchased in a record eighteen minutes) when Ariel's mother showed up.

"They had a great time," Sunny reported. "But Ariel didn't eat anything."

The woman's smile brightened. "All she ever has for lunch is frozen mac and cheese. I was wondering what she'd do if you tried to feed her something else."

Oh. Sunny contemplated the bags on the broken-tiled floor of the kitchen. For the sake of the environment, she used plastic bags, which she then recycled as garbage bags, but that made the transporting itself less than ideal. The bags had no shape, and boxes and cans and bottles tumbled awkwardly every which way inside, straining at the inadequate plastic, which thinned to transparent crescents here and there.

Leon strode in. His eyes were lost in black sockets; his skin was gray and unhealthy-looking, as pitted as old cement. His hair was lying flat on his head; his blue shirt was wrinkled; and he was running to fat. He said not a word to Ariel's mother. Nor did he speak as he sat in front of the computer screen. He was still silent as he grabbed first his quart of beer and then his twelve-ouncer. He did not play "Drop Me Off in Harlem."

"What's wrong with Daddy?" asked Linc at dinner.

"Nothing," said Sunny. "He's thinking. And Ruth, would you please take your vitamin."

Leon didn't read aloud before bedtime. He paced up and down as he filled the dishwasher. He turned on the television and plodded methodically through the channels, stopping when they started to repeat. He was still staring at the ceiling when Sunny fell asleep. In the early dawn something woke her; she was sure it was external rather than internal, but maybe it was just the intensity of Leon's glare at the ceiling.

"Honey?" she said.

Leon began to speak. He talked straight for an hour. They had to sell the house immediately, no matter what the offer, because they couldn't count on keeping it if all his real estate corporations were forced into bankruptcy. Strictly speaking, it was the co-op that was still collateral on the most troubled of the outstanding loans. By the time they'd sold it, he'd already been at odds with the various banks involved, and he'd been in no mood to change any terms voluntarily. So they might be able to fight foreclosure on the house. But it was a risk. It would be better if they put what money they could salvage into a smaller place in Sunny's name.

The room was illuminated enough by the promise of the sun so that Sunny could make out a few light-glazed surfaces among the dark shapes as he spoke. The columns supporting the mirror above the dresser, the scroll top of the cabinet, the bookcase she'd painted and polyurethaned with Linc. The comforter was warm and familiar, as was Leon, who talked on and on beside her. Soon the radiator started up in anticipation of the morning, snuffling and snorting and stinking happily of burning dust. A first few lonely cars passed by out on the road. A whole palette of grays emerged. And Linc burst through the door, tearful, holding out his palm, wailing, "The Tooth Fairy *forgot to come.*"

chapter 17

JEAN AND GEOFFREY WERE GOING TO A DINNER PARTY AT
Matt Crough's house in Riverdale. Crough had called Jean down to
his office as if he had another assignment for her, but instead, out
from behind his slight rich-boy stammer emerged this invitation—
a first. She had been to a few vague quasi-social gatherings there, and
as far as she knew, no one else at the firm had been to anything more
intimate. Although Jean did not admit to Geoffrey how truly
thrilled she was, she did tell him—in what she considered a formidable concession—"I bet it's because of you. Because I'm married, I
mean. I've become proper dinner party material." Who knew? It
could be only the first of many such meals. At Christmas parties, she
had met Crough's wife, Beth, a buxom brunette with a resolutely social manner punctuated by an odd giggle. Not a bad sort at all.

"Well, we've been married for a while," Geoffrey pointed out,
then added, "But I'm glad I can be of use to you."

"Yes, it's about time," said Jean.

Oneika, fortunately, seemed to have no social life herself (somewhat like her employers, Jean could now think generously) and so
was available to stay as late as necessary that night. Jean arranged
to send her back to Queens afterward through the Crough & Co.
car service.

Jean's embarrassment over the home visit was still keen, although it was fading. Amanda Pennington said that she had rarely seen such a positive report. "'Despite a surface flippancy, Crossley exhibits a deep attachment to her niece'" was the part she quoted. Everyone liked to think he was reading between the lines. Anything a sucker discovers on his own will be fervently believed. Phalen, put off by Jean's jokes, had responded to her tears. Typical emotional nonsense: Weakness, not strength, was rewarded. If only this had been the result of scheming on Jean's part, she would have been crowing. As it was, the incapacity revealed had been all too real, at least for the moment. Besides, what was the woman going to do—cut off her source of income by giving one of Pennington's clients a bad report?

Geoffrey drove to Riverdale. He was as good a driver as Jean was bad—steady, unflappable—and his car was a late model Buick, as silent as a raft on a lake. A brief spat sprang up over who exactly had directed them down a wayward side street, but it didn't amount to much; Geoffrey spoke little when he succumbed to the hum of his car. When Jean finally spotted the right street, she put her hand on his thigh and, in an excess of high spirits, said, "Thank you, thank you."

The house was a good-size Tudor (two and a half stories high, seven windows wide) on a narrow but surprisingly busy street. It reminded Jean of a sepia-tinted photograph. The large, immaculate lawn was winter brown. The decorative timber framing the house was the same dark liverish color as the tall wooden fence enclosing the side and back yards. The wood posts used to construct the raised beds in front of the fence were grayish tan, and the budless bushes scattered among them were an even lighter dusty beige. Even the evergreens looked as if something may have gone awry in the color process.

It was Beth Crough who opened the door. "I'm so glad you could come," she said with her giggle.

Her husband was right behind her. As he took coats in a hospitable fashion, Beth slid a pointed tongue out between her lips just long enough to reveal a white bump on the tip—a canker sore?

Jean looked for Geoffrey, but his attention was elsewhere.

"Valium," said Beth in a confidential tone. "I let one dissolve under my tongue all night."

A faint frisson passed through Jean—repulsion mixed with an overwhelming warmth. She couldn't believe that Beth was being so open with her. Maybe it was because of something complimentary Crough had said about her.

"I'd love a beer in pill form. It would come in handy during certain meetings with clients," said Jean.

"We're expecting one of your clients tonight. Gilbert Blakely?"

And why hadn't Crough mentioned this? "Ah, Gil Blakely," said Jean. "He knows my father-in-law."

"Really," said Beth brightly.

"He sent us an ice bucket as a wedding present," said Jean.

"Oh, yes, we were at your wedding. Very nice. A most interesting place for a reception, if I remember correctly."

"Yes," said Jean.

"Young people are so imaginative these days," she said.

The reception had been at a hall often used for that purpose, but Jean nodded. Perhaps Beth was referring to the address, which had been over by the Hudson River. They beamed at each other.

"I was considered quite artistic when I was younger," Beth confided with that giggle of hers.

"I can tell," said Jean, "from your house."

"Let me show you around." But this turned out to mean nothing more than a sanctioned glimpse of the elaborately set table in the dining room, an unsanctioned glimpse of uniformed young people bustling about in the kitchen, and a settling in the cavernous living room, where Crough served them drinks from a tray behind the couch.

Crough talked to Geoffrey about Scotch, a safe subject for both of them. Geoffrey looked annoyingly awkward in his old sports coat. Jean had learned not to mention his clothes, which, after all, could be worse. She hoped others would credit his wardrobe to upper-middle-class indifference, which was at least partly true. The two crumpled jackets he wore all the time were Harris Tweeds, purchased in London the summer after he'd graduated from Vanderbilt. With these items of clothing, he had dismissed the whole wardrobe question. He simply didn't think about it, the way he didn't think about his parents.

Funny how Geoffrey's family connection to the other (more important) guest must have been responsible for this invitation. He hadn't wanted to invite Blakely to their wedding at first, but Jean had persuaded him that the alternative would be too much of an insult. Already she knew Geoffrey would be susceptible to this argument. He seemed uncommonly used to gritting his teeth and bearing whatever came his way—though none of his hardships seemed like much to Jean, who found it difficult to take any problem but poverty seriously. Plus both of his parents were living, as was his sister.

When Blakely arrived with his wife, he advanced immediately upon Jean. "Ms. Crossley," he said. "My favorite recruiter. Just the person I wanted to see." He had clearly known that she would be at the dinner, even if the converse had not been true. Jean purposefully did not look over at Geoffrey for his reaction. He would not be happy that Blakely was there, but he would be civil. He was always civil. It was his most effective weapon.

Blakely kept his eyes on Jean. "So you caught him, after all."

"He was running backward," said Jean. "And he fell into my arms."

Blakely chuckled. "I was the reason they met," he said to his wife. "I should get a marriage broker's fee."

The wife, a pale, square-headed woman, didn't react. This time Jean inadvertently glanced at Geoffrey, who was looking grim. She realized now that it wasn't just Geoffrey who was dressed wrong. Beth and Blakely's wife, Patsy, both were wearing dresses. Not evening gowns, but still remarkably smart-looking cocktail party–type dresses. The sort of thing Sunny might have once found secondhand. Not at all like the suit Jean was wearing, which suddenly seemed stiff and déclassé. Well, Jean was sorry, but she worked, and she was proud of it. On-the-job clothes were going to have to be acceptable garb.

"Did you drive here?" Jean asked Patsy.

Patsy looked at her as if she might not answer, but the tone of her response, when it came, was perfectly friendly. "Gil did," she said.

"Oh, yes, of course," said Jean.

The truth was, she was more comfortable with the men, and she was relieved when Blakely returned his ferocious attention to her. "What do you think of the merger?" he asked. HealthQuest's tender offer had recently been approved by the SEC. "It may be that we can fatten up certain employment contracts. We can't let investors be the only ones who profit."

"What a great idea," said Jean, hiding her real enthusiasm behind an ironic version of it.

"I'll bet you think it is," said Blakely.

"Sometimes we do get some happy news," said Crough, beaming on them both as if Jean were his daughter and Blakely the favored suitor.

"Shall we eat?" asked Beth.

Jean was seated between Crough and Blakely—or, as she would have to remember, "Matt" and "Gil"—but she dutifully addressed her first words to her hostess. "What a delicious salad," she said.

"Oh, really," said Beth with her giggle.

Maybe you weren't supposed to compliment catered food.

Patsy asked after the Crough children—Jean couldn't believe she had forgotten to do so—and both Beth and Matt, especially Matt, nattered on about them for a while.

"They are very nice kids," said Patsy to Jean. "And I should know, because I am not a nice person myself."

The simple truth, Jean was sure.

"Do you have any children?" Beth asked Jean as the uniformed young people substituted plates bearing slabs of chicken for empty salad plates.

"I'm adopting my niece," said Jean.

"Oh, that's right," said Beth, glancing over at Gil.

"She is a very nice baby," said Geoffrey, speaking to the party at large for the first time. "And I should know, because I *am* a nice person."

No one paid any attention to him that Jean could see. She smiled at him, hard, then set about appeasing the wife.

"Do you live around here?" she asked Patsy.

Beth giggled again.

"I'm not very good at distances," said Patsy.

"They have a really incredible place," said Beth. "Nothing like this one."

Gil rose, putting his napkin down right on the remains of food on his plate. "You will understand if I take Jean into the next room to discuss a little family business," he said.

Lots of giggles. Suddenly everyone was in a good mood.

"I promise it won't take long," said Gil.

"I will time you!" cried Beth.

"Well, well," said Jean. "Duty calls. Can I take my wine?"

The living room seemed darker. Maybe a lightbulb had burned out. Certainly the souvenir lobsterman with the miniature trap hadn't been throwing those shadows on the mantelpiece before. Gil mistook the object of her gaze. "You like the painting?" he asked of an arrangement of green and blue squares above the lobsterman.

When in doubt, praise. "Oh, yes," said Jean, her voice still pitched for the liveliness of the dinner table.

"You ought to. It's worth three million dollars." With his open palm Blakely indicated an unusually tall gold-brocade wing chair on the far side of the couch, then pulled its twin closer to it.

"Then it's even more beautiful than I'd imagined," said Jean gaily.

"Yes, it's not always easy to gauge value," said Blakely.

"How true," said Jean.

"But that's what I want to talk to you about. That, and bloodsuckers."

"Bloodsuckers?" echoed Jean, realizing for the first time that maybe she should shut up.

"Malpractice lawyers, I mean," said Blakely.

HealthQuest must have acquired Bridget's hospital in its merger.

chapter 18

L<small>EON AND SUNNY WERE IN THE OFFICE FOR THE LAST TIME</small>, packing up. Gloria's desk, Luisa's, Brianna's—they were all empty now. St. Vincent de Paul was coming to get them and the chairs later on this morning. The rest of the furniture was going to be hauled up to Rockland County in the van and rental truck parked out front. Right now Leon was going through his files, and Sunny was packing up whatever he handed on to her. An article in the *Amsterdam News* that morning had quoted a tenant activist attacking Leon as a "typical speculator." "In the end, what do the residents have?" she'd said. "Higher rents and an interruption in service." Gloria had called from the Columbia Library, where she'd recently started working full-time, to tell Leon it was nonsense, but Sunny would have preferred that he hadn't heard about it at all.

Leon talked little as he shoved file folders into piles. Sunny spoke more because she had to ask about what to do with old copies of *Inside Real Estate* and whether she should count the petty cash. A few times she looked over, about to speak, and saw him reading a paper with an expression that kept her mouth closed. It was an expression of suffering, yes—also one of wonder. Leon was giving up a whole world he had created. Sunny was sacrificing something, too, but in a more secondhand manner.

Leon did most of his packing in a straightforward and busi-nesslike way, however. There was a lot to do. A few tenants stopped to say good-bye, but most of the pedestrian traffic on the sidewalk was sheer rubbernecking. People would peek through the windows, craning their necks this way or that to see better. Leon seemed to be oblivious. Everyone outside was wearing black.

The phone rang. Sunny picked it up. After a moment, she said, "You want your money? But you have the whole building! Don't you realize that?"

Leon laughed. "Even when you're being mean, you sound so nice."

Sunny laughed, too, gratefully. "Where's Luisa?" she said.

"I haven't seen her."

"I at least want to say good-bye."

Leon nodded absently. "She's probably looking for work. Another of her clients, the dry cleaner, closed down last month."

Sunny shook her head.

It was fortunate they were busy. Also that they both, instinc-tively, had dressed well, not fancily, but in fairly new, clean, well-fitting casual clothes, despite all the dust they would be fanning up today. Leon snagged his rugby shirt on a dolly, but the rip was tiny.

The phone rang again. This time it was Jean. "Leon's partner has filed a petition seeking to adopt Jade. What do you know about this?" She had a contemptuous, ferreting-out tone in her voice. It would be infuriating if it weren't so irrelevant.

"Jean," said Sunny.

"Well?"

"He is about to withdraw it. He probably already has. It was just a way to pressure Leon over the business."

"You mean he's not the father?"

"No, I think that part's true."

"Did you know that Leon was paying Bridget off every month?"

"Paying her off? What do you mean? Are you talking about the checks we gave her?" What a jerk.

There was a pause.

"Why did you give her all that money?" asked Jean warily.

"Because she needed it," said Sunny.

Jean's voice when it came was a comic drawing out of the syllable: "Oh-h-h-h-h-h."

Sunny knew that Jean would be impressed. Jean took money very seriously. It didn't matter that she had plenty of it. She couldn't help dropping that exaggerated but nonetheless sincere "Oh" into the conversation. The note struck was ancient and resounding, no matter how many layers of irony it sported.

Sunny's part in the conversation was false, but she enjoyed the small, spurious moral victory. Yes, they'd given Bridget money and would again, if only they could. But that, too, was irrelevant. Sunny informed Jean only to make her feel bad, which she was sure it did. Jean, she was beginning to see, was the most severe when feeling the guiltiest.

The information Sunny withheld during this conversation—making it all a lie, and so what—was that she had to get a job. She'd been hoping she could wait until after the adoption hearing, but the possibility looked less and less likely. And once she was employed full-time, she would lose her chance at Jade.

The Dane financial situation was dire. Leon, in the midst of declaring bankruptcy, was still wrangling with his creditors. He didn't have much time to look around for contracting jobs right now. Besides which, lawyers had moved in (not Henry, thank God), and financial arrangements with the banks had not yet been worked out. Leon's wages might be garnisheed.

It was Sunny who had first brought the suggestion of her employment into the open air, but Leon had accepted it so matter-of-factly that she figured it must have been around for a while, waiting like water vapor to turn to rain. She even pretty much knew what she would do, although that plan she had yet to pass on to Leon. She would go down to Skyline Realty and talk to Nita. Presumably it took some time to obtain a real estate license, but Sunny had no doubt that once she started she would be as successful as Nita and that she too would be able to send her daughter to "Vassar College." She had put off calling only because there had been so much to do to dismantle the business.

Instead of stopping to get a sandwich, Leon and Sunny decided they were almost done and kept drinking some warm Diet Coke that had been left in the bathroom. They said, "We're just about there," several times that afternoon, and each time they were, indeed, closer to being finished, but odds and ends kept popping up. The supplies in the basement had been dealt with, but should they leave the old pipes on the street? How about the empty plaster buckets?

And Sunny had to sit out by the truck to keep the contents from disappearing. In this neighborhood you couldn't put your trash out in a trash bag without the bag getting stolen. "Why bih, why bih," muttered the drug dealer from the first floor next door, as if she cared what talking scum like him thought.

Leon did not usually stay past 4:00, but it was considerably past that now. Twilight was starting to gather, and Sunny was getting worried about the baby-sitter, a high school girl who had to get home early to study for a test. Sunny decided to go ahead in the van. Leon would follow as soon as he could.

The van drove as if it were made of concrete. It always took a while to come to life; now that it was laden down, Sunny felt she was dragging it forward at every stop sign. Which might be why she was still going slowly enough over on 112th to recognize Luisa and Alba on a stoop. Sunny honked a little from her balky vehicle, but Luisa was sitting with her ear against the black iron railing and so didn't hear her. On impulse, Sunny pulled the van over—it was happier parked, anyway—and hopped out.

"Luisa!" she cried. "Alba!"

Luisa looked awful, not exactly blue or gray or purple, but some very pale suggestion of all three.

"Are you all right?"

"She didn't have any money for medicine," said Alba.

"My God!" Was she having a heart attack?

"I'm fine," gasped Luisa. She moved one foot in a ruined black loafer, then went still. "I'm fine."

"Can you get to the van?" asked Sunny, trying to fit her hands under Luisa's arms. There ought to be room, if she moved the bag of recyclables to the back. She didn't know where Luisa was going to put her feet, though. "Do you think you can stand up?"

"Yes," said Luisa, lifting her head with effort. "The feeling . . . I am sorry . . . This is not the first time. It goes away when I have my medicine again. My head . . . If you make me a loan . . ."

Luisa had *counted* on the income from Leon's real estate business.

"I'm going to get you to the clinic," said Sunny, hoping against hope they would take American Express. *Why hadn't she ever gone out with a doctor?*

"Keep your elbows at your sides." Sunny, who was stronger than she looked, helped Luisa rise, using her upper arms for leverage. "Alba, can you open the door, honey?"

chapter 19

At 10:15 on Sunday morning the pews in St. Catherine's are dotted with a few patient, lonely parishioners, heads bowed in the sunlight streaming through the immense glass windows. They are waiting for the third mass of the day. At 10:25 comes the surge: topcoats, some caps, a few pairs of jeans. By 10:30 the pews are full, the organ starts up, and everyone stands. At 10:33 the priest, the lay readers, and the choir are three-quarters of the way down the aisle. At 10:35 two laymen in sports jackets and white turtleneck shirts try to shoehorn latecomers into the seats. Today there were so many stragglers that some had to look for spots in the crowd themselves. Jean saw one woman, rebuffed on her original attempt, rebound twice in a jagged Z down the aisle. But then a quick kneel, like an opening of scissors, and the row of openmouthed singing parishioners closed in around her.

Jean had learned about the early birds recently because she had started to drop Jade off with the baby-sitters from the CYO as soon as they were available. Before the advent of the baby, Jean had never arrived before 10:28, riding the crest into the pews.

The 10:30 was the most pleasant of the four Sunday masses, because it was the one with the choir, but there was nothing leisurely about the service. Because Catholics have to attend mass every week, they value efficiency above all. The challenge is to speed up the ceremony without letting a fast walk break into a run. Jean expected to be back out on the sidewalk by 11:30 at the latest.

The organ sounded as if two accompanists were wrestling each other for the keyboard—or maybe the organ was wrestling with itself. This was usual. Organ music steps eventually from note to note, but within this limit it has the chaotic shape of a burlap bag with two cats fighting inside. Oh, no, the suit Jean was wearing was the same powder blue as the choir robes today. She felt like a woman who'd wandered into a wedding wearing white. The greeting: done. The confiteor: done.

As the mass raced on, Jean's thoughts went round and round. The vile Blakely had said, "Naturally you have a responsibility to your niece. I understand. That's why God invented settlements." His very words. Copying Jean's manner, of course. They all did sooner or later. "HealthQuest would think highly of anyone who made sure an offer was accepted quickly. That would show real decisiveness. I could sit right down and give Crough and Company an ironclad contract for the next five years, a contract that would name only one individual specifically: Jean Crossley. It's been done before, and it can be done again." Like she even believed him. It was too much of an offer, too soon.

Lord have mercy on us. Christ have mercy on us. Blakely's face had been so close to hers that she could see little bumps on his cheeks. Maybe shaving abrasions. She couldn't get her eyes off them. She was afraid they were going to make her sick.

The "Gloria" was sung by a relatively young woman—young, that is, in comparison with the rest of the congregation. The choir, which was lined up to the left of the sacristy, looked presentable. The right-to-life bouffants, the Mafia-inspired jewelry, the IRA-set jaws, the leprechaunlike red beards—none of that was found among the singers.

"In the long run it could mean a lot more money for the baby." Doubtful. Even if Jean didn't mind getting pushed around (which she did, and maybe she should stop the thought right there), Blakely would never take her seriously again if she let him do it.

The epistle was about running a race. Good. But the gospel was one she hated. She recognized it as soon as the ruddy-cheeked priest, heavy with vestments, began to read. Early one morning a householder hires some laborers to work in his vineyard, promising them a certain sum of money for the day's work. Throughout the day he hires more laborers, promising them all the same amount of money, no matter what time they started. When the pay is distributed, the laborers who worked all day object to the arrangement. Their objections, however, are ill considered, according to the householder, i.e., God. But why shouldn't the harder workers complain? As a child, Jean had been enraged by the unfairness of the story. Now at least she could see one good side to it: You got credit for Sunday mass whether it lasted fifty-two minutes or stretched out into an interminable seventy-eight, for a chatty visiting priest who talked in circles about birth control as if anyone were listening to him anyway.

Jean would never drop the lawsuit. They *owed* Jade that money. They owed her fine down pillows to rest her head on and clothes with securely finished seams and a leather grip whose handle never, ever broke, no matter how many years you used it. They owed her all the comfort that the Crossley girls had never had growing up.

The priest stepped forward to the rail to give the sermon, which he did with his hands raised to keep him from going on too long. His voice was medium range and carried well. He strung his sentences together as if they were sections of a fence. You could hear every pause separating period and capital letter, but all the words in between remained completely level. They were not held together by any meaning that Jean could discern.

Odd that Blakely would have even noticed an individual lawsuit. Here was a man who could not pass up an opportunity for petty tyranny.

A woman in the pew in front of her looked at her watch for a second time. The mass must be running a few minutes late. Several years ago, the church had started running an admonition in the program: "Kindly respect our custom of standing in place and singing the complete Recessional Hymn."

Jean had been *great* with Blakely. Given the circumstances. "Nothing like a little business to spice up a social event," she'd said. And she'd made all sorts of small talk as she and Geoffrey were leaving. She noticed that the Blakelys made no move to go as well, damn that Crough, who must have known all about Blakely's threat when he provided such a perfect vessel for it. Jean didn't think he'd gone so far as to tip Blakely off about the lawsuit, but he must have at least confirmed its existence—without informing Jean.

Geoffrey had said, out in the Buick, "Did Blakely come on to you or something? You don't look so hot." But Jean had straightened him out fast enough, letting him know that she could take a lot more than anything Blakely could conjure up and that Beth had said it was "very nice" to see her.

I believe in one God, the Father Almighty, creator of heaven and earth. . . . The man to the right of her had to look up the words. When was the last time *you* went to church? Jean wondered. Sunny had asked her once if she believed in God. As if anyone except a kid thought about stuff like that. It was like worrying whether the earth was really a giant's eyeball or whatever. Better to get over it young, so you wouldn't end up in a mental institution.

The laymen in turtlenecks swept their long-handled baskets up the aisles posthaste. If you weren't fast with your check, you could rot in hell.

The one thing Jean was not going to do was give up her career so that she could pursue some ephemeral advantage for Jade. She would not even give up her business relationship with that asshole Blakely. It brought in too much money. Movies were full of ardent souls who threw away health, wealth, or reputation for their families. Imagine how those households ended up—pinched and bitter. Or dead. The Blakelys of the world were always there to take advantage of such high-flown nonsense. Jean's ear caught the word *sacrifice* in the priest's singsong. How had she never noticed that word repeated over and over at this point in the mass? Very unpoetical. Downright redundant. *Sacrifice . . . sacrifice . . . sacrifice . . .* Well, forget it. She wouldn't do it.

chapter 20

Sunny stood in front of a window that was twice as high as she was and three times as long. Impossibly huge, too close to be real, the Brooklyn Bridge rose from behind her and sheered off toward Manhattan. In the foreground were two gargantuan bridge legs breaking up the deserted riverfront, some buildings of crumbling stone and crooked wood, a boat nuzzling the shore. Then an unfolding of river, a sweep of sky, and in the distance, at the end of the bridge: Manhattan, frosty, regal, skyscrapers crowded smack up to the water like penguins at the edge of an iceberg. Imagine living with a view like that, she thought. Imagine thinking that you could see up close and far away at the same time.

Jade, in her arms, was pointing with her little baby hand, knuckles indented, index finger splayed. They were at the housewarming for Paul and Clare's new loft in Brooklyn.

The Danes had had very good luck with traffic on the Saw Mill that morning, so Sunny suggested they stop off at Jean's before the housewarming. A grumpy Geoffrey directed her to St. Catherine's, which Sunny planned to check out for a second to see how much of the mass was left. Instead a shadowy curved stairway in the vestibule beckoned her down, and there in the red linoleum-floored basement were a number of babies, including Jade.

"Time to go," Sunny said, lifting her up. Sunny's heart turned over as she realized how familiar Jade was—her weight, the texture of her corduroy pants, her damp face. She drew her head down over the little body. Her heart was rolling faster and faster now. She prayed it was not visible on the outside.

A teenager wearing a navy blue spaghetti-strapped tank top cried, "Wait!"

Sunny stopped.

"You forgot your baby bag," said the girl. (Spaghetti straps in church? In February?)

"Oh, look," said Leon when he spotted Jade. He was turned in the driver's seat of the van, one arm draped over the steering wheel, the other draped over the top of the passenger's seat. He was shaped like a huge, welcoming embrace.

At the other end of the long, light-filled, L-shaped room in Paul's loft was a spread of lox and bagels, freshly squeezed orange juice, and champagne. Among these provisions murmured well-dressed guests: men and women she'd gone to college with, gotten drunk with, crashed parties with, discussed love with, made love with (where was Dennis, by the way?), argued about justice with, spent money with, taken subways and cabs and planes with— even a limousine once, across town. And here she was now, out of kilter, a criminal, she supposed. Jade was growing heavier in her arms, but Sunny didn't want to move. She had managed to slip in without speaking to anyone, thank God, and she wanted to keep it that way. All her old friends seemed very far away.

No one had looked right since Sunny had brought Luisa to the clinic. Luisa was going to be okay, but Sunny could not forget the color her face had turned. She could not forget how she and Leon had let Luisa down.

The people in the room whom Sunny did not know she found even more disquieting than those she did. She assumed they were all bankers who had redlined her family out of existence. Look at the way Paul was laughing with them, his rubbery mouth splitting open like one of those old plastic coin purses with a slit down the middle. She had to find a telephone.

A locked door. Since when had Paul started locking the doors in his house?

There: on the nearly empty night-table top in the bedroom. The phone was hard to miss. A foot wide, it resembled a light board. At the last minute Sunny had told the girl with the spaghetti straps to pass on the message "Jade is with Sunny," but that didn't mean it had gotten through. Her heart raced as she pushed buttons, shifting Jade slightly. At the sound of Jean's voice on the answering machine, relief turned Sunny's bones soft. She leaned forward and breathed in the fresh baby smell of lotions and powder and shampoo. Jean—or her nanny—must have been taking pretty good care of her. But certainly a normal child wouldn't be clinging to her like this. Sunny was able to leave all of her message before Geoffrey picked up, saying, "Sunny? Sunny?" She couldn't tell whether he knew yet or not. She had not said where she was. All she'd said was that Jade was fine. Which she was. Sunny wondered whether the police would be waiting for her back in Rockland County. Was Jade clinging to her, or was she clinging to Jade?

Linc and Ruth peeked into the room as she hung up. They could find her anywhere. A quick grimace convulsed her features; for a moment she thought she would cry, but she didn't. Linc and Ruth asked if they could have some soda, since it was a special occasion.

"A special occasion?" Sunny echoed.

They nodded hopefully. "Baby Jade is here," said Ruth.

"Of course," said Sunny. "It's a very special occasion."

She carried Jade back out to the view. Strange that Sunny should think of something so expansive as good cover. Being mesmerized by it—so mesmerized that she preferred it to chatting with old friends—would not be looked upon as suspicious, she hoped.

Linc and Ruth, as the oldest children in evidence, were hogging the huge apricot-colored couch in the center of the long room, their limbs spread like starfish. A few other offspring were scattered here and there among the partygoers, but they were closer to Jade's age. No one had had kids as early as Sunny. Glancing into the crowd had been a mistake, because Sunny's eyes snagged on Clare's as they traveled back to the view. Next thing she knew, Clare was approaching. Small face, sharp collarbones, delicate wrinkle on her brow. Sunny knew why she didn't get a job, but why didn't Clare? "Bridget was such a sincere person," said Clare in a low voice. Then she indicated Jade with her chin and slowly closed her eyes—which made Sunny's heart leap to her throat, until she realized this was universal language for "The baby in your arms has gone to sleep."

"Here they are," said Paul. "My two favorite girls." Where had he come from? He gave both Sunny and Clare large smacking kisses.

And now Henry Clark! "Has Jean come to her senses?" he asked in his soft, gray-flecked voice. Henry would be more shocked than anyone at what Sunny had done. He was so particular about the law. He had been offended by the air traffic controllers' strike in an annoyingly fastidious way. With this one stroke she had declared herself irrevocably different from every normal, law-abiding citizen.

"I have to get a job," Sunny blurted out.

Henry drew his face down in concern, put his hand on her shoulder, and looked around before speaking. Fortunately, Paul and Clare were greeting a newcomer. "That doesn't mean we give up," he said. "We just change our strategy."

Sunny nodded silently, believing none of it. Jade stirred but slept on.

"Really, Sunny, I don't want you to lose hope," he said. He was one of the few men in a suit. Most were wearing clothes that obliquely suggested a hike or a climb. Henry looked like a doctor. He had good hands. Through her sweater Sunny could feel the soothing warmth of his touch next to the fierce damp heat of Jade's face. He continued to talk in such an encouraging way that Sunny thought her brain would crack right there on the spot. And Jade had gotten so heavy.

When Sunny could stand it no longer, Leon appeared and exchanged a glass of champagne for the baby. He began to talk about the corners in Paul and Clare's loft. "You never see perpendicular lines like this anymore," he said. "Old buildings have had too many years of painting, chipping, and painting again. Even in the best restoration jobs, when all the old paint is stripped away, the wood itself will have soft and blurry edges. Beautiful ones. Walls never settle at exact ninety-degree angles. My renovations were mainly Sheetrock, and when they were new, none of the lines were as crisp as they could have been. You've got to use what you have. Work this precise is very unusual nowadays."

Eventually Henry moved on. When he did, Leon said, "I'm sorry, Sunny. Sorry for everything. I know I've let you down. You deserve better than the roller-coaster ride you've been subjected to lately."

Sunny would have jumped in at this point, but he went on in his slow, unruffled, and now apologetic way, "Does Jean know where Jade is?"

Sunny clutched the baby tighter to her breast.

"I think it's time to bring her back," said Leon.

chapter 21

Stone staircases bracketed the huge empty vault that constituted the Surrogate Court Building. Jean recognized Henry Clark as his face came into view above the stone slabs. He looked . . . game. Behind him were Sunny and Leon, who were getting the unhealthy pallor of poor relations. No kids. Jean wondered how Sunny had been pried away from them. Jade was in Jean's arms.

For one horrible and illogical moment, when Jean had first realized Jade was gone from the church basement that Sunday, she'd thought Blakely had snatched her. No reason he would. He figured he had Jean where he wanted her, anyway. But in the next moment the teenage baby-sitter had said, "Jade is with Sunny," and fortunately Jean had had the presence of mind to say, "I want you to remember this, because you may have to swear out an affidavit. This is no better than kidnapping." And from a church. Hard to imagine a scenario that looked worse.

"Jean," said Henry, nodding.

"That the girl who took Jade?" hissed Oneika.

Jean's nod answered Oneika and greeted Henry at the same time.

Sunny had showed up at the apartment with Jade a couple of

hours later. While Jean was waiting, she'd said several times that she was going to call the police, but she'd let Geoffrey dissuade her. She had *wanted* him to dissuade her. This was a new use for a husband. If you wanted to employ a creaky old Freudian analogy—which, after all, had yet to be replaced by anything more compelling—she and Geoffrey temporarily played different parts of herself: Jean, the ego, and Geoffrey, the superego. Then they smoothly divided back into the separate people they were supposed to be.

Jean had met Sunny in the lobby instead of letting her up. "Don't let her out of your sight," she'd said to the doorman. A small act of revenge. Sunny had been crying. Her face was blotchy, and her eyelashes were wet. Her voice was still a little shaky when she said good-bye to Jade. It must be hard to discover you're not a whole lot better than anyone else.

Amanda Pennington pushed forward. "I don't believe we've met," she said to Henry. And when she introduced herself, she made it clear that he had to be familiar with her work if he knew anything at all. Then she herded her side into the courtroom, pretending to hold a conversation with Jade over Jean's shoulder.

The two parties sat on opposite sides of the huge open room. The letters of "IN GOD WE TRUST" on the signboard behind the bench had been rearranged to read "IN GOD WET RUST." Mr. Crossley was not there. Jean had called him after Sunny snatched Jade. Jean! Who had never tattled in her life. But he'd said, in a voice so low she could barely hear, "I thought you didn't want me to get involved." So much for him.

When a room was as big as this one, it was hard to maintain your bearings. Were those windows two stories high? Three?

Leon came over to talk, leaving Sunny all by herself, but no exchange of any interest took place, except he spoke in the hopefully conciliatory way you might to your executioner—and he soon rejoined his wife. "See you around," he said when he left them. *See you around?* Why was it that everyone in this world except her was completely stark, raving mad?

The proceedings took place in a small room off to one side, the judge's chambers, which was similar in feel to the little curtained spot where the Wizard of Oz hid. Oneika, not being a party to the suit, had to wait out in the open courtroom. Jean had decided she could not risk telling her what she was about to do, and she felt bad about it. Although not too bad, because she was only going to do what was necessary.

The judge sat at a huge mahogany desk. She had lines between her eyebrows and at the ends of her mouth. Her first name was Lily. Hard to imagine a little girl named Lily wanting to grow up to be a judge. Jean was a much better name for a person with any kind of authority.

The judge addressed Henry first. "I received your amended affidavit just yesterday. I understand your client is now seeking employment?"

"Yes, Your Honor."

"Then I assume your position about working mothers has undergone a change. Am I right?"

She was addressing Sunny, who continued to look blank.

"I'm speaking to you, Mrs. Dane."

"Oh, yes, Your Honor," said Sunny.

"It's all well and good that you have been able to stay at home with your children so far, but I think that the sixty-five percent of mothers who work today would be surprised to learn that their parenting is necessarily inadequate," said the judge.

See, Jean thought a little smugly. She would have won even without the kidnapping.

"I never thought that," said Sunny faintly.

"Good," said the judge. "Now, have you two sat down together and tried to work out a solution?"

It was Amanda Pennington's turn to speak. "Your Honor, my client is withdrawing her application for adoption and is seeking to have the record of that withdrawal sealed. Instead I have drafted an agreement to protect Jade Crossley's financial interests."

Gasps. Astonishment. The whole farce was almost worth it to see the look on Sunny's face. Naturally she'd thought she would lose. Leon was in the midst of bankruptcy proceedings. In any normal world Sunny wouldn't have a prayer against a person like Jean. Who was sure Jade couldn't understand what was going on.

But Jean's arms had grown weak at her lawyer's words, and she may have tightened her embrace too much. Jean clenched, and Jade cried out.

"You can let her down," said the judge.

Jean was seized with the fear—the totally irrational fear—that Jade would run to Sunny. But she did not. She balanced herself on Jean's thigh, then inched her way around to her knee. Jean mastered the impulse to hug her again.

Everyone was still looking at them, stunned, except Geoffrey, who was sitting without apparent concern beside her. Jean had not made the same mistake twice. She had told him about her new strategy even before her decision was firm. Not that he had been a big help, having got hold of a wild notion that she should stop speaking to Blakely. What was the victory in that? "I'm going to miss her" was what he finally said. Jean assumed that the statement contained either more or less emotion than the simple surface of his words indicated. With Geoffrey, it was hard to tell which.

Happiness broke through Sunny's initial shock and lifted her whole face. Then Leon said, "Jean." Another man of many words.

The idea had come to Jean the week before as she ate breakfast at her desk. She had been idly wondering if she could persuade Sunny to pretend to take custody of Jade. That would certainly fake Blakely out. Then she tried to think of various other ways she could make it look to Blakely as if Sunny had custody. The records of the proceedings would be sealed, so Jean could pull all sorts of monkey tricks in chambers. Finally she thought, as she bit into her bagel, Let Sunny have legal custody, to protect Jade from Blakely, but keep the baby as much as possible. Jean's heart flinched a little, but her mind opened. If a few corners were cut, the details could be worked out. She dropped the bagel to the blotter. The cream cheese tasted funny.

"My client requests that arrangements be made so that the baby can visit her on Saturday and Sunday," said Pennington.

Let Sunny worry about all that baby-sitting nonsense. This way Jean would see Jade nearly as much as she ever did. And she wouldn't be losing all financial authority, either.

"Although we know that the court demands an accounting of

all expenditures from a child's estate," Pennington continued, "we feel that in this case extra precautions should be taken. The agreement allows for my client's participation in all major financial decisions, although her role is not to be disclosed publicly."

"I'm sorry," said the judge, although she didn't sound sorry, just exasperated. "What are we referring to here? I thought the mother was essentially broke when she died."

"The child will likely receive a sizable judgment from the wrongful death suit instituted on her mother's behalf."

"She deserves every penny," Jean said loudly. Because this was the key part. Jade would be safe from Blakely now. Blakely would never know Jean hadn't fought tooth and nail for custody, and he could not expect her to influence the actions of a sister on the other side of such a bitter contest.

The judge frowned. Geoffrey took Jean's hand.

"May I see that agreement, Your Honor," said Henry. After skimming it at his seat, he added, "I'm not sure that it's in the best interests of my client to go along with this."

"Oh, Henry," said Sunny, tugging at his sleeve. "I'm sure it's okay."

"I suggest you read it before you sign," said the judge dryly.

Jean could have told the judge that it was impossible to insult Sunny that way, but at least she was trying. Not even Jean's amended affidavit was going to succeed, although she had done her best to sneak in a zinger or two.

At the end Sunny had trouble saying good-bye. The proceedings were over, and she seemed more anxious than ever. Fear was overwhelming happiness, no doubt. Maybe she was finally asking herself how she was going to take care of a baby on top of everything else. As the others stood up around her and collected papers in a professional way, she thanked them all: Jean and the judge and Geoffrey and Amanda Pennington and Jean and Henry Clark and then Jean again. And again. Finally she picked up Jade.

"I didn't do it for you," said Jean.

Sunny nodded, although she couldn't have had any idea yet what Jean meant.

"The hospital was trying to use me to get at her," said Jean. "There was tremendous pressure on me to settle."

"Oh-h-h," said Sunny in an oddly flat and rueful tone, as if she'd been blackmailed every day of her life.

"I fought you to the bitter end," said Jean archly. "Understand?"

"Okay," said Sunny.

"You I'll see the day after tomorrow," Jean said to Jade as if she were speaking to an adult. She'd told Jade earlier that she was going to get to visit Sunny a whole lot in the future. A slight exaggeration, but an excusable one.

"Thanks anyway," said Sunny. "I know how hard it must be for you."

Jean was about to argue, but she was stopped by the sight of Jade's little arm, chunky with stripes. Jean remembered it hooked around her neck. She found she couldn't speak. She had been so careful—so canny and strong—but she suspected that she'd ended up sacrificing herself anyway. It was perplexing. She just couldn't figure out where she'd gone wrong.

chapter 22

IT WAS A SATURDAY AFTERNOON IN MAY. SUNNY SAT ON A concrete retaining wall, Linc and Ruth on either side of her and Jade in her lap. Sunny's feet dangled a few inches above the sidewalk. Linc said, "If you ever find yourself trapped behind a picture window, you can take a statue that's bigger than you are, throw it at the glass, and then step through the hole."

Their new house, a small ranch untouched since the fifties, featured a "picture window" in its living room, along with other items like chrome railings and aqua paint more commonly found in retro coffee table books. Once Leon had returned most of Sergey's investment, there wasn't much money left for a place that could be put in Sunny's name. The house was similar to the Crossley childhood home, but it was smaller, and it was the happy version.

"I'll have to remember that," said Sunny.

For several days after the move, she had put off calling Nita Altman. Finally, she'd gone down to the Skyline Realty offices but had been unable to open the door. No matter how much she admired Nita, Sunny could not become a smiling guide for rich people. So instead she'd called around, and Dennis had told her about a city job helping to find homes for people who were HIV-positive. Anyone who'd never left Paw Valley could have done the work, which didn't pay much, but it suited Sunny fine for now, and she was soon able to tell Luisa about a full-time clerical position up on the fourth floor. Sunny traveled all over the city, conducting interviews in shelters and hospitals, inspecting apartment buildings, talking to landlords. Recently she had been asked to deal with the city council on the housing issue. Her boss called her "a force of nature." Leon was at first too depressed to object to her working for his old enemy, the city; lately he'd been more vocal, but also more forgiving. He was consulting on a low-income housing project in Westchester. It was not popular with its neighbors, and Sunny foresaw that he would soon get embroiled—in his low-key way—with the coming fracas.

A couple of teenage girls were waiting for the bus in the pocket parking lot the concrete wall surrounded. They kept jackknifing with excitement, stirred up by the fresh spring air. You could hear their heels clattering on the cracked asphalt. Sunny didn't mind the excuse to sit in this dusty, weedy, overlooked spot. As soon as Jean picked up Jade for the evening, Sunny had to . . . well, there was no point in thinking about all the stuff she had to do.

A slight wind ruffled a spiral tress of Jade's hair, then dropped it in her face. The silky lock was still warm to the touch when Sunny smoothed it back. Jade was enrolled in day care in the basement of a home not too far from the bus stop. It was called Pebbles, and Ruth, upon first seeing it, had complained that Jade "got everything," because it had snakes, hamsters, rabbits, lizards, and fish. Linc and Ruth were in after-care at Kindle; next year they would attend a similar program at the public school.

Folding Jade into the family had been easier than Sunny expected. Leon had always liked to show off for babies. And the kids' reactions had all been wonderful, even after their first noisy welcome had died away and they had discovered many slights and injustices in the new arrangement. "Jade gets everything" was said about more than just her day care. But jealousy was a tribute, if you thought about it. A little bit probably made Jade feel special. Now, the three children seemed to have settled into a fitful variation on sibling rivalry, Jade mostly admiring the older ones, as Sunny, long ago, used to look up to her sisters.

Jean, wearing a dark scarf and a trench coat, looked like an international spy when she stepped off the bus, though Sunny was not tempted to spoil her by telling her so. Both women were always coolly cordial when Jean picked up Jade on Saturday and returned her on Sunday. This state of affairs was probably thanks to Jean, who'd said to Linc and Ruth at their first rendezvous, "Don't you believe anything bad about your aunt Jean. I have a piece of paper that says I'm the best person who ever lived. I'll show it to you sometime."

Sunny supposed she should be grateful that Jean was so distant and calculating. If Jean could have been carried away by her emotions, she'd never have shaken her rage over Sunny's spiriting away of Jade from the church basement. Ultimately, Jean believed, like Sunny, that you could deal with people. Jean may have had very different ideas of *how* to deal with them. Her "best person in the world" claim—to children, no less!—fell short of actual communication. It bridged no gap. Its intention was deflection rather than illumination. Still, if Jean never said what she meant, you could interpret her as you wished. Whatever ugliness had been lurking behind her words these past several months was gone.

Today, as Jean approached the wall, she said, "What are you all in such a good mood for? Didn't you hear the bad news?"

"Gee," said Jade, pointing up with her little baby hand, arm extended.

"My God!" cried Sunny. "She said 'Jean'!"

At Pebbles, Jade may have uttered plenty of other sounds that could be counted as first words, but this was the only one Sunny had witnessed. Her exclamation had been spontaneous. Now, of course, she'd never hear the end of it.

"You're talking!" said Ruth, giving Jade an exaggerated strangle of a hug that looked uncomfortable for both of them.

"Watch the hammer hold, honey," said Jean, and then continued, as she took the baby from Sunny, "I guess we know now who rates a first word around here."

As if she'd have recognized it without Sunny to point it out. To keep her in line, Sunny said, "A first word always describes something essentially foreign," but Jean wasn't paying any attention.

Sunny couldn't believe how much of the kids' childhood she

was missing because of her job. And half of it was a waste of time. Easily half. While she was still at home with the kids, Paul had told her, with the offhand authority of someone who always expects things to go his way, that no one ever looked back over a long life and thought, I should have worked more.

Maybe. But when she was with her kids, she hadn't always been cuddling with them, or making them laugh, or seeing their little faces light up with wonder. Mostly she'd done the wash. Or arranged for a man to fix the oil burner. Or cleaned up after a nosebleed.

"Don't you want to know the bad news?" asked Jean, looking at her watch. The bus always waited ten minutes before turning around and heading back to the city. The teenagers had already boarded, but Jean lowered herself gingerly next to Ruth. Her feet rested flat on the sidewalk.

It turned out that the lawsuit against the hospital was going to have to be settled for far less than they'd hoped. The undetected electrical interference had probably been a factor in Bridget's death, but her herbal tincture had contained echinacea and ginkgo, which can interfere with healing and increase bleeding. The doctors claimed she hadn't informed them of her use of these supplements, which she probably hadn't. It would also have been hard to prove that the surgery was unnecessary. Although the medical establishment was coming around, many physicians still believed that the womb was superfluous once childbearing was over. In that case, it might as well be taken out at the slightest pretext. The poor had unusually high rates of hysterectomies—but so did doctors' wives. And if Bridget had had strong views on the subject, she'd kept them to herself.

It was hard for Sunny to continue to sit calmly and listen as Jean spoke with her characteristic mix of logic and sarcasm; behind it was such an absolute acceptance of authority. If only Sunny had read up on the risks before Bridget's surgery . . . If only she had listened to her describe her herbs . . . If only she had paid *more attention*. She would have researched, pestered, even interfered for Leon or the kids (three, now). Looking back, she could not bring herself to regret snatching Jade. She regretted only what she had not done.

"When in doubt, scream and shout," said Jean. "Remember that?"

Sunny did not. Maybe it was an old saying of their mother's. Sunny could never remember any of those. Fear slipped like a knife into her heart. Was Jean going to make trouble? But no, she was surprisingly unruffled, considering that she'd given Jade up rather than endanger the baby's claim on the hospital.

As if reading the question mark on Sunny's face, Jean said, "I've quit Crough and Company."

"What? You're out of work?" Had they switched places in life?

"Hardly," said Jean. "I've gone out on my own."

Imagine being able to choose your hours. Then Sunny wouldn't have to make the white-knuckle journey home from the city each evening, afraid the bus would make her late to pick up the kids, her mind skittering back and forth between which place to go first—the school or the day care center.

"I got tired of being taken advantage of," said Jean. "Also, Crough double-crossed me once, and I never forgave him." She laughed. "I stole his biggest client. A real piece of work named Gil Blakely."

No wonder Jean's mood was so cheerfully opaque. Her decision about Jade may not have paid off with respect to the lawsuit, but it had prompted such a shaking and rattling and upending of position that she'd emerged much farther up her career ladder.

Having silenced Sunny, Jean now divided her attention between the kids. "The Crossley feuds go back over a hundred years," she said. "It's an old Irish tradition. Your mother and I tried to keep it up, God knows. But no one in our generation can live up to the standards established by our forebears."

An impossible woman. Better just to let her rattle on.

"Of course, you two could always try," Jean continued. "Do you like to fight? When you know you're right?"

"Jean!" cried Sunny.

"It was just a suggestion," said Jean with an injured air.

"Your aunt is joking," said Sunny.

The children were watching them without comprehension.

Jean took Jade from Sunny's arms and briefly held her up to her face. Sunny at first thought Jean was going to kiss her, but no, it was as if Jean were trying to read the inscription on a trophy. At moments like these Sunny had to remind herself that she was the one who had triumphed in the adoption hearing. It was hard to believe. With Jade on one hip, Jean stepped up through the accordioned door of the bus. Sunny saw her stop by the driver to calculate exactly which was the best seat before heading straight for it. The bus, engine running, patiently shivered on.

THE CROSSLEY BABY

A Reader's Guide

JACQUELINE CAREY

A CONVERSATION WITH
JACQUELINE CAREY

DEIRDRE MCNAMER *is the author of the novels* Rima in the Weeds, One Sweet Quarrel, *and* My Russian, *which is a Ballantine Reader's Circle book. She lives in Missoula, Montana, where Jacqueline Carey lived for four years in the late nineties. The two have been friends for many years.*

Deirdre McNamer: I know I'm supposed to ask the questions and you're supposed to do most of the talking, but I feel I must jump in at the outset and tell readers something about our long-standing conversational arrangement.

Jacqueline Carey: Jump away.

DM: For at least a dozen years now, Jacqueline (I call her "Jay") Carey and I have spoken on the telephone for an hour or so at a set time each week. We refer to it as "meeting at the Phone Bar," although sometimes it is the Phone Cafe. Or the Juice Bar. Sometimes we've met at the Phone Bar when I've been in Montana and Jay has been living in Manhattan, Brooklyn or, most recently, Montclair. We also met there when she lived in Missoula, four blocks from my house.

JC: Because neither of our homes had a jukebox.

DM: But you always complain about the jukebox!

JC: Not as much as I do about the noisy underage clientele on my end.

DM: Still, I thought we might conduct this conversation at the Phone Bar because we're used to the place and tend to do a lot of our mutual mulling there. We'll stick to the topic at hand. Invite interested company. Ignore the distractions.

JC: Practice a certain restraint.

DM: Those sisters in *The Crossley Baby*. Let's begin with them. Because Bridget is absent from the novel, except in retrospect, we find ourselves wondering most about the differences between careerist Jean and stay-at-home Sunny. Whom do you identify with more?

JC: I know this is going to sound cowardly, but I have to say I identify with both. When I was writing from Jean's point of view, for instance, I wasn't secretly rooting for Sunny. I was thinking, "That Sunny, she thinks she can get away with anything." To keep myself true to each voice, I would work on a number of Sunny's chapters all in a row and then a number of Jean's.

When I originally conceived of the book, I identified a bit more with Sunny. That is, I thought of arguments for Jean's side without really feeling them. But once I actually started to write, I found the Jean chapters more fun, and my loyalties became entangled on an emotional as well as an intellectual level. I always found it easy to look through one sister's eyes and see what was wrong with the other.

DM: Which sister do your friends identify with?

JC: I was surprised at the great variety in my friends' responses. Some identify with Sunny because she is, at least on the surface, nicer, more pliant, more generous. Others recoil from her because of her passivity or the way she uses men. Some career women identify with Jean somewhat ruefully, recognizing her greater anxiety or her self-justifications. Others, just as dedicated to their jobs, dismiss her for her single-mindedness and her ambition, saying, "I just don't get people like that."

I've been thrilled at how different the reactions are. They are just as complex as I hope the book is. Even better has been how very emotional the responses have been. People really care about these characters and have vociferous opinions about them.

But I don't think I know who you identify with.

DM: Neither. For me, it's baby Jade, all the way. She's got all her options before her, and in a certain deluded state of mind, I like to think I do, too.

But I did, I admit, identify very much with Sunny at one point. She is watching her husband, Leon, being interviewed on television about his real estate projects in Harlem, and she feels, at that moment, that she has the best of two worlds: access to the realm of consequence and physical proximity to her child. It seems to me that many of us, parents or not, want a realm of consequence and some sort of pivotal, warm relationship with another human, pure and simple. Do you think it's possible that this is, finally, what Jean wants, too?

JC: Jean wants more than access to a realm of consequence; she wants to tell people what to do there. But I do think women on different sides of this question might be forgetting how much they have in common. And readers can lose sight of the ways in which Jean and Sunny are, finally, like each other. Both sisters do what they have to do with great energy and enthusiasm. They don't whine; they just keep going; they're both great company. Their marriages are very different, but they're basically successful. And the sisters get more like each other in other ways, for better or worse, as the book progresses.

DM: Where did you get the idea for this novel?

JC: I've long been fascinated with the bitter feuds that split some Irish and Irish-American families apart—feuds that often last decades. My own father, for instance, did not meet one of his uncles until the older man was close to eighty, even though they'd both lived near Boston for a good part of their lives. It was hard for me to imagine what could cause such unrelenting enmity.

Then I had my first child, and overnight questions of time and money, career and family responsibilities became unbearably fraught. At last there was something I could imagine fighting over—fiercely and at length.

DM: I think rage can be wonderful fuel for a novel. And I'll step out on a limb and say rage of a sort might be what makes *The Crossley Baby* feel . . . well, the only word I have for it is . . . large. Are you enraged about anything?

JC: You name it. The gap between the fabulously rich and the rest of us is mind-boggling. The only thing worse is how most Americans accept it. But, really, I couldn't possibly list all the things I'm enraged about. A peaceful, contented person wouldn't write fiction. It's simply too hard.

I aimed for a large scale in the book by including characters from all sorts of different economic classes and ethnicities—perfect mouthpieces for rage, I guess, as long as you can see everyone's point of view. The conflict comes built in.

DM: The tone you take in talking about big topics like race, class, suffering, and social inequality is witty, lithe, even disarming. Yet you never sound dismissive. How do you manage that? Are there other writers you admire who do something similar? Or who have had some other kind of influence on you?

JC: Big topics are big only because they are important to lots of individuals. Once you get to the personal level you can see all the funny little quirks behind these abstract ideas.

Philip Roth is hilarious about social questions. It may be hard to see his influence in my novels, but I admire him a great deal, and certain of his scenes often come to mind as I work. I love the Zuckerman trilogy.

The two authors who probably had the greatest effect on *The Crossley Baby,* though, were Leo Tolstoy and Agatha Christie. I reread both obsessively while I was writing the novel. They may seem absurdly different, but I very consciously imitated certain things they have in common. Chapters are usually scenes with individual shapes and payoffs. Every moment is grounded in the physical world. If a character is getting key information from a book, say, you're going to hear where she's sitting as she's reading it. And every sentence has to have at least two reasons to be included. On the simplest level, in an Agatha Christie, that means that everything has both a narrative purpose and a role as a potential clue.

DM: Do you try, consciously, to create characters who work against stereotypes? I mean, if stereotypes are both boring and inaccurate, as they surely are, then a writer isn't going to want to go near one, right?

JC: Going against stereotype in a simple-minded way is usually laughable. Take the bestselling novel about a female boss who sexually harrasses her male assistant. That to me sounds more like a male fantasy than anything that would happen in real life. Okay, maybe it happened once in the history of the world. But some things are uninteresting precisely because of their singularity.

On the other hand, no one is merely a sum of probabilities. A person who looks like a certain type can display amazing twists. For instance, the only person I knew who came to the defense of O.J. Simpson was white. He'd played football in college, and obviously that meant far more in this case than the color of his skin.

I try to make my characters both believable and surprising. According to the polls, stay-at-home mothers tend to be more conservative than career women. Tilting the lens slightly made more sense to me, though. It seemed to open things up a bit. I could have gone further and had both Leon and Geoffrey quit their jobs to devote themselves to the raising of children. But I'm not interested in fantasy.

Jean especially makes all sorts of pronouncements about types of people only to acknowledge some kicker in the end. Like when she's sitting in the bar, hiding from her prospective in-laws, and she thinks, Jews don't drink alcohol—except for the ones she knew.

DM: Although the research in your novel is not intrusive, I know you did plenty of it. You write so clearly and engagingly about the nuances of real estate transactions, for instance. How did you get so interested in, and knowledgeable about, that whole realm? And how did you manage to make me and a whole slew of others interested, too?

JC: I read all sorts of stuff about real estate, executive recruiters, laparoscopic surgery, and adoption procedures. But in some ways interviews were even more important. It was from them that I got a real feeling for the emotions behind the facts. I don't think it's too hard to interest readers in real estate, say, as long as you stick to the human ramifications. What defines you more than your home? A house or a co-op is most people's biggest investment. Leon just works on a bigger scale.

When I was trying to decide on a way that a character could lose a lot of money, I remembered reading in the *New York Times* about a woman who had transformed a section of East Harlem real estate in the eighties. I was living in Montana then, so I flew to New York to see her, and she kindly spent two mornings with me, reminiscing. She was even more extraordinary than the articles had led me to believe: brave, persistent, far-sighted, and generous-spirited. I was surprised at how much time she and lots of other people spent talking to me.

After doing the research, you have to live with it a while, so that it sort of gets under your skin. You have to know lots more than you use on the page. Readers assume that you can write most convincingly about something you've experienced yourself, and there is some truth to that. But research that you've carried around in the back of your brain, half-forgotten, as if it were simply another part of your life, works just as well. Better, since it can break you out of your little world.

DM: Another sort of research is a lot less formal and basically involves a sort of writerly observation of the circumstances of your own life. You have two children, a girl and a boy. And you are a writer married to a writer. How have those conditions influenced the way you write, and what you find yourself wanting to write about?

JC: My career and my children have become entwined in my mind because I had my first success as a writer not long before I had my first child. In fact, I sold my first book when I was pregnant and so sick I was afraid to leave the house. It's easy to see children as a threat to your work, because of the demands on time and attention. But children can shake you out of yourself, make you think more deeply and widely. In that way they can be a boost.

My experience has been similar, oddly, to both Jean's and Sunny's. Statistically speaking, I am a mother who works part-time, but it is hard to think of something as all-consuming as writing as "part-time." I brood as much over my work as Jean does, if not more so. And since I'm usually at home and available, at least to some extent, I can be as aware of my kids as Sunny is. Well, almost as much. I draw the line sooner than she does. There are too many parents prowling the halls of the schools these days, anyway.

But here I am talking only about my own life. I purposely kept both my children out of *The Crossley Baby*. They didn't get their choice of mothers, so I give them a free pass. I figure anyone else is fair game, though. I'm amazed, really, at the stuff people tell me, people who are perfectly well aware of how freely I borrow from others.

My husband (Ian Frazier) has influenced my work mostly as an example. I can see firsthand how incredibly hard a successful writer must work and how courageous and honest he must be.

DM: Would you have written this book if you were still living in Montana?

JC: Don't forget that I was living across the park from you when I started the book. My husband says I do my best work in Montana, but that's probably because he's always dragging me out there. It's true that it's easier to see what makes a place itself when you're at a distance from it. By that logic, there's no better place to write about New York City than Montana, which always manages to feel farther away than anywhere else. But I'm glad I also wrote part of the book back east, because there are always details that you forget when you're not living with them.

DM: Why is Jean a practicing Catholic?

JC: Well, why not? She grew up Catholic. She always defined herself as a tough Irish-American girl. She's very tribal. Catholicism is a tough religion, so she would admire it and feel at home with it. She feels its heft. She may look with a skeptical eye upon certain aspects of the mass and her fellow worshippers, but she's no rebel. She likes the church's rules, even if she doesn't follow them all.

You may remember that during the mass she dismisses Sunny's criticism of the church as immature and literal-minded. Jean may be more open to the central mystery of Catholicism than many. Temperamentally she's not suited to any other sort of Christianity, as she's much more likely to find a spiritual dimension through ritual—through historically developed structure—than through personal enlightenment or any line of reasoning.

For people like you and me and Jean, it's Catholicism or nothing. And Jean couldn't countenance nothing. But she's Jean, so anything she'd say about the subject would be flip.

DM: Do you think mothers should work outside the home?

JC: As much as they can. But the important thing to remember is that most women do not have the choice. For economic reasons they have to work.

DM: I happen to know that you clip stories from the newspaper that don't make it to the front page. What are you clipping now?

JC: My new book is about the wife of a white-collar criminal, and you couldn't pick a better time to find relevant articles. Lately I've been taken with the monetary scale of the various frauds—who, in which position, got what. Some of the numbers are incomprehensible, they are so high.

I also always clip articles on outrages that seem to be particularly characteristic of a time. Recently it was the conviction of a mother in Meriden, Connecticut, whose son hanged himself in his closet. Although he had been bullied at school, the jury decided the hanging was her fault because her house was such a mess. This was a woman who had to work sixty hours a week, mostly at WalMart, to support her family.

DM: How much money is enough?

JC: In my new novel, a young corporate striver says to his boss's wife, "You have enough money so that you can tell everyone to go to hell." The boss's wife laughs and says, "I wonder how much that would be."

DM: There are moments of piercing tenderness in *The Crossley Baby,* and they are often attached to the most ordinary physical things. Just one example: Sunny, lying in utter contentment next to Leon, listens to the radiator "snuffing and snorting and stinking happily of burning dust." Are you trying to suggest that our best moments may have nothing to do with what we want?

JC: I think we are all very lucky that they do not.

Sunny is not exactly lying in utter contentment at that point, as her life is falling apart around her. But she does have a gift for appreciating the pleasure to be found in the stink of burning dust that I for one envy. It brings to mind Brecht's definition of happiness: "comfortable shoes."

DM: Comfortable shoes—and a session at the Phone Bar.

READING GROUP QUESTIONS AND
TOPICS FOR DISCUSSION

1. Carey does not organize *The Crossley Baby* as a straightforward chronology but freely interweaves current developments with episodes from her characters' past lives. How does it affect your attitude toward the conflict between Sunny and Jean to see them in younger incarnations?

2. Do you think the novel comes to a clear conclusion about what sort of mother would be best for Jade? Were you pleased with the way the custody question worked out?

3. In her interview, Carey says that Jean and Sunny become to some extent more like each other as the novel progresses. In what ways? How else do they change? Did you notice any similarities in the pressures that they react to?

4. The sisters come from a family in which lengthy feuds are part of the family lore. Why are feuds good fodder for fiction?

5. Did the identity of Jade's father surprise you? What effect did that mystery have on the way you read the book?

6. What part does the city of Manhattan play in *The Crossley Baby*? Would the story change in essential ways if it were set elsewhere?

7. What effect does the style of a novel—right down to the way an individual sentence unfolds—have on your enjoyment of it? Are there particular sentences in *The Crossley Baby* that seem stamped with the author's sensibility? How would you characterize that sensibility?

8. Reviewers have repeatedly praised the combination of wit and gravity that Carey brings to her writing. Can you think of other writers who tell serious stories in a comic and disarming manner?

Jacqueline Carey is the acclaimed author of *Good Gossip* and *The Other Family*. Her short stories have appeared in *The New Yorker,* and she is the recent recipient of a Guggenheim Foundation Fellowship. She lives in Montclair, New Jersey, with her husband, writer Ian Frazier, and their two children.